To
Candice,
With love -
Light + dreams d
Raya
follow your
remember to
always
journey d
stand up for
women!

10-11-18

a novel

Mahsa Rahmani Noble

ARCHWAY
PUBLISHING

Archway Publishing books may be ordered through booksellers or by contacting:

Archway Publishing
1663 Liberty Drive
Bloomington, IN 47403
www.archwaypublishing.com
1 (888) 242-5904

Because of the dynamic nature of the Internet, any web addresses or links contained in this book may have changed since publication and may no longer be valid. The views expressed in this work are solely those of the author and do not necessarily reflect the views of the publisher, and the publisher hereby disclaims any responsibility for them.

Any people depicted in stock imagery provided by Getty Images are models, and such images are being used for illustrative purposes only. Certain stock imagery © Getty Images.

ISBN: 978-1-4808-6421-4 (sc)
ISBN: 978-1-4808-6420-7 (hc)
ISBN: 978-1-4808-6422-1 (e)

Library of Congress Control Number: 2018907773

Print information available on the last page.

Archway Publishing rev. date: 7/30/2018

This book is dedicated to my best friend Sanaz Dasmah

CONTENTS

PART III *Soraya*

INTERLUDE *Raya's Version*

PART IV *Soraya*

PART V *Raya*

ACKNOWLEDGEMENTS

"A bird sat on a tree branch,
Wind blew
The tree shook
The branch swayed
The bird remained still
Because she knew how to fly." Kazem Rahmani (my father)

To Baba, my father, whose love of literature, poetry and philosophy is endless. Thank you for teaching me how to fly--to you I owe my love for storytelling.

To my warrior mother: you are the ultimate female role model who taught me how to love unconditionally and to be fearless in the face of all challenges. Thank you for all the stories of the past, and reminding me how important family and heritage are.

To my siblings for their constant support and encouragement; Maryam, Reza and Mehdi you are my rocks.

To Catcher Block- I will always love you.

To my best friend Patrick Ross for his limitless support and guidance--I am eternally grateful to you.

To my incredible editor Gary Brozak without whom this book would not have been possible.

To my producer Gary Foster who's encouragement and support in believing in me and this story has made me overcome so many obstacles.

To the amazing team at Archway Publishing for their guidance and hard work.

To all my friends who have stood by me and supported me through thick and thin. I am so very blessed to have you all in my life.

To His Excellency Ardeshir Zahedi for granting me so many intimate and informative interviews at his villa in Montroux. Your providing me with first-hand stories from the time he lived at court while Soraya was Empress and after provided invaluable insight.

To Madam Lili Clair Saran and Clairie Saran for granting me with an interview and stories of the late empress who was the closest friend of Madam Saran for over thirty years.

To Myrna Olivar, my second mother and grandmother figure to my children. Your love and care has kept us whole all these years. Thank you from the bottom of my heart.

Last but never the least I wish to thank my children Paris and Kian. For the last ten years you have taken this journey with me and have shown tremendous support, patience, encouragement and love. I could not have done it without you. You too should never be afraid to take flight, despite the strongest of winds. Never give up on your dreams.

I love you so…

PROLOGUE

October 2000
Sitges, Spain

Ignoring the security cameras in the foyer of my fiancé's villa, I slipped out of my new silk chemise and went upstairs. The sound of my high heels on the terrazzo tile was drowned out by the music coming from our bedroom. I smiled half in pleasure and half in disappointment as the tender strains of *"Solamente Una Vez"* ("Only Once") came to my ears through the slightly ajar door. Sergio was such a romantic that he believed that only once in your life do you find your true soul mate, the single person who makes you whole. Given that he was playing our song, I guessed my attempt at surprising him had failed.

Still, I comforted myself that at least he wouldn't expect me to walk into the room fresh off the plane from New York City completely naked.

Beneath the music, I became aware of another equally familiar sound. I stood frozen in place, wondering if the whispers and murmurs and less appealing guttural sounds of sexual pleasure were only my fevered imaginings. Suddenly I wanted to turn on my heel, run from there, wrap myself in the trench coat I'd discarded at the bottom of the stairs—flee from that place, erase the scene from my memory, ignore his prewedding dalliance—chalk it up to his one and only last-chance fling.

More than that, I wanted to see who she was. I needed to release the venomous outrage that was rising along with the bile in my constricted throat, souring my mouth. An image of my hands around her neck, her lifeless body splayed across the bed, invaded my vision.

Those twin impulses—flight or fight—flashed through my body in an instant, flushing my skin. At that moment I was an unthinking animal, fueled by adrenaline. Instead of turning my back and running away, I eased the door open. The room was ablaze with candles. For a moment I thought I'd stepped into a cathedral and the bed was an altar.

Sergio lay on his back. From a distance it looked as if he was in great pain. His face contorted in spasms that made him nearly unrecognizable to me. It was as if he were a figure transformed—a torture victim hung on a cross, a hero stretched across a rack, a body clamped in a set of stocks. For a moment, I imagined that our eyes met and he was beckoning me to rescue him, release him from what bound him.

A moment later, my heart rose to my throat. In the flickering light of the candles within, I was at first uncertain of my vision. I stepped closer, and when the shapes took a more recognizable form, I stifled a cry. The two other figures were both young men, no more than eighteen. My stomach churning, I gagged loudly. All three of them turned toward me, and their eyes met mine. I couldn't tear my gaze away. Sergio's body shuddered in the unmistakable throes of his release.

I wanted to scream, but I had no voice. I wanted to run, but my legs wouldn't move.

I have no idea how I made it down the stairs. The next thing I recalled was standing in the drive. I heard a crackle of static from a communications radio and the sound of a door being slid open. I ran blindly through the garden and into the vineyard, scraping my hand on the rock wall that separated the pool from the tennis courts and orange grove. I stumbled into a trellis and collapsed onto it, my chest heaving from exertion, sobs clawing my throat.

I tried to will my legs to move, but they refused. The smell of damp earth and the garden's aroma mingled in the night air. I shut my eyes and then opened them again when the image of Sergio invaded my mind.

How could I have been so stupid?

Growing up, I had always been told that the heart knows what it wants. As I stood there shivering, debased, and humiliated, I knew I could never trust my heart again.

PART I

Raya

Chapter
ONE

*A*s the early December rain slanted down, I imagined it as a slash mark separating then from now—wishful thinking on my part. For me, then and now were always inextricably linked, even more so given recent events with Sergio.

Although the rain was stinging and cold, on the verge of sleet, I didn't hoist an umbrella as a defense against it. I suppose I hoped that somehow the cold would numb me, that the chill would silence the febrile workings of my brain, obscure the images that pierced me behind a veil of dripping water. In the month since I'd uncovered Sergio's deception, I'd fled one former object of tangled desire and was in pursuit of someone else, someone whom I thought might help me sort out the answer to the question that clung to me like my sodden clothes.

Now that my vision of how my life would proceed was shattered, what was I to do next?

I'd just exited the Metro at Abbesses, my heart still beating quickly after climbing the narrow spiral of stairs that led to Rue Yvonne La Tec. There I merged with the few commuters heading home early and the even fewer tourists enjoying a Parisian holiday. My eyes downcast, I bumped into a young couple. I looked up and mumbled an apology, but their only response was to offer a cell phone to me. Their long hair adhered to their foreheads like cooled candle wax but didn't hide the light of love in their eyes. I nodded and took the offered phone to take their photograph. The man began to gesture instructions on how to use the device in a heavily German-accented French. Although I'm of Persian and not Parisian ancestry, I wasn't surprised that he made that assumption. In recent weeks, my already somewhat fair skin had gone even more sallow from lack of sleep and sunlight.

"There's no need," I said to him in German. "I know how to use this." I reached into my jacket pocket and showed them my own.

"You're from Germany?" His quizzical expression was no doubt a result of my non-Germanic appearance.

I shook my head. "It's complicated."

They didn't press the issue. Instead, they inclined their heads in an A-frame and flashed their newlywed smiles. They thanked me, and I shrugged and looked away, grateful that the rain and my tears were indistinguishable. Walking away, their enormous umbrella was a red daub of paint receding in an impressionistic mist. Later, while sharing their honeymoon photos with friends, would they recall our encounter and wonder at the brief intersection of their lives and mine?

I made my way to the funicular that would carry me up to Sacre-Cour. Gazing up into the rain, seeing the cars trundling their way skyward, I made a quick decision and began the long trek up the stairs. I'd decided that given the unexpected turn my life had taken, I would "go with the flow," as the expression went. Since my turn had been for the worst, I decided that I should simply assume things were going to be difficult for the foreseeable future. Each step was, if not painful or hard, a little penance. The fact that I was on my way to a Catholic cathedral and was thinking of a mild form of self-flagellation was not because of my own religious inclinations. Rather, the man who had just thrown me into a tailspin had owned one of the great design firms in Spain—everything from architecture to interiors, packaging to postcards. His work had aroused my interest in Moorish influences on the arts and design.

Less than three months ago, I'd traveled from Manhattan to Barcelona, where we'd spent a few hours at La Sagrada Familia, Gaudi's great and as-yet-incomplete masterwork of a cathedral. We watched as Sergio's crews applied gold leaf to a few of the pillars in the forest-like nave. Although the place was crowded with workers and tourists, the site was woodland-quiet and soothing, the only sounds a few murmurs and the occasional rasp of a trowel. We held hands, and he genuflected and crossed himself, even though the building was not yet consecrated.

If only I'd been able to see the forest for the trees, I wouldn't have been in Paris, climbing my way toward another great building, a tribute to the Sacred Heart and France's war dead. If only I'd understood then just how hollow and unholy Sergio's gesture had been.

Perhaps I was mixing the sacred and the profane, but I couldn't help but think of Pat Benatar's song about love being a battlefield. There I was, one of the walking wounded, seeking neither comfort nor commiseration. What I was looking for was insight as well as the satisfaction of making a long-held dream come true. After being thrown over by Sergio, I felt as if I'd come unmoored and was drifting along in a fog of regret and longing. I had no idea what I was going to do with myself for the next few weeks, let alone the next few years. On New Year's Eve, I was supposed to have gotten married in Barcelona. Since that event was no longer on my calendar, I needed something to occupy both my days and my mind. More than that, I needed to figure out how I was going to go on with my life.

Although I hadn't told anyone the real reason why I'd canceled the wedding, my friends implored me to return from Barcelona, to New York, where I could be immersed in sympathy and comfort. But right now I preferred to be alone. The very foundations of everything I'd ever believed in were shaken. How could I have been so wrong about someone I thought I knew so well? I had to reexamine everything I'd ever believed in, everything I'd taken for granted. I had some acquaintances in Paris as well, but I hadn't gotten in touch with them yet. This seemed like a place where I could be anonymous for a while until I figured things out. Since I'd run away from Spain in complete shock, I had no clothes other than the ones on my back. My closet as well as my identity had become melded with Sergio's, and now I felt completely lost.

As the limousine carried me back to the airport in Barcelona on that horrid evening, wending its way through the streets of the city that rightfully was known as the St. Tropez of Spain, I wondered about the woman after whom I'd been named.

Ever since I was a little girl, I was fascinated by the stories I'd heard of Soraya Esfandiary-Bakhtiary, a distant relative who had once been the queen of Iran. Like most little girls, I'd gone through a princess phase of my own, fueled by fairy tales and my family's desire to let me know that I was special. Our sharing a name ("Raya" was a shortened form of Soraya, and an endearment her father frequently used) had been a burden when I lived among Persian families in Iran. The presumption seemed to be that my parents must have been compensating for some fault in my character, and were hoping to give me a kind of leg up over others by linking me to this legendary figure in our culture.

There may have been a bit of jealousy involved as well. Though we certainly weren't as wealthy or influential as Soraya's family, before the Revolution we were solidly upper middle class, secure in our future, and grateful that Iran had provided us with so much to be thankful for. The events that unfolded marked another before/after in my life, one more act of betrayal acted out on a larger scale.

Later, as a young woman, and having fled Iran with my family, I realized that though I learned as much as I could about Soraya, what I knew of her amounted to little more than basic biographical information. That was fine with me then. All that Iran and Soraya meant for me and my family was a veil of sorrow, a bit of black lace through which one peered, mindful that dark forces were always at work and must be respected—that in aspiring to rise too high, one risked a greater fall.

Now that I felt there was little left to lose and my life had entered a phase very much like what Soraya had experienced in her failed marriage to the shah, I wanted to reach out to her. Maybe in hearing firsthand from a woman who'd suffered a heartache far greater than my own, I'd be able to shake my fear that I would wind up as she had—an emotional vagabond doomed to carry her grief and regret with her always, a woman both fleeing from and completely held prisoner by her past.

As I climbed toward the top of Montmartre, the fog increased, matching both my mood and my sense of dislocation. My mother had made some preliminary inquiries on my behalf, trying to find out if Soraya was still living in the same section of Paris where she'd been residing in semiseclusion for some time. Mama had not heard back from anyone, and she told me that I needed to be patient, but of course I couldn't be.

That was why I found myself wandering the neighborhood outside Sacre Cour, the view of Paris at my feet obscured in clouds, the object of my desire equally shrouded in mystery.

At one point, I walked down a street near the Lapin Agile, and for a moment I imagined that I caught a glimpse of her. A woman stood in a small cemetery across from the cabaret. The grounds angled sharply upward, and the headstones were askew as though they'd resigned themselves to their inability to defeat gravity. The woman stood in one of the helter-skelter rows of plots, a basket of white lilies standing out in stark contrast to her heather coat and black scarf. Something about her prominent nose reminded me of photographs in profile that I'd seen of Soraya. My distant cousin was a great beauty, and though I'd speculated about the ravages of time on her, I presumed that she was still possessed of the same elegant, if not regal, bearing that I'd always admired.

I decided to edge my way through the gate of the burial ground, hoping to get a better look at the woman. I couldn't make a pretense of simply being a genealogy-entranced tourist and wander about haphazardly. I strode purposefully to a grave marker uphill from the lily-bearing woman. I discovered that I was shivering, not fully from the cold, but from my sense of expectant anticipation. When the woman heard my cough, she raised her head, and I could see that what I thought was a scarf wrapped around her head was a nun's wimple— not unlike those the nuns at St. Margaret's in St. Moritz wore. I also saw that her face bore the scars of some disfiguring skin condition, and I thought of some crone from a fairy tale who might cast a spell on me. Startled, I blanched and blinked my eyes like a just-woken child. I scurried away, even more downhearted than when I had set out that morning, berating myself for how silly I had been.

I found a café and sipped an espresso while staring at my phone, wishing for some confirmation from my mother that she'd made contact. I had hoped that soon I'd be sitting across from Soraya, hearing all the details of her great triumph and ultimate humiliation. The phone's screen remained blank, but my mind did not. The caffeine roused me, and instead of heading back to my hotel via a cab, I trekked back uphill toward Sacre Cour and the metro stop there. The rain had diminished while I was in the café, but after a few minutes of winding through the streets, I was just outside the Musee de Montmartre when the skies opened again. With my head bowed against the onslaught, the rain ran in cold rivulets down my neck and back. Whether it was the caffeine I'd ingested on an empty stomach or the beginning signs of a flu, I felt lightheaded and weak.

Since it was a Monday, the museum was not open, and feeling a desperate need to sit and get out of the rain, I ducked into the nearest doorway. At first I was hoping to just remain there, but the wind-whipped rain drove me inside. As it happened, I stood in the entrance-way of a restaurant, dripping voluminously on the wide-planked wood floor. The place was empty of patrons but not of charm. I had the sense that I'd stepped into a French farmhouse. A fire blazed in a stone hearth, and white Christmas lights dripped from a fragrant pine tree. Twenty or so small tables sat in no discernible pattern about the place, and the informality of that arrangement appealed to me. I caught a glimpse of someone moving at the rear of the space beyond an arched doorway, from which emanated an enchanting mix of cooking smells.

A moment later, a spotted dog trotted toward me, its nose in the air, its masked eyes alight with curiosity. It stopped just short of where I stood and sniffed at the expanding puddle I'd created. I knelt down to let the dog smell my hand, and it immediately curled into me and invited me to pet it. As I stroked its fur, it looked up at me, giving the appearance of smiling as its tail beat a steady tympani against my raincoat.

"Roger!" Someone shouted from the back room.

The dog's ears pricked. I stopped petting him and he looked at me, seemingly aghast at my insolence. I resumed my attentions.

After the call came a second time, I said, "He's out here, monsieur."

The man who'd been calling for the dog came bustling out of the kitchen, pulling his arms through a cardigan as he approached. As he entered into the firelight, I could see that he was what the English call a ginger. His reddish hair was tightly curled around a pleasant face. His smile was gap-toothed and broad, and the soothing timbre of his voice seemed in keeping with the environment.

"I'm so sorry," he said as he took Roger by the collar. "He thinks he's the maître d'. If I could actually get him to seat you and hand you a menu, that would be one thing ..." He stopped, and his expression went from amused to alarmed. His sharp intake of breath seemed to fill the room. "Listen to me, babbling on while you stand there sodden and no doubt shivering."

He stepped behind me and said, "Please let me help you get this off."

"Thank you very much," I said, shrugging out of my coat.

The man held it away from him like it was the hide of a freshly slaughtered deer.

"I'll put it here by the fire, and you must sit as well." After he hung up the coat, he pulled a table within inches of the fireplace. "You must be frozen."

I brushed a lank strand of hair from my face, and he shook his head.

"This will not do. Come with me." He held out his hand. Feeling very much like a child and enjoying that sensation, I took it as he led me into the kitchen.

"Marie, we have a guest. Please fetch some towels. This poor woman has nearly drowned." He turned to me and once again his expression softened. "I'm sorry, but I've failed to ask your name."

"I'm Raya."

"How lovely. I take it you are not from Paris."

"No." As I shook my head, more rain dripped down my face and onto the floor. "I'm the one who should be apologizing. I'm making a mess."

"Not at all. My name is Eric, and this is my wife Marie. We own and cook here at Bistro Lepicuriene. Welcome."

Marie stepped toward me, her chef's toque slightly askew. With her dark hair and pale skin, she reminded me of a less waifish Audrey Tautou. "Hello. I'll see about those towels."

"Roger. No." Eric wagged his finger at the dog, who sat staring up at a steaming pot on an enormous iron range. "I hope you don't mind Roger. Normally he stays in the living quarters, but today with all the rain, I wasn't able to take him for his usual walk. I was letting him stretch his legs."

"Not at all. You're being so kind."

Marie returned with a towel, a large cowl-neck sweater, and some leggings. She ushered me toward a bathroom. "You can dry yourself in here, and please do change your blouse for this. It can dry while you eat."

I was beginning to feel a bit like Alice, fallen down a rabbit hole. I was too tired to resist their hospitality, and found myself in the cornflower-blue bathroom inhaling the smell of lavender. The sweater was made from luxuriant alpaca, and I felt as if I was swaddled in eiderdown. At first I was hesitant about removing my jeans and pulling on the leggings, but none of what they'd offered seemed in any way immodest. I had been feeling the universe's indifference all day, and it was nice to know the opposite still existed.

When I left the bathroom, Eric took my wet clothes and hung them near the stove. Then he led me back to the fireside table.

A glass of wine and a basket of bread awaited me.

"I thought a red would be best, but let me know if you'd like white."

I took a sip and felt the warmth trickle down my throat. "This is wonderful. Thank you." Eric pointed toward a blackboard framed with holiday lights. The menu was written out in white chalk.

"This is our luncheon menu." He pulled up the sleeve of his cardigan to consult his watch, "I'm afraid we won't be serving dinner for another two hours."

I scanned the offerings, trying to think of the last time I'd allowed myself to eat a full meal. I came up blank.

"It all looks so wonderful. I don't know if I can decide."

Marie, who had joined us, said, "Then you don't have to. Allow us!" She shrugged her shoulders and inclined her head in a typically Gallic gesture.

"Of course. I trust you will take care of me."

And for the next hour, they did. From an exquisite *terrine de canard aux pruneaux* starter to a lovely *tarte tatin aux pommes*, I was reminded that life still had its pleasures. Eric and Marie took turns preparing the courses and sitting with me. They were amiable luncheon companions, and I enjoyed the fact that neither asked me why I was out alone in Montmartre in a torrential rain. They did ask if I'd been to Paris before, and for the first time since I was a teen, I considered taking advantage of the fact that I was a stranger in a strange land. As far as Eric and Marie were concerned, I was a blank slate. I could spin any tales I chose about who I was and what I'd done before.

In shedding my clothes, it was as if I'd also shed some of the burdens I'd been carrying. For the first time since those awful hours in Barcelona, I hadn't thought about Sergio at all. Yet while I could be free of those thoughts momentarily, that didn't mean that I could change my essential self. As the meal wound down and Eric and Marie spent more time in the kitchen preparing for dinner, my spirits flagged. I'd had two glasses of wine, and perhaps it was the depressive effects of alcohol, or perhaps it was self-pity. I found myself staring into the fire, on the verge of tears.

I realized that my cash and credit cards were still in my jeans. I was reluctant to leave, but knew that I should. Eric and Marie had been wonderful hosts, taking me in and caring for my needs—much like Sergio had done until he decided to cast all that aside. After things ended so horrifically, I'd vowed that I'd go back to being the independent woman I'd been, not allowing myself to be tended to by anyone. This afternoon had reminded me of the pleasures of having some choices made for you. The simple act of not having to decide what to eat, having the food prepared, recalled those deeper pleasures of Sergio's companionship and love.

My mother always told me that I was far too headstrong to ever find a man. We were coming up on the second year of the new century, and I was still haunted by the beliefs of my Persian ancestors. If I couldn't become more *najib*—literally "ladylike," but in my mind "submissive"—I wouldn't find happiness.

I pushed away from the table and made my way to the kitchen. Eric looked up from a prep counter and smiled at me. His words were punctuated by the sound of his knife chopping vegetables.

"I hope you enjoyed your meal. I'm sorry we couldn't spend more time with you."

"You've both been more than kind to me. I don't know how to thank you."

Marie hefted a steaming cauldron from the stove to the sink. Over the splash and hiss of the water, she said, "Please stay for a while longer. Chat some more. We've been together so long, our stories have worn dusty paths in our brains. Take us somewhere new."

"I really should get going." I trailed my fingers along a stained butcher-block table.

"If you must," Eric said. "But I hope you'll return." He scooped a pile of carrots across the table with the knife's edge, and they thudded into a plastic container. "How much longer will you be in Paris?"

I leaned my hip against the table and traced a scratch. "Indefinitely." For some reason, I added, "I suppose."

Marie asked if I was staying with friends, and I said no. In fact, I had several friends, former colleagues and schoolmates who lived in Paris, but I'd chosen not to tell any of them of my arrival. I'd imagined that Sergio might try to track me down, and the less I contacted anyone, the less likely it was that he'd be able to. In my anger I didn't want him to find me, and yet in the recesses of my mind, somehow I was hoping that he would, that he'd have some logical explanation for being in bed with two other men that would make the whole thing go away.

In my imagination, I was a tragic movie heroine, hiding out in the fabled city of lights. As I'd walked the streets earlier that day, I'd continually peered in the shop windows, paranoid that I might see Sergio's or one of his employees' reflections as they tailed me. I knew I was being foolish, both hiding and wishing to be found, but I'd been knocked so completely off balance that my inner compass was spinning.

"Where are you staying?" Marie asked.

Thunder crashed, and lightning lit the dark sky. The lights flickered; the refrigerators fell silent for a moment and then clicked and whirred. Eric looked to the ceiling and shook his head. "I don't mean to pry, but …" He gestured with the knife toward the kitchen's lone window and the heavy weather beyond it. "I'd hate to send you out alone again on a night like this."

Marie picked up the thread. "You're welcome to stay here."

She had no sooner finished speaking than another fusillade of thunder and lightning darkened the room. We stood in silence for a moment. The quiet was broken by the sound of Roger's panting breaths.

We made our way into the dining room to retrieve the votive candles that sat on each of the tables. Amidst much giggling and barking of shins and dog, we returned to the kitchen, where Eric lit the candles. In the warm glow of candlelight, we sipped wine as Eric and Marie regaled me with stories of their meeting, marriage, and eventual partnership in owning Le Bistro Epicuriene. They mentioned that they'd both worked for the legendary French chef Jacques Pepin, as producers and sous chefs on his television cooking shows. As a result, they'd lived part-time in Paris and San Francisco and had managed to save enough money to buy the restaurant only two years ago. While they were both trained in haute cuisine, their real passion was the casual but delicious French fare that they offered.

As Marie put it, "Once we both had dreams of chasing stars of the Michelin variety. But here we have pleasures of a different kind. Not better or worse—just different."

They asked me about my work, and I told them about the years I'd spent after school working as an investment banker in New York. I didn't tell them that my passions lay elsewhere, in arts and design, that given my Persian family's intractable demands, becoming a doctor, banker, or lawyer were the only suitable career paths for a woman unless she chose to be a homemaker.

"I stopped working in 1998." I paused to consider whether or not to talk about Sergio, and decided to demur. "I took some time off to do some travelling. Some time off led to more time, and here I am." I shrugged.

"Well, we're glad you're here." Marie raised her glass to toast me. "To our mutual good fortune."

After an hour or so in the darkness, Eric and Marie asked for my help in storing the food they'd been preparing. Not wanting to allow too much warm air into the appliances meant that we had to stand close by while one of us quickly opened the door and then slammed it shut. Rather than being angry at the loss of a night's revenue and the prospect of a further loss in food waste, Eric and Marie laughed and operated well as a team.

I couldn't help but think of the times that Sergio and I had worked together in the kitchen. We couldn't produce anything of the quality that my new friends could, but we did craft some passable meals. More than the eating, I enjoyed the spirit of cooperation, the teamwork that the two of us managed. Those occasions were somewhat rare, however.

Sergio traveled frequently, and when I accompanied him, we dined out. He also had a personal chef who prepared most of his meals in Barcelona. His housekeeper, a woman of indeterminate age but obvious affection for her employer, frequently baked sweets for him.

Often I felt as if I spent more time with Señora Amaya than I did my fiancé. The two of us grew very close, and it was nearly as hard not to be in contact with her as it was the rest of his family.

When I first met Sergio, his parents had been pestering him for years to settle down. We became engaged after having a long-distance relationship for over a year. I'd given up my job in New York City, which admittedly I'd become a bit bored with, and gone to live with him in his villa in Sitges. Because Sergio traveled frequently for business, we were apart much of the time. I spent my free hours going to art museums, restaurants, and shops with my friends and redesigning an older section of his home. Señora Amaya kept the place clean and running properly. Everything was taken care of; all I had to do was enjoy my surroundings and be an adoring lover when he returned home from his travels.

When Sergio was at home, he was the perfect partner—warm and affectionate. I appreciated the times that we could be together, never suspecting that there might be another reason for his frequent absences. I made myself into a sweet little housewife, never complaining or demanding anything. I'd surrendered fully to him like a proper Persian woman.

I wondered what story Sergio might have concocted to explain our wedding's being cancelled. I had simply told my family and best friends that I'd suffered from a severe case of cold feet. I wasn't ready to let them know what I'd discovered that awful day in his bedroom. In some ridiculous way I hoped that if I didn't tell anyone, it would all vanish like a bad dream.

"I am indeed fortunate," I said as I lifted my glass.

After midnight and a lovely meal of salad and salmon cooked atop the wood stove, the lights finally came back on. We had moved into the living quarters and sprawled amiably over cushions tossed onto the floor. The space was dominated by another impressive stone fireplace. The antiquated boiler coughed and gargled but produced little in the way of warmth, so we stayed as close to the fire as possible.

Although none of us had spoken the words, it was clear that I was going to be spending the night. Rain still lashed the windowpanes. The thought of trekking downhill toward the Boulevard Clichy, the main thoroughfare, and trying to hail a cab held no appeal. As a part of my imagined schemes of evasion, I'd taken a room at a nondescript two-star hotel across the Seine near the forbidding monument, Les Invalides. The room was cramped and musty. After first seeing it, I'd nearly chucked all my plans to deny myself the pleasures of the flesh. Yet although the suites at the five-star George V beckoned to me, I didn't give in to their siren's call. Sergio and I had stayed there a couple of times, its proximity to the Louvre and the Jardin du Luxembourg offsetting his frequent absences while he attended business meetings. In hindsight, I wondered if some of those late-night appointments were actually assignations with male lovers. The thought chilled me to the bone.

That night, I was glad for more companionable accommodations. Eric and Marie stumbled to bed just after the lights came back on. They did a quick check in the kitchen and then waved their adieu in unison as Marie hopped on Eric's back for a piggyback ride. Their laughter cascaded down the stairs. A moment later, Marie trundled down, her arms laden with blankets and pillows. She dropped them in a pile at my feet and then bent down and rested her hand on the top of my head.

"Things will seem better in the morning. Sweet dreams."

I bid her the same.

As the fire died in the grate, I wondered what I had said or done that had indicated I was troubled. I'd thought that my skills in hiding my emotions had enabled me to evade detection. Somehow Marie saw through me, and I speculated on whether or not there was some sisterhood of sorrow that linked us—just as I sensed that Soraya and I shared a similarly shattered soul. Putting those thoughts aside, I fell into a deep and untroubled sleep, the first of which I'd enjoyed in a month.

Chapter

TWO

Over the next few weeks, I began spending more and more of my time with Eric and Marie. It was apparent that they were taxing themselves by keeping the staff to a minimum, with only one server and themselves to handle the tables. They shared the work equitably, but with the run-up to the holidays and the increased patron traffic, they were stretched to the limit. It became clear that if nothing else, I could assist them by taking reservations or occasionally waiting tables. I asked for no pay, and only after many assurances that their friendship was worth far more to me than francs, they granted my request. The only proviso they insisted on was that I worked only on the days I wanted to.

They did insist, however subtly, that I learn my way around the kitchen. The first morning after I'd spent the night, I'd been awakened in the predawn darkness by thumping sounds. I found Marie and Eric hard at work at the ancient table, their fists pounding as clouds of flour rose. In time, I came to love arriving early in the morning to help bake the day's baguettes. Eric and Marie were born teachers, able to use just the right metaphors to aid someone in the art of bread-making. Well, not always the best—but certainly memorable.

On my first day of training, Eric told me, "Before the first rise, the dough should come out of the mixing bowl like a woman's breast. Not as firm as an adolescent's, and not as saggy as an older woman's."

I managed a weak smile and looked at him as he flopped the dough out of the bowl and onto the table. With the flat of his palm, he began kneading the white mass. He waggled his eyebrows at me and said, "That is why men have been the best bakers for centuries. They have the right touch for these things, based on their experience." He grinned at Marie.

Marie held out a freshly rolled baguette. It held firm for a moment before drooping, and she gave Eric a purse-lipped smile.

"Yes, well. A woman's touch is also required."

We all laughed.

My hours with Eric and Marie were punctuated by frequent moments of hilarity, but other interactions tested my patience.

I'd been relying on my mother's assistance to help establish a contact with Soraya Esfandiary-Bakhtiary. As a member of the two tribes composing the Bakhtiari people in Iran, we hoped to use our family connections to make a meeting possible.

My people come from the mountainous southwest part of Iran and have a long history as both political reformers and rebels. Growing up, I constantly heard about how proud I should be of my heritage.

Although I didn't have the remarkable green eyes of the shah's former wife, I grew up believing that we shared many other traits. Like many little girls, I went through a period of fascination with princess stories, but many people both within and outside of my family commented on my similarities to the former empress. Whether it was how I walked or held my head, how even as a young girl I firmly knew my own mind and wasn't afraid of expressing my opinions, or how at times I could seem to withdraw from those around me and enter my own private world, I was made conscious that I was somehow set apart.

Like the empress, whose mixed Russian-German and Persian ancestry produced her nobly beautiful features, I too was not typically Persian. My freckled complexion was often a source of embarrassment. My parents and younger sister teased me that since I was the only one in our family who had freckles, perhaps I was adopted. I knew they were joking, but sometimes I felt a kinship to Soraya that went beyond merely being a namesake.

As I grew older and my changing body made me self-conscious, I was even more drawn to learning about this legendary woman. Of course, by the time I entered my teens in 1986, Soraya had not been queen for twenty-eight years. I had learned the basics of her life: that she had been queen of Iran—the young bride of the handsome Mohammad Reza Pahlavi, the deposed and now-deceased shah—for only seven years. To me, raised on both her story and other romantic tales of love, unrequited and doomed (Romeo and Juliet, Tristan and Isolde, the king of Persia and his wife Scheherazade), she loomed large in my imagination as I suffered through my first early crushes and heartbreaks.

I knew other young girls who fell under the sway of the stories of Cinderella, Sleeping Beauty, and the like. Those happily-ever-after tales didn't arrest my attention in the same way they did my playmates and schoolmates. Now, as I considered my fascination with Soraya in light of recent events in my life, I wondered if my name had served as a self-fulfilling prophecy. I'd heard people refer to Soraya as a reverse example of the life of Grace Kelly. Was there nothing but tragedy that awaited these women, and why was I so drawn to their stories?

Before Sergio had so shocked my system, I'd never thought of myself as a heroine, tragic or otherwise. Now, here I was stumbling around Paris, hoping that by chance I'd magically run into the former queen and find answers to my questions from a woman who in my imagination kept company with others like her—people of fairy tales and folklore. Had my discovery of Sergio's sins made me lose my mind? Or was there some method to my madness? Was this quest going to lead to my salvation?

Worse, I'd grown up believing that blood tells all and doesn't lie. Our path in life was predetermined by the one our ancestors and elders had trod. Since I had the same first name and ancestry as Soraya, did I have no choice but to continue down the path that I had just begun to share with her? That thought frightened me, made me want to curl up in a ball and let the fates take me where they might. The only other option was to hear her version of those tragic events. I needed to confirm that I wasn't wrong to have defended her all those years to people who criticized her for giving up and becoming a recluse, for not doing more with her life. I sensed that there was more to her story than any of us knew. Just as I'd invented a story to buffer myself from Sergio's betrayal, surely she must have felt the same fear of disclosing everything. She had to have experienced the shame, embarrassment, and self-doubt that any woman would have felt when rejected so coldly by the love of her life.

My mother was frustrated with me since I'd let her believe that I'd broken my engagement for no good reason. As a result, she vacillated between a you-made-your-bed-so-now-lie-in-it toughness, to a more tender but still tenacious get-back-on-the-horse encouragement. Whenever we spoke, she reminded me that we were Bakhtiaris. Our ancestors were made of stern stuff; we'd seen and survived far worse than what I was currently going through. She was certainly trying her best, and her reminders that I was a Bakhtiari convinced me that searching for Soraya was the right thing to do.

The word *Bakhtiari* means either "companion of chance" or "bearer of good luck." I was hoping that either of the two definitions would prove to be another self-fulfilling prophecy. However, I would have to wait to see if those meanings proved true. In the weeks leading up to the end-of-year holidays, each call to my mother for a progress report resulted in disappointment: "I've left a message for so-and-so, but they are away in the Seychelles. So-and-so promised to phone about putting you in touch with Soraya, but it will have to wait until they get back from St. Moritz."

At first, I suspected that my mother was only pretending to try to arrange this meeting. After all, I still hadn't explained to her what happened between Sergio and me, and the wedding cancellation colored every conversation, giving a suspicious nuance to even the most casual of comments. But I just couldn't tell her that I was so naïve, that I hadn't realized Sergio was bisexual. I felt it reflected on my own femininity, the essence of my womanhood. If I couldn't even keep my fiancé interested, what did that say about me? And a part of me still thought that if I didn't talk about it, the crisis would somehow go away and I could resume my fairy tale life.

At times, as I stood folding a squared bit of dough into thirds like a written letter, as Eric had instructed me, I wondered if meeting Soraya could ever live up to my expectations. What if my mother did get her phone number, and I spoke with the woman once and that was it? What would I do next? How would I get through the holidays, knowing that I should have been getting married on New Year's Eve? The future was a yawning chasm of which I stood on the brink. Although my thoughts of Soraya were a rickety bridge across it, at least that flimsy hope was a better alternative than the plunge. Still, what would I do once I got to the other side?

The bistro was closed for Christmas, and rather than impose on Eric and Marie, I told them that I was spending the day with friends. To make my commute to the restaurant easier, I'd left my hotel in St. Germaine and moved into a hostel right off Avenue St-Ouen. I was by far the oldest boarder in a place favored by backpackers and Eurail pass holders, but it was one of the few that offered long-term accommodations. Also, by lodging there, I was outside the sphere of detection by Sergio. I frequently walked to work, and my route took me past the Cimitiére de Montmartre, where I could feed my morbid sensibility like the elderly feed their local park's pigeons.

I spent a desultory Christmas Day. I considered staying in bed and reading, but the thriller someone had left in the common room did little to thrill me. I decided to attend mass at Notre Dame. The combined smells of wet wool, candle wax, and incense were nearly too cloying for me, but seeing everyone's ruddy cheeks and the bright-eyed wonderment of the children, and hearing the choir in full voice, made me glad that I'd come. By the time I'd made my way back to my room, after wandering along the Seine past the Louvre and the Tuilleries, night had fallen. My murmured *"Joyeux Noel"* to the driver was the only words I'd spoken all day.

In my room, I opened the present that Eric and Marie had given me the night before. Their gift brought a smile to my face. It was a box of exquisite French chocolates, encased in a red box with a white cross emblazoned on it, along with the words "Survival Kit."

I savored two of them, and then left the remainder on a small table in the lobby with a note wishing everyone a happy Christmas.

Chapter

THREE

he best holiday gift I received came on the twenty-eighth. As I was preparing for bed in my little hostel room, I felt my back pocket vibrate. My heart did the same until I saw the number displayed. It was only my mother calling me to wish me an early happy New Year, and not Sergio. I did my best to hide my disappointment, but it leaked into my voice when I asked if I could speak to my father.

"I'm sorry, dear. He is indisposed at the moment."

I blanched at my mother's formality and use of such a cliché. We both knew full well that he was still so angry at me, at the shame I'd brought down on the family, that he'd not spoken to me in weeks.

"Well," I said, doubling the frosty formality of my mother, "please be so kind as to pass along a message to him for me. Greetings of the season, and especially for a bountiful new year free of disappointments and grievances." I sounded like a petulant brat, but if that was how he was going to view me anyway, I may as well be an arsonist and add fuel to the fire.

"Raya. Don't be this way. Patience. He will come around. He always has in the past."

I shook my head and rolled my eyes. My continuing not to work had shattered my father. In my mind I could hear him, his basso pro-fundo voice rising. "At least when she was going to marry a wealthy and influential man, I could take some comfort. But my daughter a vagabond? Working at a restaurant? What fresh horror is this?"

"A fitting way to end this year, no?" I made every effort to filter any bitterness out of my voice but took no further steps toward an apology. After all, what had I done, and how could my father judge me instead of support me?

"Well, I do have some good news for you. My cousin finally called me back. Someone who runs in the same circles as Soraya—a woman named Annette Lentze—is having a New Year's Eve party. Apparently the ex-empress gets invited to this party every year. Now, I'm not so sure she will show, as I was told she rarely goes out these days, but it's worth a try. My cousin will set it up for you to call Annette and attend as well." I thanked her profusely and hung up the phone, feeling ex-cited about the possibility of finally meeting my lifelong idol.

When I called Annette, she admitted that Soraya rarely went out in public, but that she'd like me to attend the party regardless. She'd said the men were not going to be in black tie, nor the ladies gowned. She wanted it to be chic but fun and relaxed. She added that she would be pleased to meet me, and hoped I would have a good time at the party regardless of whether my reclusive relative showed up.

The day before the party, I headed to a boutique I'd scouted out on the Rue d'Orsel. There I found a buoyant gored skirt in brightly colored silk stripes designed by Dries van Noten. I already had a funnel neck sweater that worked perfectly with it. The outfit had a fifties feel to it—my own way of paying tribute to the era when Soraya reigned.

To further cement my anticipated good fortune, in a small book-shop I found a copy of the Persian and Bakhtiari poet Fereydoon Moshiri's *Ah Bahran*. In English the title means "Oh, the Rain."

Considering how it was the rain that led me to Eric and Marie, I thought my choice was most appropriate. That night, while listening to a Sima Bina CD, I immersed myself in Moshiri's poetry, remembering the times I'd spent in Iran, feeling the spirit of the place fill me with sadness and longing. What I felt about Iran paled in comparison to what Soraya must have felt in her exile. I hoped that somehow we'd find solace in our shared misfortune.

Earlier in the evening of New Year's Eve, I nervously dressed for the party. I had remembered an official portrait I'd seen of the queen in which her hair was cut short, parted on the side, her bangs brushed back in a lustrous wave. My hair was too long for that, but I managed a chignon that was a fair imitation of Soraya's signature look. I indulged in the childlike pleasure of dressing up as my namesake, and was glad when I saw the results.

As I took one last look in the mirror, my cell phone jitterbugged on the bureau. When I looked at the phone's display, I felt as though I was in a car cresting a hill. It was Sergio. Suddenly I realized that I'd been trying all day to forget that this was to have been my wedding night. Feeling my stomach clench, I flipped it open.

"Raya?"

My stomach turned and my vision narrowed. All the pain, anger, confusion, and humiliation hardened into a ball in my throat. I couldn't speak; I couldn't get rid of the image from the last time I'd seen him.

"Who is this?" I asked coldly.

"Don't play games, Raya. I just need you to listen, allow me to explain …"

Even though nothing he could say would make any difference, I still felt like I was entitled to some explanation.

"Go on." I sat on the edge of the bed.

"What you saw wasn't what it looked like."

"Are you kidding? I'd expect something more original from some-one like you."

I heard Sergio sigh heavily. "Raya, you know how stressed I've been with work, the expansion. If you love me, you'll …"

"I cannot fathom the thought of what I witnessed in Spain. I do not know who it is I am talking to and why …"

I had imagined this call for weeks, had loaded myself with am-munition to destroy any rationale he might offer up. I saw him as he was—a coward.

"Raya, *amor*. Can't you understand? I need your help."

I dropped the phone and kicked it under the bed.

I sat there with my head cradled in my hands. Sergio had not offered any kind of apology and not taken any responsibility for his actions. That hurt nearly as much as what he'd done. I'd expected that I would have gotten a small measure of satisfaction from our phone call. Instead, I felt much worse than if I hadn't heard from him at all. Be careful what you wish for, I'd been told dozens of times before. Now I saw how true that statement was.

I never wanted to see or hear from him again. A line had been marked in my life; I would not cross over it again. For the last few weeks, I had wondered if I'd been fated to play the role of the wounded woman. Worse, I'd martyred myself by keeping silent about what he'd done.

His despicable behavior and his even more reprehensible justifica-tions for it outraged me. Why had I even thought of sparing his repu-tation? Why had I acted so properly when he had done the opposite?

Yes, a Persian woman must act *najib*, put on an air of pretense, take one for the tribe. But to do so for a man who was a coward was an appalling display.

I owe nothing to no one, I realized. *I am the one who is owed. I'm a Bakhtiari*, I reminded myself. *We aren't defeated that easily.* I blotted tears from the corners of my eyes and repaired my makeup. With one last swipe of lipstick, I went out the door.

On the way to Annette's apartment, I stopped by the bistro. Marie and Eric stepped back from their cooking stations and clapped their hands, smiling widely as they appraised me. For most of the time I'd spent with them, I'd worn nothing but frumpy oversized sweaters with jeans, barely mustering the energy to slash a line of lipstick across my mouth. I'd looked as dowdy and disowned as I felt. Their response had me biting the inside of my lower lip to keep it from quivering, but I couldn't hold back a few tears that leaked down my cheek.

Foolishly, I titled my head back, thinking that somehow I could return my tears to their source.

"Your eyes aren't a drain, Raya," Marie said, embracing me. "Let them go. Let them water your lovely garden. No matter what, you're beautiful."

The rough cotton of her chef's jacket scratched my chin. I pressed her closer to me. Looking up, I saw Eric cast a glance our way. He hoisted a glass of wine and nodded, clearly pleased with my burgeoning relationship with Marie. She was six years older than me, yet I felt a closeness and ease with her similar to that with my younger sister Darya. I wished that Darya was here with me now, but Marie's affection would more than suffice.

"Thank you," I whispered to Marie. And then I said to them both, "I don't know how to express my gratitude."

Marie held me at arm's length and smiled her coquette's grin. "It's lovely to have you with us. I hope you will enjoy tonight. Fresh starts, and all that."

"There is so much more for me to say; so much to thank you for." I dabbed at my eyes with the handkerchief Eric had produced. The three of us embraced and didn't part until Eric said, "All the moisture from these tears might ruin the soufflé." I gave them both a parting kiss on the cheek and went out to flag a taxi.

The door of the apartment was opened by a uniformed maid who led me over to the hostess. Annette Lentze was a tall, overly thin woman with a bronzed complexion. Her long neck and patrician nose gave her an aristocratic mien. She held out her hand haughtily. "Good to meet you, Raya," she said in a husky voice.

"Thank you again so much for inviting me," I replied. "Your home is beautiful." I indicated her glittering apartment, filled with elegant French antiques.

"Please have some champagne and make yourself at home," she said as a waiter came around with a tray. I took a glass, and Annette went on to greet other guests. I introduced myself to an older couple, and we chatted for a while about the delights of Paris, but I was distracted. Surreptitiously, I glanced around the rapidly filling room to see if Soraya had by some miracle decided to attend.

As I tried to focus my attention on the sophisticated conversation of the French people milling around me, the atmosphere in the room shifted. I sensed her, although I realized later that her entrance had gone unnoticed by most. I saw that Annette was standing next to a woman with coal-black hair. She gestured me over. I approached, my heart pounding.

"Raya, I'd like to introduce you to someone," she said.

In the next moment I was holding the hand of Soraya Esfandiary-Bakhtiary.

The woman who'd fascinated me all my life stood before me. Although age had taken its inevitable toll on her, she was still the same great beauty I remembered from old photos in *Life* magazine. She wore a violet peau de soie ball gown that I guessed was by the couture designer Givenchy. Her face was wrinkle free but loose, her dark hair streaked with some white; her full lips, sharp nose, and chin as distinctive and regal as I recalled. Moreover, her luxuriant green eyes were as full of depth as in pictures. Soraya regarded me for a moment.

"Raya. What a beautiful name." She smiled.

Annette laughed at her friend. "Vanity becomes you." Then to me she added, "Her pet name as a child was Raya. In complimenting you, she compliments herself."

"I'm aware of that." I blushed and used my hand to erase those words. "What I mean is that I was named after you. My parents knew of your father's endearment."

Soraya ran her finger around the rim of her wineglass and looked up at me. Again, those eyes were more amazing than I'd imagined. This time I noticed that they were striated with faint red lines. Folds of ivory skin pooled at her throat. I wondered if her erect posture was a mark of regal bearing, great pain, or as a defense against nosy intruders.

"You're a lovely young woman. It's good to meet someone from our country, particularly someone your age. The only ones I know from there"—She paused and looked away momentarily; I noted that she didn't use the word "Iran"—"are from my generation or older. I'm told we can be so dreary. My brother lives in Paris, too, but we just tell each other the same old stories."

"I'm so happy to finally meet you, Your Imperial Highness."

"Please call me Soraya. I've been dragging around that title for so long, I've grown weary of it." There was nothing but pleasantness in her voice, and her friendly tone put me at ease.

The conversation turned as several people came up to join us. As they discussed the latest, she rolled her eyes slightly. She leaned toward me and said, "I haven't been to the cinema in years. They may as well be talking about Eskimo artifacts. I understand that you are, like me, a Bakhtiari?"

Before I could respond, the first notes of "Auld Lang Syne" began.

We all linked arms and sang. After a toast was made and we exchanged kisses and wishes for the New Year, Annette pulled me aside.

"Soraya is a recluse; I have to encourage her to get out. She needs to be around young people occasionally. Bijan is here in Paris, but how many times can you go out with your brother? She's still a vital woman with a lot to offer. She normally won't stay in any conversation for this length, but it seems like she is fond of you."

"She's a lovely woman. Someone I've admired from afar." I looked back at the table where everyone had dispersed but Soraya. She sat gazing into the middle distance, nearly oblivious to the scene going on around her, sipping another drink.

"So, good then. Keep her company. It isn't like you'd be doing charity work by seeing her. I think she's fascinating, but then again, I think *I'm* fascinating! But the two of us bore one another to tears, trotting out the same old stories time and again."

I wanted to tell Annette how much I wanted to hear those stories, how much I felt as if I needed to do so. My parents' bitterness about how they'd been treated and their desire to return to a transformed Iran someday had created an identity crisis for me.

"Here's what I'm proposing. Soraya still loves to shop. She probably wouldn't meet you on her own, but the three of us can have lunch at your bistro next week, and then we can go to the shops. Does next Wednesday work for you?"

"Oh, I'd love that," I replied.

By the time Annette and I had firmed up our plans, Soraya had disappeared. I hoped that she had another party to attend, but somehow I knew that she was on her way home, the glittering lights of Paris passing by as distant as stars.

Chapter
FOUR

I was surprised and glad to discover that Soraya was my only companion that following Wednesday. Madame Lentze had the flu but still sent her car and driver to bring the empress to the bistro. I had walked the short distance in yet another drenching rain.

I'd filled in Eric and Marie about my plans, which entailed telling them about my real reason for coming to Paris. They were intrigued, entirely sympathetic, and pleased about the role they'd played in helping me. They said they would busy themselves in the kitchen and not intrude as we had our lunch. I still couldn't believe that Soraya had come into my life, but I didn't want to think too much of that, fearing that I'd somehow trip over the opportunity.

Soraya appeared hale and hearty, the damp weather having brought color to her cheeks. Beneath an enormous fur coat, she wore a black sweater and a cream wool skirt, set off with black tights and an Hermes scarf. Despite her dark palette and natural coloring, she didn't look severe but instead, serene. The pallor and suggestion of illness that I'd seen in her eyes that first evening was gone, and I was left wondering if I'd imagined it. I took her coat and hung it up, and we sat at a table upon which I'd already laid out our salads and leek tarts.

She immediately put me at ease, and our free-flowing conversation swirled mainly around our impressions of Paris. Although we could have spoken Farsi, we kept to French. I imagined that she used her Persian tongue only with close intimates such as her brother, and that this was a way to hold me at a distance. That was fine; I didn't want to force any kind of unnatural affiliation.

I had always presumed that when her marriage ended, she was free to settle wherever she wished. Along with the obvious, the cultural offerings, food, and fashion, I asked what most fascinated her about the place.

"Why, the French people themselves, of course. Where else in the world would a group of people get together and march en masse, hoping to bring about the end of prisons in the country?"

"Really? They did that?"

"Yes. Shortly before you arrived. November, I believe it was. Quite absurd." She leaned back in her chair and gazed out the window. "Quite ironic, too."

"Have you felt that way here?" I asked, avoiding the word *prisoner*, hoping not to offend her but also wanting to take advantage of the opening she provided.

"Here or there or anywhere, really. It doesn't matter the location. One makes oneself a captive, I believe. And most of us do so."

I let the thought hang, hoping that she might say more. She did. "Do you remember the movie *Papillon*, with Steve McQueen? Why they cast an American, I cannot fathom."

"I don't believe I've seen it."

"It's quite long, but good. Exhausting, actually. It makes one feel as if one has been through all that oneself. The constant attempts to escape from an island penal colony. The odd friendships that developed. The love of routine. The insensibility of so much." She tugged at the collar of her sweater. "Their chains made my neck uncomfortable for weeks after."

"Do you go to the cinema much?" I asked.

"Not at all anymore. I see an occasional film on television or a rental. Story seems to have taken a back seat to spectacle nowadays, I'm afraid. I don't like to have my senses assaulted at every turn. That's the first line of attack, and then the brain softens."

She realigned the bracelets on her left arm and shook her head. "Listen to me, sounding like a cranky old woman. Movies are for younger people these days. I do not share their tastes, nor should they share mine."

"I don't think you sound cranky at all. Just a woman with a certain aesthetic."

Soraya pushed a leek across her plate, her face devoid of expression. It was clear she was no longer really in the room.

"Would you like coffee?"

"Thank you, Raya. A coffee would be lovely."

Back in the kitchen, I took a moment to assess our first real meeting. It had a lurching quality about it, as if we were two people who'd been injured and were just now learning to walk again unaided. Our minds knew what to do, but our bodies were halting and uncertain. Yet we recalled with a mixture of fondness and regret what we'd once been able to do naturally.

When I returned to the dining room, Soraya was not at the table. I set the cups down and peered around the partition that separated the entrance from the rest of the space. Her coat still hung there, bear-like and imposing, so I assumed she'd gone to the restroom. The rain had ceased, and sunlight reflected off the puddles. I remembered a joke that my father was fond of telling us when we were children: It's raining cats and dogs; don't step on the poodles. Mostly, he was trying to teach some English idioms. My father was not one to joke without purpose.

When Soraya returned, she took a sip of her coffee without sitting. "Let's walk. The weather seems much improved."

As we exited the café, she dismissed the driver with a barely perceptible shake of her head. The temperature had risen, and she shrugged out of her coat. I offered to carry it for her, and she agreed. I slung it over my arm, feeling its heft tilting me toward her. I shifted it onto my other side, and Soraya linked her arm in mine.

Soraya asked me about my family. I told her our story of exile and loss, our eventual resurrection in the United States. I described my sense that for all my parents' success, they still longed for home and the past.

"Such sad talk from such a beautiful girl."

"I'm sorry if I've overstepped. It's just that sometimes I can't help but wonder what might have been. Such a toll has been taken on Mama and Baba. I don't hear it from them often, but I sense that they are not fully well; that as they get older, they long for the past even more. They always speak of the mountains on the horizon."

Soraya nodded. "Ah yes, I completely understand. Please do not worry about saying too much or too little. We exiles have a duty to one another."

We stopped and I looked at her, hoping she would explain more fully. Her gaze met mine and then flitted away.

"To keep the past alive. To not let what those people did to our country become the end of the story, what most people will remember."

We'd only gone a short way when Soraya stopped and pointed at a bench outside a *fleuriste*. Bunches of peonies, petunias, and water lilies exploded like fireworks against the dark backdrop of the kiosk's canvas. I excused myself and then returned with a bundle of petunias, which I presented to her.

"Petunias are an exiled flower from South America," I said. "Here's a third exile to join us."

My gesture seemed to move her in a way beyond what I'd hoped. She wouldn't look at me when she whispered her thanks.

"I hope I haven't offended you." My voice and my heart were full of worry. The last thing I intended to do was to hurt her.

She shook her head. Clearly what I had done and her response were somehow mismatched.

I wanted to take her hand and tell her that it was all right. I reached for it and held her fingers in mine. She smiled at me briefly and then looked away.

We sat in silence for a moment. The sun had gone behind a cloud, and I saw Soraya shiver slightly. I placed the fur over her shoulders like a shawl.

Laughing softly and inclining forward, she said, "Are you going to tell me a bedtime story now?"

I took my chance. "I was rather hoping that you would tell me one. After all, I shared some of mine with you."

Soraya sighed, leaned back and extended her legs, lifting her heels off the ground. She sat for a moment with her brow furrowed.

I waited.

"When you mentioned the mountains in winter, something came to mind, but then I saw the lilies." The cellophane wrapper of the petunias rattled as she held my gift up unsteadily. Was she upset because I'd gotten her the wrong flower?

Soraya went on. "Another image intruded. I was standing at the top of the staircase in the *Kakhi-i-Marmar*. A gala of some sort. Have you been? The Marble Palace, I mean?"

I shook my head and murmured no, not wishing to disturb the moment by reminding her that I was only a little girl when we fled.

"Hundreds of guests arriving, ball gowns, coat and tails. They filed through the entrance hall. I can hear the sound of the fountain splashing, my pet seal barking. I had to hide my smile behind my hand when I saw their startled looks at my guest in his bow tie and sleek black suit. Most would smile and laugh, the ladies clutching their gloved hands to their chests. The guests rose toward us, ascending the grand staircase and into the Hall of Mirrors. The chandeliers mesmerized me. Flecks of lights dappled the walls, a starry vault like in a planetarium."

A car's horn signaled the end of her reverie.

"It all sounds lovely," I said, hoping that the moment could be restored.

"Oh, it was."

My spirits lightened when I saw that in speaking of those days, it seemed as if years had been subtracted from her appearance. "I was only twenty, you understand, so everything was heightened romance for me. Can you imagine standing there as your husband is greeted by dignitaries, bowing in front of him and kissing his hand?"

A note of wistful bitterness entered her voice for a moment. She must have caught herself, for as she continued, the recitation took on its previous happy tone. I was happy to rejoin her in the pleasurable reminiscence.

"We had lilies that night. Hundreds and hundreds of them perfuming the air, all in malachite bowls or Steuben glass. The containers were all gifts from Stalin, from Queen Elizabeth, from the such-and-such from so-and-so. I can still hear the sound of the *santur*. You know its sound, I'm sure."

In my mind's ear I could hear the dulcimer-like tones of the ancient instrument, precursor of the European piano.

"Yes. Its sound is so …" I struggled to find the word.

"Romantic. Evocative. Transporting." Soraya ran her fingers along the edge of her throat. I was struck by the way her face and neck resembled the stem and petals of a flower.

She closed her eyes and her expression soured, the corners of her mouth drooping into a frown. "Listen to me. It was all just a girlish fantasy. Reality intruded."

She sat up, gathered the coat about herself, and hugged her arms to her chest. My heart quickened, thinking that our encounter was ending. I didn't want to return to the present and all its concerns. My own worries had diminished when she'd taken me back to that time. How awful, I thought, that what might do me good was hearing about things that might cause her pain. Guiltily and greedily, I longed for more; however, I couldn't press her too strongly.

"Still," I said, "You must have some wonderful memories."

"Of course I do, although I see now that the times before I was made queen were really the best years—the times I miss the most."

"Do you and your brother talk about those days much?"

"Bijan and I?" She laughed. "He talks. I mostly listen, or pretend to. When you've known someone your entire life, you speak in shorthand—a kind of code. He can say very few words, and then I just fill in the blanks. A lot like music in that way. A few notes, and we're taken away."

We sat and watched as an articulated bus slithered up the hill and around the curves, its brakes squealing as it stopped in front of us. The vehicle hissed and the door swung open, the driver regarding us impatiently. I looked up and saw the sign that indicated the bench's true use.

"Would you like to go?" I asked Soraya, feeling as if she were a child and the bus an amusement park ride.

Soraya stood and walked past me and into the bus. I gave the driver my best smile, and his eyes softened. My bit of kindness achieved the desired effect. He waited until Soraya and I were seated before taking off.

Soraya scanned the advertisements above us. The bus was empty save for two elderly women with nearly identical shopping carts, stocking caps, and yellow rubber rain boots. They sat, hunched by age, staring into the middle distance. At the next stop, I realized that they were twins.

I inclined my head toward Soraya. "As a child, I always wanted to have a twin sister."

"What made you think of ..." Soraya turned away from the signs and saw what I had noticed.

"Ah, yes." She folded her coat in half and laid it on the seat. "I don't know if I would have liked to have someone with whom I shared so much. It may have been wonderful, but it may also have been frightening."

"Frightening. How so?"

"Losing one's sense of self, one's identity, being unique." She shrugged. "I don't really know. I hadn't thought of it much before you mentioned it."

We bounced along for a few moments, crossing a paving stone intersection. Out the window, I could see the dome of Sacre Cour in the distance. I thought if the bus took us there, we could take the funicular down and do our shopping.

Once the bus's rattling quieted, Soraya said, "I was to tell you another story, wasn't I?"

I was encouraged that she had decided to pick up the thread of our earlier conversation. I wondered if I had come across as too much of an interrogator instead of a curious friend in the making.

"It's funny how both the magical and the mundane stick in the mind. That gala was one thing, but this is quite another." The bus rolled and pitched, and I had the impression that Soraya and I were at sea, wiling away the hours of an Atlantic crossing back at the start of the just-ended century.

A few minutes later, the bus came to a halt at Sacre Cour, and we dismounted. We made our way to the boutique, but something had been palpably altered since our ride had ended. Soraya brightened a bit as she fanned some of the clothes from the small racks. "He's quite ethnic, isn't he?" she said of the designer I'd worn. "He's as eclectic as could be. I like that; it's a bit unpredictable."

Moments after we left the shop, a car pulled up to the curb. The door swung open, and Soraya stepped toward it.

"I must say goodbye now. Thank you for the day. I really enjoyed it."

With a quick wave, she ducked inside the car and was gone. I stood there for a moment, feeling puzzled. I wondered if the car had been following us the whole time, or if Madame Lentze had given the driver the address and our itinerary. In either case, Soraya's departure was abrupt. And it made me sad to think that her life had become so circumscribed that someone knew where she was at every moment. I briefly considered the possibility that she was still under some kind of protective custody or monitoring. With the monarchy long since gone from Iran, I doubted that was the case, but based on what my parents had told me, who knew for certain?

All I did know was that I was left feeling unsure about whether or not I'd ever see Soraya again.

Chapter
FIVE

*M*y fears were justified. For the next two months, I didn't hear from Soraya or from anyone within her circle. I was disappointed and left with the sense that I had been nothing but a pleasant diversion for a wealthy woman, a way for her to fill an afternoon. It made me feel doubly rejected, first by Sergio and now by Soraya. In order not to be overcome with mourning the end of my relationship, I had to turn my attentions elsewhere. I told Eric and Marie that I was going to take a break and leave the city for a while.

I spent a few weeks with my parents in Manhattan. My mother was thrilled that I had gotten to meet Soraya, but her elation lasted only a few moments.

"Now what are you going to do about getting your life back on track?" she asked. She was voicing not just her own worries, but my father's as well.

Her concern was understandable, but I was still stinging from not being able to tell them about Sergio. I felt as if I were a kind of leper, keeping my distance from my family so as not to infect them with my shame. Admittedly in a state of denial, I didn't want to let go of my old life yet. I still clung to the idea that perhaps Sergio would somehow come up with an explanation that made sense and I'd be able to return to my former existence. Deep down I knew this was impossible, but I couldn't quite let go of that sliver of hope.

I now regret making my mother the target of my regrets and frustrations, but I did. "I have no marriage, no children. I'm going to go back to Paris, throw myself into a new job, and enjoy my independence."

"How easily you concede." My mother made it sound as if she was referring to the game of backgammon we were playing while waiting for a delivery from a local Middle Eastern place.

"What is it that people say? 'You can't really be called a quitter if you don't play the game.'" My relentlessly upbeat mother shook the dice and rolled. "Double sixes!" She moved two more pieces home.

As I was reaching for the dice, she took my hand. "Seriously, Raya. Time is your friend. All will be well. Just keep your chin up."

On the flight from New York to Paris, I tried to read to keep my mind occupied. Somewhere just past Greenland, I looked out the window at the vast expanse of steel-gray water. I wished that my mother was with me then, helping me to pick up the pieces of my life and reassemble them into something far more satisfying than what it had become.

Without her to buoy me, my efforts to find employment and a place to live were half-hearted at best. Every time I started to send out my CV or get in touch with one of my banking contacts, I imagined that they thought of me as "that girl" who'd broken the engagement. Sergio's network ran deep and wide, and he might be vindictive enough to put me on a blacklist, even though I was the wronged one. I did manage to find a semi-permanent residence, a sublet near the Gare du Nord train station. The housing arrangement was unofficial, and that met my ever-more-paranoid desire to not have Sergio or anyone else track me down. I spent the next few weeks going to interviews. I also realized that, given what I now knew about Sergio's sexual activities, I needed to schedule a checkup.

One morning in late April, I walked up the stone steps to l'Institut Curie. The hospital was an imposing yellow brick building with a mansard roof whose arched dormers topped massive windows. It gave the impression that serious work went on there. I hoped that wasn't going to be necessary in my case.

A few hours later, having endured the paperwork and probing, I was given some assurances, but needed to wait a day or two for the test results. I walked out, feeling a mixture of relief and worry. As I stood at the bus stop, examining the map, my phone rang, but the caller immediately hung up. Curious, I pressed a button to redial.

"Who is this?" a woman's voice asked in French. To my surprise, I realized that it was Soraya.

"This is Raya. Did you just call me?" I replied in French as well.

"Oh … I was dialing my doctor's number. Blasted cell phones. Annette had put your number in mine. When I didn't get the receptionist, I hung up. All this technology frustrates me. I'm sorry, that was very rude."

On impulse I decided to ask if I could see her. The worst she could do was say no. "I've been out running errands. Could I stop by your apartment? I've been wanting to talk more ever since the day we had lunch."

"I don't see many people," Soraya said in a hesitant tone of voice. "I've been leading an exceptionally quiet life for a number of years."

"I really wouldn't take up much of your time. It's just … I've read your memoir many times, and I find your story fascinating. Since we're from the same family …" I held my breath.

"I guess you could come for a little while," she finally said.

"Oh, that would be wonderful! I promise I won't stay long. Thank you."

Soraya gave me her address, and we said goodbye.

My heart in my throat, I flagged down a cab and fumed when we got stuck in traffic. Finally I exited at her door.

In the light of day, Soraya looked much more fragile than when I'd last seen her. I could see that her mascara had run and that she'd applied a fresh coat of lipstick, but the right side of her mouth was untinted. The uneven aspect this created made me feel protective of her.

She took a deep breath, clearly making an attempt to compose herself. "Well, now that you're here, come in."

I followed her down a dark, narrow hall and into a sitting room brightened by a fire's glow. She indicated an armchair and sat with ramrod posture on the sofa opposite me. A silver tea tray and some cookies were on a low antique table. "Thank you," I said when she handed me a steaming cup.

"I really meant to call you," she said. I knew that wasn't true, but appreciated her lying on my behalf.

"This fire is so nice; it's freezing outside. I was just at the doctor's for a routine checkup," I said. My stomach dropped for a moment when I realized how clumsy my attempt to make conversation had been.

Soraya looked out the window, and in profile she was the same beautiful woman whom I'd seen in pictures. "Bijani made me go the other day. I detest doctors, but they're a necessary evil, I suppose."

My concern must have been more obvious than I realized because she added, "Please don't worry yourself over me. I'm well enough." Her voice wobbled.

Immediately I moved to her side and went down on one knee. Soraya stroked my hair, which made me feel as if I was the one being comforted. It was almost as if she couldn't accept a kind gesture.

"Is there anything I can do?" I asked.

Soraya slumped in the chair. "I just want …" She leaned back, shut her eyes, and shook her head slowly. "What I really would like is nothing."

The rest of her words spilled out of her in a torrent. She told me that she was ill; that her liver function was deteriorating. The doctors told her she drank too much and had to stop. Bijan hounded her about her diet, her drinking, and nearly everything else.

"I'm an adult," she said. "I've made my choices, and I'll live with the consequences." I wished that I could convince her that Bijan was right, but she was so agitated that I'd only make her feel worse if I said so.

"I don't have a death wish, mind you. I simply want to live out the rest of my days on my own terms. If I want to drink, I'll drink. I can't bear being around Bijan when he looks at me so disapprovingly."

She took a small bottle from the side table and poured herself a drink. "I simply refuse to be cowed into submission. Not this time around."

"*Najib*," I said, applying the concept of one's proper behavior with men more widely.

Soraya's expression softened for a moment, and then she caught my meaning. She laughed a great guttural guffaw. "Exactly! I knew there was a reason I liked you. To hell with najib!" Soraya chortled and sat there beaming at me.

I wasn't shocked to hear those words come from the mouth of a woman her age, let alone the epitome of refinement. But I was surprised at her opening up to me so honestly. "I'm glad to hear you say that."

"Too little time and too many rules. I can't be bothered anymore." Soraya stood unsteadily, went to the window, and pulled the curtain back. "I'm sick to death of hiding my condition—not letting anyone know about my affliction. I feel doomed to relive the past and damned by my efforts to forget. I keep running away, but I seem to take my troubles with me. So many people have criticized me for my acting career, although it was short-lived. For not running some global charity or other organization." Soraya turned to look at me, and her expression softened. "You don't seem to judge me, though. Why?"

I shrugged. "I've admired you for as long as I can remember. I see no reason to judge you."

"I find some young people insufferable, with their smug self-assurance that they'll get everything right, be the best at everything. But you're not like that."

"At one time, I may have been like them, but I've made enough mistakes now to know better."

"Odd how that works, isn't it?"

"Yes."

Soraya's voice softened to a whisper. "It seems a bit schoolgirl-like, me wanting to run away."

I wanted to assure her that I felt the urge to flee very much like she did. After all, I'd fled to Paris. "Completely understandable. Admirable in its own way. Perhaps this is a means by which you can undo the wrongs of the past. All the other times you wanted to escape, but didn't."

"You sound as if you have some experience with such trouble."

I smiled a tight-lipped grin, secretly pleased that she sensed my own hurt. "For now, let's just say that my being here is part of my own walkabout."

There was so much more that I wanted to say about myself, about Annette Lentze, about Bijan (and why had she made it seem as if he was persecuting her). Questions about the previous fifty years of her life sprouted like mushrooms from the damp earth, but I didn't give voice to any of them.

"But back to the idea of escaping: Just say the word, and we'll be off," I said, scarcely hiding how thrilled I was at the prospect.

"What do you mean? You want to go away with me?" She chuckled.

"Wherever you'd like. It doesn't matter." As unrealistic as my offer may have seemed, I felt that if she said no, then nothing was lost.

"And what would a girl like you want to do with someone like me?" Her tone was almost flirtatious, teasing, and it warmed my heart.

"I have a bit of a confession to make."

Soraya's eyes narrowed and she pursed her lips. She wagged her finger at me, then broke into a laugh. "I'm listening."

"It's perfectly natural, isn't it, for someone to want to get to know better the person they're named after? As you know, from the time I was a little girl, my parents told me about your life. I've read a bit more, but how much of it is the truth?"

For a moment I thought I read panic in Soraya's eyes. "It depends on how one defines it. You know what they say—there are three sides to every story: his, hers, and the truth." Her sarcasm juxtaposed with humor eased my fears.

Pleased beyond words but keeping in mind her awful circumstances, I said, "I've been grounded here long enough by bad emotional weather. I have no real agenda, really. I would love to take you away somewhere, if you'd like. I would like to offer any comfort, any support I can." In order not to scare her off or come across too eager, I made it sound as if I was doing this solely for her. In some way, I suppose that was true.

I wondered briefly if my comments had offended her, my presuming to have experienced anything at all like what she'd been through.

Soraya was far too intelligent to not realize that I, or for that matter any Persian girl, would give their right arm to accompany the late empress wherever she desired to go. But like me, she responded in the Persian manner, each of us going back and forth telling the other person how it is your pleasure, even if it's not.

"I have been wanting to get away for a while, but sans everyone in my circle. And you know how hard that can be for someone like me. 'Birds of a feather' I think the expression goes." Soraya smiled ruefully, indicating her displeasure with the tightly-knit community in which she lived. "It would be my pleasure to take a few days and travel with you, somewhere near that is close enough to Paris should there be an urgent need for my return."

"Where would you like to go? I'd need to make some travel arrangements. That would take a day or so."

Soraya wasn't completely without opinions regarding the trip. She wanted to avoid the usual tourist spots as much as possible, and she wanted to travel incognito, in a fashion. No luxury accommodations, keep off the beaten track; that sort of thing. She preferred that we not go directly to Marbella, Spain, where she had a second home, but at some point she hoped to.

"The simple pleasures will do," as she put it, "preferably by car."

Her last request was going to be a bit of an obstacle. I'd left the BMW sedan that Sergio had provided for me back in Barcelona.

"Of course," I said, mentally scrambling to come up with a quick solution. "I love road trips." I paused and considered the lifestyle that Soraya had enjoyed. "Have you ever taken one?" She shook her head, then shrugged. "A few hours, yes, but anything longer than that, no."

"You're in for a treat then." I said the words with as much conviction as I could muster. They aroused a feeling that I had perhaps bitten off more than I cared to chew.

Chapter
SIX

After a few days' searching, I located a 1987 Mercedes roadster. At one time it was considered to be a posh convertible, but the one I found had lost a bit of its luster. Still, even in its faded glory, it would be more than serviceable, and with the approach of spring, I thought we'd both enjoy being able to take in the air while motoring. My friend suggested a mechanic to evaluate the car's prospects for a lengthy journey—how long was still to be determined—but with a few minor repairs, it was deemed to be in good health. A week later, and hopefully roadworthy, the car was in my possession.

As I knew they would be, Eric and Marie were thrilled with the developments, although sad to see me leave. Marie's pronouncements about how fated all these encounters were charmed me.

"Are you sure you're not Persian?" I teased her. "We are great lovers of signs and omens."

"Please," Eric said, smirking. "I've enough trouble already getting her to prepare the squab without her trying to divine the future from its entrails."

Marie mock-scowled at him and said, "I foresee many lonely nights ahead for you." Then she turned to me and said, "And for me as well. Hurry home, my dear."

Whatever additional misgivings I had about my selection of a car and whether or not it ran counter to our no-luxury edict, were immediately gone when I saw Soraya standing outside her building. She clasped her hands in front of her face and rocked back on her heels. When I got out of the car to help her load her suitcases in the trunk, she exclaimed, "How did you know?"

My puzzled expression spoke for me, and Soraya continued. "But you didn't! I once owned one just the same. Except mine was white." She ran her hand along the sun-faded red fender. "I love the black leather. The car reminds me of a ladybug! I haven't driven in years, but at some point, I must. No license and no recent experience be damned!"

It took some time for us to pack her six pieces of luggage. Soraya stood and directed the operation while I hefted them about. Rather than take umbrage with my lowered station in life, I counted my good fortune in being able to see up close her vintage Hermès suitcase in a buttery leather and weathered canvas, held firm by brass tacks. I was most interested in a black Chanel makeup case that rattled noisily when I finally found a spot for it in the back seat.

Although the day was brightly sunlit, the temperature was still only in the low sixties. But Soraya assured me that she wanted to keep the top down. As we set off through the crowded streets of Paris, she wrapped a scarf around her hair and put on an oversize pair of sunglasses and a wide-brimmed leopard print hat. I felt as if I was chauffeuring about Sophia Loren or some such glamorous movie star. Feeling a lightness that I hadn't experienced in months, I drove along the Champs-Élysées, luxuriating in the glorious bit of freedom. Even the noisy, nerve-wracking clamor of the Arc de Triomphe's roundabout couldn't drag down my high spirits. I honked the horn for no reason other than to join the reckless revelry, and once we were safely past and on our way down the Avenue de la

Grande Armée, I realized I wasn't so much lost as I was without any idea where we were going.

Taking a couple of deep breaths, I decided that the first sign I saw for a major road would serve as a guide.

That first sign gave me the option of heading toward Versailles or Antony, and I chose the latter. Not only had I already been to Versailles, but its gloomy history held little appeal. Besides, one of my first real boyfriends, a young man from another boarding school with whom my own school scheduled dances, was named Antony. Let the past be your guide, I supposed. The weak sunshine warmed our faces and encouraged me to continue south.

"Human beings are capable of so much, yet we often fall so short of the mark." Soraya and I stood in the center of the labyrinth at Cathédrale Notre-Dame de Chartres after she had asked to stop there. I knew that she'd converted to Catholicism, but I was surprised at what she had said when I asked why. "I suppose I did it as an act of rebellion. Islam was a disappointment to me. For a woman, how could it be anything but?"

Those words came back to me as we walked arm in arm among the tourists, all of us gazing upward at the vastness.

"I wonder how many of these people are pilgrims?" I asked.

Soraya stopped for a moment. "All of them, in their way."

I wanted to ask her what she meant. I stopped for a moment in a square of colored light filtered through the stained glass of a clerestory window, enjoying the prism of illumination.

"You're a vision, Raya," Soraya whispered, covering her mouth like a schoolgirl to hide her laughter.

We resumed walking, and Soraya seemed pleased to act as my tour guide. "I've always been fascinated by the Mary story," she said. "It was one of the reasons for my conversion, I suppose. The Sancta Camisa, the tunic that Mary wore on the day of the Christ child's birth, is here. I love the idea that a woman is so venerated in Catholicism."

We made our way to Our Lady of the Pillar and stood in front of the statue of the Black Madonna. The Mother Mary's ebony visage stared out beatifically. It struck me as so at odds with most of Christianity's depicting of Christ as someone Western in appearance.

I was about to comment on that when Soraya said, "They wanted to destroy the cathedral, you know."

"Who?" I expected her to describe a savage group of medieval plunderers.

"The Americans, during World War II. They thought the Germans were using it as a lookout post."

"That can't be."

"Men can be both remarkably cruel and unthinking, and also remarkably kind. Some American soldier stood up to his orders and convinced his superiors that the Nazis were not occupying the cathedral. I believe he undertook a surveillance mission to prove he was right."

I stood for a moment, turning a tight circle, marveling at the stone arches that rose like hands folded in prayer. "Can you imagine if this place had been bombed? Such madness."

Soraya laughed ruefully and quietly. "Unfortunately, I can."

We stayed the night at a small inn in Chartres. Whether it was having passed the day at such a stunningly beautiful place, or whether Soraya was feeling expansive at being out of Paris at long last, we spent much of the evening in conversation that ranged widely. She demonstrated again that she had an active and curious mind. At first, she seemed content to talk more about her adopted religion, wondering why it was that so many people placed such an emphasis on Christmas Day and Easter. The latter was approaching, just three days away, on April 15.

"Jesus' mission wouldn't have been complete without his death and resurrection, but why do we celebrate his birth so widely? I mean, practically everyone participates in Christmas in the West," she commented.

I'd had a few hours to think about some of these issues myself, and my thoughts tied in neatly with my desire to hear more about her life as well as with the story that she'd told me about Chartres and its importance.

"People like beginnings and endings. Maybe because they are more dramatic, but we remember those bits the best. In law school, a professor in a litigation class told us about the theory of primacy versus recency. He said that in presenting evidence, remember that jurors will recall what they hear first and what they hear last. What's in the middle frequently gets lost."

Soraya arched her eyebrows. "I can see how that's true. Still, that irritates me somehow. So much of our lives are taken up with other things besides births and deaths. Nearly all of it, in fact."

"But think about this. If that tunic that Mary wore was just one that she wore any time and not on the day she gave birth to Christ, would people care as much?"

"They should!" Soraya's voice took on an unfamiliar sharpness. She was rarely so critical of other people. I wondered why this subject troubled her so.

"But human nature fixates on the beginning," I said. Adding myself to the list of those Soraya distrusted, I went on. "For example, any time you are with someone, dating them or whatever, don't people always ask, 'So how did you two meet?' Or if you talk about a past lover, then they ask the other inevitable: 'So what happened at the end?'"

"That's true." Soraya finished her glass of wine and leaned back, looking at the bottle. I refilled her glass.

"I suppose we build monuments to beginnings and endings of people as well. So-and-so was born here. So-and-so died here."

"Maybe that's because we travel so many different places in between, we do what's easiest."

I was coming to realize that Soraya was well practiced at hiding and disguise. For every revelation she made, every entry point she allowed me into her life, she covered it up with the brush of other references and allusions.

Soraya smiled, clearly pleased with my taking hold of her remark and fashioning my own response.

"You're quite right. My mother was one; quite expert at it, too."

"How do you mean?"

"My mother seemed to erect a shrine to the circumstances of my birth, and to the rest of my life as well." Soraya drained her glass and straightened in her seat, "But as the saying goes, that is a story for another day. If we're going to visit any more shrines this trip, I'm going to need my rest."

I sat at our table for a while after Soraya left, rehashing much of what she had said to me. I was eager to share my story about Sergio with her, but I didn't dare to interrupt her once she got talking openly. I also suspected that she sensed there was more of a connection in our circumstances than simply sharing a name.

I wondered what it felt like to constantly be talked about, as she was. There was much that I admired about Catholicism, but when it came to God's forgiveness of his creation's sins, I struggled against the feeling that someone like Sergio, a regular churchgoer, abused that privilege. Did Soraya feel the same way that I imagined Sergio did—that God's love was so infinite that he would offer absolution to anyone, and that we all should do the same? Could humans' love ever be so unconditional?

As I prepared myself for sleep that night, I kept thinking about the tunic that was enshrined in Chartres. Soraya, like many others I knew, seemed so devoted to Mary. I didn't share their faith, nor their belief in the Virgin's story, but I did see one connection. In my own way, I had venerated Soraya for much of my life, had held her up as a figure not just of great importance, but someone who was different from all other women. I was beginning to see that she was a human being like the rest of us, one who grieved and got angry.

Soraya's feelings made her human, I suppose, but as she herself said, humans often fall so short. Yet in other ways, they rise to great heights. I was beginning to understand that beginnings and endings, high points and low points, zeniths and nadirs tell only part of the story.

Chapter
SEVEN

*O*f I learned one thing in the first weeks that I spent with Soraya, it was this: While you can travel a great many miles, it is still possible to make very little forward progress. As we meandered our way from Lourdes to the Atlantic coastline and then to Madrid, I heard Soraya speak of many things. At Lourdes, she saw a blind man and his family seeking a cure. That brought to her mind a poor man in Tehran who came to one of her public appearances to thank her for the work she did on behalf of the poor. Seeing a group of cyclists pedaling their way up a pass in the Pyrenees, she wondered about the Italians and the French and their obsession with the sport. That led to a lengthy story about a time in Monaco when an outing was delayed by a race there. At times, I felt as if I was one of those riders, struggling up a steep mountainside, hoping that the downhill would bring both speed and relief.

That's not to say that I didn't enjoy her company. Soraya seemed to be reveling in the opportunity to talk about herself. At times she was preoccupied with her girlhood in Berlin, her grandfather Karl, and their walks through the Volkspark Friederichshain and their trips to the zoo. She was proving true the statement that I had made about our propensity to build shrines. Soraya's early days spent in Germany were a memorial she'd erected to the time before. I could understand why she would want to fondly recall those days before her world changed, but I found conspicuous by its absence any mention of the war and the rise of the Nazis to power.

I suppose that, in a very real way, I had done the same thing as we drove along. With the great exception of Sergio's betrayal, I found myself not truly behind the wheel of the car so much as with him, skiing in the Alps in Torino; happily sunning myself on a motorboat off the Isle of Capri; lounging on a beach in Rio. For Soraya and for me, it was lovely to think that those painful moments from our pasts were easily erased. In reality, they formed a great part who we were.

At one point, tired of doing all the decision-making, I asked Soraya if she wanted to go anywhere in particular.

"I've never been to Andorra, and it has always been a great curiosity—like a landlocked little island."

Grateful to have a destination in mind, I pointed the car east out of Madrid. With Bosch's painting of *The Garden of Earthly Delights* fresh in my mind from our visit to the Museo del Prado, I hoped to find some of those earthly delights for myself. I was feeling like one does after a fever breaks. Nearly five months had passed since I ended things with Sergio. My passionate disillusionment and heartache had calmed, but I was still feeling weak and ineffectual. The novelty of following one whim after another still kept me amused, but it was also contributing to my lethargy. While I was traveling with Soraya and learning more about her life, I wasn't actively doing anything to press her for more than a mere set of holiday snapshots.

For a few days, the Mercedes had been difficult to start, and it sometimes did its own version of trembling and hesitating as if it had taken on some of the characteristics of its occupants and their halting journey. Late one afternoon, as Soraya sat dozing, I completely lost my sense of direction on a narrow road following the twisting path of the Ara River. At that point, left and right, north and south, might been advanced topics in calculus. Just past the town of Ainsa in the province of Huesca, I let my instincts take over and turned left at a crossroads. Passing onto a small wood-and-stone bridge, the car lurched to a stop. All my efforts to restart it failed. The tank was three-quarters full, so that wasn't the problem. Soraya was equally out of her depth, but she did suggest that I put the car in neutral and allow it to coast to the other side of the bridge to allow others—we hoped there would be others—to pass.

We sat there for an hour, the rushing water and the furious whining of locusts the only sounds. Finally, a farmer in a rusted relic of a tractor came upon us. After we explained and he stood staring at the car's engine for a while, he attached two stout ropes to the fender and towed us into the next village.

After several dozen miles of more winding roads and nothing but trees and fields, we crossed under a small archway that said "*Castejón de Sos.*"

"That's about as close to a castle as we're likely to find," Soraya said as she craned her neck to look at the hand-lettered banner strung between two flagpoles. We'd been hoping to find a parador, one of the system of castles, monasteries, and palaces that had been converted into tourist hotels.

"This is definitely not the way to Paradore de Oroel," I said, watching as more open fields passed by slowly.

The road turned from tarmac to dirt, and we bounced along the ruts. As we made a sharp turn, we could see the town center that ran for the equivalent of two city blocks. Our progress was halted at one intersection by a flock of sheep. The town's school had just let out as well, and the children all stood, the girls in plaid jumpers and the boys in white dress shirts and blue pants, waiting patiently.

One of them noticed our car and nudged his friend, who passed along the nudge, and soon they were all staring at us. The shepherd and his dogs had finally entered the crosswalk, and he stopped and said something to the children. Whatever he said must have worked. The kids all turned away from us, and none dared look our way when they passed in front of us.

"How remarkable," Soraya said. "They went from boisterous to reverent in an instant. Whatever else goes on here, they should bottle the water. The young people I know could stand a bit of that kind of training."

The farmer towed us a few meters further, past a municipal building on our right, in front of which flew the flags of Spain and Aragon, the state in which the Huesca province sat.

"I love the boldness of the red and yellow stripes," I said, "They stand out remarkably against the blue sky."

"I know we both tend to romanticize," Soraya said as she lifted her sunglasses off, "but I feel as if I've gone home." She inhaled deeply and sighed. "This place so resembles Gahveh-rokh, the village in the Bakhtiari region. Have you ever been?"

"I was very young the only time I was there. I don't remember it at all. But I have seen pictures and heard tales of the place."

Soraya circled her hand above her head. "The mountains, the streams, this valley." She laughed her great laugh. "And the smell of the sheep!"

I wasn't certain who or what had guided us to this place, but I was glad for it. Soraya seemed—like the flowering plants that lined every windowsill—to have budded, offering the promise of a graceful blooming to come.

We came to a stop in front of a small stone-walled hotel. It wasn't possible for the tractor to get us into the parking lot. The farmer dismounted and raised his index finger to signal that we should wait.

He entered a small tavern and came out a moment later with several other men. They pushed the car up the slight incline, where I parked.

Before we exited the car, an older woman bustled out of the entrance and stood by the trunk, waiting for me to open it. She wore a housecoat and a pair of black shoes that I always associated with nuns. Standing erect with one hand on her hip, she gave off the same no-nonsense, there's-work-to-be-done air as those women. Before I could protest, she waved me off and hefted both my bag and one of Soraya's under one arm. In the meantime, the men had all gathered around the Mercedes. Its hood was propped open. One at a time, each took a turn at bending over to inspect the engine. It was as if they were expecting the motor to tell them what was wrong. Clearly, the Mercedes spoke German, but none of them did.

I was torn. I stood in the middle of the parking lot, watching the older woman toting our luggage and these men inspecting the car. Soraya cast her vote with her feet and went inside the hotel. I walked over to the men.

I may have surprised them with my fluency in Spanish, for their eyes widened when I asked them if they had any idea what was wrong.

"The distributor," one of them said.

"The fuel pump," chimed in the next.

By the time they were through, I'd had five different diagnoses.

"Can anyone fix it?" I asked.

On this, there was complete agreement. As though embarrassed at having been caught at something, the men all folded their arms across their chests and said softly, "Miguel." Amidst their nods and their eyes avoiding direct contact with mine, I managed to get them to explain to me that Miguel was the local mechanical genius. However, he was out of town doing some repairs to the ski lifts at a nearby resort. When he would be back they couldn't say because only Miguel could do the work at the resort and who would know how long it would take.

I was nearly in tears, thinking that we were likely hundreds of kilometers from any major city with a mechanic who had experience with a Mercedes. And if the car required some parts to be replaced, who knew how long that might take?

I thanked the men and headed inside the hotel. In ornate hand-painted letters down the pinkish stucco façade of the building was painted "Hotel Plaza." In time, I would learn that the older woman, Delores, ran the place since her husband died twenty-two years previously. The Hotel Plaza had been in existence for more than a hundred years, and was so named because at one point it sat in one corner of the town's plaza. She couldn't remember exactly when that square had been razed, but she thought it had something to do with some horrible dictator and his army and columns of marching soldiers. She and her daughter Estrela were the latest in a long line of family members who had owned the hotel.

Estrela came out of the kitchen, wiping her hands on her apron and smiling widely. She was in her fifties, judging by her salt-and-pepper hair, so Delores must have been at least seventy. Although the place was called a hotel, it was really an inn. Estrela explained that meals were included with the cost of the room. I was wondering where Soraya was. For the entire trip so far, more than three weeks, Soraya had only picked at what was on her plate. Therefore, I was surprised to find her sitting at the dining room table, all alone, happily eating olives and serrano ham along with a crusty bread that would have made Eric and Marie envious. A large glass of red wine, the shape and color of a rhododendron blossom, sat half-filled in front of her. I left her to her pleasures and followed Estrela to my room.

The two women were in the late stages of renovating the place, and the spacious rooms felt more like bedrooms in a private residence than ones in a hotel. Each was tastefully and distinctively decorated, echoing one another with small splashes of color. My room looked out on a substantial garden, and beyond that the rolling hills and pasturelands. I seemed to have exhaled my concerns about Soraya's health in the fragrant air of this tiny enclave in the Pyrenees foothills.

After dinner, Soraya and I sat out on a tiled porch abutting the garden. Wisteria and roses that were twined around two enormous trellises scented the evening air. Twin pairs of citrus trees, lemon and lime, were lit by fireflies.

"This place very much reminds me of the house my father built in Isfahan. It was his pride and joy. All that is missing is a fountain," Soraya said, taking a sip of her Rioja. I'd come to learn her body language. As she rested her arms on the wicker chair's side bolsters, splayed slightly to the side and her head tilted back to take in the stars, I saw how relaxed she was. She began to describe her family's summer getaways to a small village in the province of Isfahan.

"In Berlin, I had never seen men with a sheep balanced on each shoulder, walking miles to take their livestock to market. But in Ghahfe-rokh, that was a common sight. Their young children trotted alongside, never seeming to complain. When we were there, we were either astride a horse or driven behind in a cart. Later on, we were the first to drive cars along the rutted horse paths. You should have seen the looks we got in our Mercedes–Benz."

Soraya smiled at the memory. "Once, when I was about ten, I made the trek from our estate to Isfahan with Bijan and my grandmother, Bibi Maryam. I rode a Bakhtiari-bred horse, a small thoroughbred related to the Arabian. I was fearless then, in many ways. A Berlin girl didn't have much occasion to ride the rest of the year, and the horses, though beautiful, were as fiery as could be. But I was determined and made a fuss about wanting to ride on my own. I had more imagination than horse sense, I suppose. Sitting there on the saddle, I commanded a view of the terrain, and something inside me seemed to vibrate with purpose and passion. This was what I was meant to be doing; not be cloistered in some stuffy classroom."

She took a sip of her wine. "I lost my concentration for a moment, and a sheep stepped into my horse's path. The next thing I knew, it reared and I fell off. I lay there, the wind knocked out of me, my chest heaving.

"I remember looking into the sky, seeing a cloud in the shape of a lounging cat drifting past. Then I saw Bibi Maryam's creased face. Bent over me, her skin seemed to drip from her skull. As the blood rushed to her head, her skin turned a deep russet tone. I expected her to kneel beside me and gather me in her arms. Instead, she pulled me by the arm so that I was standing unsteadily on my feet. Scowling, she roughly dusted me off and led me toward the horse, which stood grazing at the side of the path.

"She cupped her hands and shook them. I had no choice but to put my hand on her bony shoulder, step into her hold, and clamber into the saddle. Only then did she hand me a bota bag and order me to drink. I could barely gag anything down, but I did as I was told. Bibi Maryam handed me the reins, and we moved on.

"A few kilometers later,"—Soraya's eyes misted over—"she came astride me and said, Raya, my love. Look at me.' She stretched out her hand to encompass all that was around us. 'This is where you're from, and who you are. Draw strength from it.' When we got back home, no mention was made of the incident. The lessons were clear. Shortly after that, my mother told us that we had to pack for our return. We begged and pleaded to be able to stay longer, but it wasn't possible."

Soraya sighed. "Whenever I daydreamed, it was always of Ghahfe-rokh. I loved that village, loved living in the tent, the feeling of both being rooted to the land and having the freedom to roam and set up quarters again somewhere else."

As she spoke, it became clear—and it was something "in the blood" that I related to as well—that no landscape would ever so captivate her as the Bakhtiari villages and surrounding region. In my mind's eye, I saw again what I had witnessed the one time I had been to that area. I was sure that it hadn't changed much from when Soraya trod the same ground. I recalled the tents rising up out of the lush spring meadows that ran with ice-melt from the Zagros Mountains. Bakhtiari women wearing sevenfold skirts and tulle headpieces jangling with gold coins. Everyone cooked; everyone herded sheep; everyone milked cows and hunted on horseback. Every way that a human being could display fortitude, the Bakhtiaris did. Family honor and pride, the chest-swelling sense of generosity and respect in hosting—these ideals had made an impression on young Soraya, and on me.

Thinking of the things we shared made me want to ask about the one big subject that she hadn't yet touched on. I wasn't sure how to broach it, but I took a gamble and said, "You know, there's more than just a fountain missing from this hotel to make it like your home in Isfahan. And there's one thing missing from all the stories you've told me so far. What's missing is him. You never mention his name."

Soraya turned her head away from me. She had heard what I'd said, but she was pretending she hadn't. Her blank expression was all the more frightening because it signaled her complete withdrawal. I was used to a certain kind of aloofness from her, but to be ignored completely hurt me. If she'd told me that it was none of my business, or had even harshly told me to shut my mouth, I would have been less offended.

In the few moments that lapsed while she sipped her wine and busied herself lighting a cigarette, I thought of our earlier discussion about the building of shrines. It was as if her life with Mohammed

Reza Pahlavi was one that she had built in a prominent location but kept locked so that no one could visit. When she didn't respond to me, I said as much to her.

From over the roof of the two-story hotel came the sound of children laughing. Every time Soraya and I saw youngsters, I'd hoped that she'd make a comment about them, providing me with some entry point into that part of her life that still confounded me. Once, in Zaragoza, we came across a wedding. Soraya had stood there, rapt in her focus on the bride as she was ushered into the church. But on that day and in days after, she never mentioned the wedding, and what she was thinking was impossible to decipher.

"I'm sorry if I've overstepped my bounds, but I've read the books you wrote, and you talk about that part of your life extensively. However, I can't help but believe that what you said was not the complete truth."

My comment roused Soraya from her reverie.

"What makes you say that?" Her tone was both hurt and haughty, a combination she often paired.

"My family talked about you so much, and told me things that I believe are true. Maybe they were rumors, but when I read your memoirs, you made everything seem so cut-and-dried. It had to be more complicated than that."

Soraya laughed, exhaling a plume of smoke before she dashed out her cigarette. "Of course it was. I did the books for the money. There was a lot of interest in me, but at the time, I was still receiving money from the shah. Surely you understand."

"I do, but don't you feel the need to share the real truth with someone else?"

"Quite honestly, no."

I sank back in my chair.

"Why does that disappoint you?"

"Because you have experienced so much in your life. For your feelings, your perceptions to pass on with you …" I stopped myself, ashamed that I had dared raise the subject with her. She didn't need to be reminded that her life was in the late stages.

"Go on. I appreciate your honesty." Soraya's voice was more tender than it had been.

"Okay then. Honestly? Maybe you don't owe it to anyone to tell the truth, but I'd like to hear it. I share more than a name with you. I know all about betrayal—maybe not on so grand a stage, but my heart is scarred too. I was thinking that maybe if I better understood what you'd been through, I could gain some insights. Maybe it would help you make some sense of things as well."

"Pardon." Soraya rose and went inside. I could hear her speaking with Dolores and Estrela. A few minutes lapsed, and I was certain that she had retired for the evening, leaving me feeling very much the fool. When I heard the door slide open, I believed it was either of the two proprietors coming to wish me good night.

Instead, it was Soraya. She had put on a heavy wool cardigan, and her arms were folded across her chest.

"So what is it you don't know already?" she demanded.

"I've read and heard so much, but I don't know anything about what you really felt."

"Such as?"

"Did you really love him?"

"Yes," Soraya said instantly.

"At sixteen, you knew what love was?"

"What does age have to do with love?" Soraya adjusted her sweater, and then sighed. "This may take some time."

The last breath of evening breeze fanned the candles and stirred the leaves. A moment later, everything in the garden grew quiet in anticipation.

PART II

Soraya

1948–58

Chapter
EIGHT

irls were different then. That's the simple answer to how I could have possibly considered being married at sixteen, let alone assuming the role of the queen of Iran. Today, girls that age are supposed to be more knowledgeable and advanced in many ways, with the influences of the media. Back then, we were less aware, but believed we were quite sophisticated, and in some ways we were. After all, at fourteen I was living in a different country other than Iran or Germany, where I'd grown up; I was attending boarding school in Lausanne, Switzerland. My classmates and friends were a menagerie of exotic species from around the world.

Now I realize how silly we were to presume so much.

They called them finishing schools. "Beginning schools" may have been a more appropriate term. We were just beginning to try on identities as if they were outfits. Our imagined maturity was a product of mass hysteria. Put that many girls together from backgrounds of wealth and means, and what would you expect? My own family had fled the war in Europe and internal strife in Iran, and if I wasn't world weary, I was at least world aware. At the same time, I was prone to dreaming.

One day, before I came to Lausanne, I was in Isfahan, looking skyward, watching a plane flying low overhead. I was with my friend Aryan, and we heard the rumble of the plane's engine before we saw it. I immediately thought of the shah and Queen Fawzieh, winging their way to some important destination. Even that brief glimpse of the plane's insignia had me rapt. I remember standing there in the courtyard while we were at recess. All the girls were running about, a few of them looking up and pointing. I had to shade my eyes, staring skyward, feeling a thrill I couldn't really explain. The sounds of the girls' chatter faded to silence. Just the plane's drone remained, mesmerizing and titillating.

I had no way of knowing then that I was hearing the siren's song, luring me. Funny the choices we make, and that are made for us. How unpredictable consequences can seem at the time, and how inevitable they appear to us later.

Back then, I certainly didn't know any better than to lose myself in dreams. Despite our differences, the girls at our school were all in the same boat. We all lived both as part of and apart from our families. I did love the companionship of the girls, the camaraderie, the competition, the life in the dormitories.

"Why do you keep your makeup under your bed? Are you afraid someone will steal it?" Madeleine Swift, the American girl, asked. "The last school I was at, there were terrible thieves everywhere. I told my parents, and the next thing I knew, I was here in dull old Lausanne."

"If you were to ask my father," Claire said, "The only thieves here are Mademoiselle Roseaux herself and the staff. He claims that I haven't learned a thing." She stood at the window and unbuttoned the top three buttons of her uniform blouse. She bared her shoulder and did her best pin-up impression, curling one leg and pouting her lips.

The other girls laughed. "That's not very ladylike," I said mock-seriously.

"If I had a franc for every time I've heard someone say that to me," Claire said, "I could pay my own tuition and that of the Persian teacher's pet." She was about to muss my hair, but I ducked and arrested her hand.

"Please, don't. My father is coming round later, and I've spent too much time already primping for him."

"Why do your parents take you home every weekend?" Madeleine asked.

"Mind your manners," Claire said, rising quickly to my defense. "You haven't been here long enough to know anything. Besides"— Claire turned on her heels, her eyes sparkling with mischief—"none of us have asked you how your calves grew as fat as sausages. Your father must covet them."

"Don't be cruel," I admonished her, managing not to laugh at the running joke about the "Pork Princess" of Chicago. Madeleine fingered the hem of her skirt as Claire grinned at me. I loved Claire, and sometimes aspired to be more like her—the witty, catty, unpredictable girl unafraid to speak her mind. The truth was, my parents' constant reminders that I needed to be ladylike in the Persian tradition had had their effect. Besides, Madeleine wasn't to be faulted for the unfortunate circumstances of her birth. If her family had made its fortune in mining rather than meat, she wouldn't have been teased.

I had tried to convince Claire to be kinder to our lone American, if for no other reason than Madeleine was a native speaker of English, the subject with which the two of us struggled the most, but also most wanted to succeed in.

Still, I wasn't pleased that Madeleine had brought up that tender subject. There I was at boarding school, but my parents had moved to Montreux along with me. It wasn't so much that I wanted to be free of them, but their presence in town marked me as different.

Madeleine stood in the doorway, her sagging shoulders and folded arms a pantomime of hurt.

Claire raised her eyebrows and sighed. "Soraya should be glad her parents take such an interest in her. When I go home for the holidays, my mother and father are off in Barbados. *Comment voulez-vous dire 'fou'?*"

"Crazy," Madeleine answered.

"Thank you. While I sit about in Lisbon, bored. Crazy."

Madeleine resumed sitting, demurely crossing her legs at the ankles—whether the result of good instruction or self-consciousness, I couldn't decide.

I thought it was best to confront Madeleine's question head-on, to put the matter to rest. "My parents live in Switzerland now. It's convenient for them to retrieve me on the weekend. I think my father is afraid that too much exposure to continental influence will damage me."

"*Comment merveilleux!* Continental influence. Such big words for such a little speaker of English," Claire said.

"She's not a little speaker of English." Madeleine adopted her schoolmistress tone. "She may speak just a little English, but a little speaker of English is someone who is physically small."

I remembered the debates my parents had held in Isfahan. The endless go-rounds about whether it was in the children's best interest to remain in Iran or in Europe. War on one side; unrest and upheaval on the other. I was elated when my father announced that the family was moving to Switzerland, less so when he said they'd live in the same city where I'd be schooled. I can still see him, sitting perfectly erect at the table, making eye contact with each of us as he made the proclamation. Then he added, "I would especially like to thank your mother for her perseverance in keeping the ship of family afloat."

In the two years since, I wished that I'd taken the opportunity to thank my mother for intervening on my behalf about leaving Iran. Although we two were allies, I had been raised to believe, doubtless more because of the Bakhtiari influence than my German roots, that women must suffer in silence. I tacitly understood that Mother and I shared the desire to live in Europe. While we both would have preferred to be back in Berlin with my grandfather Karl, where I lived until I was six, such an arrangement was not possible. The war had been over for three years, but Berlin was still essentially in ruins. To go back was to have our hearts broken, but I knew that one did not speak of such things.

"However you phrase it, I'm working on my English. By the way, what time is it?" I jumped to my feet and went to the window. "We don't want to be late for the movie. Let's get going!" The three of us shrugged our purses over our shoulders and dashed out the door.

Two hours later, we exited the darkened theater into the fading afternoon. Tugging on our white gloves, smoothing our skirts, and adjusting our hats, we thought we were the very picture of glamour.

"Why couldn't they have split the money as they'd planned and just gone on and been happy?" Madeleine stepped into a crack in the sidewalk, stumbled, and shouldered Claire.

Never one to resist a pratfall, Claire walked unsteadily for a moment, her long legs splayed to the side, her hand clutching her hat to her head. "Would you want to see that movie? Did you not understand the title, *Treasure of the Sierra Madre*? The mother mountains. Greed is the mother of all men."

"Ach, Claire, how cynical!" I said, "Besides, Bogie is not a bad man like the rest of them."

"Oh, to have such beautiful eyes, but not be capable of the seeing." Claire shook her head forlornly. "Blinded by Bogie. Someday, I'll write a book about you with that title."

"You have to admit, even looking so dirty, he is a handsome man." I heard the sound of male laughter, slightly high-pitched and annoying, coming from behind us. "I fear our friends are tailing us."

The girls laughed at my use of the term. "They're cute but little boys," Claire said. She reached into her purse and tossed three wrapped toffee candies down an alley. "This will throw them off the trail." She looked expectantly at us.

We clapped politely. "Very good use of the idiom," Madeleine said.

"I told you. I pay attention in the movies and learn much for the English."

The sound of running feet made us turn around. The three boys came rushing up.

"I don't think your plan worked," Madeleine muttered out of the side of her mouth.

"Oh, you have so much to learn," Claire said, tossing her luxuriant brunette hair over her shoulder.

"*Bon soir*, fellas," she said in a ludicrous but appealing manner.

The three boys had been seated behind us at the film. In the dark they were difficult to distinguish, but in the daylight, it became clear who was who and where they were from. Each wore a burgundy blazer and gray pants. Even without being able to read the crest emblazoned on their chests, we knew they were from the St. Nicholas school.

From the way they'd been acting, having to be shushed throughout the film and noisily belching and punching one another in the arms, I had assumed they were lower form boys, maybe eleven or twelve, around Bijan's age. They were likely doing their best to impress the three of us, who were fifteen.

I was slightly surprised and even more disappointed to realize that these were upper form boys—our age chronologically, but far less mature.

We stood several feet apart, regarding one another as other pedestrians filtered around us. The boys each held up one of the toffees.

The tallest of the bunch, a redhead, stepped forward. Whether

76

from the brief run, the cool air, or his embarrassment, his cheeks were aflame.

"Pardon me, ma'am," he said, pretending to doff his hat. "I believe one of you ladies dropped this." His attempt at a Western American accent was foiled by the lilt of his Irish brogue.

"And I believe," Claire said, snatching the candy back from him, "That you dropped your brain there." She pointed to a spot on the sidewalk where some garbage had fallen.

Everyone except the red-haired boy laughed. He raised a finger to his forehead and saluted. "Touché, Madame."

"You may call me Fifi." Claire held out her hand as though expecting him to kiss it.

"My name is Eamon," he said, edging toward her, looking as if he were approaching a pit viper. To everyone's surprise, "Fifi" did not pull her hand away or smack him across the cheek. When his lips touched Claire's skin, I could have sworn she turned demure.

I didn't have much time to consider my brash friend's transformation. Another young man stepped into the group. He spread his arms and ushered us out of the flow of walkers and into the entrance to an alley. Unlike the others, he wore a light sweater offset with a black dickey, the color of which contrasted sharply with his pale skin.

"Are these gentlemen," he said, his voice dripping with sarcasm, "causing you ladies any trouble?"

"No, Archie, they are not," I said.

"Good. Then when are we going to finally go on that date?"

"That date that we have never once discussed?"

"Oh, Soraya," said the young man, ignoring my objection and launching into a rather feeble Bogart impression. "Of all the schools in all the cantons of Switzerland, you had to come to a sister school of mine?"

I regretted previously revealing this celebrity crush to my

friends, but this latest assault was far too much. How could the fact of it have spread so far? The truth was, I adored Humphrey Bogart and wouldn't have minded being Lauren Bacall, Ingrid Bergman, or any other female movie star. It wasn't just that I was enamored with Mr. Bogart; I was in love with the whole idea of Hollywood and fame.

Worse, I couldn't understand why Eamon, and now Archie, had both thought it clever to do impersonations. Surely they didn't believe that the way to win a woman's heart was by pretending to be someone they were not?

I stared at Archie stonily, assuming this would switch off the impression.

"All right then, seriously, what do you say to a rendezvous next Saturday?" he asked.

I found it convenient to channel the tone my father Khalil Khan took when admonishing me about respectability, as he did constantly.

"I must inform you, dear sir, that I am forbidden to go on dates. Your expectations would surely be disappointed, in any case. My father says that I am like a painting in a museum. Admirers may look and appreciate, but they may not touch."

"You wouldn't say that to Bogie, now, would you?"

"Of course not. I would immediately swoon and fall into his arms. But so far as I know, Bogie is thousands of miles from here." I liked the way I'd managed to deflate him, à la Claire.

"Well, if you'd prefer to be admired from afar your whole life, I dare say there's nothing I can do about it," Archie said in a wounded tone.

Eamon and the other two boys headed back toward the theater, clearly not enjoying the live performance in front of them.

"It's too bad that's the only wit you will ever have about you. You've proven yourself completely charmless."

Archie's expression grew angry and then faded into blankness. Without a word, he shouldered past and continued down the sidewalk.

"Bravo, Madame Soraya," Madeleine said appreciatively. "You put him in his place."

"Yes. She certainly did." Claire frowned at me. Claire understood, and when our eyes met, her suspicion was confirmed. I had acted with my brain and not my heart. I thought Archie was attractive enough, with his aristocratic nose, high forehead, and gelled bangs.

I'd been told for so long that unsupervised interaction with boys was out of the question, that I had responded automatically to rebuff his innocent flirtation. That said, Archie had been entirely too forward, asking me on a date in front of the others. From my father, I knew that relationships between men and women were frequently arranged and not subject to one's choice. From my mother, I learned that as far as matters of the heart were concerned, I was the one to be in control. She was far more subtle than my father, so frequently his point of view dominated.

Still, here in the free air with the panoramic lakeshore vistas of Lausanne, it was easy to be a Western girl, to sample chewing gum, and even try a little makeup. Well, it was easy, up to a point. I glanced at my watch, realizing the appointed time of my pick-up had come. I frantically buttoned my blouse and vest to the very top, wiped off my lipstick, and put my hair up in a conservative bun. When the transformation was done, Claire hugged me before stepping back to kiss my cheeks.

"It is so hard saying goodbye to you and hello to your other self."

I felt my throat clench and my eyes begin to tear. "Please, Claire, don't say that." Claire shrugged, "I can only trust you about this. It makes me sad."

The car pulled up. "Oh, I almost forgot. Everyone—spit out your gum!"

I couldn't bear the thought of having to endure another of Khalil Khan's tirades against the degenerate youth of the West. He would surely take one look at the short dresses and painted faces of my friends, see them standing slack-hipped and snapping their gum, and forbid me to have anything further to do with them. At least, I thought, let him see them without their hopelessly Western chewing.

Two wads of gum were immediately deposited on the sidewalk. Crouching down to look through the window, to my relief, I saw that my mother was behind the wheel.

"Sorry," I said, turning back to my friends. "False alarm."

"You owe us," scolded Claire jokingly. "Mine was Wrigley's—imported."

The parental disagreement over the worth of such friends that had played out in my head was a disagreement about Western vs. traditional ways. It mirrored the battle lines my parents had drawn as my time at finishing school neared its end. I'd hoped that as I'd gotten older, the tug of war between the opposite poles would end. Instead, the battle regarding my impending womanhood and my proper role only intensified.

"It is our duty, I don't need to remind you," Khalil began one such confrontation, "to safely deliver our daughter to the next stage of life, which should be marriage. Learning and education is all well and good, but you don't want—do you?—for Soraya to wind up unmarried at age twenty-one? An age when, as the saying goes, 'Fetch the vinegar—it's time for her to be pickled.'"

My mother burst out laughing at this traditional Persian aphorism regarding a young woman who has gone past her "freshness date." It seems silly to me now, to think that twenty-one could be considered "expired." Back then, I simply sat in my room listening to the two of them through the walls. I'd heard variations on this theme for so long—well before I had any real notion of what it truly meant to be married—that the concept held no real meaning to me. I knew that men and women got married, that it was the expected thing to do. But beyond that, marriage was so common a thing as to be unknowable. It was like thinking about what it meant to breathe.

I heard my mother's tone softening. "I'm sorry, Khalil, I don't mean to make light of the situation. Why, I myself married at age eighteen. But times are different now. Girls have more opportunities, and if Soraya wants to follow her passion, I think we should encourage her."

"But she keeps saying she wants to be an actress. That's not a passion. It's just nonsense! Acting?" My father's tone sent a shiver through me. Unlike marriage, I'd thought a great deal about becoming a performer. I didn't have to wait for my father to express it; I knew his disapproval was forthcoming. I mentally recited the litany: It was completely inappropriate for a young lady of a reputable family to pursue this folly. For me to study toward such a "career" was no different from running away to join the circus. A convent, yes; a group of frivolous fornicators? No!

"I want her to learn to act *properly*, and not vagabond about."

"I know, I know," my mother said with a sigh, her tone expressing the slightest mockery with a good deal of sympathy and understanding mixed in. I was comforted to know that she, too, knew the remainder of the litany.

"If she is going to remain unmarried, she should at least study something worthwhile, like medicine," he added.

"But what if she isn't interested in medicine?" my mother asked.

Lying in my bed in our Swiss apartment, I rolled over and wrapped the pillow around my head. Why must a Persian woman only be allowed to become a housewife or a doctor? Why must she always be someone serving the needs of others ahead of her own desires? But I knew the answer: It was because traditional Persian families considered these professions respectable.

This philosophical impasse came to a head when we were summering at Lake Lugano. The four of us sat around a table at a café, sipping our drinks, and gazing at pedestrians wafting past on the Piazza della Riforma. Bijan and I sat with our heads tilted back, taking in the sun, while Mater thumbed through a magazine beneath a wide-brimmed hat.

The calmness of the scene was shattered by Khalil's introduction of the Great Question—his daughter's choice for the future.

"Soraya," he intoned. I let one eye flicker open and saw him glaring at me. I sat up straight. Bijan and I looked at one another, knowing a lecture was in store. "As you know, we have moved here so that you and Bijan could have the opportunity for a better education than our country, with its current upheavals, could allow. Still, although we are here in Europe, I want you to understand the importance of your roots, your upbringing, your culture. Soraya, you are at a sensitive age, when it behooves you to make an important decision."

Why, father, I thought, *does it "behoove" me to decide on your terms?* Nothing good ever came from the word *behoove,* I realized.

Bijan had shared a sympathetic glance with me at first, but now switched to the mode of bratty little brother. Throwing down the spoon with which he'd been gobbling his *gelato misto,* he cried excitedly, "Aha! They're marrying you off. Finally! But as the brother of the bride, I would like to make one thing clear: I refuse to be the ring bearer. I'm too big for that." A look from our father induced Bijan to take up his spoon again.

"*Baba,*" I began, "you know I want to improve my English, and …"

"English, the language of Hollywood?"

"It would at least enable me to study performing arts, perhaps in the US."

Khalil turned his head, staring in silent aggravation as tourists in their fashionable resort wear strode past the café.

82

Here my mother intervened with a compromise. "English," she said, "is spoken not only in Hollywood. It is also one of the major languages of international business and world affairs. And besides, shouldn't the people of Iran, including our daughter, be able to speak the language of the country so interested in controlling Iran? Couldn't Soraya at least go to stay in London with your cousin Bibi Shoakat? Her sons are studying in an intensive English-language program. It would just be for the summer."

"My dear, you know very well that London is no place for a proper young lady who is unattended."

"But she wouldn't be unattended. Her male cousins would be by her side every waking moment."

After some hashing-out of details, this was agreed upon. As we filed out of the café, Bijan whispered to me, "I hope you do make it to Hollywood. I'd rather be the brother of the Persian Olivia de Havilland than of just any old bride."

I tousled his hair affectionately. "Thank you, little brother, but you may be aiming a bit high." Though I spoke modestly to my brother, in my heart of hearts, I hoped that he was right. I wasn't blinded by my desire to lead a glamorous life, but those bright lights certainly held a powerful allure. In some ways, I'd been very sheltered. What could be more the opposite from that of the life of an actress?

I knew that Claire would be unhappy when she learned of my departure, but the thought of us one day sharing a flat in London, starring together in a West End production, and being discovered by a Hollywood agent, erased whatever misgivings I might have had.

Many years later, a friend gave me a collection of American poetry. One line I remember so well is this: "They who go feel not the pain of parting; it is they who stay behind that suffer." I'm ashamed to say that I never contacted Claire again. Given how my life evolved, I know that she was aware of what happened to me. I'd like to blame my lack of continuing our relationship on my being so frequently uprooted. But that's no excuse, and it saddens me to think that I have a clearer recollection of some of our family pets than I do of my childhood friends. Now that so many of my memories have parted from me, I feel the pain in earnest. Strange that even at this age, the recollection of those happy times makes me feel the sting more acutely.

Chapter
NINE

"Come on, Soraya, don't dawdle!" my cousin Amin shouted.

"I'm walking as fast as I can." I was pleased to be wearing a curve-hugging short skirt and heels, but the outfit wasn't the best for hustling around Coventry.

"Please hurry. The light is wonderful now, but it won't last for long." As Amin spoke, his camera swung wildly about his neck, and he clutched it. I had heard his endless stories about this Pentax, one of the first exported from Japan following the war, and the remarkable speed of its lens. At that moment, I wished that Amin were obsessed with something else beside rapidity.

When we turned off Earl Street, Amin broke into a full-on run. I slowed and then stopped. Removing my shoes, I sat on a nearby bench to massage my aching feet. I pulled out my compact and examined myself in the mirror. Tiny beads of sweat appeared on my upper lip and hairline. Unhappy at being hustled about the city, I was also frustrated that I'd finally been given some time to explore, and yet was stuck here. I tamped the moisture away with the sponge and a bit of powder.

My heart rate returned to normal as we walked up Bayley Lane and onto Priory Street. Rounding a bend, I saw the lush lawns of Coventry University. A few students sat on spread jackets, smoking cigarettes and furtively passing a silver flask that caught the late afternoon sunlight. I wondered what it would be like to be at university somewhere, anywhere. The language school I attended with my cousins was fine, but spending all day learning English among a small cadre of students very much like me could not hold my attention forever.

Despite that, I felt more vital and energized than I ever had. Even though Amin and Ali were overly protective and accompanied me everywhere (I wondered when they'd start tasting my food for me), my parents were on the continent hundreds of miles away. I loved the freedom that entailed. Every morning when I left the family's rooms at a boarding house near St. James Park, my cousins and I would walk along the Thames, leaving the serenity of the area around Buckingham Palace for the din and energy of Fleet Street and the Livingston Language Academy.

My arrival in London coincided with a marked improvement in the city's revitalization efforts. Three years after the war's conclusion, the city was hosting the summer Olympic Games. Many remnants of the destruction that rained down on the city from the Luftwaffe's bombers remained, and construction continued throughout London. However, the tube stations at Balham and Euston, destroyed during the Blitz, were now open. For the most part, I had been insulated from the war's destructive forces, and the London I saw was more of a tourist guide's vision than what most natives experienced. Of course, I was torn. Being half-German but decidedly anti-Nazi, I still harbored some appreciation for my mother's home country.

For that reason, when I caught sight of Amin standing in front of the ruins of St. Michael's Cathedral, I drew in a sharp breath. Although one tower still stood, the remaining walls scratched jagged lines across the trees and sky. Amin was down on one knee, snapping away, the shutter's clicking audible in the still air. Conscious of the sound of my heels tapping on the sidewalk, I took them off and padded barefoot until I was standing behind him.

"Do be careful," Amin said, frowning and nodding toward my feet. "There's bound to be glass. The last thing in the world I need is for you to come up lame and bleeding. Your father would have my head."

At the mention of Khalil, I sighed. Placing my hand on Amin's shoulder, I stood on one leg and then the other to put my heels on again.

"Thanks a lot," my cousin said. "You pushed me and ruined the shot." He began rewinding the film. "I want to take some of you. I have one more roll."

"Don't you tire of using me as your subject? How sad this place seems." I tried to reconstruct the structure mentally, but I couldn't.

"Yes, but I need a human in the picture's foreground to help establish scale. Besides, you've never minded me shooting you before. The camera is your friend."

"That's true, but how does the expression go, 'Familiarity breeds contempt'? I think that's true, even among as good friends as me and your Pentax. I can't even imagine what this place looked like before." An oppressive melancholy settled over me.

"Less talking and more posing, please."

I felt silly posing like some kind of glamour model in front of the ruins. Better to appease Amin and use his good will to my advantage later on than worry too much about it. After he was finished, I made him promise that we'd take the route I selected to get home. When we exited at Charing Cross, I led him south and east.

"You have no sense of direction, my cousin. Why didn't we get off at Piccadilly Circus? It's much nearer to home," he commented.

"The answer is simple: I can't say that name without laughing. Besides, the evening is pleasant and there's much else to see." I'd been so under his thumb, only slightly less oppressive than my father's, that I had to take advantage of the opportunity to explore.

"But we're wandering about like we're lost."

"No we're not. I know exactly where I'm going."

Eventually we arrived at Queen's Walk on the edge of Buckingham Palace Gardens.

Amin stopped and pointed at the red and blue sign. "Can you read that, Soraya? I know it's English, so sound it out for me."

I refused to take the bait and continued down the Queen's Walk.

"The sign for the tube says 'Green Park.' If you'd intended all along to come here, we could have exited right here and saved ourselves much time."

I didn't like it when his exasperation turned into whining.

"I didn't know that I wanted to go this way until I got here." As much as I enjoyed the bustling street scenes, there was something about the treed meadows along the pedestrian-only route that I enjoyed even more. I needed the serenity of that green space to quiet my adrenaline rush. Here the sounds of traffic were reduced to a sibilant whisper. Without my senses being assaulted, my mind was free to roam. Something about the scene, in stark contrast to what I'd seen at the cathedral, lifted my spirits. I spent some of my time wondering what it would have been like to be an English queen strolling these grounds, my own private reserve of solitude and fresh air. Short of that, I wondered what it would be like to have played the queen in some costume drama for the cinema.

"My mother will be wondering where we are. I told her we'd be home in time for dinner." Amin's words broke my reverie. I was so deep in thought that even he could tell I was far away. "What were you thinking about?"

I hesitated for a moment. "I was thinking about America."

"Hollywood, no doubt." Amin used the same tone one would

reserve for an impoverished slum. "Why the fascination with that place and those movies?"

"I believe it would be fun. An escape. A way to live other lives, but still have one's own to return to."

"What do you have to escape from? You've been given everything you've ever wanted."

"Precisely."

He looked at me quizzically, then shook his head and escorted me home in silence.

A week later, Amin came into my room with his ever-present camera. "I'd like to take some shots of you."

Something about his expression, the way he ran his tongue across his lips and his hand through his hair, was very different from his usual self-involvement. I also had the clear sense that he was hiding something from me.

Amin brought in an elegantly carved wooden side chair, its cushion covered with a needlepoint depiction of a parrot.

"I know it's your favorite. Reminds you of the bird you had in Berlin, right?" He went over to my closet and pawed at my clothes. "I'm not sure any of these will do."

"Enough! I won't let you point that thing at me until you tell me what's going on."

He sank into the chair. "You know my mother's cousin Forough Zafar, right?"

"Of course. She's the lady-in-waiting to the queen mother of the shah."

The Fleet Street tabloids had been running stories for weeks about the shah and his wife Queen Fawzieh getting divorced. As the sister of King Farouk of Egypt, Queen Fawzieh was especially fertile ground for the British press. The most recent developments were the shocking—to the British anyway—revelations that the shah was publicly seeking a new wife. Not only was he the "Shopping Shah, So Soon?" but also he was seeking photographs of beautiful women, specifically Persian woman, from which he could choose his next mate.

Amin explained that Forough Zafar and his mother had decided to submit my photo for "consideration."

Even before he was through explaining, I began to smirk. When he finished, I burst out laughing. "You can't be serious. The Bakhtiaris would never stoop to serve the Pahlavis." The age-old enmity between the two tribes was an old story we both knew so well.

"In this case, it pays to keep one's enemies closer than one's friends." Amin nodded at me. "But can you imagine? You as empress!"

"And what's so funny about that?" I pretended to be insulted, realizing full well that the odds in this game were astronomical. Still, I mused, if one was going to play, one should at least try to win—especially that great a prize.

I tried to bring to mind an image of the current shah. My family kept a photograph of the young man's father, Mohammed Reza, on the wall in our house in Isfahan. In the picture, he was a handsome man, someone whose almost stern smile exuded confidence. His military bearing and greatly decorated uniform gave him substance, something that even at sixteen, I could appreciate. I'd had my fill of schoolboys and their uniforms and immature ways. At thirty, the new shah seemed very much his own man, fully in command of his identity.

"I meant no offense," Amin replied. "Once I get these developed, I believe I'll send duplicates to Buckingham Palace. Perhaps King George will be in the market. He's a bit old for you, of course, but as long as you're in town, it's the polite thing to do."

"Oh, by all means," I said, matching his ironic tone. "And if there are any other members of royalty seeking a mate, do feel free to send my photos along."

I felt as if I was entering some silly drawing, and just as I would have for a school fundraiser, I quickly forgot about the matter. Or so I tried to tell myself. Truth be told, I found myself staring out the window and daydreaming instead of listening to my teacher go on about conjugating irregular verbs.

The following week, I returned from school as usual. Morad Khan, another of my father's cousins, stood in the center of my bedroom, his hands folded behind his back. A dozen unfortunate circumstances ran rampant in my mind. Why else would Morad Khan be here? I tried to speak as calmly as I could.

"Is it my mother? Is she not well? Bijan? My father?"

Morad Khan held up his hand, "I'm here to deliver a message from your father. Tonight you will accompany me to the embassy. There is a party being held in honor of the shah's sister, Princess Shams. It is three o'clock now. We leave in precisely four hours. Make certain you are prepared."

Morad Khan nodded pointedly and left the room. My legs went weak beneath me, and I felt the hairs on the back of my neck stand at attention.

Princess Shams.

I could scarcely believe it. I would be in the company of the glamorous woman I'd read so much about. The princess had lived in exile with her father, the deposed Reza Shah Pahlavi, in Mauritius and South Africa. I remembered how bitterly my father complained of how the British and the Soviets had treated Iran's leaders. From my father, I also knew that Shams, her mother, and sister had met with Adolph Hitler in Berlin. Grandfather Karl and Khalil had strenuously disagreed about the appropriateness of that visit. That Shams was back in the good graces of the British government was clear, but how she'd managed this was a mystery.

To be honest, at sixteen, I didn't care about all that. What wasn't a mystery was why she was a society page darling. She was stunningly beautiful, her dark hair and complexion giving her an exotic allure. She was no native princess emerging from some backwater, however. Shams prided herself on presenting an image of utter elegance. In every photo I had seen of her, at some gala in Europe or Iran, she was dressed in the most tastefully stylish clothes from the leading haute couture designers. I suppose that she was the Princess Caroline of Monaco of her time, minus the three marriages. If my father read about her in the news, I followed her exploits in the various European gossip magazines. When I showed my school chums the articles and photos, she became the woman that many of us aspired to be.

But I didn't have much time to think about palace intrigues or what the princess might be wearing. I had a closet full of clothes to consider, and only less than four hours to select something that would let the princess know that this particular Bakhtiari girl belonged in the presence of royalty.

After showering, I curled my bangs and applied only lipstick and eyeliner—too much paint would not be proper for a sixteen-year-old girl. As I put on those small touches, I thought of Claire and how fun it would be to tell her and all my friends about how I'd met the princess. I also thought of the shah's father and the cruelty he'd meted out against the Bakhtiari tribe. I put aside all those thoughts and simply decided to have an enjoyable evening out. Anything would be preferable to another session of feeling like I was being stalked by Ali and Amin. Still, I was haunted by the thought that one of my girlhood fantasies might come true.

The first obstacle I had to overcome was Morad Khan. When he came to the family's room, he stood in the entryway, looking as if he had been assigned to gather up the trash and not me. I expected that he'd be delighted to see me all dressed up in my finest, but his expression was dour and emphasized his rigid posture. He might as well have been a statue in comparison to my fidgety presence. In trying to close the clasp on my beaded purse, my fingers trembled.

Riding in the cab to the embassy, I asked him questions to help settle my stomach. "So, what do you think the princess is like?"

"I have not made her acquaintance."

"Still, you can have some opinion, can't you?"

"I don't think about people I don't know. It's tiresome and wasteful to speculate. I do not think you'd like to hear my opinion of any of the Pahlavis. I'm appalled that your father would waste my evening, and for that matter yours, in the company of those traitors."

I pressed my back against the seat more firmly, the better to stifle an urge to throttle Morad Khan. Why was he ruining this night for me, bringing up such a long-standing tribal grudge? The young man sat staring ahead, as if what played out ahead of the driver was a movie.

Outside my window, the streets of London seemed luminous. The streetlights spotlighted the passing cars and danced on the rain-slick roads. After a brief summer's evening shower, everything felt and smelled fresher, as if everyone in London had donned their finest for this event.

"I wonder," I asked, vowing this would be the last attempt I made to engage Morad Khan in conversation, "who else we're going to meet at this party?"

But he seemed not to hear me.

Keeping to my promise, I gave up, turning my attention instead to my own reflection in the window. I wore very little makeup, like the proper Persian girl that I was. My dark shoulder-length hair was parted to one side, and I had pinned it back with the diamond clip that my grandmother Bibi Maryam had given me for my sixteenth birthday. Since Princess Shams was a fashion icon, I wanted to look my best, but I had very little to work with. My parents had shipped me a dress only two days prior. It was a long dress that seemed more suited to a much older woman, with its empire waist, heavy lining, and chiffon peach color. Since I was tall for a Persian woman, I was told I couldn't wear heels so I wouldn't appear taller than the petite Shams. Therefore I put on flat shoes.

I could not help assessing my appearance from the point of view of someone else—someone with a demanding eye. Did I measure up? Measure up, for that matter, to what? I hadn't spent a great deal of time considering what the shah and his minions might be looking for. I decided that all I could do, and should do, was to be myself.

The cab pulled up to the front of the embassy. The offices were located in a bland-looking building situated among a row of typically British brick and stone slabs. From atop the pillared and roofed entryway, an Iranian flag hung over the balustrade. I suddenly felt a bit of disappointment. I had the impression that I was paying a visit to the family's solicitor or doctor. Morad Khan walked two steps ahead of me. Only when I got to the double glass doors did I receive the first impression that I was somewhere special. Two men, both in formal Iranian military attire, opened the doors with white-gloved hands.

The artificial breeze of air conditioning brushed against my flustered face. I imagined (and then confirmed in mirrors lining the entryway) my cheeks to have reddened. The foyer had dark, wood-paneled walls, with a musty dampness that surrounded me in the imposing old building. Above all, I was struck by the enormous portrait of the shah presiding over the space. For a moment, I seemed to make eye contact with the monarch and, intimidated, cast down my gaze. Then I chided myself for my superstitious fear. I looked again at the portrait. This time I saw it only for a moment, before a group of other guests converged in front of it.

Upstairs, guests were mingling at the entrance of the great ballroom. The light from the crystal chandeliers bathed everything in a warm glow as if candles lighted the space. Men in black tie and women in ball gowns, all older than my father and mother, all with thinning or silver hair, greeted each guest. I had no room in my mind for their names. Just as quickly as one face smiled at me, the name and the image passed out of my consciousness. I had room in my mind for only one person—the handsome man whose portrait hung in the foyer. I had no expectation that he would be attending, but I could always hope. It wasn't as if spending time with Princess Shams was going to be only a small consolation. In the constellation of stars that hung in my imagined glamorous sky, none was brighter than her.

Beyond the receiving line, I noticed a cluster of women in the center of the room. Princess Shams sat on a burgundy velvet sofa. As if they'd been rehearsing all day, the group of women turned as one to face me. At first the princess had the same slack expression on her face, but when she saw me, the corners of her mouth turned up in pleasure. She lifted her chin slightly and turned her head a few degrees. She looked at me with a sidelong and appraising glance—part wary, part pleased, all practiced. One of the women seemed to be nattering on. The princess merely raised the index finger of her right hand, and the woman stopped. I felt my cheeks and ears burn.

Princess Shams arose from her seat and walked toward me. Every bit of moisture went out of my mouth, but I dared not run my tongue around my lips to moisten them. I marveled at how still the woman held her head and body, yet managed to propel herself across the room. For a moment, I was reminded of a puppet show I'd seen as a little girl, although Sham's performance was anything but stiff or halting. She was more like a sailing vessel.

"I'm so pleased you were able to attend," she enthused, shaking my hand and kissing me on both cheeks. The smell of wine and violets mingled in my nostrils.

I was flattered, and of course agreed when Princess Shams invited me to sit with her for a bit. As we moved to a table more secluded from other guests, I felt as if every pair of eyes in the room was fixed on me, scrutinizing my every move.

"Would you like something to drink?"

"Oh, no," I answered, discovering a strange hoarseness in my voice. "Please don't get up on my account."

An attendant immediately approached the table. An embarrassed heat washed over my face again.

"Oh. Ice water, please."

Not looking at the attendant, the princess smirked faintly. She held up two fingers and the server hustled off.

"How lovely to meet the granddaughter of the man who was a key element in the constitutional movement. You should be very proud to be from such a family."

Still, I was not sure if she was trying to compliment me, or make me feel as though I was worthy of her time because of the great Sardar Asad, the head of the Bakhtiari family.

"I am indeed," I said, nodding for emphasis. I made sure to bring my chin back up to level. The princess continued to speak to me as though she were talking over a hedge. When she did lower her chin, I noticed why she always held her head high. The skin of her neck collapsed into little folds, and the faint traces of a wattle hung like a droplet of water. The mischievous part of me wanted to touch it, set in motion like a fleshy metronome.

"And your mother is German. How wonderful for you."

The princess spoke the last statement in German, and I followed suit. "Yes. Thank you. Being a part of both worlds has always been something I'm grateful for."

I hoped that the harsh tones of the language could mask any insincerity from my response. Truth be told, sometimes having those dual identities frustrated me.

I was glad that the attendant returned with the water; I needed something to do with my hands. A moment later, a round of applause rippled across the room.

The princess turned toward the door, and I marveled at how her chin cut an arc, as if she was watching the takeoff of a bird.

"I see our special guests are here." Princess Shams looked back at me. "Our Olympic team is also being honored here tonight."

"I see. I didn't know …"

"Not to worry. If I didn't have my people around me constantly reminding me of these things, I probably wouldn't remember either. I suppose I should greet them, put the poor boys out of their misery. They look so uncomfortable standing there. Please excuse me, but do stay here. I'll return in a moment."

While she was away, I sipped my drink, barely able to constrain myself from swallowing it in one gulp. My tongue felt as thick and rough as burnt flatbread. I dared not lick my lips or let them make contact with the glass's rim. My awkward motion allowed a few drops of water to drip down my chest. I was glad that no one could see me. How silly of me to be so overwrought, but at least the water helped cool my flush.

I turned back to the banquet hall, where Morad Khan was standing with a group of athletes. I had to look twice to be sure that the man I saw was in fact my cousin. He was laughing with the men, throwing his head back in great gusts of mirth. I wondered if personalities were being offered on the trays that were constantly circulated.

"Have your eye on someone in particular?" Princess Shams sat across from me. She crossed her legs in a great stir of fabric and motion. I had the sense that the princess always posed, and a moment later, I understood why. A photographer stepped toward us and asked her permission.

"So," she resumed after the bulb's flash had cleared from my vision, "you didn't get a chance to answer my question."

"I was merely locating my cousin," I said, keenly aware that I shouldn't point. I nodded my head demurely in the direction of the cluster of men. "He's the tallest of the men there."

"Is he a sportsman, then?"

"Not that I am aware of."

"He does seem quite taken with our Olympians." Princess Shams laughed softly and suggestively. Back then, I couldn't have guessed what she was hinting at, and her next words masked her intent. "Hero worship can be a difficult thing to manage. So much possibility for disappointment."

I shivered as a bead of perspiration ran down my back.

"My dear, are you well? I can see you have gooseflesh."

"I just felt a little chilled for a moment."

"It is quite cool in here—these drafty old monstrosities. Would you like to go to another room? I know that sometimes it takes getting used to being in front of all these prying eyes." Princess Shams moved her gaze from side to side indicating the assembled guests, who seemed to be trying very hard not to have their noticing be noticed.

"Oh, no. I'm fine here. I like attention—when it's deserved, of course."

Princess Shams sighed and smiled, "Well, when one is as attractive a young woman as you are, the attention is always deserved. Whether or not it is welcomed is your choice."

"You're so kind."

Even today, I am struck by the disjointed nature of the conversation that followed. At times I felt as if I was chatting with a friend about music, recent events, favorite places. At others, I felt as though I was being interviewed for admission into I wasn't sure what. Princess Shams frequently asked me a question a second time, always well after the first occasion, as if she was trying to memorize everything for a test. Only later did I wonder if she was trying to catch me in an error or an omission.

Eventually the interview took another turn. Instead of asking about my family or the upbringing that was the basis of my entire character, the princess focused on my two years of finishing school and my ability to name-drop poets and artists. It was, after all, my parents, my upbringing, and the challenges of living between two cultures in Europe and Iran—not the courses in superficial refinement—that had made me a person capable at such a young age of sitting beside a princess without feeling intimidated. But I also understood that the princess had a specific agenda: to find a suitable wife for her brother and a woman refined enough to be queen. As much as I had tried to tell myself that this was a fun night out, my first among members of Persian and British society types, it was much more than that. As if I needed a reminder, throughout our conversation that evening, Princess Shams dropped in statements that spoke highly of the shah's character.

"My brother is the kindest, most compassionate king. He loves his country and will do anything to prove his loyalty and commitment to the people of Iran."

Like the foyer, the ballroom featured an enormous portrait of the shah. At the princess's mention of her brother, I glanced nervously at it. It seemed somehow friendlier than the one downstairs.

The princess lamented the unfortunate divorce from Queen Fawzieh.

"It does not look good for a king to be without a wife. However, this time around he must marry a Persian girl, one of our own kind. The people of Iran would want that."

The whole evening had seemed something out of a film. She had gone to such effort to put the shah in a favorable light that I could not help being filled with thoughts of becoming the candidate in question. I wondered if the princess had spent as much time with other women as she had with me. Were any of these other elegantly dressed, disdainful-looking women at the event ones who'd also been initially considered? If so—and I felt certain they were—then I had triumphed. I derived a great deal of pleasure from the fact that Princess Shams had left my side only briefly the entire evening and had always returned to me.

When it was finally time to leave, Princess Shams took my hand firmly and whispered into my ear an invitation to have lunch the following day. Bursting with curiosity, I agreed with an overeager, horsey nod of my head.

"I'll have a car brought round to take you and your cousin home. The driver will retrieve you tomorrow."

"Yes, Your Highness. I very much look forward to it."

Princess Shams bustled off, leaving a trail of admirers and aides in her wake. By the time I found Morad Khan, it was well after midnight. He reeked of expensive whiskey and cigar smoke. We stood at the curb, Morad wobbling slightly, me gazing up at the night sky. A light blinked and I nudged him. "Look! A shooting star. What a wonderful omen!"

Morad squinted and then shook his head. "It's just an airplane."

Leave it to a Persian man to let you down, I thought. Suddenly I felt lightheaded and anxious. The high of the evening had wound down, and now I was beginning to question what was at stake.

Chapter
TEN

he next morning, I woke before sunrise. Although I'd left the party giddy with the promise that something extraordinary might be afoot, I'd awakened in a funk. This was to be the first of my non-alcohol-induced hangovers; the sense that I'd invested too much of myself and overdone my expectations. I had the lunch with Shams to look forward to, but I still felt as if my life hadn't changed in any significant way. The impatience of youth, I recognize now.

As much as I was enamored of the fairy-tale aspect of my being among the chosen ones, and as much as I was hopelessly in love with an image, that love was accompanied by a small seed of doubt—about my fitness for the role I was aspiring to. Perhaps I was overthinking it all.

As I lay there that morning after, as much as I remembered the glittering people and the elegance of the place, I also remembered Amin's comment about my always being given everything. It was impossible for another person to truly understand what I'd experienced in my life. Amin was likely basing his assessment of me on assumptions more than fact. Still, the difficulties our family endured, the times in Berlin when money was tight, and my father's anxiety about the Nazis' encroachment were like spice added to our increasingly spare meals, not something that anyone could have known. Here in London, while memorials would be built and the passing of loved ones remembered, everyone seemed eager to put the war in the past. However, that didn't change what had happened, or diminish the suffering—not to mention what the Jewish people had endured.

Prior to this, as I walked the streets of London, I'd occasionally come upon a lot heaped with rubble. It was as if people wanted to forget the past but remember it all the same. So they piled up the bad memories in order that they could one day pick through them. Since I had not suffered through the blitz and the threat of invasion, those piles were little more than brick, wood, and concrete. To others, they excited painful reminders: the sudden and unpleasant buzz in the stomach, the sharp intake of breath, the heart's momentary unsteadiness. Once, I'd seen a child's pram, crushed and misshapen, poking out of the ruins, its rent fabric flapping in the breeze. Its poignant reminder of the casualties of the war saddened me immensely.

The liquid gray light of morning often brought out such thoughts in me. Morad Khan would have been surprised to know I had my introspective moments. I was prone to thinking more deeply than Claire and my other friends. I seldom acted rashly, but as I'd heard for my entire life, that was likely because I "knew my own mind." I was frustrated by that expression. After all, whose mind could anyone know the best but one's own? If I was somewhat willful, a little too self-involved (if I believed what seemed to be said about me), then wasn't I simply behaving normally?

I had so much to think about, and with my father's constant reminders of the importance of making a future for myself, to constantly have my mind in the present while considering all the repercussions in the future, wasn't I doing exactly what everyone expected of me?

Outside, a foggy rain wreathed the streetlamps, and the London bankers' black umbrellas negotiating the roundabout moved like dim hands on a darkened clock face. If only I could get time to move as quickly.

Along with my contemplative nature, I had an active imagination. Although I couldn't literally speed the day forward, I thought of what my life might be like in the years to come. Even with these most recent developments, I hadn't given up on my dreams of being an actress. Now, instead of co-starring with Claire on stage or on the screen, I imagined my saucy friend at court in Iran. She'd scandalize everyone with behaviors and pronouncements hardly fitting for a lady-in-waiting. I laughed softly at the irony of that title. Wasn't I just then a lady-in-waiting as well? Wasn't that the fate of any young Persian girl? Truth be told, unlike most—even the upper class and educated of Iran—I was fortunate that as a female eldest child, my parents hadn't been disappointed by my gender. They were pleased with me from the start, and as I heard the retelling of my birth, their words became a kind of litany.

The story about the origin of my name always stuck with me. When I was born, my mother had joked with my father that I would require another six sisters, since "Soraya" was another name for the constellation Pleiades, the Seven Sisters.

In Persian culture, the Pleiades were considered a sign of good fortune, as was the number seven. One of the nurses had commented on my name and the connection to the Seven Sisters and said, "May this lucky number bring her good fortune for years to come."

And I had been very fortunate. I suppose that was why I'd been invited to meet Shams and, hopefully, the shah. I grew up believing that despite whatever downturns my family had experienced, I was destined to have good things come my way. I didn't debate the difference between having been given and having earned them. Who was

I to say? Opportunities were there for us all; some took advantage, while others did not.

That morning in London, as sleep overtook me again, I wondered if my real wish would ever come true—that I might be able to determine the course of my own life. I was being given an opportunity to perhaps become the shah's next wife. I was doing my best not to be too giddy at the possibility, to not put too much pressure on myself. I understood that what one did with an opportunity was far more important than how it came about. No one would care about the behind-the-scenes machinations. I hoped only to have the opportunity to meet the shah and let nature take its course.

Hours later, I walked into the lobby of the Savoy Hotel feeling positively ebullient. Although the weather hadn't cleared, my mood remained upbeat and extremely curious. I decided that my youth and my energy should serve me and not make me question myself. So I breezed up to the front desk and asked for Princess Shams's room as if I'd done so hundreds of times before.

Riding in the elevator to the penthouse, I stared ahead at the William Morris cabbage-and-vine motif wallpaper. The operator shifted from foot to foot, casting furtive glances at me, but I kept my face composed. As soon as I stepped out of the elevator, I stifled a laugh. I'd been admitted to the Princess's suite. In the sitting room, a rack of clothes, new by the tags hanging from them, were draped over a chaise lounge. Peering around to make certain that no one was watching, I gingerly reached for one of the tags. Having almost managed to turn it over, I started when the bedroom door flew open. I let go of the tag and snapped to attention like a dutiful soldier.

Shams swept into the room, an empty cigarette holder pinched between two fingers, a bunch of folders under one arm. As she regarded me, she dropped the folders into a maid's hands. "Soraya, my dear, come with me. Let's eat—something simple. I'm famished. You?" Without waiting for my response, she ushered me out the door. We took the lift to the ground floor, where "something simple" materialized as a table laden with delicately plated food: buttery scones, fresh strawberries, melon, mango, smoked salmon, quail eggs, and the rarest of teas.

The hotel staff had cleared the Afternoon Tea Room for us. I was overwhelmed by the luxurious setting, by the staff's almost telepathic attentiveness, and, most of all, by the fact that here was the famous Shams, again engaging me in non-stop conversation.

"I never understood all the fuss about Coco Chanel. A 'collaborator!' What nonsense. I find it ridiculous. At least someone had the good sense to intervene on the poor woman's behalf."

I nodded. "Yes. King George showed admirable courage in that regard."

"I'd nearly forgotten your German ancestry. I suppose your view makes sense."

"Regardless of my ancestry, to persecute her, as you said, makes little sense."

I could see that Shams was impressed with my knowledge about the scandal involving the famous designer and the German spymaster who'd hoped to use her connections to get a message to Churchill.

"Quite right, and from what I understand, they all merely wanted to bring the stupid war to an end."

As the meal progressed, the princess touched on other aspects of fashion, movies, art, and poetry, all the while punctuating her discourse with frequent mentions of her brother, His Majesty Mohammad Reza Shah, his likes and dislikes, his love of travel and sports. This was a variation on a theme from the previous night.

"I don't understand the fascination with polo, to be quite honest. Do you ride?"

"Yes. I learned to ride when we first returned to Iran," I said. "I love it."

"Riding is one thing. Riding while swinging a club at a ball is another." Shams looked at me expectantly, but I wasn't sure how to respond.

"For those who enjoy it, it makes sense," I said at last.

"Mohammad adores it. If he had his way, he'd be in Saint-Tropez one week and Buenos Aires the next, all for the sake of watching. It is a good thing that affairs of state sometimes take precedence. Otherwise, I fear, he'd never be at home."

"I understand he also loves to fly. As a young girl ..."

Shams threw her head back and laughed, "Loves it? *Adores* it. Myself, I find it boring but useful. How do the English put it? 'A necessary evil.'"

I shrugged my shoulders, "Necessary, yes. Evil? I wouldn't quite go that far." Screwing up her face into a mask of anger, Shams said, "Do you dare disagree with me?"

I blanched and was about to speak when Shams cut in. "Please, Soraya! I was joking. My brother could use someone who disagrees with him from time to time. Privately and discreetly, of course. And frequently, if only to get him used to having the bit in his mouth. Can't let the horse have its own head too much, can we?"

After a pause, Shams leaned forward in her seat, assessing me. "That's how it should be with the woman who marries my brother. Fiery when it suits him, but also willing to be controlled. After all, the purpose in polo is to score as many points as possible, is it not? Style is one thing, but results are what matter."

Somewhat nervously, I joined Shams in laughing, but the disquiet in my stomach would not still.

During the rest of Princess Shams's weeklong sojourn in London, I met with her three more times. On each occasion, she gave me to understand how taken she was with me. She also added how fortunate she felt that mine had been the last of several names added to the list for the "scouting trip." She felt more and more certain that, as she put it, "this young Bakhtiari girl" was the closest to what her brother was looking for. I knew full well that I possessed outer beauty, as constant male attention had repeatedly reminded me. But I was determined to show Princess Shams my inner self. I never questioned her about why she always pointed out my tribal affiliation. And I knew the shah wanted and needed to marry a Persian girl since the Iranian people had been disappointed that his first wife was an Egyptian whom he'd married for complex political reasons.

All I knew of such things was a vague recollection of my father and other males in our extended family cursing Reza Shah the Great for what he had done to us—torturing, imprisoning, and beheading Bakhtiari Khans for refusing to turn their oil fields over to the British.

My confusion was extended when she mentioned that I was surprisingly composed for a young woman of eighteen. I knew enough to not correct her. My birthday was in June, and I'd only just turned sixteen. When I mentioned this discrepancy in a phone conversation with my mother and father late that evening, I sensed that I had hit on a sore subject between them. They seemed unwilling to discuss the issue, and only later did I learn that they had altered my birth certificate, setting back my birth year to 1932. Based on that falsified document, Shams was correct.

My father seemed particularly eager to move on from that subject to how the process was progressing. My mother was strangely silent. I was too caught up in the moment to consider fully what Eva's silence might mean.

At the end of the week, Shams and I sat sipping tea at the Palm Court in the Ritz. The Princess's gold cashmere dress nearly blended in completely with the upholstery and draperies. I had the impression that the woman was a chameleon.

"I'm leaving on Friday for Paris—a bit of a shopping spree. Last minute decision, but I'd love it you'd join me."

"Your Highness, I would need to ask …"

Understanding dawned on Sham's face, and she held up her hand to cut me off.

"I should tell you: This wasn't really an invitation. My dear, your father is well aware of all that is going on. Forough has been keeping him completely up-to-date."

I was stunned to hear how far the plan had developed behind my back, but I managed to hide my surprise.

My father later told me that the queen's lady-in-waiting, Forough, had played the part of matchmaker, specifically drawing the queen mother's attention to my photographs. And she had expressed a preference for a Bakhtiari girl. Such a match would strengthen Pahlavi ties with our esteemed tribe and help heal the damage that had been done to the relationship between the two powerful clans in recent years, in particular by the shah's father.

"So, Paris it is, then." I raised my cup to my mouth to hide my smile.

Back at our family's flat, I went immediately to my room and collapsed on the bed. I lay on my back staring at the intricate rosette pattern that ringed the light fixture, not caring that my shoes were still on.

I had to admit that my childish fascination with royalty had led me to speculate about the prospect of being the queen. The young woman in me was fearful of what that suddenly real possibility would mean for my happiness. Even more, I mused about the role that my father had played in the machinations that brought me to this place. I thought of this in terms of my friends and the amorous pursuits of some of the boys. My girlfriends and I, with the exception of Claire, played the game of opposites. By not showing an interest in a particular boy, we hoped to let him know that we were attracted to him. On the other hand, boys could never be subtle about their intentions, but they demonstrated their interest in frustrating ways. A leg thrust out from a desk to block one's path, a derisive comment, or some other form of irritant was intended to attract a girl. Neither sex could ever be direct, and I supposed it was the same for the Bakhtiaris and the Pahlavis.

What my father had done in going round the fence rather than through the gate made sense. If he'd approached me directly and told me of his involvement, I might have been more tense around Shams. Knowing what was at stake would have only increased the pressure on me. Far worse, though, was the feeling of disappointment I experienced in learning that my father was angling for this on my behalf. I'd taken great pleasure in believing that I'd forged my own way. I hoped that I had won Shams's favor purely on the strength of my own personality. I'd also hoped that this prospective direction was outside the realm of my father's thinking and control. Until now, I believed that I'd gone ahead with this plan that was, if not of my own making, at least of my own execution.

True, I'd been given the opportunity, but I'd seized it myself. My father wanted me to marry, and the usual routine of considering cousins and family acquaintances was the well-trod way. I'd veered from that route and struck out in a new, and I thought surely surprising, and perhaps even disappointing (to him) direction. That had pleased me in a way I could scarcely explain. If my father thought that the sole thing I was capable of doing was being a wife, then how would he feel if I took for a husband a man that many in the family despised?

Now, knowing that my father approved of the match, I was far less certain this was what I wanted to do. My father did nothing without first calculating all the possible outcomes and repercussions. That he'd defy tradition and choose to pursue this matchmaking in secrecy confused me. At that moment, as I drowned in questions and doubt, I wished I had my mother's opinion as a lifeline.

Chapter

ELEVEN

I wouldn't have thought it possible, but Princess Shams made Paris the City of Tedium rather than the City of Lights. After a week spent bustling from one fashion house to the next, scarcely having time to look at the clothes on offer, I'd nearly reached my limit. Even enamored of fashion as I was, by the fourth day I'd heard enough about the return of body contours and tight silhouettes, and how if you thought last year's bare shoulders were all the rage, you hadn't seen anything yet. I realized that I was beginning to think of taffeta (one of Shams's favorites, and which she insisted I wear) as a moral obligation rather than a fabric. The pressure to be on stage at the nightly dinner parties further exhausted me. Instead of a fairy tale week spent having fun and being dazzled, Paris was a forced march—one done in pumps, and with a servant toting shopping bags.

I tried to keep things in perspective, but woke one morning with the thought that if this was Thursday, then that meant another day listening to Madame So-and-so's dissertation on the wonders of the double flounce.

Shams seemed indefatigable in her desire to conquer every street in Paris's fashion district.

"You know," she said, reminding me for not the first time that she'd spent the last two years living in the US, "compared to Faubourg Saint-Honoré, Fifth Avenue or Madison seem like streets in quaint country villages."

I thought of saying that Shams's exile hadn't exactly been to a cultural or economic wasteland, but thought better of it. Traveling with anyone for an extended period of time can cause tension. I had to admit that my concern about what might happen next had me on edge. Perhaps it was simply the eagerness of youth, but I just wanted to get on with it. If I was to meet the shah, then I wanted to do it as soon as possible. Having the decision made, the die cast, seemed preferable to this endless waiting and wondering.

One morning we strolled up Place Vendome, Shams's pace slowed by the ingestion of three chocolate croissants. She asked me for the first time how I was enjoying the trip.

"As much as I've enjoyed the shopping, I'd been hoping to see something more of Paris." Shams turned toward me, a look of shock stretching her features. "Really? Why didn't you say so?"

"I didn't think it was my place. You've been so generous to me, and I didn't want to presume."

"Nonsense. Where would you like to go?"

I knew that the Louvre was nearby, and suggested the museum. Shams agreed, and her driver soon had us walking through the galleries. I had studied art history briefly, so the names of many of the paintings and sculptures were familiar to me. There were the three great ladies— Venus de Milo, the Victory of Samothrace, and Mona Lisa—but seeing them in person underwhelmed me. I hoped the same wouldn't be true of Mohammed Reza. Unfortunately, someone can be built up so greatly in our minds that he inevitably must fall short of our expectations.

Fortunately, we can also be greatly surprised by the unfamiliar. I was much taken with a painting I came across, the massive *Wedding*

Feast at Cana by Paolo Veronese. More than twenty feet high and thirty feet wide, it made me feel as if I could step inside and join the celebrants in Verona.

Having converted to Catholicism, Shams was familiar with the story of Christ's first miracle. She was glad to tell the story of how the Savior had transformed water into wine to prevent the newlyweds and their families from embarrassment.

Reading from the museum's catalog, Shams went on to explain the various motifs and symbols. All I could think of was the market in Isfahan, and how the painting's colors and the active scene resembled its fevered motion.

"Interestingly," Shams read, "here, seated at the table with the other wedding guests is Kanuni Sultan Süleyman, otherwise known in the West as Suleiman the Magnificent."

After she finished the recitation, Shams said, "Suleiman spoke Farsi, you know."

Of all his accomplishments, I thought this was the least impressive.

We sat on a low bench and scanned the painting for a few moments in silence. The hall was empty but for the two of us.

"The bride and groom seem unhappy to me," I noted, hoping that my statement might open a conversation I'd been longing to have.

"I suppose that's because they ran out of wine," Shams said distractedly.

"I've always thought that weddings should be joyous."

Shams laughed derisively. "Not always."

"Was yours not?" I kept my tone as neutral as possible and continued to stare straight ahead at the painting, feigning disinterest.

"The first one was not. Actually, the wedding was grand, the marriage less so."

My father had told me that Shams had been married briefly to a man who was the son of the prime minister of Iran at the time.

Counting on Shams's love of the subject—her own life—I kept quiet.

"Mahmud Jam was a fine man, I suppose. I don't really know, since I scarcely was acquainted with him. I certainly made little effort to learn more about him. My father was adamant that the two of us wed. So we did. As soon as my father died, Mahmud and I divorced. I'm glad my father did not live to see that day." Shams's voice was scarcely a whisper.

"I'm sorry."

The princess shook her head and sighed. "Listen to me, Soraya. I know why you're asking these questions. I'm letting you in because I like you and because I understand a bit about what you are experiencing now. Even though I loved Mehrad and he was my choice as a husband, I was still nervous on our wedding day, wondering if I was making the right choice. Enough wine convinced me I had."

I smiled at the joke and her honesty. "Thank you for telling me. I know it can't be easy for you, acting as a go-between for your brother."

"As long as the bills get paid for the dresses and things, I'm happy to be of service."

Shams's words stung me, and I sat staring at my hands folded in my lap. I thought that she had made some personal connection with me, but now she was telling me that I was one more item on her to-do list.

She must have read my thoughts. She took my hand and said, "There are obligations, and then there are obligations that turn into pleasures. Getting to know you has been very much the latter. I wouldn't be here"—she gestured around the room—"if that wasn't the case. Nor, for that matter, would you be."

"Thank you."

"Enough thanks. While we are on the subject of obligations, I have been ordered to take you to Tehran with me. There is someone who is very eager to meet you. Would you be so kind as to accompany me?"

By way of answer, I looked Shams in the eyes. Then I inclined my head slightly and raised it, hoping that I looked the part of a queen. Although my face was serene, dozens of thoughts careened around in my head. Part of me was joyous at the thought that I'd won. I can be as competitive as the next person. Part of me was pleased that I might be able to do the Bakhtiari people some good. Still another was thrilled that a childhood dream could be realized, the fairy tale made real. It seems funny to me now, but none of those thoughts centered on the fifteen years' difference between my age and his.

Back then I believed—and in some ways I still do—in the purity of love. I hoped that the two of us would share that emotion, feel that pulse-quickening sensation that I thought was love. I had no way of knowing what romantic love was, except from what I'd seen in the movies. I discounted my parent's relationship, as most young people do. What they had, as good as it was, was not something I aspired to. Meeting Mohammed Reza in this carefully orchestrated manner put our potential relationship at a higher level. I just hoped that I would like the view from that rarefied air.

As soon as the wheels of the shah's private aircraft touched down, I felt my skin prickle. It wasn't just the typically cold weather for the eighth of October that had me shivering. I looked at my father, who had come to Paris to accompany me to Tehran. He was craning his neck to see outside the cabin's windows.

"I didn't think I'd ever see Iran again," I said.

My father nodded. "I had faith that we'd be back. As a Bakhtiari, you should have known that. We can be shunted aside, but not forever. We've staked our claim in places of prominence before and will continue to."

My father's words were dripping with pride and indignation and certainty. What he said didn't really comfort me as much as increase my anxiety. Could I meet these expectations? I leaned further into him and watched the propellers stop and briefly reverse.

"I only meant to say that I'm pleased to be back."

"I am as well. I don't think I could have ever predicted under what circumstances we'd arrive."

We watched as an airport attendant dashed under the plane's wings to chock the wheels. Princess Shams was already in the aisle, and she nodded at us.

"Good luck."

Not waiting for a response, she ducked her head and exited the plane. This was like a scene out of a war picture. I had been recruited for a dangerous spying mission, and now my handler was leaving me to my own devices.

From outside the cabin, I heard the high-pitched voice of a woman calling my name. A moment later that voice was joined by a body—a rotund, round-shouldered woman's body bundled in an enormous fur coat. Atop that was a fat-cheeked face crowned with a thick head of curly, dark hair. She ambled down the aisle toward me. I had the distinct impression that a bear was about to devour me. I wasn't being left alone; I was merely being passed on to someone else.

"Welcome home, Soraya," the woman said, wrapping her arms around me. "How wonderful to have you here again."

She stepped back and held me at arm's length. Her features were anything but fierce. Her round cheeks sandbagged her watery gray eyes, but did not diminish their softness.

"Come along, come along."

"Forough Zafar," my father said in greeting to his relative. "It is wonderful to meet you. A pleasure to make the acquaintance of a Bakhtiari woman whose legend precedes her." Forough waved her hand in dismissal.

"I am pleased to meet you as well, *ameh*," I added, emphasizing the Farsi word for "auntie."

"Never mind all that. I want to fill you in a bit on what to expect," Forough said, taking control in her role as the queen mother's lady-in-waiting. "We've arranged a greeting for you. Despite the custom, I'd like you to exit the plane first. Khalil Khan, you will follow. I'm sure you understand." Her tone suggested that even if Khalil did not understand this breach in etiquette, he'd better get used to it.

"Of course," my father said. He straightened his necktie and pulled his overcoat around his shoulders, buttoning the top button only, to form a cape.

"Either on or off, but not both," Forough scolded. "The runway is packed with photographers, so look sharp and smile." My father buttoned his coat all the way and forced his arms through the sleeves.

As soon as I walked up to the plane's doorway and tentatively set foot on the stairs, it was as if I'd stepped into midair. The assault on my senses was nearly as intense. Flashbulbs blinded me, the first stirring strains of the Iranian national anthem were belted out from the band, and an honor guard snapped to attention and began slapping rifle barrels and stocks. Soon their weapons were spinning in the frigid air as the white, green, and red flags snapped in the stiff breeze.

A group of men in Western suits all stood in a row. They were little more than a composite of flashing teeth and slight pressure on my hand and as I passed from one to another. It was as if I was back in Lausanne at the Theater Luminaire, watching a newsreel, everyone moving stiffly and formally. All that was lacking was a narrator's intoning voice.

Those flashbulbs blinded me, but they also opened my eyes. This scene was real. What had been a private affair among the shah's representatives and me was actually something quite public. I hadn't thought far enough ahead to worry about what my future would be like if I failed. I didn't think of it in those terms. If I'd thought of measuring up, it was as a wife, and not as a queen. Unlike my father, I didn't focus on the politics.

I wasn't worried about being rejected so much as I was hoping that this man and I would truly love one another. I didn't want a marriage that was all fanfare and pretense. As much as I had once dreamed of being a princess, I still very much wanted to find a soul mate—a man with whom I could share a life and not just a title.

Finally, as the band wound to a conclusion, a short, handsome man with a pair of round spectacles that gave him an owlish appearance stepped forward. "Welcome to Tehran, Miss Bakhtiari. I am Dr. Ayadi."

Something about the man's noble demeanor calmed my jangling nerves. Whether it was Dr. Ayadi's presence or the absence of the band's clamor, the way he took me by the elbow and led me to a second group of dignitaries helped immensely. Still, I kept seeking out my father, and every time I caught a glimpse of his beaming face, I was reassured.

I would have loved for my mother to be there with me, but she had obligations at home with Bijan. In addition, her being German made things complicated, given that country's relationship with Iran during war. Still, I felt I needed her calming presence, and I sensed that she was more objective than either my father or I could be.

I moved through the second line more quickly, and despite my best attempt to put names with faces, I abandoned all hope of doing so. I was tired, having spent two hectic nights packing and then traveling. There'd been a great deal of turbulence, and though flying didn't usually trouble me, I couldn't sleep. Add to that my anxiety about meeting the shah for the first time, and I was on the verge of collapse.

Fortunately, the mass introductions ended, and I, along with Forough and my father, were whisked into a waiting limousine. I had hoped to speak with him about the reception we'd received and my need to get some rest before making any significant personal appearances. Any thought of that was dashed an instant later.

"Soraya, dear," Forough said, her eyebrows knit in concentration, "tonight is a very important night. The country waits with great anticipation." She produced a newspaper, and showed me the front page headline: The Shah's Future? Underneath that banner headline was a photograph of me, smiling easily and looking relaxed. Somehow they'd gotten ahold of one of the photos Amin had taken in London. Before Forough could snatch the paper back, I had a chance to scan part of the photo's caption: "Escorted by Princess Shams, the fiancée of the shah is to arrive in Tehran …"

"My picture. In a newspaper?" I felt numb.

"Not in *a* newspaper; *all* the newspapers." Forough sounded as pleased as if she'd just delivered the news that I had been granted eternal life.

"But I'm not even his fiancée yet!"

Before Forough could respond, Khalil interjected, "Well, you know how much people like to speculate. I'm certain the editors thought it wise to feed the hungry with something they desire. Everyone wants the king to marry, of course, and they want to know as much as they can about his personal affairs. Don't read too much into it."

Forough folded her arms across her abundant chest. "Ever the diplomat, aren't you, sir?"

My father shrugged his shoulders. "I'm merely trying to help the girl see all sides of this. If that's diplomacy, then so be it."

I was struck by my father's use of the word "girl" to describe me, as if I was no longer his daughter.

"You know, Soraya," Forough added, "you should be very honored to even be considered his fiancée. Perhaps after dinner tonight at the queen mother's residence, you will realize how fortunate you are. If, in fact, His Majesty approves of you."

I shut my eyes and leaned my head against the window. The glass was cold and soothing to me. I felt the beginning of a fever coming on, but it would be useless to register any objection to that night's affair. I thought of Bibi Maryam and some advice she'd given to Bijan and me when we played near Isfahan and the summer's melt from the spring snow was at its highest. I was caught in a fast-running current, and trying to grab at any branch or head for the bank would be a useless expense of energy. Better to point myself downstream and wait for calmer waters.

Any idea of getting a few hours' rest was dashed when the limousine pulled up to a small house within the shah's residential compound. I had hoped we might stay in one of the hotels in Tehran, but Forough's quarters were our destination. Though the house was small compared to the one I'd lived in in Isfahan, it hardly lacked for comforts. The floors were a gorgeous patchwork quilt of exquisite rugs—Tabriz, Kashan, and Kerman. I immediately identified the one from Kerman by its silk pile and ground weave and its central motif of a huntsman on horseback pursuing a lion. How I wished I could lie down on its field of tall grass and sleep!

"Follow me," Forough instructed. "They have set up a room for you back here."

I walked into a bedroom only to find it missing that one key piece of furniture—a bed. Instead, someone—I couldn't believe it was the conservatively dressed Forough—had purchased racks of clothes and had them hanging on a bar that stretched the length of the room. I recognized several as ones I'd seen in Paris, but how they arrived here was a mystery.

The rest of the afternoon was spent trying on clothes. Forough and my father oversaw the tornado of outfit-changing, and neither of them was easy to please. I could scarcely believe that my father, a man whose only prior concern was that his daughter appear proper, suddenly had developed an eye for fashion. Each time I stepped behind the Japanese *noren* to change, Forough joined me. I felt strange disrobing in front of a woman I barely knew, but soon I became used to standing in front of Forough in just a bra and slip. I was so exhausted I could have paraded around in front of the whole population of Tehran in that state of undress without a second thought.

After the final selection was made—a taffeta dress in crimson—I was allowed to bathe. An attendant ran the water and stood by, expecting to hand me a towel when I was finished. Instead, I asked the woman to leave. I sank into the steaming water, bunched a towel behind my head, and nodded off. When I awoke, I was even groggier from the heat and the brief nap. The water was still warm, so I knew I hadn't slept long. A knock at the door—Forough's reminder that we were to leave in an hour—struck me like a hammer's blow.

"Well, what do you think?" Forough asked, gesturing toward the royal residence. Before his death, Reza Shah Pahlavi had ordered many of the Golestan Palace buildings to be razed. He had great plans to build a new palace at Niavaran. Construction had begun, and his son Mohammad Reza would one day occupy the new structures. In my fog, I considered all the possibilities. Was Forough herself in favor of the new site or the old? Should I answer in a way that would please the lady-in-waiting or the shah?

"It is obviously very beautiful, I said, "But beauty can always be improved upon, can it not?"

I watched as my father slowed his pace a bit, allowing Forough to get a few steps ahead.

"Very diplomatic, Raya," he whispered. "You have been paying attention all these years."

Golestan Palace was aptly named. Even in October, the air was redolent of roses. As we made our way through the arched main entryway and into the palace proper, the odor went from fragrant to cloying. It had been hours since I'd eaten a few figs and pistachios, and I felt light-headed. The vibrant colors of the tiles and mosaics were rendered as Monetesque blobs of color. After a seemingly interminable walk down a labyrinth of corridors and hallways, we arrived. Too exhausted to consider the import of what was about to take place, I took a few deep breaths and tried to gather my energy.

The shah's brother, Gholam Reza, and his older half-sister Fatemeh greeted us. Like the shah himself, they were each born non-royals, prior to Reza Shah's initiating the dynasty's rule in place of his brother. Mohammad was the oldest of eleven children, and I was glad that not all of them would be in attendance for that night's dinner. After a few minutes of small talk, the shah's twin sister Ashraf joined us.

If Shams could sometimes seem to put on airs, I sensed immediately that Ashraf felt no one else worthy of breathing the same air as she. She swept into the room wearing a dress that heightened one's awareness that she was stick-thin. The way it hung from her bony shoulders made it seem as if the dress was still on its hanger. One eyebrow was permanently raised, giving her plain face a sour aspect. Her pinched, nasal tone added to the unpleasant effect.

"Is he not down yet? Must I always arrive before him?"

The three other siblings shifted uncomfortably. The men folded their hands and looked at their shoes.

Shams had warned me about Ashraf, filling in the details about the woman known as the "Black Panther." But her opening statement was anything but stealthy. Her reference to her being born shortly before her twin was a not-so-subtle reminder that the circumstance of their birth was a bad omen. In Persian culture, a man should always precede a woman. Worse, according to Shams, Ashraf coveted her position as the shah's twin. She felt that this privileged position meant that the throne was partly hers, and she relished the idea that she had the shah's ear on all variety of matters. Rumor had it that she had been partly responsible for the dissolution of the marriage between her brother and Queen Fawzieh.

"Soraya, how fortunate to finally make your acquaintance." Ashraf extended her hand and withdrew it after the barest of touch of mine.

"Where's mother? I thought we dined at seven." Ashraf squinted at her diamond-encrusted watch.

"Have you somewhere else to be this evening?" Fatemeh asked blandly, but with clear intentions. Clearly, she thought her sister rude.

The youngest brother, Ali, took Fatemeh's arm and said, "Excuse us for a moment. I must speak to my sister privately."

The pair stepped aside. If there was any tension between them, it was not apparent from their smiles and pleasant tone.

They were interrupted by the arrival of the queen mother, escorted by Shams. The fourth and favorite of Reza Shah's wives, she was of Quajar descent. Her presence instantly changed the atmosphere in the room. Suddenly, they weren't in the royal residence assessing a prospective mate; they were a family about to be seated for dinner.

"Soraya," Shams said, putting her hand on Ali's shoulder, "this is His Majesty's prized possession. I know you've met already, but this is the guy you really have to impress. A kid brother's opinion means a lot."

"Very funny. Soraya, please forgive my siblings. Apparently I'm the only one who shares my brother's penchant for being charming." Ali placed his hand beside his mouth and whispered overly loudly, "I really don't know who these other impostors are. Foundlings, I suspect."

I was immediately fond of the "kid brother," and saw in him qualities reminiscent of Bijan. Although I was considerably younger

123

than the twentyish Ali, I immediately felt the same kind of protective affection for him as I did my own brother.

I appreciated the brief respite from the tense exchange that Ashraf had begun. I was still feeling off-center, trying hard to balance my impressions of these people and my own tendency to be guarded. The queen mother and Ashraf were treating me coolly. On the other hand, I was certain that Ali, Fatemeh, and Shams liked me. But I knew that I couldn't count on them to win the others over; I'd have to take on the opposite faction directly. But before I could gather my wits, the queen mother and Ashraf fired their opening salvos: a series of questions for which they had little interest in my answers.

"What a delightful dress. Who designed it?"

"It's interesting, really …"

"Why could your mother not be here with us?"

"She's back in …"

"How did you find your studies in Switzerland?"

Caught off-guard, I repeated numbly, "Switzerland."

"Yes. Where you went to school, I'm told."

"Oh," I stammered, a bit surprised that I was expected to provide an answer and not field another query. Reeling, I grasped at the first platitude I could come up with. "It was lovely." All the while, I kept looking toward the doorway, hoping that the shah might appear and put an end to this madness.

Soon enough, an attendant announced the shah's arrival. We all rose from our seats.

I steadied myself, my hands on the back of my chair. My heart was pounding, and the other guests swam in and out of focus. The room had fallen completely silent. As I stared at the candles' flames, I could hear their flickering gasps.

A man appeared, clad in a white military jacket with a high red brocade collar and gold-trimmed epaulets. A series of medals dripped from his chest. Rather than being taken aback by his overly formal appearance, my heart went out to him. Not only was he dashing and handsome, but I immediately sensed that despite his square-shouldered stance, he was uncertain of himself. In dressing this way, he'd gone to great lengths to try to impress me. I thought of those boys back in Lausanne, imitating movie actors. The shah was performing a variation on that theme—he was dressed up as a gallant soldier. I was charmed by his effort to appear heroic.

I also imagined him in his room, trying on various suits and finding none of them satisfactory. Something about the wrinkles that flanked his eyes softened him, made him appear vulnerable.

He immediately went to his mother and kissed her proffered hand. The queen mother gently pulled his head down and kissed him on the forehead. Next, he strode toward my father. I watched as my father bowed. Seeing his cheeks flush, I wondered what Khalil Khan was thinking.

Finally, Mohammed Reza approached me. The shah came into sharp focus, and my head cleared immediately once I looked into his eyes. All the tension in my body eased, and I became keenly aware. I noticed that one buttonhole on his jacket was slightly frayed, and a thread waved in the breeze as he walked toward me. I looked up at him, tilting my head slightly to the left.

When Mohammed Reza took my hand, I felt as if I'd been immersed in a warm liquid that suffused my body inside and out.

"I must confess," he seemed to exhale rather than merely say, "I have eagerly awaited this day, and it has well been worth it."

"Your Majesty." I was surprised at the feelings welling up inside me, as well as the composure in my own voice. "I can only say the same." When he spoke to me, it was as if everyone else in the room disappeared. The other members of his family gave off a nervous energy, but not so Mohammed. His serenity wrapped me in a cozy blanket. I felt none of the anxiety that had preceded this first meeting. His voice was warm and kind and soothing; although he'd spoken only a few words to me, it felt both instantly familiar and appealingly new.

"I'm given to understand that we have much in common, you and I." The shah smiled, still standing next to me.

"I am told the same, Your Highness."

"Our Swiss education, for one thing. I was a student at Institut Le Rosey. One of the finest in the world, I like to think. I'm a sportsman, and the slopes at Gstaad were my friends. As a young man, I spent a great deal of time in the Zagros Mountains, your tribal region, and took on its magnificent slopes. They're finer than the Alps, I'd say."

I felt my cheeks reddening at his schoolboyish bragging.

The shah continued, but I was too pleased to really hear what he had to say. I realized that even though the man was fifteen years my senior, he wanted to impress me with his exploits and education. Despite his lofty position, the insecurity I first sensed couldn't be hidden behind his bravado.

I refocused and heard the shah talking about his love of the arts. I had just begun telling him about my recent visit to the Louvre when the queen mother said, "You have all the time in the world to talk later. I am told that our dinner is growing cold. Soraya, would you mind terribly if my son permits our guests to be seated so that we can start our meal?"

The shah took his seat, and everyone else followed suit. I sensed immediately that the queen mother and I would never be on friendly terms. As a possible wife of the shah, I'd have to share my prospective husband's time and attentions with an entire nation, but the reality that I'd have to wrest some of the same from his immediate family was a new revelation.

Throughout the meal, the shah regaled me with stories.

"So, I've lost a ski pole and veered off course. I don't know which way is up. Just then I hear a rustling in the bushes beside me. Remember, my boot is still stuck in the snow. A wolf emerges from the tree line. I try to free myself, but I can't. The wolf is no more than two feet away."

The shah paused for dramatic effect.

"What happened next?" I asked eagerly.

If I had resented the rules that forbade me from associating with the men in my family as a young child, I did benefit in one way. I knew that men like to talk, as much about themselves as any other subject, and that all I had to do was listen to the shah. Yet, I wasn't merely feigning interest. Unlike my father, who too often resorted to preaching and pontification, the shah was a wonderful raconteur, interested in entertaining more than educating. He had a pleasant speaking voice, his eyes sparkled and danced as he spoke, and he gesticulated animatedly, adding to his stories' impact.

If nothing else, I felt sure that if we were to end up married, there would be no lacking in communication between us. For as much as the shah went on about himself and his adventures, he stopped at times and asked me questions and probed for more details if I cut my responses short.

For much of the time, it was again as if the rest of those in the room had disappeared. I was so taken with the shah that the faint buzz of their conversations barely registered in my mind.

Unfortunately, just as the shah was about to cap his wolf story, Ashraf shattered the moment. "Are you sure," she asked, her voice dripping with sarcasm, "it wasn't three feet away? For that matter, are you sure it wasn't a baby lynx stalking you?"

The shah kept his eyes on me as he said, "Spoken like a woman who wasn't there. It was indeed a wolf, my dear sister."

The spell broken, I tuned out for a moment, troubled by the feeling that I was being watched. Looking up, I saw the stony face of the queen mother, staring daggers at me from across the table. Strangely, when the older woman saw me looking back at her, she raised her wine glass in salute. Not wanting to back down at all, I mimicked the gesture and the look. I then returned my attention to Mohammed Reza, feeling a small thrill of triumph at having stood up to the queen mother. I'd taken a risk in possibly offending her, but what of it? The ignorance of youth was guiding me.

After dinner, the two of us were able to retire to a formal sitting room for tea and fruits. Left alone for the first time, I expected to feel uncomfortable. Instead, I was even more at ease now that we weren't on display. It seemed that the shah was equally smitten, but Persian custom and upbringing caused the tone of our conversation to change. The shah was no longer as jovial as before, but the seriousness of his tone and our private discussion was entirely appropriate.

Our conversation ranged from the recent establishment of the state of West Germany, to the film *The Third Man*, to T.S. Eliot being awarded the Nobel Prize in Literature. In reference to the last, I quoted "Do I dare to eat a peach?" as I reached toward the bowl of fruit.

The shah laughed delightedly. "You are a clever one."

Blushing, I felt a longing for this man to touch me, to make more tangible the feelings that coursed through my body. Yet it was one thing to match witticisms with the shah, but obviously an honest expression of one's feelings was not appropriate. Several times I had to remind myself that I should do my best to appear disinterested in him. Yes, I could seem rapt as he spun one of his stories, but merely as a polite audience might in the presence of any great performer. The rules dictated that the line was not to be crossed. The absurdity of it frustrated me. However, to cross that line—to blur any lines of distinction between pleasant familiarity and attraction—would ruin my chances. As the shah escorted me to another part of the residence where my father had been entertained by the others, I wondered when the Iranian soul would be allowed to roam freely.

As we said our goodbyes, I could not escape feeling as if I had been just another guest at a state affair—a privileged guest to be sure, but still. I knew what protocol demanded, but I'd been under the influence of romantic films and my schoolmates' tales of their adolescent romantic assignations. Why did we have to retreat into formality? Deflated, my adrenaline rush in decline, I supposed that was to be expected. After all, we were no longer alone, and there was no way he could kiss me. I wondered when I might hear from him again. When the shah took my hand and told me goodnight, it was as if he was a shy schoolboy, struggling with his own feelings and desires. We weren't a king and his possible queen; we were simply two people caught up in our very real emotions. The politics of the heart are quite different from the politics of the state. For that night, and for some time to come, I was concerned only with the first. He was a man and I was a young woman. He was experienced and I was naïve. But that was as it should be, at least as far as fairy tales go. "Once upon a time" is the way they begin, and as we were driven back to Forough's residence, I was already writing the rest of our story.

Chapter
TWELVE

Of course, as soon I had started to mentally write that story, I had revisions in mind. Back in my room, I changed out of my dress into my nightgown. I was glad that no attendants were there to assist me. I left the gown puddled on the floor, exacting a bit of revenge on Shams for her reverence for the fabric. I laughingly thought of my mother telling Bijan and me that the pick-up fairy wasn't going to visit our rooms.

I'd spent most of the day wishing for a chance to rest, but now that I had one, I was wide awake. With the passing of each minute, I shifted restlessly in my bed. I also moved from one emotional position to another. Finally, I settled into place.

What had passed between the shah and me was real and special. What convinced me was something seemingly trivial. Ashraf interrupting his story proved my case. He had rejected whatever propriety response was necessary in a public setting and had shown real irritation with his beloved twin sister. That was no act; neither was her sense that his attention was focused entirely on me. When I shut off my brain—something I often struggled to do—and let my heart speak, I agreed with what it was telling me. Despite the clumsiness of the situation, the two of us had made a deep and personal connection. I tried to imagine how the evening might have gone if we were allowed to be completely alone, to let our guards down without reservation. That imagined scenario was a bit different from the one that had occurred.

While no physical intimacies had transpired between us, I had felt a spark each time his hands neared me. Even though skin had not touched skin, it was as if some force, something electromagnetic, had literally passed from one to the other. I'd been in close proximity to boys before, some of whom I found attractive, but nothing like that had ever happened to me before. In that kind of situation, all I felt was the fear that my father might find out. Instead of being made fearful by close proximity to the shah, I was exhilarated.

I pulled the blankets tighter around my body, hoping to trap the pleasurable sensations coursing through me. I wished that I could speak with my mother, fill her in on every detail of the evening. That wasn't possible; the hour was far too late. I also wished I could know what the shah was thinking, how he was spending these hours, how his mind was occupied.

I didn't have long to wait for the answer.

A light tap came from the bedroom door. "Raya, my love. Are you awake?"

"Yes, Baba." I arranged the pillows and sat upright.

"May I come in, if you're decent?"

"Of course."

My father sat on the edge of my bed, his back partially to me. He appeared to be fumbling with something in his hands.

"Is everything all right?"

"Yes. I don't mean to alarm you." My father shifted so that he was now facing me fully. I could see that he'd been crying. His eyes were red-rimmed, and he'd been fumbling with his handkerchief. My heart fell for a moment, but not daring to give voice to my worry, I kept silent.

My father cleared his throat, "You know how I am; I always must have the right words in place. Perhaps I should have waited until morning."

"Nonsense. I was hoping you'd come in. I wanted to hear what you had to say about this evening."

Khalil smiled at my understatement. I think he could tell I was about to explode from eagerness. "I thought it went very well. Very well, indeed. The two of you seemed to be enjoying one another's company immensely."

I tugged at the blankets and brought them to my chin. "I'm so glad you thought so. It's true, I really did. I was starting to doubt my own sense of things."

Khalil took one of my hands in his. "Listen to me, Raya. You should never doubt yourself. You're a bright girl, a sensitive girl." He paused and shook his head. "What am I saying! You're a young lady, and you proved that over and over again tonight. Every bit a lady."

My stomach buzzed with empathy when I heard a slight catch in his voice and saw his Adam's apple rise and fall. I'd never seen my father so emotional, and the sight of him this way both pleased and saddened me.

"That's why I've come to you tonight. I have a question for you, and I want you to consider carefully before you answer." Baba leaned into me, his eyes widening.

I nodded. "I will."

"I received a phone call a few minutes ago. It was the shah. He has asked for your hand in marriage."

I slid down and pulled the covers all the way over my head. I kicked my legs, feeling both a giddy delight and disbelief. Heaving a sigh, I emerged from my hiding place. "After an evening's encounter? In those few hours he …"

Baba raised his hand to quiet me. "The heart knows what it wants, Soraya. A hundred thoughts can be shouted down by a single feeling."

My father had put it more eloquently than I had, but we had come to the same conclusion.

"Are you prepared to be the empress of this country?" The weight of that question was not evident to me then. I didn't consider the importance of the answer I was about to give, or how my life—the life of a sixteen-year-old girl—would change in that moment forever. How naïve I was; how little I read into what I'd experienced!

Without hesitation, I answered, "Yes."

Khalil Khan pushed himself to his feet. "I will deliver your answer to the king."

"Baba, wait. Don't leave yet." I held out my arms, and my father bent to hug and kiss me. I could feel his shoulders quivering slightly. He held me longer than he had in years, and I enjoyed the time it took for him to compose himself.

When he straightened, I asked, "Have you spoken with Mater?"

"She is aware of the situation."

"What did she say?"

"That she trusts her daughter to do the right thing, and that she will support your decision no matter what it is."

"Are you pleased?"

"I'm always pleased with you Raya. Well, nearly always." His smile let me know his intent. "I'm pleased for you, our family, for the Bakhtiari people. This bodes well for us all."

Baba paused at the door. "More than anything, I'm happy for you. And so very proud."

I got out of bed and threw my arms around him. My father stood there unnerved by my display, but when I let go of him and walked back to my bed, he followed me. Once I lay down, he helped pull the covers up and then kissed me on the forehead as if I was a young child before he rushed out of the room.

I scarcely slept that night; visions of the handsome man I was to marry invaded my every thought. I pushed away any intrusive thoughts that threatened my happiness.

I dined with Mohammed and his family again the next evening. As we had the night before, we barely acknowledged the presence of the others. After a few minutes together, my cheeks felt numb and puffy. It was as if someone had sculpted my face and permanently given me a giddy smile. The shah and I came out of our trance only when first Ashraf and then the queen mother pointedly interrupted our conversation.

"I'm quite certain," Ashraf said, "That when the novelty wears off, the two of you will appreciate the presence of others around your table."

The shah rose to my defense as he had the night before, but was quickly cut off by his mother. "Your Majesty. Your baby sister is quite right about one thing. It is ill-mannered to leave everyone else out of your conversation, my son. We'd all love to hear more about the girl that is to be your wife. I don't relish the idea of having a stranger about the palace."

I was glad to hear that unpleasant exchange. By vocalizing so clearly the disdain they obviously felt, the two women were achieving quite the opposite of what they'd hoped. Mohammed and I were now even more united in our defense of what we saw as our natural right to develop a much closer bond.

In the weeks that followed, we saw each other nearly every day. The moments I treasured the most were the quiet ones we spent simply talking in his favorite room at Ekhtesasi, the building that housed his private office. During those times, I felt the urge to kiss my future husband. I did not dare, but my mind was filled with dreams of that moment.

The shah had made arrangements for Bijan and Mater to join us in Tehran, and they were housed in a villa near the palace. Bijan was ever the little brother, secretly proud and pleased for his sister, but outwardly teasing and torturing me. I don't know if the changes I noticed in him were real. Maybe I was just imagining things based on my need to feel older and more mature. He seemed heavier, chunkier even—more of a boy who'd yet to develop any muscle on his frame.

I would have appreciated my mother's counsel, but we spoke only of arrangements and details. She did ask me if I loved him, and I told her yes.

"That's important," she said. I was confused by her saying that, as if it was just one of a number of things on a checklist. I wanted to hear more, but she said that no one could prepare me for what was ahead. I'd simply have to figure out how best to adapt on my own. In saying this, I can see how someone might think her to be indifferent, but in the end, she was right.

One morning, Mohammed called and instructed me to pack a bathing suit. Although I pressed him for more details, he playfully evaded my questions.

When I hung up the phone, Bijan stood in front of me, his arms folded across his chest. "So, where are you off to?" he asked, trying to sound more like a parent than a younger sibling.

"He wouldn't say. It's some kind of surprise."

Bijan collapsed onto a sofa. "How can anything be a surprise these days? Everything that's happening is a surprise, so even when it isn't, it is."

"What are you talking about?"

"You get it. You just don't want to admit it." Bijan pinched a pillow between his toes and flung it at me. "What's he like, really? Does it feel strange that he is so old? I mean think about it, when you were born …"

"Bijan, stop. It's not like that. I don't even sense the age difference."

"Does he treat you well?"

"Of course he does. And he's actually sort of shy with me, even awkward in a way." Bijan threw his head back and laughed, "Shy? The shah is shy? With all the women he's had?"

"Bijan," I began, impressed with the imperial tone I was able to produce that startled my little brother. "I won't have you talking this way. Teasing is one thing. Being malicious is another. Respect, please."

Bijan frowned and pouted momentarily. Rather than apologize, he picked up a magazine and leafed through it. A moment later, as though completely absorbed in the reading material, he walked out of the room, his eyes still riveted to the page.

I was left alone with my thoughts about my future husband. I was surprised by how I rose to his defense in the face of Bijan's teasing. I had to admit, I was troubled by some of Mohammed's insecurities. He'd continued to tout his adventurous spirit and ways, frequently reminding me that he was a pilot and that he was eager to fly off with me when we had the chance. A number of times, we'd walked through one of the out-buildings that housed a collection of his cars and his airplanes.

I didn't mind the show and tell at all, and was moved by his passion for speed and flight. His frequent mentions of his late father and how he'd disapprove of such frivolities worried me. Mohammed Reza's father was a man who used a club to ascend to power. Although he'd been sent into exile during the Russo-English occupation and later died in exile in South Africa, the elder Pahlavi had still held considerable sway over the family he left behind. The man had made ambitious plans for the country, wanting to modernize it while still holding it in his iron fist, and Mohammed Reza spoke highly of his father's vision. I understood that my future husband hoped to see his father's hopes through, but I felt that he did so more out of fear than respect. It wasn't as if his father was going to come back from the dead and overthrow his son. Still, it seemed as if he was haunted by his ghost. Maybe that's true for all sons and fathers in some way, but I hadn't seen anything like this before.

Mohammed Reza had been handed the reins of the country during World War II, when his father was deposed, and yet he seemed uncertain about which direction to lead it. During the years the son had been in power, I'd heard my father and some of his confidants talking about how the start of this dynasty was troubled. In living memory, the people of Iran had known only the tyrannical Qajar rulers. They had been in power for centuries prior to the Pahlavis, in large part due to British protection in exchange for a percentage of the profits from the country's oil production. Mohammed's father had tried to modernize the country and to enact many improvements, including women's rights, but he also used the law to punish his personal enemies and allowed people in his administration to accept bribes. I was led to believe by my male relatives that the good old days, as bad as they may have been at times, were at least predictable.

My father had advocated for patience, but I'd overheard more than one guest, even in their new accommodations in Tehran, say, "It is the first knots that determine the quality of the weaving."

My musings were interrupted by the bleat of a car horn.

The November sunlight was blinding, and as I stumbled along the walkway, I held my hand up to shield my eyes. I immediately wished that my vision hadn't cleared. As much as I liked Ali, I had hoped that Mohammed and I would be spending the day alone. My disappointment was brief. When I saw the two of them beaming at me from behind their sunglasses from the front seats of a convertible, and then saw Mohammed wrap his arm around his little brother's shoulder, my heart softened. Ali didn't spend much time in Tehran, but Mohammed wished he did.

"It is a glorious day, isn't it?" Ali said. "Who would have thought a day at the beach would be in order?"

"I agree," I said. "When you mentioned a suit and swimming, I didn't think of the beach. A nearby pool maybe."

"We're off to Ramsar. We have a villa there. It's November, and no one will be about. We'll have the place to ourselves."

I couldn't help but think that the shah had to be a bit dense to use those words in connection with this outing. If ever there was a chance for the two of us to be alone, to really be free to express ourselves, maybe even physically, having Ali along seemed like an opportunity wasted.

"Aren't you afraid it will be cold?"

"Come on, Soraya, get in. We are burning daylight," Ali said. He stepped out of the convertible, and instead of climbing in the back, he lowered the seat back so that I could clamber in the rear. There was so little room for my legs that I had to sit sidesaddle, with my legs stretched in front of me.

The shah turned to face me. "Don't you love this? It was just shipped over. It's an Austin, A90 Atlantic. The first off the assembly line. Caspian blue, can you believe it? As if they named the color just for us."

"It's lovely." I was swept up by his enthusiasm.

The two hundred kilometers to Ramsar and the Caspian Sea passed mostly in wind-enforced silence. Ali and Mohammed spoke briefly, and the only word that I could catch was "delightful." I felt certain that although it could have been spoken in relation to the day, the car, or the roads, Mohammed had said it about me. This was not vanity on my part, but an honest assessment of the brothers' opinion of me. In some ways this was better than any first kiss that I'd imagined Mohammed and I might exchange, but in others it fell far short of the mark.

The villa was a colonnaded sprawling monstrosity that seemed to date back to the Romans. The marble floors of the portico still held a chill as I padded out of the changing room in my bathing suit. This would be the first time my husband would see me in this state of undress, and I hoped he would like what he saw. I had fully expected that he'd be waiting on one of the wicker lounges that had been pulled into the patch of sunlit lawn astride a wavering palm tree. The wind carried the sound of voices over the surf's clamor. I lowered my sunglasses from atop my head and saw two men splashing and diving in the waves. Disappointment again gave way to bemused appreciation for the shah's way with his siblings; his ability to shed his royal duties and demeanor. I'd never considered that the shah of Iran would submit, however grudgingly, to a less-than-kingly dunking from his younger brother. To his credit, Mohammed came up spluttering and splashing frantically, trying to blind his attacker. When that attempt failed, he strode toward shore.

I heard him shouting my name and waving at me to come join them. I walked toward the beach, and said, hoping that my voice wouldn't carry, "No, thank you. I'll just lie in the sun for a bit."

Unfortunately, Mohammed heard me and didn't have to come any closer. I retreated to my spot in the sun to watch the boys at play. The light at the shore was intense, sharply drawing the outlines of everything. The crystalline quality to the air and to my vision was something that I realized I had missed about Iran. Everything I saw was clearly defined, whereas in Berlin, Lausanne, or London, I was shrouded in fog. It was as if in those other places, I was peering through a veil. Here that veil was lifted. Also, the air felt and smelled fresher. The sharp scent of the ocean, the fragrance of the gardens and the lawns were so different from the muted and dirty smells of those big and industrialized cities. With visions of smokestacks and gloom in my mind, I fell asleep.

I woke to a cool breeze and shade. The shadowy figure of the shah was standing several feet away, dripping wet and shivering from the sea. Clearly he appreciated what he saw. I slowly pulled a towel over myself and drew my legs up. I hugged my knees to my chest and rested my chin on them.

"I thought we might take a walk." The shah extended his hand and I took it. He led me toward the villa, but only to help me into his shirt. The sun-warmed broadcloth oxford caressed my skin. We strolled the beach for a while, and then turned back toward the villa. My hopes fell, but as we neared the portico, the shah tugged at my sleeve and led me through a hedge and into the garden. Before I could say anything, he bent to me and kissed me. His lips were warm, and tasted of salt. They were living things moving on me as he pressed my body close to his. Without our lips parting, we sank to the lawn.

The first kiss seemed to last for minutes, and we only broke apart when I winced involuntarily.

"Are you all right?" Mohammed Reza asked.

"Wonderful." I held up my hand to show him the imprint of the sharp blades of grass on the palm of my hand.

"Does it hurt?" He kissed the spot tenderly.

"Just a bit. But it's better now."

"Wait here."

Mohammed returned with a pair of towels that he spread out for us to lie on.

"I wouldn't want your memories of this moment be anything but pleasant."

I felt myself transported. I could faintly hear the trees rustling and smell the sea on the wind. My fiancée alternated between tender brushes of his lips against mine and more forceful crushing kisses that had me arching my back and stifling a gasp. When he ran his hands along my sides, I was in a thrall of exquisite sensations. I entwined my fingers in his hair, wanting more. But for that, I would have to wait.

By the time we returned to the villa, the sun was setting. My lips felt swollen and raw, and Mohammed's were bright crimson. I touched my finger to them and he winced.

"A price I'm willing to pay," he said.

We'd forgotten all about Ali, but he had the good sense to write a note for us advising us of his return to Tehran. He'd taken one of the cars the family left at the beach house. The shah read the note and smiled ruefully as he handed it to me.

"The last line," he said.

"I trust that Soraya will keep you on the right road and that you won't wander off in the dark as you have in the past." I felt a lump developing in my throat. I bowed my head and handed the paper back. "He's sweet."

"Ali is a good man. Even if he weren't my brother, I'd say that of him. That he's family makes it even better."

On the drive back, Mohammad said, "I forgot to mention earlier that tomorrow we'll be having lunch at my mother's."

I was glad the darkness hid my frown. Mohammed sensed my discomfort.

"Tell me."

"I could use a little more notice, is all. I need to prepare myself."

"Well, consider this your notice." His voice had a sharp edge that I didn't like at all. "My mother considers her Friday family luncheons to be an important ritual, and I'm inclined to agree."

The matter settled, I drew the towels more tightly around myself to ward off the chill.

That coolness was nothing compared to what I stirred up the next day at lunch.

"How was your day at the shore, Soraya?" The queen mother asked.

"Oh, the beach was lovely, but it was too cold to swim. I did spend a lot of time in the garden and loved it," I said, nearly giggling.

The shah gave me a wide-eyed stare, warning me that I was treading a fine line between cheek and catastrophe.

"Soraya, would you care for some cardamom tea?" Princess Ashraf said. She sniffled softly and added, "We have it flown in all the way from ..."

"I'm fine with just water, thank you, Lady Ashraf."

An awkward pause ensued as Ashraf waved off the servant girl. The queen mother resumed her exploration of the previous topic. "I find the Caspian too drab this time of year. I hardly consider it to be worth the travel time."

"Oh, how can you say that?" I replied, the intensity in my voice capturing everyone's attention. "It's marvelous. A very special place. Of course, the company makes an enormous difference." I reached for the shah's hand and beamed at him.

Mohammed Reza withdrew his hand. I could see that his face had gone ashen. In the span of less than a minute, I had managed to refuse the offer of a rare tea, demoted Princess Ashraf to a "Lady," and contradicted the queen.

I knew what I'd done, but I felt that they had it coming to them, regardless of whatever position in my future husband's life they occupied.

"I believe you owe everyone an apology," the shah said as he wiped his mouth with his napkin.

"I meant no offense. I merely wanted to make clear how much I loved your villa." I knew they wouldn't understand the subtext of my near-apology. I hated the residence in Tehran. As far as I was concerned, it was an over-decorated clutter of silver candelabras and crystal vases stuffed with silk flowers. The room we sat in seemed to suffocate its inhabitants with wall tapestries and damask and heavy brocade curtains. The place was as oppressive as the Qajar regime had been, and the queen mother seemed to revel in her anti-modernity.

Looking at her self-satisfied, round little figure, fingering the silver flatware and the bone china as if they were her pets, I could not help thinking, *Please, don't let me end up like her.*

I was taken aback when Ashraf said, "If you loved our place in Ramsar, the two of you simply must go to Shemiran. The last girl you took there to ride the horses loved it so. What was her name? Beautiful girl. We all thought the world of her."

The shah looked at his sister coldly. "That's a fine idea. Soraya is an accomplished equestrienne."

"Oh, I'm sure she thinks she is, but at her age, she can't possibly have experienced enough to earn that label." The princess blinked slowly as if sending a semaphore message, "It's settled then. We'll go, the three of us, tomorrow. We'll picnic and make a grand day of it. Perhaps you'll find those gardens to your liking as well."

At midday the shah and I were seated on the lawn at the secluded Pahlavi estate outside Tehran. Before us, on a traditional *sofreh*, were platters of grilled meats, watermelon, honeydew, a basket of lavash, and mints.

I tugged at the waistband of my new jodhpurs to get comfortable. "Strange that your sister left us to ourselves."

Ashraf had said that she didn't have much of an appetite generally. This was obvious considering how her riding clothes draped her bony frame. She'd gone inside to read. I kept thinking I saw the princess's piercing dark eyes peering out from behind a curtain, but I dismissed the thought.

I turned my attention to the real scene in front of me. Mohammed looked resplendent in a checked shirt and a pair of corduroy trousers—a far cry from his usual Iranian Air Force uniform. Beyond him, a team of grooms slathered the horses with soapy water as the animals chewed at the grass, occasionally nickering their pleasure.

"I wouldn't say that anything my sister does these days is

strange—it's all of a piece. At least she was good enough to prepare all this for us. Except," he wrinkled his nose at one of the containers, "she knows I detest yogurt soup. Everyone in the family insists that I should give up my title if I can't be a proper Persian and eat the stuff."

"Give it to me, then. I can be Persian enough for the both us." I savored the richness of the dish.

I had to spend the rest of the afternoon riding alone. Mohammed was called away to a phone conference to handle some urgent matter. I'd pouted for a moment when he informed me, but quickly put on a brave face, knowing that I'd have to reconcile myself to a life dictated by imperial duties. As my mare galloped about the grounds of the estate, my old riding lessons gradually took hold. I lost myself in the rhythms of the trot and the canter, but the occasional gallop had me feeling lightheaded and queasy. Worse, I could hear Ashraf's words from the previous night about the other girls with whom her twin brother had gone riding, and about my inevitable lack of experience as a rider. I felt a wave of something like dread rumble in my belly.

"You look unwell," remarked Ashraf when I returned to the house.

My legs wobbled beneath me briefly, but I regained my balance. Ashraf's comment seemed laced with malice. "I hope one lovely young mare didn't wear out the other," she added.

I smiled thinly. "Not at all. I'm not in the best riding condition, but I know that in the future I'll have ample opportunity to improve."

A stabbing pain gripped my stomach. I tried to keep my expression neutral, but I recoiled nonetheless. "If you'll excuse me, I'd like to bathe before we return to Tehran."

"Whatever will make you comfortable," Ashraf said. "I have to make a few phone calls. Let the staff know if you need anything."

The princess placed the back of her hand on my forehead. I flinched at her touch. "You're a bit warm. The water will do you some good. I believe that there are some salts. One of the ladies will get them for you."

At that point, I could barely stand up the pain was so intense. All I wanted to do was to get inside the lavatory and shut the door. Ashraf led me to a bedroom and then picked through a closet. I could have sworn the woman was torturing me, enjoying every second of my discomfort.

"Please, Ashraf, I need a moment alone." I finally said, nearly breathless from the pain.

"You really need to toughen up, fair one," Ashraf said as she stepped out of the room. "Enjoy that bath."

I shut the door and slid the bolt. The ache was so intense that I sank to my knees and rested my head on the cool porcelain of the bidet. My breath came in ragged rasps, and I thought I wouldn't be able to keep the contents of my stomach from rising past my throat. I reached for the taps above the tub and turned them on, hoping that the sound of the water might obscure my retching. As much as my stomach heaved and the acrid taste of bile filled my mouth, nothing came forth. I peeled off my sweat-soaked clothes and lowered myself into the tub. After a few moments, my vertigo ceased and my stomach settled. I'd never experienced anything like that sensation before, and was grateful it had ended.

The drive back to the palace was agonizing, but I battled the waves of nausea in silence. I noticed that Ashraf kept her eyes glued to the rearview mirror, assessing me. I suspected that somehow she was enjoying my misery.

Overnight, my condition worsened. I lay in bed, alternately shivering and calling for more bedclothes to wrap myself in; and then sweating, hurling the blankets off me and calling for a basin and cool water. Baba and Mater were in an agitated state, wondering aloud what they could do for me.

My mother sat up with me throughout the night, moistening my brow and wetting my lips with a damp cloth. At times the pain wracked me so badly that I bit down on the hand towel she offered me. In the mirror across the room, my face was wizened and red like a shriveled plum. At one point, my mother slipped into a half-sleep. When she woke, the room smelled of my waste. I was too weak to even call out for help. The heat rising from my body was so intense that the room's temperature seemed to have gone up.

Eva called for one of the maids to assist her, and they carried my limp body into the bathroom and lowered me into the tub. I merely moaned. Finally, the fever seemed to break and they carried me back to bed. As soon as they did, my fever spiked again. I lay writhing on my sweat-soaked sheets, tearing at my clothes.

During a calm period, my parents, thinking me asleep, sat together in my room talking quietly.

"How is she?"

"Not well at all." My mother's voice was strained, as if each of her words were cracked and on the verge of shattering. "She needs a doctor."

"We've put it off as long as possible. Mohammed Reza must know."

"Consider the hour. It will be sun-up soon. No need to rouse them all."

"But if he finds out we were up all night with her ... Besides, she needs a doctor as soon ..."

Mater nodded. "Of course, you're right. I'm not thinking clearly at all. I must get back to her."

When she was gone, my father sagged into a chair, his head in his hands, cursing. After a moment, he pulled the phone to him and dialed the number.

I imagined that I reached for the phone to stop him, but after that point, all was darkness.

Chapter
THIRTEEN

"As far as I can tell, Your Majesty, she's been poisoned."

Even in my febrile fog, I could feel the electric charge in the room. Mohammed Reza's face hardened into a mask of outrage. "What do you mean? Who are you accusing?"

Dr. Ayadi's magnified eyes grew even larger behind his round spectacles. He pushed his glasses back into place and brushed a handkerchief across his nose. "Let me rephrase that. I mean to say that she may possibly have food poisoning. Something she ate has set off this reaction."

The shah shook his head wearily. "Learn to express yourself more clearly, then." He walked up to me and smoothed my damp hair from my forehead. I tried to smile gratefully, offer him some assurance, but all I could manage was a weak whimper as another wave of pain and nausea crashed into me. I so wanted to tell him I was sorry for worrying him, that I appreciated his concern more than he knew.

Turning back to Dr. Ayadi, he asked, "There is nothing to be done then?"

"In most cases things should …" the doctor paused, "work themselves out in twenty-four to forty-eight hours. Of course, if the fever gets worse, I need to be called."

"Thank you."

Mohammed's words were a clear signal that the doctor should leave. He hesitated near the door, fussing with the clasp on his medicine bag. He removed his glasses and squinted back toward us.

"Is there something else?" Mohammed's voice was filled with frustration.

The doctor pursed his lips. "There's always a chance that I could be wrong, that something more serious is at work. An allergic reaction perhaps. I suggest that she review everything she ate on the day in question. Perhaps avoid such things in the future."

Doctor Ayadi lingered longer, and I suspected that he had more to say. The closing of the door behind him put a period to the end of his sentence.

"How are you feeling, my love?"

Mohammed's endearment gave me temporary relief from the spasms that stabbed my stomach. Not wanting to add to his worry, I said, "I'll be fine. I just need a bit of rest."

Mohammed Reza looked at the bedside table and the plate of lavash and pot of tea. As he poured me a cup of the mint brew, the sound of the water splashing into it nearly made me gag. I hid my mouth behind my hand and feigned a yawn.

"You need your strength. Eat something. Drink some of this." Having the man I would soon marry acting as a nursemaid touched me. I didn't know how to say to him that I'd become like a funnel. One could pour things into me, but they flowed right out.

I took a tiny sip of tea and held it on my tongue, hoping it would be absorbed there.

My head was pounding, and it seemed as if someone was holding a seashell to my ears. I felt my eyes closing, and a moment later the shah's lips brushed my eyelids.

The next four days proceeded much as the first had. I needed to be carried into the bathroom to be bathed and, too frequently, perform bodily functions. Eva and Khalil took turns sitting with me, my mother knitting and my father reading. I appreciated their presence and their silence. They spoke only briefly and as necessary. An ounce of thin broth and a few crumbs of bread were all I could manage to eat. My skin felt hot and papery, and even the mildest of foods smelled powerfully strong and unappetizing.

On one occasion, I saw myself in the mirror and started with fright, clutching the bedsheets. Even that touch caused my fingertips to burn. My skin had a ghostly pallor, and my eyes were sunken, my cheekbones sharp ridges on a snowy plain. I plucked at the skin of one wrist, and it was limp and spare.

I hated for anyone outside my family to see me, but keeping them away was impossible. Shams and Ashraf paid their daily visits, but it was my account that was charged. The two women were absolutely wearisome, nattering on about one thing or another, making a passing reference to their future sister-in-law's health before launching into one story or another about someone at court I'd never heard of. I had wondered why I'd never met their husbands, and after a few days of their bedside torture, I understood why. The men were probably as far from Tehran as they could get.

Even my daily visits from Mohammed became a bother—not because he wasn't as sympathetic as he could be, often bringing me small gifts of single flowers, but because I could read in his eyes and his face how his worry about me was taxing him. I had no idea what events were taking place in the country. My concerns were more personal. I feared being sick was a sign of weakness, a frailty that suggested I was unsuited for the task of being the queen.

On the fifth day, I lay asleep when the shah came in and sat beside my bed. I stirred briefly, but my lethargy grabbed at me like the undertow and dragged me under.

Later, I lay in that unpleasant zone between sleep and wakefulness. My body ached, and every moment was an agony. I was vaguely aware that others were in the room. Through heavy-lidded eyes, I saw two men standing near the window.

The shah stood slump-shouldered with his brother Ali. The two men embraced and then sat.

"Brother," Ali said, "I can see how these days have taken a toll on you. It's no wonder. With everything else going on, you've got to worry about her. I also understand that you're running yourself ragged making wedding preparations. Whatever for? You need to expand your energies more wisely."

"Ali Reza, these all may seem separate to you, as if I could cast one aside for the moment, but it is far more complicated than that."

"You only think …"

"Brother, please lower your voice. And no, I don't only think. I know that a shah's choice of mate is more than just a matter of love, and so is his wedding."

"I know that you have fallen deeply for Soraya. She's a lovely girl, and will do well by you. I'm only suggesting you hold off the wedding plans until this crisis has passed."

My heart skipped a beat when I heard the word *crisis* used in connection with me. I thought briefly of rising to ask what it was they knew, but the conversation took a different turn.

"I'm hoping that our marriage will put an end to the crisis. With the Bakhtiari factions satisfied and on our side, the opposition may back down. I know that there will always be extremists, but it is the *bazaari* we must be concerned about." He was referring to the uneducated religious commoners who did not accept the shah's attempt to modernize.

"If only those damn merchants would be happy in their stalls," Ali said.

"If only it were just them. You know as well as I that a country's business leaders exert a powerful influence over public opinion."

"I assume you saw the headline?"

"Of course. 'Outrage.' The bastards at the Anglo-Iranian Oil Company are going to be the death of me yet. Who else could have the balls to hang signs saying, 'The entrance of Iranians and donkeys is not permitted?' Whose oil fields do they think these are?"

"They say that our people live in the Dark Ages, and resist modernization."

"Well, who can blame them if they do? If this is what modernization means, being worked like dogs and treated like less, then we'll never achieve the reforms I have in mind because I won't be their leader for very much longer."

"Political expediency. You don't wear it very well. I saw your tears, Brother Mohammed."

"As you said before, you know how I feel about Soraya, but I must take all these things into consideration."

"You're certain the Bakhtiari will support you if you marry her?"

"As certain as I can be of anything in these uncertain times. If nothing else, thoughts of a royal wedding will be a pleasant distraction. If the threatened strikes come to pass, they will need something to think about as they sit on their asses and gossip in the squares."

I had never heard Mohammed sound so bitter when discussing the people of the country. My illness was taking a toll on him personally, but I hadn't thought about what effects it was having on him politically. Earlier, when I overhead him haranguing Dr. Ayadi for not curing my illness more quickly, I thought this was just a case of a man being impatient and wanting things restored to good working condition, as he did with his airplanes and automobiles. It was naïve of me to believe that he—and for that matter, I—could separate the personal and the political. As a result, I could love Mohammed Reza without reservation, but as real as his love for me seemed to be, it would always be freighted with conditions.

Instead of being angry at this dawning understanding, I felt a deepening empathy for him. I'd entered a fairy tale, a place where nearly everything existed in black and white, good and evil. I'd come to understand that it was the shades of gray that made life both more complex and more wonderful. I decided to will my body back to normalcy, no matter the cost.

Although Dr. Ayadi seldom spoke to me about my condition, I decided to ask him what he suspected was going on. Gaining private access to him proved complicated since my mother and father hovered about me. I decided the matter was best approached directly.

Following one of Dr. Ayadi's brief examinations, I turned to my parents and said, "I have something I'd like to discuss privately with the doctor. Will you please excuse us?"

Whether it was because I had just strung together more words than I had for a week, or the forceful tone of my voice, or my father feared that I might need to discuss some matters of female physiology, he quickly escorted my mother from the room.

From the time that we'd been introduced at the airport until that moment, I had implicitly trusted and liked the doctor. His owlish appearance and deferential manners were far different from the coldly officious doctors I'd known in Germany. Even though he directed most of his remarks to others in the room, he always cast a sideways glance at me. I sensed that there was always more that he wanted to say, but couldn't.

"Dr. Ayadi," I began, "first, I want to thank you for everything you've done. I'm feeling much better."

"My child, I've scarcely done anything. A few tinctures, a few herbs."

"That's not what I mean exactly. You've offered reassurances to my family and to my fiancé that I will recover shortly, and that what happened to me is common enough."

The doctor shifted on his feet and looked around the room.

I patted the edge of my bed. "Please sit down." Knowing that he wouldn't be comfortable with such familiarity, I added, "It pains my neck to speak to you otherwise." He sat, and I could see that his shirt collar was frayed and nearly threadbare.

"I want you to know that whatever you tell me I will hold in the strictest of confidence. I suspect we understand one another in this regard. I apologize for my fiancé's behavior. I know that he is quite agitated, and that is no reflection on you or your expertise."

"I appreciate that." Dr. Ayadi nodded.

"I'd like you to tell me what you believe is wrong with me."

"Well, as I said to the others …"

"I don't want you to tell me what you said to others. I want to hear what you really think."

The doctor sighed and nodded his assent. "As you know, your symptoms point to some kind of poisoning. Food poisoning could result from something as simple as eating an unripe or unwashed fruit. Some foreign entity such as a bacteria that was in something you ate, or something you touched with your hands and then introduced via your mouth."

Dr. Ayadi paused. His expression clouded, and I could sense he was struggling internally. "Yes?"

He exhaled loudly and rubbed his chin before launching into an unpleasant description.

"Then why have I been sick for so many days? Why can't I eat anything that stays within me?"

The doctor scratched his cheek. "All I can say is that without examining any of the things you ate or the remnants of what you ate, I can't draw any conclusions. Let me put it this way: Weak in and weak out. Strong in and strong out. In other words, if all you had done was to eat something that was spoiled, that would have been weak. The irritation would have been slight and the symptoms would have cleared up fairly soon."

"So, what you're saying is in my case it's strong in and strong out—greater irritation, longer recuperation."

The doctor's hangdog look touched me. Surely he would have rather been anywhere else at that moment, but I appreciated his honesty.

"I'm glad that you understand and that I didn't have to go into greater detail about such matters of delicacy."

His words confirmed what I had suspected. The doctor *did* believe that I'd been deliberately poisoned.

I thought back to the day of the picnic and realized that the only thing that I had eaten that Mohammed Reza hadn't was the yogurt soup. Ashraf knew that her brother despised the dish and wouldn't be likely to eat any of it. Also, if she knew that he didn't like it, why would she have requested that it be prepared for our lunch?

As I sat there watching the doctor grow more uncomfortable, I grew more agitated. I didn't want to believe what the doctor had suggested, however indirectly, but I had no other choice. If I was in a fairy tale, then having an evil sister-in-law bent on poisoning me seemed almost laughably predictable. I didn't want to think of who else might have been involved or what I'd done to make them want to hurt me. Shams had indirectly warned me about her sister—about how Ashraf thought of herself as the shah's closest advisor. She'd always had her brother's ear, and now I stood in the way of her enjoying that privilege.

"I thank you for your honesty and discretion."

"Again, please understand that although the 'strong' may have gotten into you, I have no idea how or what it was."

I was no longer touched by the man's difficult position and his repeated insistence that he say only things that he could deny later on.

"You may leave now, doctor. I would like to rest."

I couldn't believe that Ashraf would try to kill me. Perhaps she'd merely wanted to spoil the day. In light of what I'd heard Ali and Mohammed speaking of, my being deliberately poisoned made even less sense. If the shah felt it important to stay in power by placating the Bakhtiaris, why would his sister jeopardize his rule? I had sensed from the beginning that the princess and the queen mother were opposed to me marrying Mohammed Reza, but why go to such lengths? I wasn't even certain I thought the queen mother was complicit in any way. Perhaps they were merely trying to delay the wedding or show the shah that I was too fragile a thing to stand up to the rigors of being queen. Or did they understand the shah's pressing political need to be married immediately, and therefore hoped that my lengthy recovery would force him to marry another woman in my place? But who did they have in mind?

At the time, I couldn't possibly answer all those questions. I did know one thing. If anyone wanted to challenge my love for Mohammed, then I would fight for him tooth and nail. By now, I also knew with great certainty that I loved him, more than I'd imagined I would in the short time I'd spent with him. That I might foil the plans of Ashraf or someone else in the family was merely dessert at the end of a wonderful meal.

Hours later, when Mohammed broached the subject of a wedding date with me, I lifted myself off the pillows and threw my arms around his neck and kissed him.

"Yes," I said. "The sooner the better."

Seeing Mohammed Reza's face light up with delight and not just relief pleased me beyond words. I decided to forget the conversation I had with Dr. Ayadi. Thinking about how I got sick would only detract from my efforts to make myself well. I knew in my heart that dark forces were allied against me. I chose to focus on the light and the goodness I assumed to be in Mohammed Reza. His words about his vision for Iran stayed with me. I couldn't be an impediment to his progress any longer.

As the saying goes, my spirits were willing but my flesh was weak. It soon became clear that the December 26 date we chose was too soon. I had fallen ill again and suffered from high fevers. Rumors spread throughout the country that I had typhoid. While I did experience some of the symptoms of that bacterial infection, I exhibited no signs of its telltale rash. As much as I hated the thought that my private business was the subject of public speculation, I despised what my body was doing to me. I'd begun to resemble a stick figure. I imagined myself a broom with a pair of half-inflated balloons where my breasts should be. While bathing, I'd look down at my hipbones that protruded sharply as if a clothes hanger was implanted beneath my skin.

We couldn't play tennis as we had before, and the few short flights that I took with Mohammed behind the controls were about as much as I could stand. I was so weak and so frustrated that my body was failing me. I was eager to help Mohammed and ease the pressure of the political situation, but I also simply wanted to be married. I was desperate to begin my new life. To that end, I was able to make some progress.

Ashraf and Shams took me on a tour of the Royal palaces, and they were glad when I chose one of the modest ones. With relish I dug into the project of redecorating the place. I was reminded of my father's preoccupation with the house he had built for us in Isfahan. I enjoyed spending days monitoring the work of the various craftsmen and decorators who helped rid the place of any remnants of what the queen mother called "its Old World charms."

"Old, old, old," I complained to my mother one day, out of earshot of any of the Pahlavis. "That's all that woman can talk about."

"Let her be, Soraya. At least her son is more forward-thinking."

I had to agree with her on that point.

"And you've better things to worry yourself about—like regaining your strength. I don't know how you're going to manage redoing that monstrosity. Look at you. You're frail as a bird."

"I'm not nearly as bad as that," I responded. "I'm fit as can be. A bit slimmer, but still."

I had a hard time convincing myself of the truth of that statement. I'd grown accustomed to my gaunt face. Seeing the rest of me that was normally covered by clothes still gave me a start.

I also had a hard time not discussing with my father my fears about being poisoned. He'd taken an active role in negotiating my dowry on my behalf. Persian men are a strange lot. I'd heard stories of cousins being bought and sold (to put it harshly) for vast and meager sums. Some men like to demonstrate their wealth, others their love and fidelity, while the rare few are more concerned with their reputations as shrewd bargainers. I looked at a dowry as a declaration of my future mate's intentions and the depth of his love for me. My father said that he looked at it as a kind of insurance policy since I'd receive the thousands of gold and silver coins only if the marriage ended. I viewed the whole thing as symbolic rather than actual. My father, pragmatist that he was, was also an idealist in this regard. Just as husbands took pride in either the greatness or the smallness of the fee, so did the bride's fathers. They treasured their daughters, and it was a point of honor to be able to state what a daughter was worth numerically.

I couldn't believe that Ashraf or anyone else would be upset by what Mohammed Reza had pledged to me. Surely, for a family as wealthy as theirs, money couldn't have been an issue. Perhaps I'd seen too many movies after all.

In truth, I also worried about how I'd be able to walk down the aisle. I loved the Christian Dior design that I'd chosen, but when I realized that it was comprised of thirty-seven yards of silver lamé, I worried if I'd be able to tow it all along. The thought of the twenty thousand feathers and the six thousand diamond pieces sewn into the bodice and train nearly buckled my knees. This was well before people's obsession with fitness, and I knew of no one in Iran with whom I could consult about building up the muscle required for the task.

I was like any bride: excited, nervous, and self-absorbed to the point of being a pain to everyone around me. My dear mother took the brunt of it, and I translated her every doubt about my health to her thinking that I was going to be less than attractive.

In addition, I had the typical concerns any young woman my age might have about her wedding night. I knew the basics—the mechanics of the act. One night in February, days before the wedding, we ate whole chickens that the cooks had split in half and roasted over an open fire. When I saw the platters of meat brought in, I suddenly felt faint. The sight of the chicken's ribs and other bones reminded me of my own body. I had focused too intently on everyone commenting on how thin I was. I sat there staring and breathless as Mohammed forked a piece of meat onto his plate, imagining that he would be splitting me in half on our wedding night.

I was like a child in their eyes, disappointing everyone by not being able to eat the meat that had been prepared. I was barely able to get a few bits of rice down. How could I have possibly explained to anyone my lack of appetite?

Fortunately, in my weakened condition, I slept well. I had to be roused from a deep slumber the morning of my wedding and felt as though I sleep-walked throughout the early part of the day.

As I dressed, my mother and my two sisters-in-law-to-be assisted me. While my stylist put the finishing touches on my makeup, Eva came into the room along with three servants, all of them lugging the dress.

"Forty pounds, daughter! That's more than half your weight. I don't see how you can do it," she said.

I was tired of my mother's preoccupation with the weight of the dress, but I managed a smile and a wave of the hand. As instructed by the stylist I puckered my lips, but not before saying, "I'll be fine."

As the three women and various attendants and servants assisted me with getting into the dress, Shams and Ashraf resumed their long-running battle.

"As the shah's twin, it is my right and duty that I accompany the bride to the palace."

"Forgive me, sister. But wasn't it I who was asked to bring the bride here? If it weren't for my diligence, there wouldn't be a wedding."

Shams looked at me and mouthed the word "sorry."

I shrugged my shoulders.

"Don't move like that," Eva warned, "I'm afraid that you'll cut right through the fabric with those bones.

"And we all know," Ashraf added, "That if it wasn't her, it would have been someone else, so please don't use that to think you rank ahead of me."

Every eye in the room widened in shock and horror. But to everyone's surprise, I remained perfectly calm.

"I would very much like it if you both accompanied me," I said. Then I added, "The only thing I ask is that you exit the car after I do. There will be ample opportunity for you each to be front and center for the photographers."

That shut them up, much to my surprise and pleasure. I liked the idea that a bride's nerves could be used as an excuse for a breach of politeness. They were obviously desperate for attention, but my patience had worn thin. This was my day and my marriage, and I didn't want to share the spotlight with anyone except my husband. He and I were what mattered today, not the needs of the others.

Before we walked out to the car, my father asked for a moment alone with me.

"A father's prerogative," he said as he watched the others exit.

"I just wanted to let you know that it is still not too late for you to change your mind."

"Baba, what are you saying? How horrible! I love him."

He smiled. "That's good. It's what I wanted to hear."

"And just so you know, I took your words under advisement. I not only love him; I know he needs me. I know that the country needs me."

"What are you saying?"

"I've heard some things. I know about the unrest. I know that the Bakhtiaris can be valuable allies."

"And this doesn't upset you?"

"Not in the least. I'm not a little girl any more. You said I should do what's best for all of us, and that's what I'm doing. I'm happy to do it. It is not a sacrifice; it is a privilege."

"Much good will come from this, Soraya. You are already a queen."

I remember all of it as if it were a movie being played on constant repeat in my brain. Snow fell in large wet flakes that accumulated on the gardens. A few caught in my eyelashes and melted, lending the scene a colorful air. The palace grounds were strung with white festival lights, which reflected the snowfall. The flash of the photographers' cameras added to the otherworldly picture. The air was heavy with the scent of white orchids, roses, and lilies—so many flowers that I imagined the Tuileries Garden had been flown in especially for the occasion. (Only later did I learn that one and a half tons of flowers had been flown in from the Netherlands.) I was especially pleased to see that several vases the size of bathtubs were filled with carnations. They are a humble flower, but my very favorite, unassuming in their beauty and fragrance.

As we waited in an anteroom just off the main hall, Eva and Khalil came up to me just as I was having my veil fixed in place.

"Raya, are you ready?" Mater was doing her best to keep from crying, and that was harder to take than if she'd been wailing.

"I am." I squeezed her hand, hoping to let her know how much strength I possessed. I was grateful that for the first time in what seemed months, I was the stronger one having to offer support to someone else. And being a Bakhtiari, and therefore never saying anything that I didn't mean, I added that I was ready—to be a wife, a lover, a partner, and to serve as empress to a nation of twenty million.

When it was time for the ceremony to begin, I was joined by His Majesty, resplendent in his finest uniform, his gold epaulettes and light blue sash a vibrant counterpoint to the uniform's deep blue. Mohammed's eyes glinted and he smiled widely. I took pleasure in his. Even in my depleted state, he still found me attractive, and that pleased me greatly.

"You look exquisite." He draped his arm around my shoulder, "Even more beautiful that I imagined." I didn't really need his words to echo what his eyes had told me, but I appreciated them all the same.

I shivered and Mohammed's face clouded. "Are you not well?"

"I'm just a bit cold. This drafty old place." I smiled, hoping that resurrecting a long-running joke between us would offer some reassurance.

"I've just the thing for that." He snapped his fingers and Dr. Ayadi came out of the shadows holding a mink jacket. The shah draped it over my shoulders. I felt the weight of it crushing me. I stepped unsteadily forward, and heard everyone gasp.

"It's too much," Khalil and Eva said in unison.

"The poor girl can't be expected to drag around more weight than an automobile might," Dr. Ayadi said.

I was surprised that my newfound friend had the temerity to come to my defense.

"Tell me what we should do," Mohammed said.

The doctor frowned. "Fetch me a pair of scissors." He pointed to a maid.

I didn't dare try to turn around to see what was going on behind me. A moment later, the sound of scissors cutting through fabric answered my question.

When the operation was complete, Dr. Ayadi came up to me holding a length of the train in his arms.

"Anything to lighten your burdens," Mohammed said.

"May the house of Dior forgive our rash actions at this urgent time," I said.

I had promised myself that I wasn't going to cry and managed to fight off the urge that began with a burning in the back of my throat. I was as vain as the next girl; I wanted my wedding day to be perfect. Yet that gesture of altering the dress at the last moment meant so much to me. Mohammed's willingness to do something unexpected to help me made me trust him even more. It was silly to think that, I suppose. I could have assumed that he merely didn't want me to embarrass us and cause a scandal by having me stumble halfway up the aisle. But that's what a marriage is supposed to be like: assuming the best about the other person, assigning the kindest motives for their actions.

Feeling energized, I entered the Hall of Mirrors and made my way to the front of the ballroom. I tried not to look to the side, but it was impossible to not know that on either side of the aisle, dozens of dignitaries and hundreds of other guests were watching our every move.

For the exchange of vows, we knelt before a large mirror. Persian tradition calls for this—I can only assume because it allows couples to see themselves as they commit their lives one to the other.

After lighting candles on either side of the mirror, the mullah read verses from the Quran. When he was through, he set the book aside and stepped toward me. By custom, he asked me if I would take this man to be my husband.

I looked down and remained silent.

He asked me a second time.

Again, I did not respond.

He asked me a third time.

I looked up expectantly. Each of the shah's sisters stepped forward and pinched my arms.

Finally, fulfilling my role and honoring the Persian custom of not answering the first two times, I simply said yes.

In my mind I added, "I will love you forever, through all eternity." I did this because I didn't like the idea that the woman had to be coerced into replying. That seemed to me to indicate that I was somehow reluctant to take that man as my husband. Nothing could have been further from the truth.

The mullah concluded the vows by asking the shah the same question. He immediately answered in the affirmative. The mullah stepped back, and the ceremony was over.

Mohammed and I turned to face our wedding guests, and for the first time, I was able to take in the enormity of the situation. As the guests stood and applauded us, I saw military officials festooned with ribbons and medals, gray-haired heads of state in formal morning clothes and their wives in ball gowns, members of royalty, and hundreds of others all beaming at us.

Later, after the reception and dinner and the endless hours of cir-
culating among the guests, I stood in the foyer, waiting for Mohammed
to join me. I was impatient, both eager and slightly fearful of the
night's last ritual. I had a surprise in store for Mohammed, and I was
anxious to reveal it. Even though most of the work was not completed
on our residence Ekhtesasi, I'd paid particularly close attention to the
details of decorating our bedroom. I felt they'd struck a nice balance
between masculine and feminine, but I'd insisted upon a canopied
bed, one draped with lace and damask. I had hoped he would like it.

"I'm sorry to keep you waiting. I had to have a few words with
Mother and my sisters. I barely saw them this evening." I took my
husband's arm. "They were tending to our guests. They're the hosts of
this event as much as we are."

"Yes. It will be nice to be alone this evening." I sounded a playful
note with my voice.

The shah took the large umbrella offered to him and held it above
us. "You've lost track of time completely. This morning is already
tomorrow. Well, it's today, but our wedding was already yesterday."

We both burst into laughter as we ducked into the car.

My wish to be alone together took a while longer to be granted. As
the driver reached the main road, throngs of well-wishers greeted us.
The thick crowds pressed in close to the car, not stepping aside until
the last moment, parting briefly, and then filling in behind us like a
boat's wake.

"Oh my God, someone is going to get hurt. What are these people
doing here in this miserable weather?" I stared wide-eyed as some of
the more eager celebrants ran alongside, pressing their hands to the
car's windows.

"They merely want a glimpse of their queen. It has been a while
since one of theirs was on the throne."

Mohammed's first wife, an Egyptian, had not won much favor

with the commoners. That I was only half-Persian seemed enough in comparison. Still, I didn't like thinking of his first wife on my wedding night. I concentrated on the fact that these people had come out to share the festivities with us. I was touched and a little saddened. All weddings are such public affairs, and ours was especially so. Mohammed and I had spent relatively little time together alone. Even those instances were often interrupted, cut short by some new obligation that cropped up. I tried to tell myself that it wouldn't always be so, but I was trying to make myself believe something that wasn't true.

It was all too much. I wondered if I was truly worthy of such adoration, and felt a little ashamed that I hadn't considered how all these people might feel about my assuming this new role. I was eager to move beyond those feelings of uncertainty.

I felt that same way about my new role as a lover. Some of my female cousins had married at my age. Because of the pain they'd described, after the excitement of the ceremony and the feast afterwards, I was left with fear about what would come next.

When Mohammed Reza slipped my peignoir off my shoulders and kissed my breasts, I felt the guilt that had marked our previous moments of intimacy slipping away along with it. As a proper Persian girl, it was my duty to remain intact until our wedding night. Given my father's sometimes overbearing guardianship and then my cousins' overly watchful control of me in London, if I had been anything but a virgin, a miracle would have had to take place.

From the first time we'd kissed in the gardens of Ramsar, I'd wanted to give in to my body's urges, had felt myself on the verge of losing the war that waged within. But the wait proved worth it.

When the shah hovered above me, I ran my hands along his arms, feeling them straining to support his weight. I looked into his eyes and nodded eagerly, urging him forward. He smiled the delirious grin of a young man who'd just been told that something he'd desired for so long was now his. I rose to meet him, gasped at the first sensation of the man I loved inside me, and buried my head against his shoulders, alternately clinging to him and floating freely. When he was through, he collapsed on me, his breathing heavy.

"I'm sorry my dear. I'm crushing you no doubt." He started to roll over and I stopped him.

"No, I like the feeling of your weight on me. Everyone keeps telling me I need to put some on, so why not yours?"

I couldn't tell him that I was worried about the sheets, whether my hymeneal flow had produced the desired evidence. I had been active in sports, and had heard that some girls had "lost their virginity" through jumping and playing roughly. My mother had warned me about the tradition. She'd endured it herself, even to the point of a crowd of females standing outside the room as my father and mother made love for the first time. When one of their representatives came inside to gather the sheets so that they could be proudly displayed, she stayed in the bathroom, her head buried in a towel to stifle the sound of her tears. I wasn't feeling the same kind of humiliation and degradation that my mother felt, but I hated the idea that something so intimate was also another part of the public spectacle.

I did as my mother had done, only I didn't cry and I didn't wrap my head in a towel. I simply cleaned myself off, neither proud of nor disgusted by the sight of my own blood on my pale thighs. I could only hope that Ashraf, Shams, the queen mother, and all the rest of them felt neither of those emotions. I wanted them to feel nothing, to be rendered blank by my presence in Mohammed Reza's life. That sounds overly dramatic, but I wanted more of the times like those dinners when the two of us shut out the rest of the world.

I stood looking at myself in the mirror. The flush of my cheeks, a bit of crimson at the base of my throat, stood out in stark relief against my pallid skin. I couldn't have put it into words then, but I had the sense that perhaps I wasn't so much being erased, but having my outline filled in. Hearing the commotion coming from my marriage bedroom was a sound so strange to me that I could scarcely believe all this was happening to me. When I heard the door close and the quiet resume, I hoped and I prayed that I could stay in the bedroom, marking out the place where one life had ended and a new one had begun. Opening the door of the bathroom, I scurried into bed where Mohammed Reza was waiting for me, once again eager. Again, I was willing to be taught. No one had to tell me that I needed to savor those moments, keep them close to my heart.

The next morning, I woke from a deep and untroubled sleep for the first time in weeks. I was disappointed that one thing had not changed—I was alone in bed. I rolled over to look at the clock on the nightstand and found a box with a card. Mohammed Reza had fulfilled the custom of providing the bride with a gift on the first day of marriage. Glad that this token of good fortune was in place, I opened the box. I held the diamond broach to the light, admiring its shimmer. It was shaped as a peacock, a bird associated with the Persian monarchy ever since Nader Shah had brought the peacock throne from the Mongol Empire in the eighteenth century.

I got up and put on my peignoir and affixed the broach to it. Wandering over to the mirror, I admired myself in it. Although my eyes were puffy and my hair a tousled tangle, I thought I looked fetching. I assumed several poses, none of which I thought of as particularly regal. Greedily I drank two glasses of water, put a record on, and climbed into bed. As I smoothed the sheets, I hummed along with the first strains of Gershwin's "Our Love is Here to Stay."

Closing my eyes, I let Ella Fitzgerald's velvety tones caress me to sleep as she sang, "Not for a year, but ever and a day."

I woke to the sensation of the shah's lips brushing my ear.

"What time is it?" The room was flooded in bright sunlight, and I squinted against its intrusion.

"It is nearly noon."

I burst into a great guffaw.

"Why are you laughing?" Mohammed asked.

"Because I am so happy!" I threw aside the bedclothes and walked toward my closet.

Mohammed intercepted me and kissed me, locking my lips on his as he walked me back to the bed. We fell onto the sheets and a moment later were both unashamedly devouring one another. When we were through, Mohammed dressed again, telling me that he had some urgent business to attend to. After he left, I thought ruefully that his love may be here to stay, but he wasn't.

INTERLUDE

Raya

APRIL, 2001

Chapter

FOURTEEN

oraya told me the story of her brief courtship and wedding over the course of our first three nights in Castejón de Sos. Each night, after our evening meal, we'd sit together in the garden, our chairs facing east, like two people at a movie. It was as if the film was so bad, we'd talk through it and not miss a thing. Eventually, her story took its place on the screen.

I think it made Soraya more comfortable that we didn't make direct eye contact. A few times, I'd catch her looking my way. I wasn't sure if she was testing me, trying to figure out if my expression betrayed some judgment I was making of her. When she started, the sunset's pinkish and violet hues colored the hillside beyond the town's limits. The grazing sheep were tinted as well, and from that distance, they looked like sweaters resting on green tissue paper. Later, as darkness covered them, they seemed to transform into fireflies.

We'd know when Dolores and Estrela were about to retire for the evening. The rectangle of divided light that shone on the peonies would go out. A few moments later, Dolores would join us briefly on the patio. The first night, she asked if we needed anything. The next nights, she set out a fresh pitcher of sangria. Soraya and I enjoyed the somewhat bittersweet drink for hours, retiring well after midnight.

As I listened, I couldn't help but think of my own life in comparison to Soraya's. I'd never been married, let alone at that young an age, but some of my cousins had been. It seemed to me that one day we were playing Barbie together, giggling and giddy, and the next time I saw them, they sat quietly and dutifully, looking slightly stooped, as if the burden of having become a woman weighed on them. As for the worry that they shared about being able to demonstrate their virginity and the other nonsense associated with their first sexual encounters, I was appalled at the barbarous nature of it all.

I may not have judged Soraya, but I did judge Persian culture. I remembered wanting so badly to escape from the Iranian Post-Revolution. I couldn't have said exactly why, other than the fact that my extended family suffered so. But I had a sense that I needed to be in America, that the new country offered me a way to escape from the fate that lay ahead of me in Iran.

As for our own escape from Castejón de Sos, we were being pleasantly held hostage by the absence of the mysterious Miguel the mechanic. Although we'd been told that it would take three days for him to finish his work at the ski resort, he didn't show up as anticipated. I knew enough from my dealings with Sergio and some of the contractors he hired, particularly in some of the areas outside the major cities, that Spanish time didn't always bear a strict resemblance to actual time. I was worried that Soraya would become restless. Since we'd arrived, we'd done little but eat, sleep, and talk. Each of those things had been splendid in their own way, and the Hotel Plaza was as pleasant a place to idle as could be. Yet as lovely as it all was, Soraya decided she wanted to explore the town and its offerings.

Saturday in Castejón de Sos was a real celebration. The town had just more than seven hundred inhabitants, but that number had to double on Saturdays. We woke early, had breakfast, and then joined the throngs at Plaza Mayor for market day. Soraya surprised me by purchasing several skeins of wool from a local dyer. I didn't know that she knitted, but she told me that she'd taken it up a few years ago for its "therapeutic value." I had a hard time reconciling my image of her as a glamour queen with such a sedate pastime.

Soraya must have known what I was thinking, since she said, "If I tell you this, it is fine. If you tell anyone else, it is not fine. I know people who can track you down." Soraya removed her battered hat and shook her hair out. Her radiant smile rivaled the sun's power to lift my spirits.

We moved on to another market at Plaza Cortes de Aragon, and then joined nearly the whole town as we paraded toward the soccer pitch. The field sat on the banks of the Rio Ésera, its waters shimmering in the noonday sun. The mood was festive; many of the residents were dressed in the red and gold of the home team. Soraya loved the uniforms of Los Tigres. Their red jerseys were ribbed with gold tiger stripes, and many of the players wore gold shoes that flashed and flamed as they ran.

Their opponents, who staked out the side of the field with their backs to the river, were from Graus, and their austere white uniforms put me in mind of hospital orderlies. That meant, of course, that Los Tigres were the lunatics set free, and though I don't claim to know much about soccer, that appeared to be the home squad's strategy.

At halftime, the players all retreated to a tree beside the river to rest in the shade. A few of the men joined them, and several dogs gamboled in the river, barking and shaking water off themselves in jeweled arcs of spray. An improvised trio—a trumpeter, a bass drummer, and oddly, an oboist—played some songs that were a mix of military and Dixieland jazz.

A woman named Anna, who was a local grocer, filled me in on some of the goings-on, and I quickly realized that she was the unofficial town historian, gossip columnist, and public relations officer. She extolled the virtues of the place, raved about the fishing on the river, and touted the exploits of its most famous citizens: a young woman who danced with the folkloric ballet in Sevilla, and a veterinarian who had devised a test for early detection of white muscle disease in sheep.

Then she said, "Oh, there's Miguel. I guess he's back from fixing the ski lift." She pointed across the field to the road, where a man was walking. The dust he kicked up clouded around his feet, leaving us with the impression that he was floating. I was eager to meet our car's potential savior.

Miguel negotiated a small rise and then ambled down onto the field. From closer range, what I had thought was a hat turned out to be a shock of thick auburn curls that fell about his head haphazardly, giving him the look of a sheepdog.

She waved frantically at him and called his name. "He's very good friends with my brother, Esteban."

"I see," I replied, thinking that she spoke of her brother as if I knew his entire history. Miguel shielded his eyes from the sun, cupping them, and then raised his left hand in a shy gesture of recognition. He then walked toward Los Tigres.

After the game had concluded, we all went back into town and wound our way to still another plaza. I would have been able to find the place by sense of smell alone—the wood fire, the seafood, the garlic, and the tomato scents all blended together into something captivating.

I'd lost track of Soraya in the crowd, but saw her talking with a distinguished-looking gentleman in a dress shirt and checked vest. They were deep in conversation, and I didn't want to interrupt, so I walked the plaza, taking in the celebration. At one point, I was watching a group of women with toddlers sitting on a bench while their children scattered the pigeons. I wished that I had a camera.

A moment later, a glass of beer appeared in front of me, its foamy head spilling over the brim.

"For our guests." Miguel stood in front of me. "This is courtesy of Anna. She asked me to deliver it to you." Miguel nodded.

"Excuse me," I said. "Are you Miguel the auto mechanic?"

"I am Miguel, and yes, I can fix things."

"Well, I was told that you might help me and my travel companion. I assumed you were told."

He shook his head, and we took a few steps toward the cooking area. "I'd like to, but I don't know if I can." Miguel stopped in front of an enormous steel pot suspended over a glowing fire. "I'm sorry," Miguel said. "Perhaps we can talk about your car after we eat."

"Certainly," I replied.

After our meal, we returned to the hotel. I heard Estrela in the lobby talking with someone. A moment later, Miguel came into the kitchen. "So, the car? It is the Mercedes out in front?"

"Yes." I told him about the symptoms, how the car suddenly died and wouldn't restart. Miguel asked about the noises it made or didn't make, and then asked for the keys. When he was through with his investigation, he stood staring intently into the engine compartment.

"There's no spark, as far as I can tell," he said. "I'm pretty sure the problem is electrical."

"Is that good or bad?" I asked.

"Both, really. Generally these parts are attainable and inexpensive. But without knowing exactly what's wrong, this could take considerable time."

"I see." I wasn't sure what he was suggesting as a next step. "I can pay you, of course, but I simply don't know what to do. We are a long way from Paris."

Miguel slammed the hood down and handed me the key. "There's nothing to do until Monday. I can make some calls about parts then."

That night, Soraya and I ate fish that Dolores and Estrela had grilled. At one point, I excused myself from the table and walked out onto the patio. Tears overtook me, and I let them come without any attempt at damming them. Though I'd been trying hard to fight off the feelings and memories, Soraya's story of her fairy-tale-like courtship and wedding had triggered the sadness I'd tried to escape.

A minute later, Soraya was at my side.

"I don't think I've ever been happier or sadder," I said when I was finally able to squeeze any words past my constricted throat.

"I know, my darling," Soraya said. "Enjoy them both. Hold them and let them go. They'll both be sure to come back again."

For the next few days, Soraya and I walked to the river each afternoon, and she'd share more of her story with me. Some nights, Dolores and Estrela joined us. Soraya didn't seem to mind, but she asked a question that had long been on my mind.

"Why is it that your mother named you Dolores? After all, the word means pain or sorrow, doesn't it?"

"I never asked her, but I did think about it. Maybe she believed that if she named me that, she was protecting me from harm. Or maybe she wanted to remind me always that life can have its pleasures."

"I'm sorry," I said. "I don't understand that last bit."

"If we didn't know pain or sorrow, we wouldn't know pleasure or happiness. So maybe my sad name would bring me happiness." Dolores shrugged.

"And so why Estrela?" her daughter asked.

"The stars," Dolores said, as if the rest was self-evident.

"You mean that we have a choice? That our fates aren't written there?"

Dolores smiled mischievously. "I can't tell you. That's for you to decide."

I already knew what I thought, and was curious to see how Soraya's ongoing story played out. As Dolores and Estrela continued redecorating the hotel, they asked our opinions on their choices. Twice, I even joined them on trips to Zaragosa to buy fabrics and furniture. Miguel kept trying to troubleshoot the car, saying at one point that it would be less trouble to shoot the car and put himself out of his misery.

Soraya and I found the serene rhythm of life in Castejón de Sos very much to our liking. We both sensed that when the car was finally repaired, we would be reluctant to leave.

PART III

Soraya

1951-1958

Chapter
FIFTEEN

There has always been something I enjoyed about making changes. Many people are distrustful of change, but I've always welcomed some types of it. At the time I didn't think much about what my desire to refurbish our marital residence meant. I can now see that it was a reaction against all the changes that were being forced on me. Not the marriage, mind you; I enjoyed giving up my girlhood for adulthood and being a wife. What I couldn't stand was the constant harping by what I'd come to think of as the Terrible Three—The queen mother, Ashraf, and Shams. By far, Shams was the least of my concerns, and possibly I was finding her guilty by association. But the other two were a pestilence.

They constantly offered me "suggestions," although they were seldom couched as such and came across as criticisms. I needed to know how to dress for court. How to speak. How to stand. How to dance. They seemed to view me as a lump of clay that they needed to mold into the image they desired.

Mohammed Reza was too preoccupied with affairs of state to even notice. If the Terrible Three had stuck to their territory—life at court—I might have been less resentful. Unfortunately, they didn't, and I had no sanctuary. Our home became their home. Their insistence on having an open-door policy frustrated me at first and later infuriated me.

At the conclusion of one tour of the house, Ashraf clasped her hands together and spun on her heels, taking it all in. "Breathtaking. Ekhtesasi has never looked better, Soraya. You've done wonders here in just a few short months. It almost feels as though you've always lived here. As if it were your very own home."

An awkward pause ensued, as the three of us contemplated the last loaded utterance.

"And while we're certainly delighted that you feel so at home here," continued the princess, "I feel the need to remind you that every house does have its rules. We realize, Soraya *jaan*, that court can be a lot to take in, especially for someone so young and unfamiliar with our ways. Which is why my sister and I wanted to take this opportunity, while it's just the three of us here, to remind you of some of the house rules. You know, things that have perhaps slipped your mind in your hectic—and understandably so!—adjustment period."

I didn't know where they got their ideas, but it often seemed to me that they'd just come from having their noses pressed into some dusty old history book. They came out sniffing and determined to stick them elsewhere, but I relished the opportunity of turning Ekhtesasi into a more contemporary home. Out went the gloomy and too-formal seventeenth- and eighteenth-century French pieces, the heavy brocade draperies, and the profusion of rugs that softened footfalls but made me sometimes feel as if I lived in a tomb. Worse, they allowed the invaders to sneak about behind my back more quietly.

Down came the ornate Victorian grand sconces and chandeliers, and in came more modern fixtures that in comparison to the old blinded the inhabitants with brilliant light. Mohammed would often reward me with a compliment on my taste when he noticed a new set of Paolo Buffa chairs, their curved shapes a stark contrast to the old rectilinear ones, arrayed in the now-less-formal dining room.

I had also irritated the in-laws by making changes to the staff, dismissing two indifferent cooks and replacing them with a pair of chefs from Le Bouveret in Switzerland. We could enjoy both French and my native German cuisine, which the others turned up their noses at but still seemed to open their mouths to during their too-frequent appearances at my table.

The symptoms of my illness had finally subsided. I was determined to eat better and have more control over what went into my body. Mohammed was pleased with these changes and immediately took notice of the improved quality of the meals. He also couldn't help but notice that the various ladies-in-waiting and other attendants had undergone some remodeling. No longer did they wear somewhat shabby native Iranian garb, but walked around the house in typically European gray uniform-style dresses. I was greatly pleased by Mohammed Reza's approval. It was what I sought most of all.

The afternoon of yet another invasion, my face registered my bafflement at Ashraf's comment regarding how I should conduct affairs in my home. "House rules?"

"Yes, Soraya dearest," offered Shams, taking Ashraf's lead. "The fact is," she shot a glance to her sister, "several times now, in greeting us, you have failed to bow."

"The first few times," interjected Ashraf, "we simply allowed the breach to pass. Should we add to the burden you bear of getting acclimated at court? Heavens no! But now it's been several months, and we fear that you've simply lost sight of protocol. Perfectly understandable, of course, given how busy you've been with …"

I had hoped to gain, if not their affection, at least their acceptance of my role in their lives. Now, nearly a year into my marriage, and still feeling the first blush of happiness I'd known since our wedding day, I decided that I'd have to take an alternative tack.

"Pardon me, Your Highnesses," I said purposely interrupting the tidal flow of Ashraf's words. "I haven't forgotten. It's just that the 'house rules,' as you call them, have changed. Superseded by a new royal decree."

Ashraf and Shams stared at me, stupefied.

"Perhaps," I continued, "in your own state of busyness, you haven't had a chance to familiarize yourselves with it. It states that I do not bow to anyone, except of course, to my husband, the king."

Ashraf was visibly stunned. "We never authorized ..."

"The decree further stipulates," I went on, ignoring her entirely, "that I am henceforth no longer required to kiss the queen mother's hand."

The room was hushed, so much so that I could almost hear the shah's sisters fuming. "All part of our effort to modernize, you see," I said in conclusion. "Changes in decorum; changes in décor."

The sisters flew from Ekhtesasi in a rage. I felt a small twinge of guilt and worried about how they would relay the exchange to their brother. But if he was upset at all, it never showed. Although I seldom saw him during the day, he was a constant and ardent presence in our bed each night. I'm sure I came across to the Terrible Three as quite a bitchy young woman who didn't know her place. The truth was, I really just wanted them out of my house.

No matter, my words had the desired effect. In the coming months, their palace stopovers ceased. The queen mother hardly visited either, and I imagined that she only continued to come around knowing that it was her primary opportunity to exert her influence on her son.

We weren't all together again until a few weeks after Mohammed and I celebrated our first anniversary together.

Ashraf spent most of the meal talking about a recent trip she'd made to Cyprus and the wonderful fish dinners she'd enjoyed. "Not that the salmon tonight isn't …" She hesitated for a moment and then said, "passable. Tasty even."

I noted Shams's stern look directed at her sister. A moment later, Ashraf's face was the picture of conciliation.

"Soraya," she offered quietly, leaning across the table. "After a cooling of tempers, Shams and I talked about our little spat."

I was determined to not make things any easier on her, "Our spat? I wasn't aware that we even had one. Perhaps you mean a spitz, like the little dog?"

Ashraf painted a smile of perfect insincerity on her face. "That's quite funny. I appreciate the levity, but I've something serious to say to you."

Just as insincerely, I responded, "I'm quite eager to hear it. Go on."

"We decided to extend a helping hand to you. A peace offering, if you will. After we took some inventory, it turns out that we have one too many ladies-in-waiting at the moment. And we wanted to offer her services to you."

"That's very kind of you to think of me, Your Highness." My tone was civil, if a bit guarded. I wondered what the two of them were up to, but also thought that Ashraf could use the extra staff to help her with her makeup and clothing choices. She'd come back from Cyprus looking very much like a down-on-her-luck gypsy. Her medallion bracelet and coin-like earrings were appalling.

Ashraf bleated on, "Especially since you've been keeping so busy lately. She's come over recently from Europe, and is certain to get the household running with the Western-style professionalism you so seem to desire. Surely you could use the extra set of hands."

"I appreciate your kind gesture, but I'm managing just fine." I turned to continue a previous conversation with Forough Zafar, leaving my sister-in-law hanging in mid-sentence. I was feeling very proud of myself. Unfortunately, that didn't last long.

"Soraya, you can't go around smiting and disrespecting my family at every turn!" Mohammed Reza shouted the following morning.

I was knocked off-balance. This was the first time I did not have my husband's complete support in these matters. But "smiting?" These could not be his own words. I imagined that he must have been getting an earful from the other side.

"My love, it is not my intention to smite or disrespect anyone. But you must realize how hard your sisters make it to tolerate them!"

"Enough!" he shouted.

My immediate, absolute, and shocked silence seemed to calm him somewhat.

"If there is tension between you and my family, this is something that you need to address. Our country has more than enough strife as it is. I will not tolerate it here at court among my own family. I will have harmony. And as you're the newcomer, it must start with you. You can begin by accepting this new lady-in-waiting as a peace offering."

I lowered my head in defeat.

I couldn't understand this sudden about-face and the intensity of my husband's demand that I bend to the will of the Pahlavi faction. Having him remind me that his reign was still fraught with political tensions and uncertainty made me feel guilty for adding to his troubles.

"As you wish."

I couldn't help but feel like a chastened schoolgirl who had to meekly submit to her punishment. Didn't anyone see my side?

My mother and father were still in Tehran, but I didn't see them with anywhere near the frequency I did the shah's family. Trying to comfort myself, I thought it wouldn't be so bad having someone else from Europe on my staff. Still, I felt I needed the counsel of a woman, someone not attached to the court in any way. I arranged to have lunch with my mother, just the two of us. The Persian way was to suffer in silence, but I was so taken aback by the shah's dismissal of me and my desire to update the way the court conducted itself that I had to do something.

I was upset that Mohammed had simply closed the door entirely to any kind of compromise on the matter. He placed the blame for the disquiet in his household squarely on my shoulders. That irritated me to no end. He could go on and on about how complicated political matters were in the state of Iran, but he couldn't see that there was more than one side to these domestic issues. I'd have to tread carefully. Although I trusted my mother implicitly, I didn't want her to think that the marriage was not working out well. With this one exception, I was blissfully happy—just not content with allowing the status quo to go on indefinitely. The Pahlavis would have to change; this Bakhtiari girl would have her way in the end, no matter what.

"Soraya," my mother said, "you have to understand something about Persian men. I know what you're dealing with. When I met your father, he was the most charming, sophisticated, and worldly of men I'd known in all of Germany. But there were times, and there still are, when he is very much the Bakhtiari, rooted deeply in the old ways."

"I'm proud of my heritage," I replied. "But I'm sometimes sick to death of hearing about the proper Bakhtiari, or for that matter Persian ways, the centuries of tradition. Every time any issue is in doubt, does it always have to turn on the old ways, on how things have always been done?"

My mother looked around the dining room. "What you've done here is beautiful. It reflects your taste and your ways so very nicely. But you have to remember that the shah is not like the rest of the people. Nor are you. You want to be the queen of these millions? Well, keep in mind that not every one of them has had the privileges that you and your husband enjoy—Western education, travel beyond the village where you were born. Your husband wants to modernize the country. I hear your father talking about his plans, but there are those who are opposed to that notion."

"But he's in charge. If he wants something changed, it should change."

"If it only were that simple." Mater placed her hand on my wrist, keeping me from tossing my napkin in disgust. "Listen to me. The shah came into power only because his father was removed from power. The British brought in his father because the Qajars had fallen under the sway of the British and the Russians. Then those same two placed your husband's father into exile. What has your husband known his whole life? Other people exerting power over him. Change is not easy for anyone, especially when it's imposed from the outside."

"But he's in power now. I can understand that things are difficult for him politically, but can't he take charge of this family? His father is gone and he's the shah, yet his mother and his sisters lead him around by the nose."

"Are you sure that's the case?"

"I see it."

"You see what you want to see, my dear."

I sat gaping at my mother, who sat calmly, pushing a bit of fish around her plate.

Finally, she spoke. "Your father is much the same way. He is as progressive as can be in some ways, but in others, he reverts back to the old ways in matters of family. I don't quite understand it, but family means so much more to him than I can ever understand. It's like a button gets pushed and something happens automatically whenever a question of family duty and loyalty arise. It's both admirable and infuriating."

"I know." I suddenly felt very bad about how I'd behaved. I could see that I'd been childish.

"And remember, your husband's father was an absolute tyrant. I can recall hearing about his rise to power and feeling chills. Imagine being that man's son! His mother was raised in a military family as well. They expect things to go their way—the established and routine way."

Suddenly, at the mention of the queen mother, my feelings of shame disappeared.

"Ah, the mother. She's one for the ages. Mohammed Reza told me that she was none too pleased when her husband took a second wife. She moved out of the residence, kept the shah from seeing his children. My husband told me that the only person in the world his father feared was Taj-Ol-Moluk."

"It must have been challenging for your husband to grow up in a house fraught with such tensions. No wonder he craves compliance and calm."

"He's certainly not like a teapot that you can hear coming to a boil. He just exploded at me."

Eva laughed. "Remember, you can make whatever changes you like to this house that the Pahlavis own. But you can't do the same to the House of Pahlavi."

"What do you mean?"

"They don't really care about this building and everything in it. They were handed it along with the title. Certainly, they may still cling to bits of it, but the rest was done by the Qajars and the dynasties before them. These are all just things. But the family traditions, the pecking order, the conduct—those they hold especially dear. Think about this: they are in a very precarious place, newly established on the throne. They need the support of a variety of people, influential people mostly. Those people are concerned about modernizing and all the other grand schemes your husband has but only to the extent it will mean they will keep their power and influence. How it will affect the money in their pockets. They cling to stability, just as your in-laws do—just as your husband does in family matters."

I stared at the china, whorls and flecks of bright colors with no easily detectable pattern. "This is all so complicated." I laughed ruefully.

"You'll find your way. You just need to be patient and concentrate on doing the things that give you both pleasure. The house, for instance. Make the changes that you can, keep looking for opportunities to do more elsewhere. Whatever you do, don't give up."

When Mater left, I was aware for the first time that things had really changed between us. We had spoken like two women, not just mother and daughter. Hearing my mother speak so eloquently about these matters of cultural differences and hearing her share her insights made me wonder for the first time about what my mother's life had been like, married to a man from such an opposite culture.

I felt a bit guilty for relaying to my mother some of the things Mohammed Reza said to me about his childhood. I'd withheld others, and it was those things that were most on my mind. As my mother had said, living in a household in which the parents were at odds couldn't have been easy. I also knew that my husband had been used as a tool by each of them: The mother took him away from his father to enact some kind of revenge on the man who took other wives; his father took him away from his mother at the age of six and sent him off to various military academies to make him more of a man. I had come to understand one thing about my husband: He was truly a complicated person. Instead of wanting to keep himself apart from the people who'd hurt him most as a child, he clung to them. Human beings are perverse, I'd realized, as subject to forces beyond their understanding as the stars are.

To my great surprise, not only was the new lady-in-waiting

European, she was German. Petra Weber was a slim blonde in her late forties. She wasn't taken aback when my first question was whether she happened to know any Schiller or Goethe by heart.

"I suppose, Your Majesty, I remember bits of *Die Jungfrau von Orleans* from school."

"Ah!" I clapped my hands joyously. "My grandfather Franz used to read that tale of Joan of Arc to me when I was little. Perhaps he is responsible for instilling in me a dream of leading a nation?"

Petra looked confused.

"I beg your pardon," I said hurriedly, "just a little royal humor. And no, declaiming from the classics of German literature won't be a part of your duties here. It's just a joy to be able to converse with someone in the language of my childhood."

We discussed everyday matters of menus and housekeeping, and I thought I caught the scent of my beloved silver fir tree. It was as if I'd been transported back to the Christmas snow globe of my early years in Berlin. In no time, it seemed, Petra became to me a kind of sister, offering me the kindness that Shams had once seemed destined to offer, but now withheld.

"I have to admit," I said to Mohammed Reza several weeks after Petra had joined us. I put down my tea. "I'm pleasantly surprised at your sisters' gesture. Petra is working out wonderfully. She hasn't been here long, but I'm thinking of promoting her to head of staff. She's proven her competence, and she is—how do I say this? In line with my style."

Engrossed in his briefing papers, Mohammed did not look at me, as he replied somewhat robotically: "Wonderful. Ashraf will be very pleased to hear that."

"I'm hoping, actually," I went on a bit more pointedly, "that Petra can handle the bulk of my daily duties. That would free me up for weightier matters."

Mohammed lowered the document he'd been studying and gave me an inquisitive, slightly alarmed look.

"It's my belief that a queen should do more than revamp and re-decorate a tired old palace. I was thinking that I could begin assisting you with matters of state and court administration."

Mohammed pursed his lips and raised his eyebrows.

"I just want to do whatever I can to make governance easier for you. You know full well that running our country means balancing a fearsome tangle of interests. Do we know, ultimately, which advisors and functionaries we can trust, and which are acting mainly in the interest of the UK or the Soviet Union?"

I was careful to omit my impression that it sometimes seemed like he could be convinced by whomever he happened to be listening to at the moment. But even without saying that, I could see I'd already gone too far. Mohammed took a sip of his tea. It was as if he needed the extra time to steel himself for his delivery of words that came out very much like a policy statement.

"Soraya, the situation in our country is extremely fragile right now. My throne is in peril. I face the threat, even, of assassination. I cannot imagine you becoming immersed in such a life, as I would constantly be distracted by fear for your safety. Furthermore, I would lose face in the eyes of my advisors if I included a wom- ... if I included you in the decision-making process. It would be best for you to engage in philanthropy, start a foundation or two, help women and children, the sick—that sort of thing."

It did not help that this policy statement was recited with the tone of a parent faced with a child's outlandish request, a parent chuckling at but clearly disapproving of a youngster's antics. I was upset to hear that my husband's life was in danger. I also wondered if he exaggerated for effect, but in the end, I was left with the feeling that I was being dismissed.

I had never expected to hear the shah so starkly express that mentality common to most Persian men, according to which women are not fit for political life. It is a matter of fact, I would later fume to myself in my bedroom, that successful rulers throughout history have had strong women behind them. As far as I was concerned, women could be far more political, in the sense of calculating, than men. But there was nothing I could do in that moment. I did agree to take charge of the philanthropic foundation started by his former wife, Queen Fawzieh.

It was a cause close to my heart, and I threw myself into the work. Fawzieh's foundation was aimed at alleviating the suffering of Iran's poor. At the time, fully a third of the country's population could be categorized as destitute. I loved children, and oh how they suffered! I undertook the construction of an orphanage for little ones whose parents could not look after them. Besides food and shelter, education would be provided. In addition to the joy I experienced at doing good and important work, I felt the swell of fulfillment that comes with independence. The orphanage was entirely my project. Aided by my secretary, I recruited a staff of caregivers, teachers, and doctors. Iranians got used to opening their newspapers to see me, clutching a shovel and beaming with pride into a camera lens. I had found a calling, and whatever unhappiness I felt with Mohammed's backward attitudes about women or his insistence that I toe the line with his family, was muted.

My pride in doing useful work also lessened the sting of the recognition of a hard fact: Whether it was my disputes with his family, the dissatisfaction I'd expressed about my role, or something else, as we passed the two-year mark in our marriage, Mohammed had grown increasingly cold toward me. As the new decade dawned, he slept most nights in his own bedroom. Occasionally, when he felt amorous, a muted rapping would sound at my door. He would enter, taking me in a fit of strangely businesslike passion. Afterwards, I would cling to him, trying to draw him into conversation. His responses on these occasions were monosyllabic, and he would typically just slink away, back to his "lair," as I came to think of his room. After those visits, I was left feeling like I was just one more item on his list of tasks to be accomplished. In addition, I kept hoping I'd become pregnant. I even told myself I was tired, that my belly was puffing out. But to my great disappointment, every month I got my period. I wondered if my failing to provide an heir had something to do with Mohammed's lack of interest in me.

Since married life had begun, Dr. Ayadi and Forough Zafar had become my most trusted companions. I spent more time with the two of them than with any other individual at court. One day I sat in my palace office tending to foundation matters. Dr. Ayadi came, asking if he could speak with me.

"Of course," I answered. I wondered why this man who exuded an even temperament now looked so worried. "What can I do for you, doctor?"

Dr. Ayadi stared out the window. "I think I see a black-shouldered kite, just there in the branches."

I turned to look, but saw nothing. I didn't share the doctor's interest in birds, but didn't want to appear rude.

"Has it flown off?"

"I may have been mistaken. I've been reading a monograph on several species of birds of prey, and ..."

"Please, Dr. Ayadi," I said softly. "I think you had something else on your mind that you wished to discuss." I closed the door because Petra was in the next room reviewing some accounts.

"Your Majesty, I beg your pardon, I don't wish to interfere, but I must warn you of the people who surround you at court." He paused as the strange words sank in.

My eyes widened. The man had gone from reluctant to brutally honest in an instant.

"To put it bluntly, you have enemies." He pushed his glasses back up onto the bridge of his nose and sighed.

I was stunned. I was aware some in the shah's family didn't like me—but enemies? How could I have seemed threatening enough to anyone to earn anyone's hatred?

"There are those among the royals," the doctor said, "who are intensely jealous of you. In their eyes, your intelligence and leadership qualities are by no means a plus. They fear, moreover, that you might involve your family in the affairs of the shah or seek to elevate the prominence of your Bakhtiari clan."

"But this is absurd!" I slapped my fountain pen down and then scowled as the ink bled across a sheet. "The Bakhtiaris have no need of any 'elevation.' They were here long before the Pahlavi dynasty." I began quoting my father, but seeing Dr. Ayadi's nervous glance, I cut off this thought.

"More to the point: In these 'complicated times,' as my husband is fond of calling them, there are plenty of things to worry about. But I assure you and everyone else at court that I am not one of these complications. My only desire is to be a good wife to my husband and to serve my country. In that order." Later on as I recollected that conversation, I wished that the order had been reversed.

I reminded myself of Dr. Ayadi's belief that I'd been poisoned. I'd been well for many months, then. In light of the passage of so much time, I wondered if I'd overreacted. After all, I was now a fully-fledged member of the royal family. Shams and Ashraf were hardly cordial and welcoming, but they weren't villainous either. Perhaps the doctor was fond of drama, and liked to stir the pot a bit.

"Of course. I understand." The doctor removed his glasses and began to polish the lenses with his handkerchief. "I see that you've broken ground here at Ekhtesasi," Dr. Ayadi began, clearly wanting to repair any damage he'd done.

The conversation lasted another quarter hour, focusing on the orphanages and other neutral subjects. I tried to put my confidante's strange words out of my mind.

The next day, I expected Dr. Ayadi to join Mohammed and me for lunch, as had been scheduled. But I waited in vain.

"Dr. Ayadi will not be in attendance," Mohammed informed me with a strangely bureaucratic tone upon entering the dining room. "In fact, he has been banned from setting foot in the palace until further notice."

I was flabbergasted. "What for?"

"My dear, I can't give an exhaustive explanation."

"Can you give *any* explanation? One that makes sense?" I was failing at my attempt to keep my tone neutral.

"Suffice it to say that in light of the political situation, it would be best if the palace did not have visitors floating around at all hours. What's more, public concern regarding the Bahá'í must be reckoned with. Or is the empress unaware of the sermons of the preacher Falsafi, who has so stirred the people?"

I was well aware that Dr. Ayadi was a member of that religious sect. I also knew about one of its leaders and the attention he'd gained. Although the Bahá'í were a small minority, they were a vocal one.

"You mean the man who has stirred the people against a threat you and I both know to be entirely imaginary?"

"My dear, facts are facts, and the existence of public concern, whether you consider it well-founded or not, is a fact."

I was certain now that Dr. Ayadi's warnings about my standing at the court were not a figment of his imagination. Mohammed's statements were nothing more than incomprehensible rationalizations. I was so upset that I slammed my napkin down and stormed toward the door.

"Oh, one more thing, my dear. I have asked Ernest Perron to join me at court as my advisor."

I stopped in my tracks. My eyes flashed with anger as I turned back to the shah.

"It's very confusing, Mohammed. One moment, you tell me the palace is not to have visitors running about at all hours, and the next, that Ernest Perron—who must be considered the strangest visitor possible—is to have the run of the place."

I had had, on occasion, the pleasure—if one could call it that, which one decidedly could *not*—of encountering my husband's phony, brazenly insincere friend. "If I understand correctly, your own wife is not qualified to advise you, but now the gardener's son you fell in with at school in Switzerland is to be your grand vizier?"

"You sound like my father," Mohammed chuckled. "He was baffled when I brought Perron back with me to Tehran. So what if his father was a gardener? The man is possessed of a keen mind, and that's all that matters."

"Then this is one instance, at least, when I concur with the opinion of Reza Shah. Perron is not someone I would choose to have advise me of anything but what roses to plant." Mohammed Reza frowned, and was silent.

"So, why is he in Tehran?" I continued, venturing to pursue the matter. "Why are you making him an adviser?"

"For the same reason anyone is made an adviser: because his advice has proved sage. Given the current situation, it is good to have someone with an outsider's perspective. He has less of a vested interest."

Sage? When I thought of Perron's tall, bony figure, his thin mustache, his reedy lisping voice, my skin crawled. What my husband said about the need for a perspective outside of a Persian's made me despise this new adviser all the more. If I knew one thing about what my husband referred to as the "complications," it was this: Many people in Iran were tired of enduring the British and what they viewed as their exploitation of the country's richest resource. Nationalization of the oil industry would be the key to ending much of the poverty that I saw all around me. But as long as the British were the ones in control of the oil, they would be in control of the country's destiny. Perron's presence did not bode well; it was just another outsider's influence.

Back in my quarters, I found it impossible to fend off the intrusive thought that somehow my husband had learned of my discussion with Dr. Ayadi the previous day. This must have been the reason for my confidant's being declared persona non grata at the palace. Turning events over in my mind, I had a sudden chilling memory. Petra, Shams's former lady-in-waiting, had been in a side room during that conversation. It would hardly have been difficult to eavesdrop. Impossible, I told myself. She couldn't have. At that point, I thought I had earned the woman's loyalty. Little did I know that loyalty is a commodity as easily bought and sold as any other. Had I inadvertently fallen under the sway of another outsider, done little better than my husband had done in anointing Ernest Perron?

Repeating such denials to myself did nothing to alleviate my suspicions. I pushed my face deep into a pillow and wept like a child. What kind of household was this? Along with fine marble and priceless vases, I had to accept spies and duplicitous "friends" who said kind things to my face, only to stab me in the back.

One day not long after the announced banishment of Dr. Ayadi from the palace, I received a letter from Bijan. I noticed a strange crease in the envelope. The seal seemed somehow off. Or was I imagining things? I hurried to the one person I felt I could ask about such matters, Forough Zafar. I admired the woman for her pragmatic if sometimes too blunt manner. If anyone would speak the truth, she could.

"Has it been opened? Who knows? But if it has, well …" the last of my confidantes looked away, as if fearing to make eye contact with me. "Then it's for the sake of security. Nothing for you to worry about." Despite speaking with the voice of experience, she hardly seemed convinced herself. Finally, having apparently gotten her nerve up, the lady-in-waiting drew close to me and whispered in my ear.

"If I were you, my dear, I would be more concerned about the gardener."

My eyes widened.

"There is a rumor," said the lady-in-waiting, "that he is a spy."

"I'm well aware," I replied. "Everyone knows that he hangs around at the bazaar, then comes back to the shah to report whatever scuttlebutt is going around."

"No, I mean, a *spy* spy. For the British."

If Forough was correct, then the situation was even worse than I imagined. I had to learn the truth, if such a thing even existed.

That night, I tossed and turned, ultimately losing my battle with sleeplessness. As the dawn seeped in through my windows, I got out of bed. Stepping outside my door, I felt drawn by some force toward Mohammed's bedroom. I hoped I might find some comfort there with him. But as I rounded a corner, I caught sight of Perron slinking his way down the corridor, clearly with the same destination in mind. The insidious new adviser didn't see me. He crept up to the shah's bedroom door and, having tapped at it lightly, almost conspiratorially, stepped inside.

For the next few days, my nerves remained on knife-edge. The sight and sound of that man rapping at my husband's door so reminded me of the shah coming to me at night that I was nearly undone by my wild imaginings. It was as if Perron was my husband's lover, a rival for the affections and time and attention that should have been mine exclusively.

As for who or what might allay my fearful state, I knew it wasn't Mohammed. I couldn't distract myself with social interaction. I feared that anyone I spent time with would be banished like Dr. Ayadi had been. Oh, I knew that with a snap of my fingers, some general's wife would appear at my table, ready to gossip. But as for genuine human contact? That seemed nonexistent.

I thought of my frank conversation with my mother. What if that had also been overheard and reported on? I couldn't imagine placing my mother under suspicion, nor could I endanger her or my father in any way. I'd neither seen nor heard from either of them since that lunch. She had mentioned that they were planning a visit to see Bijan, who was now in school in France. If so, that was a good thing; better for them not to entangle themselves in what was going on at court.

I racked my brains for ways, outside the foundation, to occupy myself, knowing that an idle mind produces too many bad thoughts. I sat in the magnificent dining hall alone, trying to appreciate my chefs' latest creations. Bored, I puttered around in the kitchen, trying to recall what my mother had taught me about cooking. In my bedroom, in front of the mirror, I put on makeup in new, inventive ways I hoped my husband might find elegant.

"You mustn't paint your face so," was Mohammed's only reaction. "You're an empress, not some trashy Hollywood starlet."

Having failed to lure him back any other way, I tried to be more direct, to engage him in conversations about the issues that faced him.

"I've seen the people in the streets, Mohammed Reza. I know the kinds of crushing conditions in which they live."

"And I suppose you're another advocating for nationalization? You know so well based on your little forays into the streets what is really going on? You understand all the implications?"

"Maybe not all, but I do know what is needed," I said.

"What is needed? What about what I need? And do you know what that is? A woman by my side who supports me and doesn't undercut me. A woman who knows her place. If I want a woman's point of view, I have my mother to challenge my every decision, thank you very much."

I saw the veins rising at the side of his head, pulsing at his throat and neck, and heard the fearful clamor in his voice.

"I want to help you," I said, seeing that he was truly fearful.

"Fine," the shah said with a fierceness that pierced me. "Then do me the favor of leaving me alone. Take care of your orphans. The only children you know."

With that, he turned on his heel and walked out. It was obvious my inability to become pregnant was a sore point with his family, but I hadn't realized that he'd become bitter about it. Apparently he considered me a failure, too. Surely this was one reason he'd lost interest in me; I wasn't able to provide an heir. My only value to him now was my ability to give birth, and I couldn't even succeed at that.

I sat staring at the Paul Klee watercolor I'd recently added to the collection. I had come to know about him on a trip to Bern, Switzerland, when I was a schoolgirl. I was sad when I heard, years later, that he had died. At least he had left something behind, something others could take pleasure in. At that moment, I took pleasure in nothing and no one. I tried to rouse some tears, but none would fall. I was empty and dry, a rasping leaf skittering along a sidewalk in the Tiergarten, a thing of little consequence to anyone. I tried to push aside the notion that Mohammed considered me a failure, that my station in his life would be determined by my ability to produce a child.

Chapter

SIXTEEN

*O*n early 1953, I, like everyone else I knew, was immersed in the news of political maneuvering. With protestors in the streets of Tehran and my husband having survived an assassination scare several years earlier, my worries about my own place in the universe seemed rather petty. As a wife would, I keenly felt my husband's stress.

"Mater, I'd had such hopes that the New Year would bring better news." I sat on the phone in an anteroom in the palace. "But Mohammed Reza is a wreck."

"Your father was shocked when General Razmara tried to persuade the parliament that the nation wasn't ready for nationalization. Telling a people that they aren't capable of operating their own oil industry didn't win him any friends."

"But he was the prime minister. He didn't speak for the shah." I knew that not to be the case, but saying so gave me a moment of relief. "I know what you're going to say: The shah appointed him. But for the man to be shot dead while praying at his mosque …" Images of what might have happened to Mohammed Reza when a gunman had fired five shots at him unsettled me. That his cheek was only grazed by the bullet was a miracle. Mohammed Reza refused to discuss it with me, saying that it did little good to talk of fanatics. Further, he believed that his surviving the attack was evidence of Allah protecting him.

Regardless of divine intervention, there were forces at work that wanted the Pahlavi dynasty to be brief. I also knew that the activity of the Tudeh, the communists behind the plot to kill him, had only intensified since then.

"The Tudeh will go to any ends." My father joined my mother on the line. "It's little wonder the shah is at his wit's end."

"Baba, what other news have you been hearing?" I'd been forbidden to read the newspapers in Tehran and was denied access to the radio broadcasts. Under my husband's influence, they had carried only vague accounts of the goings on anyway. For that reason I had to rely on my parents' honest appraisals.

"From what I hear, the Tudeh is organizing a strike. You know what the communists can do when they put their mind to it. The British and the Americans are nosing about. Since we nationalized, Prime Minister Mosaddegh has few friends outside the country and more than few enemies within. I don't see how he can last. I'm sorry to say some of these things to you, but I must."

I heard the genuine anxiety in my father's voice, and in a strange way that comforted me. I had wondered why the shah had turned so cold toward me, had withdrawn from our marriage bed and kept me isolated from the political realities. My lack of fertility was one reason he'd turned against me, but how could I become pregnant if we didn't sleep together? Perhaps his ban on my listening to the news was only because he was being protective of me. After all, that was what one did for loved ones—kept them from truths that might injure rather than enlighten. In my father's case, he saw no other option but to educate me, even at the risk of making me even more anxious. Regardless, all the information I received was filtered by men.

"Not to worry, Baba. If you hadn't told me, I would have learned eventually. Better to be prepared."

After our conversation ended, I tried to gather my thoughts. I'd been married for only three years, but something had changed in my relationship with my father. He no longer held in reserve for male ears only his opinions on politics in his homeland. It frustrated me that having a husband was necessary for my father to now think me capable of understanding the larger picture. My work with the foundation had only begun my political education. Mohammed had given me the task to keep me out of politics and governance, but seeing the horrific conditions under which many of our subjects lived had awakened me to another reality.

While I still enjoyed the benefits of my royal standing, I perceived that a fundamental change needed to be made in how monies were distributed from the oil royalties. Why couldn't some of the riches be distributed to those lower on the social scale?

I wasn't so young and naïve to not understand that the British had reaped huge rewards on their "investment" in the country. Iranian efforts to change the terms of the agreement had angered our English friends. According to the terms, it was to last until 1993, forty years hence. Every chance I got, I discussed politics and history with members of my staff. I read as widely as I could and tried to get a grasp on what the future might hold. The one thing I wasn't able to do was to discuss these issues in any depth with my husband. He still clung to the old notions about women and their place, but something had changed in recent weeks. He was more willing to open up and discuss how troubled he was by recent events. He spoke vaguely about pressure being applied from outside agencies.

But that was as far as he went. I was not allowed to interject any opinions or comment on his choices, or ask any questions. He kept saying that the Cold War had heated up, but little else.

My suspicions about my husband's horrific state of mind proved untrue. The man whom I met later that evening after my phone call with my parents appeared to be anything but haunted by the news that the protests against the Prime Minister had intensified. Rumors of a coup abounded. If Mosaddegh was on the way out, what did that mean for us?

"I've suffered through worse, Soraya. As a child I had typhoid, whooping cough, malaria, diphtheria. None of the them killed me, and these men and these circumstances won't either."

"Surely you need to take some precautions. Perhaps it's best ..." I stopped, aware that I was crossing the line again. I'd learned a thing or two in the passing years.

"Go ahead; tell me what I ought to do—how we should run away." Mohammed Reza pulled angrily at his tie as he unknotted it.

"Not run away. Just get away for a while. You've been under coercion ..."

"Did I tell you about the time when I was a child and I was thrown from a horse? I lost consciousness, yes, but when I woke up again, I told everyone that I'd seen Imam Ali, one of our saints." He continued changing out of his suit into more comfortable slacks and a polo shirt. "Ali kept me from dashing my head on one of the rocks. God has been by my side since I was a young boy, Soraya. I've seen other visions. This will end well for us, let me assure you."

Mohammed Reza thought his visions prophetic. If so, in the months that followed, it appeared that perhaps the saints were focused more on the distant future than the near. I was no longer able to safely attend to my duties for the foundation. The unrest grew from a rumbling to spasms of violence. The shah forbade me to leave the grounds for anywhere but the palace. I could only meekly agree.

In time, I learned that my husband's concerns were warranted. The British had responded forcefully to nationalization of the oil fields, and the stalemate between the two resulted in the people suffering even more than they had before. With Iran's oil essentially blockaded, the production nearly stopped, and the money coming in slowed to a trickle. The workers who were once underpaid were then not paid at all. Prime Minister Mosaddegh's efforts had improved their lot initially, but now the Tudeh and others were leading the unrest. Little of the recent developments made sense to me at the time. What did these protestors really want? Who was leading them? Why was Mosaddegh's dismissal being called for? Only later would the pieces fall into place.

Mohammed Reza seemed baffled by the developments. "Years ago, I tried to tell them that nationalization was not something we were ready for, any of us. Did they think me stupid? Did they not understand that the British and all their allies in the United Nations, within the US, and elsewhere wouldn't let us get away with this? The West has invested too heavily to simply comply with any of our demands for sovereignty."

I didn't say a word in response. I'd learned that it was best to let him rant and reserve my judgment. I agreed with the people that the only way for Iran to truly be independent was to gain full control of its oil production. What was happening seemed in some ways worse than the days when the British were in total control. I also wondered why Mohammed kept making references to the British and the Americans. What did they have to do with our people marching in the streets?

"And now Mosaddegh has learned the cruelest lesson of all. The Majils will not let him enact his reforms. The National Front is once again trumpeting their nonsense against the upper class. And Mosaddegh has the balls to think he can assume my duties and name a minister of war and a chief of staff! He can rot in hell, for all I care."

This made sense to me. If the prime minister and my husband were squabbling over matters of power, then those who called for

206

Mosaddegh's removal were on Mohammed's side. As much as I thought I'd matured in my understanding, I realized now that I knew little. And not being allowed to read or listen to the news kept me even more out of the loop.

Later that evening, I watched as my husband was escorted from the dinner table by Ernest Perron and a few other advisers. He returned a few moments later.

"What news do you have for us?" the queen mother asked, regarding her son with a mixture of impatience and thinly veiled disgust.

"Mosaddegh has resigned, the coward. He doesn't get his way, so he leaves."

"Why didn't you give him his way?" Ashraf asked. For the last few months, she'd been an infrequent visitor, spending much of her time in various meetings around the capital as well as in the provinces. When I asked him about the nature of those meetings and her absence, the shah had met my question with a blank stare. "I have no idea what you're talking about." If that was the case, I had thought, he was the only one in Tehran who didn't. One of my great frustrations with Mohammed was that he refused to see his twin sister as the manipulator that she was.

"The fact is, there are many interests at work here." Mohammed rubbed his forehead tiredly.

"*British* interests?" Ashraf emphasized the first word.

"I'll admit that the British influenced me in some of my appointments previously, dear sister, but the times are changing."

"And you will go in whatever direction the political winds are blowing?" Shams asked. "What do you mean?"

"The Majils elected the man prime minister, even though he clearly opposed your view on nationalization. You ended up appointing him premiere. Now you have nothing good to say about him?" Shams shrugged.

"The man refuses to negotiate. He has resigned abruptly. Tell me whose interests he really has at heart, his people's or his own."

"Why should we negotiate?" Ashraf asked, pounding her fist on the table. "These people think they are entitled to everything. Who's done the work, really? They're hurting themselves, putting into jeopardy plans they've no idea of. If they had any patience at all …"

"The people who are suffering aren't the ones who made these policies and deals," I said, my voice rising. "We sit here eating these fine meals and talking about these events as if they have no consequences for them. The people will speak, whether you listen to them or not …"

"Another voice to add to the clamor," the queen mother said. "It was Marie Antoinette who said, 'Let them eat cake.' But that's a dish too good for these …"

"Enough!" Mohammed rose from the table. His napkin clung to his waist, and I though it looked very much like a diaper. "I will not endure this for another moment."

After he'd stormed out, Ashraf looked around the room. "I suppose he's gone to get another round of advice from that stick of a man, Perron."

"I don't see how he can bear to be in the presence of such an unfortunate-looking person," the queen mother said as she rang the bell for dessert. "I should think that he'd long since worn out his welcome."

"Politics makes strange bedfellows." Shams seemed to take particular delight in her remark.

"I'm going to have a talk with my brother; that vile little toady be damned," Ashraf said. "Something has to be done about that power-grabber Mosaddegh. Can you believe the man actually thinks that the illiterate have the right to vote?"

Nowadays, the few times that I got to talk to Mohammed was mostly about politics instead of our dreams for our future. Still, I was grateful for any moment with him, At one time I was frustrated by not knowing about the affairs of state. Now a small part of me longed for those years of ignorant bliss.

For the next five days, I woke to the sounds of rifle shots, chants, and wailing sirens. The shah had appointed a new prime minister who announced his intention to open up bargaining talks with the British. The people responded with strikes and protests. My husband insisted that I travel to Ramsar, the Caspian Sea residence, where I would be safer.

At the conclusion of five days, I listened to the radio as it was announced that Mohammed had reappointed Mosaddegh to the post of prime minister and granted him full control of the military. What on earth could be going on? What kind of deal had Mohammed worked out with him?

I had made a ritual of spending those nervous days consuming cup after cup of Turkish coffee. Sometimes I'd turn over the empty cup I'd just drained. The gesture reminded me of the move that a chess player makes when conceding defeat—toppling the king. I tried to interrogate the future from the dark patterns left in that saucer. Could anything head off the clash of wills between Mosaddegh and the Western powers that were seemingly allied against Iran's nationalization efforts?

Through the months of turmoil, I'd seen my husband vacillating between one uncomfortable political position and another. I'd also seen his emotional state do the same. From his bravado and words about his visions and the protection offered by the voice of God, to his late-night visits with Ernest Perron, to his not infrequent outbursts of anger and demand for silence, he clearly was not comfortable with the power that had been bestowed upon him. Changing one's mind may be a prerogative, but it comes with the danger of appearing weak. If Mohammed seemed that way to me, what must those in parliament and elsewhere have been thinking of him?

To see a man like Mosaddegh, a long-time player in Iranian politics, rising to such heights of popularity must have been difficult for him. One afternoon I found a copy of the American news magazine *Time* in his office. The cover story hailed Mosaddegh for his advocacy on behalf of his people's interests. At heart, Mohammed wanted to be a reformer, to be seen as his people's savior. Unfortunately, a shah is not an elected official. He can't enjoy the feeling of being popularly elected. As simple as it may sound, Mohammed Reza had no faith in his political power. He wasn't respected. Worse, he wanted to be liked.

It became clear to me that much was at stake, possibly even the question of whether the country would transform itself into a republic and do away with the monarchy entirely.

One night that question was brought home to me when Mohammed paid me one of his nighttime visits. Before he climbed into bed with me, he'd taken a pistol from his robe pocket and placed it underneath a pillow. As he buried his face in my neck and thrust away, I was glad that he couldn't see the look of stricken panic on my face. Had it come to this? Did he mean to use it on himself, on me, or on some extremist bent on ending both our lives?

I was dismayed by what I saw as weakness. But what could one man have done anyway, with so many different forces at work? His father had wanted power and gotten it. Mohammed Reza was put in power after his father was exiled, so he was in a position not of his own making. So many different interests to keep happy; such a tenuous position.

Later that same week, I suspected that perhaps my husband had another target in mind for that weapon. The household was in an uproar, with Ashraf leading the charge. She and Shams had retreated to Ekhtesasi to escape the unrest near the palace and parliament.

"Mosaddegh's an idiot! Months ago, he proved it by officially declaring the British an enemy. As if we could go to war against them!"

Ashraf swept around the room like a bird, alighting upon one piece of furniture for a moment and then another. "And now he is asking the Iranian parliament again for emergency powers so he can do whatever he wants."

"What does Mohammed Reza say?" I was no longer ashamed at having to ask someone else about my husband's views.

"What does he say?" Ashraf laughed. "What he always says: 'There are many sides to this.'"

"The Majils have granted the prime minister emergency powers time and again. He can decree any law he wishes," Shams added. "He's virtually a dictator."

"And now the Islamist Kashani is their speaker. What's next? An Ayatollah to oversee us personally?" Ashraf sighed and shook her head, "Women can go to sleep tonight knowing that with that Islamist influence, our interests will be well represented."

"Communists and Islamists," Shams said. "What strange bedfellows."

Ashraf turned on her. "You seem awfully fond of that phrase lately. Should we be concerned about you and your husband?"

I smiled thinly. "I wonder how the British will react to this? They're already afraid that the Tudeh will lead us right to the Soviet's front door and offer them up our oil."

Shams crossed to the window and peered outside as if she was concerned that her words might fall on the wrong ears, "It's not the British I'm so worried about; it's the meddling Americans. First Harriman, then that Roosevelt relation. I should think ..."

"You should think before you speak," Ashraf said, spit spraying from her mouth. "You haven't any idea what any of this really means. What's at stake for this family?"

Their conversation was interrupted by the arrival of Ernest Perron. "Princess Ashraf, your brother is in his office. He would like to see you on a matter of some importance." Perron seemed even more shriveled in recent weeks.

"Tell him I won't have any more of his closed-door meetings. If he wishes to speak to me, he can say what he must to us all. In fact, where is Mother?" Ashraf looked around the room as if the woman in question was capable of sneaking in undetected.

"I think it best …" Perron said in his gratingly smug way.

"I really don't care what you think." Ashraf spoke between gritted teeth. Even the normally composed Perron seemed to shrink at her fierce tone.

A few moments later, the shah came into the room, carrying a sheaf of papers and a glass of clear liquid.

"I'm guessing that's not water," Shams said.

"No, it's not." He patted the couch cushion alongside him, "Please, my dear, sit here." Ashraf and I both stepped forward.

Mohammed Reza pinched the bridge of his nose and then took a long swallow from his glass. "I should have said 'my dear wife.'"

After a pause during which everyone was seated, he began.

"I'm afraid that I have some bad news for you, Ashraf. The prime minister has expelled you from the country."

I felt as if the air had been sucked from the room. Months ago I would have been overjoyed at the news, but that night I felt myself on the verge of tears. What did this mean for the rest of us?

Ashraf sat smiling, looking quite pleased, "Well, Mosaddegh has finally executed a shrewd move."

"Don't you want to know why?" Shams asked. She'd gotten up from her seat and poured a drink. She carried it to her sister.

"I think I know. In point of fact, it doesn't matter. Given his new powers, the man can do essentially anything he wishes." Ashraf hoisted her drink. "To the new ruler of all Iran."

If Ashraf's cruel comment had any effect on my husband, I

couldn't detect it. When I heard what he had to say next, it seemed apparent that Mosaddegh was completely in charge.

"Just so you know that you're not alone in this, Ashraf, he has further decreed that I cannot directly communicate with other national leaders, their representatives, or third parties." The shah leaned back and put his arm on the sofa's back. He crossed his legs, and his foot twitched nervously. I wanted to still it, but didn't dare.

Mohammed Reza swallowed and pursed his lips. "He's also taken it upon himself to seize royal property with the intention of giving it to the state."

I didn't move my head, but scanned the room with my eyes. We were all so still, it was as if we had all been participating in a kind of *tableau vivant*. The only one moving was Perron. He had stayed on the periphery in front of a glass cabinet examining some of the crystal objects I had purchased. Now he left the room.

"I'm sure that there's more to come, but for now that will suffice." Mohammed's voice sounded unnaturally shrill.

I took my husband's hand. To my surprise, he drew me into him.

"What will we do?" Shams's voice was vacant. It seemed to me as if she was back in boarding school and one of the girls had asked that question on a boring weekend night.

"I can't tell you where to go or what to do, Ashraf, but it is clearly in all our best interests if you leave as soon as possible. We will do the same shortly."

I sat up and gave him a quizzical look.

He set his glass down on the table, and it was as if the sound of glass on glass shattered the façade of calm he'd erected. A few moments later, he composed himself. "When we return, we may have much to celebrate, God willing."

Ernest Perron reentered the room and bowed obsequiously. "Your Highness, the documents are ready for signing."

Mohammed Reza pushed himself up from the sofa. "Then it is done. Let us hope it is as swift in the execution and the result as it was in the drafting."

We watched as the man we loved walked out of the room, his arm wrapped around the shoulders of a man none of us trusted.

"Uneasy lies the crown," Shams said.

Ashraf sighed. "I must pack my things. I'll say my goodbyes now."

The sisters embraced while I stood nearby, chewing at my bottom lip nervously. If I understood things correctly, this was the beginning of the end for the brief Pahlavi dynasty. Stripping my husband of his powers meant that we were to be little more than figureheads. The next logical step was to end the need for a royal family entirely. How could Mohammed Reza have seemed so calm? What was really going on behind the scenes?

Dozens of other questions flowed in my mind, but I held them in reserve. The night when Mohammed Reza announced our departure for Rome, he sought solace in my flesh. I was more than willing to share in it with him. He was an eager and tender lover, more in tune with my body and the rhythmic movements his touch produced in me than he had been for months. That strengthened my sense that something had been set in motion. He seemed more decisive in a way, more resigned to let matters play out. His relief was that palpable.

The next few days were taken up with preparations for the journey and goodbyes with Ashraf and the queen mother. She felt strongly the sting of Mosaddegh's actions and decided that she didn't want to stay in a place where such a man exerted so much influence. Forough would stay behind to oversee the properties in our absence.

On our first nights in Rome, we stayed in the Hotel Excelsior, just off the Via Veneto. As we lay in bed in a post-coital embrace, I finally asked one of the questions that had been troubling me. The shah had mentioned Ashraf, and I seized the opportunity.

"You didn't seem very upset when Ashraf was forced out. As her twin, that must have been difficult."

"I know that it is only temporary. Painful, but temporary."

Something in the shah's tone told me that there was far more to it than that. I let the silence lie, knowing that if I waited long enough, he would resume. In the meantime, I wondered how he could sound so certain that the ban was only temporary.

"She had become a political liability as well. We didn't need any more attention focused on us."

"Why a liability?"

Mohammed Reza had been running his fingers through my hair throughout the conversation. When he stopped, I was certain I'd asked the wrong thing. He rolled onto his stomach, propped himself on his elbows and looked at me.

"She was always out expressing her views. I know she despises the role women have to play. She can't understand that while we are twins, I was the one granted the privilege to lead the country."

"I was out there as well."

"Your foundation work, you mean? That's not the same, my dear."

I felt hurt by the implication that what I was doing was of lesser importance than the shah's twin. My husband's expression was neutral, as if he had simply stated a fact with no intent to hurt me. In some ways, that made me even angrier.

"How do you mean?" I asked, feigning a calm I didn't feel.

"Think of it this way. You are applying a dressing to a wound. Ashraf wants to destroy the weapons that cause the wound."

I thought about it for a moment, and had to admit his explanation made sense.

"But to see her be shunted aside …" I fumbled for the right words, knowing that it didn't make a great deal of sense for me to empathize with a woman who'd wanted to destroy me. I was beginning to understand a little better the kinds of games that Mohammed Reza had to play and how difficult it was to determine who was friend and who was foe.

"I understand what you're hinting at, and at the time, I didn't want to explain. I know it seems as if we're running away, giving in." Mohammed Reza rolled onto his back and folded his hands across his chest.

"You have to understand that I am a military man. Sometimes it is more important to make a strategic retreat than it is to charge ahead. Believe me, there are many battles being fought on many fronts. Sometimes it is a soldier's duty, especially a commander such as I, to make a decision to do what's necessary to fight again another day."

I thought again of the image of the chess master capitulating by toppling his king. Didn't that mean that the war was over? That prisoners would be taken?

I was confused by the shah's words, but didn't want to press him for a further explanation. His breathing had slowed and taken on the regular rhythm that I knew preceded his falling asleep. While he lay softly snoring, I slid out of bed. I was uncomfortable with the idea that someone as close to him as Ashraf could be so easily dismissed, even if the promise was that later on she'd be recalled. So much might happen in the interim.

I padded out into the sitting room. I'd added espresso to my list of favorite things, and with all the caffeine running through my system, I was unable to sleep. Though this wasn't the first trip we'd taken together, it felt as if it was. I laughed at the thought that instead of him being loaded down with worries, I was. I thought again of our delayed honeymoon, how the affairs of state had always intruded on our lives. At first I was envious of the country, as if my husband had another lover. I was angry at the time it stole from us both. Now I longed for those days when it was merely an annoyance. I wondered if we'd ever go back there again.

I considered myself a fairly optimistic person, more than most other people I knew. My natural buoyancy was something I counted on to help me get over the rough patches. But it was hard to act positive when we were exiled.

We'd discussed the need to put on a pleasant face while on our Roman holiday. Once the journalists got wind of our presence there, they were sure to hound us. Mohammed Reza told me that it would work in our favor. The two of us hadn't fled in a panicked moment. Instead, we were so carefree that a few days in Rome seemed just the thing. Let the others fight it out. We were secure enough in our station that we need not be bothered with nervously watching the blow-by-blow from a near distance. According to him, things would get sorted out, and we'd return to Tehran to pick up our lives just as we'd left them.

The truth was another matter entirely. As soon as we'd arrived at the hotel, Mohammed Reza had been on the phone, presumably with Ernest Perron, who had remained behind to be the shah's eyes and ears.

If Mohammed required that I act the part, I was more than willing to assist him. Rome was a lively city, and I felt the pulse of it rising up through the foundation of the hotel and into the floor of the penthouse suite. I was eager to explore the city, hopeful that the time away would help my husband and me reestablish the close bond we'd enjoyed in those early days of our marriage. Still, the longer I sat, and as the sun began to rise, I wondered if the sensations I felt were the energy of the city or the more distant rumblings of the disquiet that had propelled us out of Tehran.

Chapter
SEVENTEEN

"*I* have failed." Mohammed Reza sat in the Café Vesuvio, swirling the ice in his drink. I peered into the shadow cast by the candy-striped awning, trying to discern just how miserable my husband was. Three days into what I'd hoped would be a kind of Renaissance for our marriage, I found myself dining in the Dark Ages. Guilt and retribution were the primary offering on the menu. I wondered what happened to the man who in recent weeks had come across as decisive and strong, spouting words of wisdom about strategic withdrawals and the importance of living to fight another day.

Although I was frustrated by Mohammed Reza's black mood, I took some pleasure in knowing that he needed my strength to help him. In the early days of our marriage, I'd assumed that a man much my senior in age and experience, the man who ruled a country, would never be reduced to such an abysmal state. If he needed me at all back then, I supposed that it was only in a carnal sense—much the same as he needed to eat, drink, and sleep. The softness and kindheartedness that had so appealed to me was also reflective of a fundamental weakness in his character, and in a way this endeared him to me. I had come to learn that love is not unlike the glittering diamond I'd been presented with; its facets both blind one from its imperfections and make it unique and valuable.

In most ways, I now knew, Mohammed Reza was anything but a diamond. He was far more malleable—not prone to surface scratches, but to much more trenchant changes.

When I reached out my hand to take his, I was responding reflexively. I was entirely empathetic toward this man and his insecurities. Certain aspects of his personality infuriated me, but I was learning to keep my anger in check.

I ran my thumb over the top of his hand and listened again to the litany of sins. "I have failed my people, my country, my family." His voice caught for a moment, and then he went on. "And you."

"No, you have not. True, some things aren't in your control, Mohammed. But the problems of the people—their poverty, their suffering—these are things that given the chance, you can do something about."

"You don't understand."

I shut my eyes in frustration. I felt that this was one of the things he could control. He could let me in and allow me to understand what it was that was so troubling him. I wanted to chastise him—better yet, take him by the shoulders and shake him to get him to reveal to me the nature of the burden he was so obviously struggling with. Only now does it seem strange to me that I was just a young lady, on the verge of twenty years of age, yet I was dealing with such a monumental issue as the fate of a nation. At the time, I just accepted this as my reality. I was alternately afraid and fearless when it came to speaking my mind. When it came to being a wife and not a queen, I knew exactly what my duty was, and what my heart told me was needed.

"It's only a matter of time before the Iranian people acknowledge your love for them. You will see. All this business with Mosaddegh—whatever it is—will come to an end. Some agreement will be reached.

The people need and want *you*. They also need to feel secure, to know that their needs are being looked after; that those governing them have their best interests at heart."

"I do. But those aren't the only interests I have to keep in mind. It's not as simple as you put it."

"Nor is it as complicated as you make it seem. Unless there's something about which you'd like to enlighten me?"

Mohammed looked up and signaled for the waiter to bring us another round of drinks. When he looked at me, I felt as if he was truly considering letting me in more completely. But like a cloud briefly passing in front of the sun, his expression altered. He was once again guarded and pensive.

We finished our drinks in silence.

That evening, we sat in our room dining in and sipping wine. It was as if the afternoon's exchange had been a matinee performance in advance of this one. The shah seemed even more glum. I attributed that to the amount of alcohol he'd consumed during the course of the day.

At one point, tired of the script, I said, "We're in Rome, and I haven't even seen the Spanish Steps."

"For that you would need to be in Spain, wouldn't you?" The shah's thin smile leaked across his face.

Glad for even a moment of levity, I replied, "I could do the Flamenco."

"I'd prefer the dance of the seven veils, if you don't mind." The shah waggled his eyebrows.

Again, the moment passed too quickly and he resumed his somber air.

"I have a feeling that I could dance on top of this table, tear off my clothes, and you would only ask me to pass you the salt." I got up and threw myself onto the divan. Kicking off my heels, I flung my shoes into the bedroom, crossed my legs with a great flourish, and reclined dramatically.

"What are you on about?" he mumbled.

"Throwing a fit fit for a queen." I laughed hysterically, enjoying the release of some of the tension that had clamped down on my neck and shoulders. "I could really do with a massage."

A knock on the door interrupted me. I scrambled to my feet and walked to the door, swaying my hips in large arcs, the ice cubes clicking in my glass. "Perhaps my prayers have been answered."

When I opened it, there stood Ardeshir Zahedi. I hadn't been allowed to see the shah's aide-de-camp in quite a while. I had missed him, since he was one of the few members of the shah's inner circle I liked and trusted.

He eyed the two of us suspiciously for a moment.

I immediately pulled myself together and, while greeting him, turned around to allow the shah to receive him. Ardeshir and I had an endearing relationship. He was kind and loving, but showed his affection and support only with utter professionalism. I knew how close he was to the shah and his little brother Prince Alireza. Ardeshir's father, General Zahedi, had served as the head of the army under Reza Shah the Great. The Zahedis were nobles to start with, but the general, through his brave acts and patriotic demeanor, had won the people's hearts and respect. His son was no less beloved.

The shah lifted his head. As soon as he saw Ardeshir, he stood up abruptly.

"To what do we owe this honor, Ardeshir Khan? Are you here to celebrate with us?" His voice carried a tone of both sarcasm and sternness.

"Then you know already?"

"That my 'father' Baba Mosaddegh has cut my allowance and sent me packing? Of course," the shah responded.

We laughed at Ardeshir's wide-eyed look of confusion.

Recovering his equilibrium, Ardeshir reached into the inside pocket of his suit and pulled out an envelope.

"What's this?" Mohammed sounded bored.

"I think you should read it, Your Highness. I think you'll be well pleased."

"I thought your job was to do my reading for me." The shah smiled to take the sting out of his remark. "Clearly," he went on, straightening in his chair, "you've read it, or you wouldn't know it was good news. Just tell us."

Ardeshir eyed me. "As you know, Your Majesty, there has been a great deal of unrest in your absence as a result of your decree. Mosaddegh has been replaced. In his stead is General Zahedi." Ardeshir paused, his delight overwhelming him. "My father has assumed the premiership. He asks that you return to Iran as soon as it is advisable. Your people await you!"

I later understood that Mohammed Reza had done a great deal of work behind the scenes to depose Mosaddegh and install General Zahedi in his new role. At the time, I thought that events were unfolding naturally and happily for us all.

The shah leapt to his feet and grabbed his aide's face, kissing his cheeks with gusto. "Ardeshir, you beautiful man!"

I rushed to my husband, but he had already turned back to the table. I stood uncertain of what to do, and chose to hug Ardeshir, our bodies forming an awkward A-frame.

"We must drink to celebrate," Mohammed said. He poured a glass for his young aide and then stepped back. He looked at the floor and then the ceiling and shook his head. "I can only think of the words that my dear wife has been saying to me these past few days: '*Il va bien se passer. Je t'aime, et ainsi de faire votre personnes.*'"

Seeing Ardeshir's incomprehension, the shah motioned with his glass toward me. "Please translate for my young friend here."

"It will be all right. I love you, and so do your people," I said. This time, when I rushed to my husband, he opened his arms wide and embraced me. I could feel relief oozing from him, but even in our joyful and slightly drunken state, I wondered what decree Ardeshir was talking about, and how all of this had come to pass.

"What's the expression they use in those Hollywood westerns? 'Back in the saddle?'" The shah was beaming, any sign of his alcohol-induced languor gone. He had conferred with Ardeshir Zahedi for a few minutes, and was now bustling around the room putting on a fresh suit as Ardeshir waited in the next room. Mohammed gestured toward my closet.

"I think the flowered one would be best, my darling. I like the notion that things are in bloom, ripe and all that."

I pulled the dress off the hanger. I'd always admired Chanel designs, and this had been one of my favorites. I was glad my husband suggested it.

"I always believed, Your Majesty." I turned my back to him, and as he zipped me up, he pressed his lips to my neck.

"I know that you did, and for that I will always be grateful in return."

He spun me around and looked at me admiringly. I felt my throat constrict a bit, tears of joy beading my lashes. I was relieved that the crisis was over, but even more so, I loved the way that he looked at me, the delight he took in seeing me. I wanted to savor this moment, savor what it meant not just for the Iranian monarchy, but also for the two of us as husband and wife. But that moment would have to wait.

"Your Majesty," Ardeshir said, peering around the doorframe, "they are waiting for you in the lobby."

"Excellent. Thank you, Ardeshir—for everything. I assume that in addition to the press, the television people are here?"

"Yes, Your Majesty. It took some doing. You know the Italians are seldom in a hurry to do anything. But the foreign correspondents have been most eager for news all along."

"Fine. We will be downstairs shortly."

"What about all our packing? I'll have to oversee it, and then there's …"

"It will all be done in good time, Soraya. Right now, we must show our faces. Our people need to know that we will not allow a vacuum of power to exist for long." He took me by the elbow and led me out of the suite. Two men I didn't recognize stood by the elevator. By the look of them, they were Americans.

I was about to comment on their sudden appearance, but was more startled when Ernest Perron suddenly joined us in the elevator.

"All is arranged, Your Highness. The pilot is on his way to the airport."

"Very good."

Perron and I eyed one another suspiciously in the elevator's mirror, our glances bouncing off one another's in the confined space.

I ended the little game by staring down at my shoes, overcome by the memory of the Hall of Mirrors, where Mohammed and I had exchanged vows. The intrusive lurking of Perron was another reminder of just how many others the shah seemed betrothed to. I looked up, and Mohammed still seemed energized, his enthusiasm infectious. I stood straighter and pulled my sunglasses down from my head and over my eyes. When the doors opened, the flashes of the still cameras and the bright lights of the television cameras nearly blinded me.

Despite that, we managed to put on our best smiles as aides cleared a path for us to the waiting limousine. Just before we bowed our heads to climb inside, we turned to face the cameras and we each waved.

Once inside the car, I experienced the sensation of having been placed inside a jar. The noises diminished, but in my ears I heard a hollow ring.

As the car wended its way through Rome's legendarily intense traffic, Mohammed held my hand. Once, as we took a roundabout amidst a clamor of taxis and scooters, the driver veered left suddenly. We slid across the leather seats against the door.

Instead of shouting angrily at the driver, Mohammed Reza pulled me closer to him and kissed the top of my head.

"I will miss you."

"What do you mean?"

"Only that while I'm away, I will be thinking of you and your absence from me."

I shook my head as if I'd been slapped.

"Where are you going? I thought we were returning to Tehran?"

He looked at me as if I was a child who misunderstood completely some simple matter of arithmetic.

"I never said that. I'm going to Tehran of course, but you need to remain behind. It may not be safe for you there. Besides, you've barely gotten to see anything of the city, and I'll be so busy there. The Spanish Steps await you ..."

"Mohammed Reza, stop!" I slammed my hands down on the seat.

The shah sat back stiffly. "Soraya, I trusted you when you told me that everything would work out. Now it's your turn. Please trust me when I tell you this is the best way now."

I refused to respond or even to look at him. I understood that our exit from the hotel had been a well-designed bit of playacting. Worse, I felt as if what had been required of me really was that I be a mere stand-in for myself, a kind of cardboard cut-out the shah and his advisors trotted out and then put away when no longer needed. I wondered what would be required of me at the airport, where there was sure to be another crowd of reporters.

I briefly contemplated remaining in the car, refusing to get out for a staged bit of propaganda instead of a proper goodbye. I was disappointed when the car skirted the airport's main entrance by way of a series of access roads and made its way onto the tarmac.

The car pulled to a stop at the shah's plane, and the two of us sat for a moment in silence. "I thought that you would be happy about what has transpired, my darling. This is a great day for us. I will see you soon, and all will be as before."

As he stepped out of the car, I was sure that he could not have spoken any more damning words had he tried.

I stood on the balcony of the Hotel Savoy's presidential suite, looking down at the Via Veneto below me. I'd decided to change hotels. I didn't like the quiet of the Excelsior or the reminders of what had transpired there. From inside, the sound of an Italian radio news program chattered on, indifferent to the events taking place in Iran. I sipped from my tumbler of vodka, wondering what it was exactly that people do in the world. Just a few hundred kilometers to the south, over an expanse of water, my husband was returning to both chaos and a chorus of voices raised in support of him. Here, people sat at cafes; strolled the shops; passed through the shade of awnings, palm trees, a passing cloud, all of them unmindful of what so preoccupied me and vice versa. I didn't like the idea of looking down on these people, literally and figuratively, but sometimes one has little choice.

I had no reason to question their presence here. After all, this was where most of them lived. I did not. That fact begged the question: What was I doing here then, and more to the point, where did I belong? Apparently, not back in Tehran with my husband. That much had been made clear to me. Just look at that distinguished older gentleman in the pinstriped suit depositing a letter in a mailbox. Royal protocol demanded that I not do such a thing myself; to display such independence would be unforgivable. (I also wondered ruefully if any letter I sent would arrive unopened, or at all.)

What had become abundantly clear was this: My influence at the palace was minimal. Court intrigues and all the maneuvering those entailed—the culturally ingrained expectation that I take a back seat (or no seat at all) to my husband—had seen to that. Maybe I could have accepted this state of affairs if I had any private life, the freedom to go where I desired and when, just like those people on the promenade below me. I wanted to turn my back on Tehran, and run away from all this madness.

That would mean, of course, turning my back on Mohammed Reza. By leaving me in Rome, he'd done essentially the same thing. Unfortunately, in matters matrimonial and monarchial, there was nothing fair about any of it. I couldn't know what the future would hold for me if I took off entirely. For me, the change of hotels would have to suffice, a small expression of my independence—a move of a few blocks, a slight change in scenery.

What so angered me wasn't so much Mohammed's decision to go alone back to Tehran. I understood that. What infuriated me was that I was just a cardboard cutout. In the early days of my marriage, I didn't like having people tell me all the time what I needed to do, how to act, how to speak. However, at least then I was doing something, playing some role. This latest outrage was far worse. Essentially, I realized that outside of being empress, I played no role at all. I was even more of a nonentity than I had thought before. It was ironic that we had been in danger of being made into mere figureheads in our homeland, but that was already what I was. What I symbolized for myself wasn't clear to me at all.

Although Mohammed had tried to use the rationale that I hadn't seen enough of Rome while on our holiday, the truth was that I couldn't go where I wanted. A small group of reporters still clung to the hotel lobby's bar like cobwebs in a disused house, a reminder of what had once been there. Even if I had the energy for an excursion to see any of the ruins or the Vatican, a cadre of the shah's staff would insist on accompanying me. My safety was of the utmost importance, I'd been reminded time and again. But rather than keep me safe, I felt as if I was being kept isolated. It was as if I was some relic, kept behind glass, paraded out and put on display only on some holy day.

I thought of my school chum, Claire. The two of us had our dreams of acting glory, or at least living the bohemian life together. We hadn't spoken in years. I wondered what Claire's life might be like, whether she, too, had exchanged one dream for another, hoping for something greater and falling short of the mark.

In truth, I had no real friends. Forough was a kind of confidante, but our relationship had not developed naturally. Ardeshir was the only person whose friendship I took comfort in, but that too was tied to my husband. When I considered the matter more fully, I realized that I could say the same of nearly everyone. What or who really did I have of my own? Even the foundation, the one thing that gave my life at court some purpose, had been founded by my husband's first wife.

I drank my vodka and muttered a Farsi proverb. "*Az injaa runde, az unjaa munde.*" She was driven from here, but not quite there.

The phone's ringing ended my dark reverie.

I brightened slightly at the sound of my mother's voice, but thought it best not to reveal too much. "I'm fine, mother."

"I'm glad to hear that the ordeal is over. Forough tells us that The shah is returning to Tehran today."

"Yes, that's true." I wasn't completely sure what "ordeal" my mother was referring to.

"Why did you not return with him?" Eva sounded worried.

"Concerns about my safety."

"I would have thought it would be better for you to be with him.

That his security people could better protect you. But I suppose he knows best."

"Yes." My vague and distracted response sounded hollow even to me. My mother must have picked up on the discordant note.

"Soraya, are you certain that you are all right? It can't be easy knowing how some people feel about what your husband has done."

I couldn't formulate a response. The static on the line seemed soothing.

"I'm sorry, dear one, for having put it to you so bluntly."

"No need to apologize. To be honest, I don't know what you mean." I sat at the writing desk mindlessly turning a pen over and over. I had a feeling I knew what my mother was referring to, but I didn't want to let on. Better that none of us knew the truth about Mohammed Reza and what he'd done.

"Let me put your father on. He can better do justice to this."

"It doesn't matter ..." I stopped when I heard the phone making contact with a hard surface. I sat examining the ends of my hair and tried to recall the last time I'd had it trimmed.

"Raya," Khalil said, his voice formal despite the endearment. "Your mother and I are concerned. I'm personally glad to hear that you are still in Rome. I suspect that there's a security contingent with you?"

"Yes, but why this sudden concern about my safety?"

"We don't want to frighten you, but things in Tehran have been ..." My father paused. "I don't know quite how to put this."

"Go on, Baba."

"Some believe that your husband's decree that Mosaddegh be removed isn't quite as legal as it seemed on the surface. There's been a great deal of unrest, given that man's popularity. Quite a bit of rioting. One has to wonder why Kashani, and a few others who were once Mosaddegh's staunchest supporters, turned on him so suddenly."

"What does any of this have to do with the shah or with my safety?"

"Well, things are never as they may seem to be. I won't go into too much detail, but there are suspicions that the Americans and the British were behind Mosaddegh's ouster. It's true your husband wrote the decrees removing the premiere and installing General Zahedi, but how much of that was his choice is …"

I thought again of how my husband had been acting during our stay in Rome. The man clearly had a troubled conscience. His actions seemed out of proportion for having merely signed a document. I suspected he'd done far worse.

"Three hundred are dead, Soraya. Mosques burned. Mosaddegh in prison awaiting trial." "Three hundred dead?" My cocoon had finally been penetrated.

"Rumor has it that the protestors had been incited somehow, and then once the violence began …" Khalil's voice drifted off. "Raya, have you a television there?"

"Yes."

"Switch it on. Find some news."

I did as instructed and watched the flickering image of my husband walking up the steps of the palace surrounded by an adoring throng, reporters, and cameramen. He walked with a sense of determination that I'd seldom seen in him lately, scarcely looking around. Only as he was about to enter the building did he turn and wave, triumphantly holding both clenched hands above his head.

"It is done," Khalil said.

"Yes." My response was more directed at my own thoughts than my father's comment. I should have been there with him, but instead, there at the top of the steps to greet him and to bask in the glory of the moment were the queen mother, Ashraf, and Shams. The royal family. The Pahlavis. But where was I? Standing alone in a hotel room half-listening as my father went on about the CIA and Brits and the oil and national interests and repercussions and international sentiment. All just a blur of words, none nearly as powerful as the ones burning into my mind. I set the phone in its cradle, sank into the sofa, and watched. My husband and his family stood shoulder-to-shoulder, once again in power, and I was hundreds of miles away.

***

"To my beautiful wife on her return home."

In the chill quiet of the Ekhtesasi dining hall, we seemed dwarfed by its immensity. The shah's words echoed, the enormous space leaching any sincerity from his tone. I thought I should look around to see if any of the press corps were present to make note of the formal declaration of my pleasing appearance, the one thing that seemed to matter to anyone.

"Thank you," I said coolly, lifting my glass.

"It's so good to see your face. I'm happy to have you back."

From me, no response whatsoever. I wasn't going to give him the pleasure—particularly since, to my dismay, Ashraf had been the one to accompany me to Tehran.

Apparently able to withstand the silence no longer, Mohammed Reza slammed down his fork. I jumped.

"I cannot believe you're being this ungrateful!"

"Ungrateful? Should I be kissing your feet, thanking you for abandoning me in Rome?"

"I've told you many times, matters of state are very complicated, Soraya. You must understand …"

"You know, Mohammed, I'm tired of understanding but never being understood. I'm sick of hearing about how 'complicated' statecraft is. I'm a human being. And thanks to you, also, a queen. I should think that along with the title comes some respect."

"That's what you wanted wasn't it? To be a queen?" Mohammed

Reza had adopted the tone that I had come to loathe: that of a superior placating a subordinate. "You have the title. You have the royal residence. The clothes. The jewels. You're well provided for."

"And do you know what? When you spoke of us maybe being forced into exile, I was thrilled." Mohammed stiffened, taken aback. "And you still think of me of as that sixteen-year-old girl. How naïve I was. Yes, at first I was thrilled at the idea of being a queen. What woman wouldn't be? But then I fell in love with *you*: not a title, not a leader of a country, but a man. And now you treat me the same as if you were just any Persian man and I was just any other Persian woman. I suppose I should have expected as much."

"You're clearly overwrought, as I suspected." Mohammed resumed eating.

I sensed that the arrow had struck home. As much as the shah was insecure about his standing at the head of his country, he was now equally uncertain about how he measured up as a husband.

I paused, striving to soften my tone. I wanted nothing more on earth at that moment than to be understood.

"So, yes, I am overwrought right now. Not because I can't deal with recent events. As an empress, I am fine. But more than that position, I covet the title and role of a wife. And right now, I'm a woman who desperately wants the love of her husband. Who wants to feel important, wanted, needed." I was almost whispering now. "Noticed."

Mohammed sat staring as tears coursed down my face, his expression a mosaic of hurt, anger, remorse, and worry.

"I would rather be your wife for one day than empress for a hundred years, Mohammed Reza. I'm sorry if that's not what you wanted or need to hear right now, but it's the truth."

Mohammed Reza slowly nodded. Relieved to see understanding finally dawning on his face, I continued, "I know the shah needs me. But does my husband want me?"

Getting up from his chair, Mohammed walked with great deliberation around the table to my side. He stooped over me, tipping my chin up so that our eyes met.

"I do want you," said the shah. "Now hear me. You mean the world to me. What you want and what you deserve will be yours. This I promise you. Let's begin again."

I nodded and Mohammed kissed me deeply and passionately. I could not stop crying, doubtful that my husband could really do the things he said. I didn't feel so much the need to begin again as I did the desire to reveal more of my thoughts. It seemed to me that Mohammed's lips pressed against mine as much to silence me as to demonstrate his love. Why must he always think that what I deserved must be given and not earned? Why did love have to be so complicated?

It is funny to me now, long after I learned what Mohammed Reza had done to preserve the role of the monarchy. I found out how he'd cooperated with the CIA and British intelligence, although there was more to that story than people speculated. No doubt the west played a role in removing the "old lion," but I also knew full well the great role General Zahedi had played in the fight against Mosaddegh. You see, the Americans or the Brits could not have done anything no matter how much money they paid. The fact was that the people needed to have one of their own take charge—one they trusted, feared and above all respected. That was General Zahedi.

I didn't think that the loss of those three hundred lives was worth the preservation of Mohammed's family's place in Iran. We all act out of self-preservation at some point in our lives, some more frequently than others. I never thought that he sold his soul to the Americans and the British. He may have let them think that, but I really believe now that he wanted to do what was best for his people. Certainly, he wanted to preserve his family's standing at the head of Iranian society.

I was a part of that family, as much as I protested at the time that I felt I wasn't. He also felt that without his presence, the people of Iran would have continued to suffer.

I think that Mohammed wanted to please me. When he spoke upon my return about all that I had been given, he was expressing deep hurt. He thought me ungrateful, and perhaps I was. He did love me. He did love Iran. I just wished then that the two desires didn't have to be in conflict.

The reasons behind the things we do for love are seldom simple. Only with the passage of time can I see more clearly this: He was doing everything he could to make certain that the promises he made to me were kept. I was to be his wife and his queen. Everything else is ashes and dust, things that hide the truth, cover the surface, diminish and detract.

Chapter
EIGHTEEN

Much to my surprise and delight, Mohammed Reza lived up to the promises he'd made. For the first time, I truly felt that we were man and wife as well as king and queen. Together we went over some of the changes I had wanted to make to the staff in the residence. I rid myself of those ladies-in-waiting who'd proved to be unreliable during moments of greatest stress. Among those I forced to pack up was Petra, the German woman who served the dual roles of spy and attendant. Although I didn't tell Mohammed Reza the exact reason for my displeasure with Petra, he readily agreed that the woman needed to go. As for the two other women who had placed the poisonous spider within my midst—Ashraf and Shams—I worked out the details with my husband regarding a new set of rules for their contact with me.

Just like anyone else, they'd have to notify me in advance of their desire to meet with me. An even more mundane set of guidelines had to be put in place as well: Their expressed desire to meet with the queen didn't mean that their request had to be honored.

"That all seems perfectly reasonable to me," Mohammed said. "I think that matters of court should be handled with decency and respect, the same as any other household."

I had to bite my cheek to keep from laughing, but I hugged my husband's neck and kissed him repeatedly for expressing such a sweet sentiment.

Like most Persians, I had learned to play backgammon as a child and was strategic enough in my thinking to employ a kind of priming game to ensure that Ashraf and Shams were frequently blocked from gaining access to me. I made sure that each day several blocks of time were reserved for undisclosed meetings; that regular appointments with a hair stylist, a masseuse, and several advisors from the foundation filled up most of the slots on my board. Shams and Ashraf would have to be very fortunate in their "rolls of the dice" in order to schedule anything.

I knew not to press my luck too much and therefore didn't immediately discuss with Mohammed one of the things I most desired—removing Ernest Perron to a more distant sphere of influence. I would have liked very much if he could have been booted back to Switzerland, but I would have settled for him being anyplace else but the palace and the inner sanctum. I don't know what it was about that man that so rankled me, but I wasn't the only one who disliked him. It wasn't because of his lack of breeding; I simply didn't trust him. I thought myself a good judge of character, and paid attention to my instincts.

Unfortunately, I was made personally aware of just how much Mohammed relied on Perron's guidance. Now that he was more open with me about matters of state, Perron's name came up more frequently in conversations. Also, since I was now a more frequent presence in the palace, I could see for myself the many opportunities Perron took to be at my husband's side.

In many ways, Perron reminded me of a roach. I always seemed to sense his presence out of the corner of my eye. The man seemed to scuttle away when I directed the harsh light of my glare at him. Also, many times when I addressed various officials and delegates, Perron seemed to be lurking just outside the periphery, his narrow face and beady eyes vigilant and vaguely threatening.

I'd learned enough to know that one of the most important ways I could spend my time was by cultivating strategic alliances. I assembled a new team of supporters. My twice-weekly receptions with various members of the military, business, and educational communities led to Mohammed's appointing several of my guests to prominent positions within the government. My talent for negotiating social situations helped me make these people feel as if they were a part of the royal family, ensuring their loyalty. That they owed their positions to me was not something I considered fully at the time, but I now see that my strategy may have been faulty. Some saw this as an attempt to gain too much favor for myself, an act tantamount to undermining my husband's power.

I instituted other changes on the domestic front. Instead of eating my meals alone or with my husband distantly brooding over some report or another, we set aside time before and after our private dinners (Friday was still sacrosanct for the Pahlavi family gathering) to discuss various projects that had been proposed.

As a military man, the shah was focused on infrastructure like roads and highways, while I advocated for schools and hospitals.

"I'm happy to report that the foundation's coffers are overflowing. We're receiving support from people all over the country."

"I'm not surprised." The shah's voice had a note of teasing in it that I had come to regard as our own secret language.

"Why?"

"How could anyone say no to an empress who is willing to join her underprivileged campers in swimming?"

"Mohammed, stop it."

"It's true. You know you've won over my sisters by doing so."

"But your mother must be horrified at the thought of me being photographed in a bathing suit."

"If she is, she hasn't said as much. I think that Ashraf in particular has worn her down. You're helping my sister advance her favorite cause of modernization for women, so she's fully on your side in this. My mother has her own notions of what a woman ought not to do. I don't know if that will ever change, but at least she's learned to turn her back on what she views as unpleasantness."

"That's progress of a sort, I suppose. But Mohammed, if she could only bring herself to show up at one of the camps to see these young girls ..." My voice trailed off at the memory of the joy I'd seen on their young faces, so different from the expressions I'd seen among the orphans.

"I'm afraid that is beyond the scope of my powers. I do know that some of the increase in contributions is due to her campaigning on your behalf—privately, of course. She'd shoot me if she knew I'd told you."

Mohammed paused, realizing that his use of the expression was ill-advised. In the aftermath of his restoration to power, Mosaddegh and several of his supporters and key figures in his government had been arrested, tried, and convicted of treason. His foreign minister, Hossein Fatemi, had faced a firing squad just months after Mohammed's return.

Grateful for the faux pas, I took advantage of the opportunity to ask again about Mosaddegh, who was awaiting sentencing.

"Any news from the military court?"

"Concerning?"

"Mosaddegh, of course."

Mohammed frowned briefly, then sighed heavily. "Rumor has it that he will be sentenced in late December. I don't think he should expect any kind of leniency."

"Do you really want to be the man known for killing those who oppose you?" I twirled my wedding ring around my finger. It was now much tighter than it had been before; a tribute to the good health I'd been enjoying. I wondered if anyone had noticed, or if they still thought of me as that overly-nervous frail thing.

"Don't try to provoke me."

"I'm not trying to provoke. I'm trying to get you to understand that there may be consequences beyond those you've considered if he is sentenced to death."

The shah grimaced. "I don't control the courts, my dear."

"Not officially, no. But your word will mean a lot. Maybe there is a way for everyone to get what they want from this."

The shah furrowed his brow. "Perhaps you're right."

Several weeks after our conversation, Mosaddegh was sentenced to death for treason. Later it was commuted to a three-year term in solitary confinement followed by house arrest. I took some satisfaction in thinking that my influence had brought about those results. I was less than satisfied when, the same month that Mosaddegh was sentenced, the American vice-president Richard Nixon made a much-publicized trip to Iran. He was there to show support for the restored monarchy.

"I really don't understand why the Americans need to demonstrate their support."

"It is always good to have allies, Soraya."

"Allies like that have a strange effect on the sentiment of your people. Everywhere we go in the country these days, we see hundreds of people in the streets waving banners, chanting their love for you." My mind was filled with an image of several placards I'd seen earlier in the day. On it, the photograph of a beaming king and queen showed the two of us. I wondered briefly how those people got hold of that image, made those placards. Pleased that we were being received in a positive light due to our recent efforts, I did not want the interference of the west to cast a shadow over us.

"The Americans are our friends." Mohammed's statement returned me to the matter at hand.

"I realize that, but an awful lot of people don't approve of what they see as their meddling. It's just as it was with the British. Do they love us or our oil?"

"Regardless, we're meeting with him tomorrow, and a state dinner will follow."

I was less than impressed by the blunt, jowly man with the rough-edged voice and demeanor. Afterwards, I sat with the shah and his sisters, unwinding and recapping the night.

"At first I felt sorry for the poor man. I thought he had some kind of stammer," Shams said. "He wasn't without his charms, I suppose. Something like a street dog."

"From what I understand, he comes from a family of no means," Ashraf said with mild disgust.

"The Americans love that sort of thing. A man of the people and all that." Mohammed shrugged, seemingly in incomprehension.

"That's all well and good for them," I said. "But I'm not convinced the Americans can be trusted."

"Soraya," Mohammed said, "I'm sure there's some wisdom in your view, but I'm too tired to discern any of it. I'm retiring for the night. If you ladies care to discuss the great events of the day, you will have to do it without your moderator and voice of reason."

The next morning I rushed into the sitting room, where the shah sat sipping coffee. "Have you seen this?" I placed the newspaper in front of him.

"Yes. Ernest brought that to my attention this morning. It's very unfortunate, of course." Mohammed Reza sounded as if he was talking about getting a stain on a new shirt the first time he'd worn it.

"Unfortunate? Three university students killed by our military for protesting Nixon's visit? 'Unfortunate' doesn't begin to describe it! How could this happen?"

"Please calm yourself. Let history be your guide. You know that we've always had our detractors and we always will."

"That doesn't mean they deserved to die. They were students, Mohammed. No older than I am." I could feel tears welling up. What could those young people have been doing that they deserved to be murdered? If we were going to build any kind of democracy, surely it would allow for people to express their opinions without fear of death!

"But far less wise than you. I don't know all the details, but you have to understand that sometimes we have to sacrifice a part to save the whole. We can't define success as achieving happiness for all. That's a battle we can never win."

I shook my head, disappointed that I was hearing a kind of lecture rather than a humane response to what I saw as a tragedy.

"Look at all you've done," Mohammed continued. "Look at all I've done. And yet, there are those who still strive to bring down the monarchy." Mohammed's tone had lost some of its measured calm. I supposed that if I wanted to be able to express my opinion and share our role, I had to be prepared for some disagreement.

"You know that I've always believed prosperity for all would lay the foundation for Iranian democracy, and build a model state for all others to admire," I said. "May it still be so. Forgive me for saying this, but this incident calls to mind Reza Shah, and not you." I knew I was pressing a button that would rouse him from his slumber. Better that than his indifference.

"Soraya, please! I'm my father's son, not my father. Do you think I instructed those officers to shoot?" Mohammed's eyes widened and his expression pleaded for an understanding that I wasn't willing to give him.

"Not directly."

Mohammed rose from his seat and walked over to a bookshelf. He stood like a browser in a store, staring at the spines. "Let me assure you, I didn't order it indirectly either. Sometimes these things happen in a heated moment. Imperfect humans; imperfections. The sooner you come to accept that, the happier you will be. That will always be the way in political life."

"I suppose, then, I'm an idealist."

Mohammed turned to face me. "You are. And that's one of the things I love about you most. You think with your heart, and that is an admirable quality, but in politics one has to think logically most of the time. Believe me, you and I have our idealism in common. The difference is that while I dream ideally, I act practically. That's how I've survived up until now."

Both of us having made our points, we dropped the subject. I was glad that this was a case of our feeling free to differ. Somehow that brought us closer.

Nearly a year later, in October of 1954, another tragedy—one we shared similar feelings about—solidified our relationship before other forces began to wear at it.

"Let me be the first to wish you a happy thirty-fifth birthday, Your Majesty."

"Thank you very much, but you know that it is not until tomorrow." Mohammed drew my face to his and kissed me warmly. "That said, I would not object if you wanted to give me a present tonight ..."

"But you're already getting what you most want," I said as I caressed his hair. "Your dear brother Ali will be gracing us with his presence here in Tehran."

"Yes, I know. You have been quite busy with the preparations."

Mohammed stepped away from me, as if the mention of his brother and our amorous exchange were incompatible. I helped smooth his lapels and straighten his tie. "Your brother doesn't like all the trappings of royalty, so I've made an attempt to make this a tasteful if not overtly elegant gathering."

"That's good of you to do so. I know he will appreciate it."

I so admired Ali and his views regarding what he saw as the family's luxurious if not ostentatious lifestyle. He respected his older brother's role and that of his mother, but wanted little part of it. I did think it odd that those luxuries and amenities he seemed to disavow didn't include the airplane that he would pilot from the north.

Unsurprisingly, the birthday gathering was a bit tense. The queen mother, Ashraf, and Shams were well behaved, but it was clear they weren't happy that instead of the fine china, sliver, and crystal, the table was laid with what the queen mother called "quaint crockery." I made no attempt to explain that I was trying to please Ali. Given his absence from court, his rejecting nearly everything to do with the royal family and its duties, I would have thought it obvious.

The evening was about to descend into familiar chaos. As much as Mohammed and I had managed to change our relationship, there were some things that just couldn't be helped. In families that trod a familiar road all the time, the tracks create deep ruts.

"Your brother should have been here by now," Ashraf said, intentionally disavowing her relationship with Ali. "His lateness is certainly in keeping with his attitude toward us."

"I'm sure that he's encountered some bad weather and has had to route around it," I said, glad to take Ali's side.

"He has the experience for that," the queen mother said, sniffing. "He has done everything he can to avoid seeing to his family duties."

"I really don't think this is the time or the place," I said. "After all, we're here to celebrate Mohammed Reza's birthday."

Shams leaned forward intently, taking me on about an issue that still clearly rankled them all even after all this time. "What better place to discuss an important family member. We're so seldom allowed to see you …"

"The boy has to understand that the line of succession …" the queen mother added on top of Shams.

"If we didn't speak of this in your presence, you'd be resentful of the …" Ashraf joined the trio.

"Good evening, your Majesty." Ardeshir's cheerful voice rose above the others. He embraced the shah and me in turn and then skirted around the table greeting the others.

After he'd settled, Mohammed asked him, "Any word on Ali?"

"I was informed that he departed on time. I would have thought he'd have been here an hour ago."

Mohammed's face turned ashen. He quickly recovered and spoke, as if to buoy his own spirits as well as ours. "As much as it pains me to admit it, he's a finer pilot than I am. And as you know, I'm a very fine pilot myself. He'll be here."

The meal began without one guest. The participants in the celebration tried to keep up the pretense, but after dinner when Ardeshir excused himself, the room fell silent. When Ardeshir returned, it was clear that the news was not good. Seeing the aide's stricken face, the queen mother burst into tears.

"I'm sorry to inform you that Ali's plane lost radio contact an hour into the flight. It is presumed that he has gone down in the mountains. There is quite a bit of fog and snow …" Ardeshir's voice trailed off.

I moved toward Mohammed, but he sidestepped me. Raising his hands to quiet the room, he said, "Everyone remain calm. Ali Reza is fine, I can assure you. Just because he lost radio contact doesn't mean he's …" Mohammed hesitated and then continued. "Radios malfunction. Planes are set down safely. He is alive, and I will find him."

The room erupted again, and Mohammed strode away. I stood stunned for a moment, and then took off after him.

"Mohammed, you can't mean to go now. What about the weather?"

"He's alive. I will find him." His voice had taken on a steeliness that chilled me.

"Then I'm coming with you."

"Another pair of eyes will do us some good, I suppose."

At the first light of morning, the plane lifted into the sky. Queasy from sleeplessness and dread, I sat with my face pressed against the window. My dry lids scratched my eyes painfully. After an hour, we reached the rugged snow-covered Alborz Sierra, where a few trees dotted a landscape packed with rocky outcroppings. The craggy peaks of Mount Damavand came into view, its volcanic dome emitting a wisp of smoke, a tiny fissure in the dark plate of the sky. Unspoken among us was the idea that the weather couldn't have been more perfect for flying, the scenery more gorgeous. Why had Ali experienced the misfortune of fog and high winds?

Both the co-pilot and I spoke into our headsets, intoning, "Nothing. Nothing," for what seemed hours and hours. Mohammed turned ever-tightening circles when I thought I saw a flash of light reflecting off of something. I blinked hard; there it was again.

"I see something. Off to the left."

"Where? You have to be more precise." Mohammed's voice was surprisingly calm. "Think of a clock dial."

"It's at three o'clock. Now four as we're moving,"

My stomach lurched as the plane banked. I had felt a moment of exhilaration at having spotted something, but when I thought of what that something might have been and what it might mean for us, my heart rose into my throat.

Though Mohammed didn't say anything, it was clear that he saw what I had. The plane descended rapidly and then leveled off only a hundred feet or so above the ground. At the sight of a plane's fuselage split in half, its wheels pointing skyward like hands offered in prayer, I gasped and sobbed.

"He could have easily survived that." Mohammed Reza turned in his chair to face me. "See if you can spot him. Look for tracks in the snow."

The sun's glare off the snow made it difficult for me to see anything. The plane banked and circled repeatedly, dizzying me. Finally, I caught sight of a dark clump in the shadow of one of the outcroppings of rock. It was a vibrant moving thing. I guided my husband toward it. Then I saw the clump break into pieces. It became clear that a group of wolves had been disturbed by the sound of the plane's engine. They ran and circled, eyeing the sky. Another pass revealed a stain of blood on the snow, and a central mass of shredded blue standing out in harsh relief from the shadows.

"I have to find somewhere to land this thing," Mohammed shouted. "To be certain. To bring him home."

"Your Majesty," the co-pilot said, "that's quite impossible. Perhaps we could land, but we'd never get airborne again."

I hated myself for having to say it, but I knew Mohammed needed to hear it. "That blue can only be one thing. Of course he would wear the royal family uniform to honor you on your birthday. He loved you so, he'd do anything for you. He wouldn't want you to risk your life for him."

I reached over the pilot's seat to comfort my husband. His only response was to circle the plane once more and ascend, turning back to the south and defeat.

The image of that broken and ravaged body has never left me. Sometimes, just as I am about to fall asleep, it comes back to me in a flash. In most ways, my mother was a very modern woman, but she disapproved of the idea of humans flying. She thought that we were tempting the fates too much. Funny her thinking that way; we so associate the Germans with logic and precision. Every time I flew anywhere after that, just as I settled into my seat and buckled myself in, I'd experience a momentary panic.

Of course, I worried about Mohammed Reza every time he flew. I wondered about it at the time, but later on it became clear to me what the appeal was. In the air, at the wheel of the plane he experienced two things that were often lacking in his life: total control and absolute freedom. When I was a young girl and saw a plane flying in the skies of Isfahan, and I shouted that it was him, I didn't think that he was the one in charge. I always assumed that he was just a passenger, sitting back and putting his life in the hands of another.

That night after we returned to Tehran with the confirmation of Ali's death, Mohammed and I sat together, leafing through a photo album. In a formal portrait, the two boys stood in front of a backdrop of palm fronds and an Ionic column, both of them dressed in morning clothes and top hats. Their chins were tilted toward the ceiling, as if they were trying to peer over something to see what lay beyond.

"You look like such little gentlemen."

"That's the word for him exactly. Such a gentle man." I felt him quaking as he tried to stifle his tears. His breath came in ragged gasps for a moment, and then quieted. "I remember how we both howled when were made to dress up for that photograph. We wanted uniforms with swords and scabbards; my father's influence I suppose, our wanting to be soldiers. Instead, we were made to look like scholars and statesmen. I fear I've made a failure at being any of those things. I'm certain Ali would have done better."

I squeezed his forearm and kissed him on the cheek. "You do yourself an injustice thinking so."

Mohammed sat impassively, staring into the middle distance. We both started at the sound of a door banging and raised voices. In a moment, the queen mother came into the room, her skin gone a spectral white, her wide eyes staring but seeming not to see. She staggered into the room as if sleepwalking. She seemed like an apparition out of Shakespeare as she raised her hand and pointed at me.

"Everything ripped, everything torn asunder! The sky's soil has fallen on us. My light, my heart, my eyes …"

Mohammed and I glanced at one another uneasily and then stood staring back at the queen mother. Neither of us dared to do anything, fearing that waking up a sleepwalker would do the old woman harm.

"My dear baby son, ripped from me! And this country … is one martyred student away from unraveling completely. Our enemies grow stronger. They will see this as a sign of weakness. No one to succeed you, Mohammed Reza. The wolves will circle." At that point, I realized that she wasn't asleep. As disjointed as her thoughts seemed to be, the woman was lucid even if gripped by grief.

"Mother. You're not well. You're distraught; we all are."

I didn't like thinking this way, but her state of mind was different from the way she'd talked about her son the night before. It was as if in losing him, she'd regained her love and admiration for him. I was worried that she'd truly become unhinged, but when she spoke next, it became clear that these were not lunatic ramblings.

"And you," she said, turning on me directly. "You have failed us miserably. Three years married, and no heir? Do you know what that means with Ali gone? No line of succession for this family. Have you any idea how vulnerable that makes us? Oh God! Oh God! Oh God!"

The queen mother began striking her own head with open palms, all the while keeping her eyes fixed on heaven. I remained rooted to the spot, but Mohammed Reza stepped forward. We'd both seen Persian women respond this way before, and each time I had, their response had riveted me in place.

"Mother. Please stop. Don't do this to yourself! You must calm down." Mohammed's tone was reassuring.

"You owe me this, my son. Produce an heir."

She broke out of her son's grasp and turned on me again. "Do your duty. Fix this!" Her expression had gone feral. I nearly shivered.

"Get someone, please," Mohammed instructed me.

As I rushed out of the room, I heard the old woman haranguing her son. "Ripe for the picking, we are. Ripe for the picking!"

The next several days, a gray cloud settled over the household. Mohammed Reza was busy with working on retrieving his brother's remains. Whatever sympathy the royal family received was insufficient to offset their sense of loss. Ali had given away much of his fortune to various charities, and so a large state funeral seemed out of keeping with his stated desires to live a more simple life. Regardless, there were arrangements to be made, affairs to be settled.

Shortly after the funeral, we lay in bed, sleep eluding us both.

"She's right, you know."

I had no doubt who he was talking about, but I struggled to accept the truth of his remark.

"Those were the ravings of a grief-stricken mother. Surely you know that."

"I also know that my mother is often right even when she seems most ... You have to look beyond the appearances to the substance of her remarks."

"And that is?"

"That with Ali Reza gone, the country has no heir to succeed me. We have to do something about that."

I rolled over and curled against him, gently nudging my hips against him.

"More than that, Soraya."

"What else is there to do?"

"I would think by now that we'd have succeeded. Perhaps you need some help. Have you seen a doctor lately?"

"I'm fine, Mohammed. Since that unfortunate time, I've been mostly well."

"Well, mostly well or not, we are still without a child."

"We're both young. There's time yet."

In the weeks that followed Ali's death, Mohammed mourned in private, not wanting anyone to see him acting weak. I don't understand why being human is viewed that way. No matter who we are—a king or a commoner—we are all still human beings and entitled to feelings and expressions of emotion. But society is structured in this way, unfortunately. If you are in a position of power, then you must put on a mask that resembles strength so as not to appear vulnerable. I'd viewed him as weak before, but this was clearly different. This wasn't a case of his will being weak; it was a case of his emotions, his grief, being strong.

One evening, Mohammed said over dinner, "I've been doing a lot of thinking. I believe that a trip will do us both some good. Relieve some of the stress and get us out of this gloom. Put some distance between us and Ali's passing."

Although I did not like this false portrait of strength, I asked, "Where would we go?"

"I have in mind a kind of goodwill tour. We received a lot of support from the West during our troubles. Enough time has passed; we need to renew acquaintances."

Although my response was muted, I was overjoyed. I was eager to travel, but more eager to get away from the queen mother. Her performance that night when she stormed in—and I was convinced that she'd been acting—had unnerved me. That the woman would go to such lengths, using the death of her son to advance her agenda, showed me just how twisted and desperate she was. While I wanted to have children, my reasons had nothing to do with keeping their dynasty intact.

"We should pay a few visits to some of the best doctors in the West as well. See if we can hasten along your pregnancy. We can do what's best for us and for the country at the same time," Mohammed said.

"Do you think there's something wrong with me?"

"Soraya, dear." He turned to face me, and I rested my head on his chest. "No, I don't. It's simply that with Ali's passing, the issue has moved to the forefront of everyone's mind. In that respect, this is both a personal and national matter."

I had come to understand that separating the two would never be possible. Still, I didn't like the idea that our reproducing was a matter of national policy. That said, I knew that my feelings didn't really matter. "I'll do whatever is necessary."

Mohammed stroked my hair, and I could feel the tension easing out of him. "I'm grateful that you're becoming more of an empress than ever before. It's essential to put your country on par with your own interests. We've been working on some arrangements. I'll get everything finalized as soon as possible."

With a kiss on the forehead, Mohammed rolled away from me. I lay awake. In my mind's eye, I saw a plane winging west where, apparently, this key issue in my life would be settled. I couldn't escape the thought that I was being manipulated. Clearly, Mohammed had given the matter some thought, and had already put into motion part of the plan. Was he the one at the controls, or were others? I tried to tell myself it didn't matter, but it most certainly did.

Chapter
NINETEEN

"Look around, Mohammed; what do you see?"

We stopped in the middle of the block on Manhattan's Upper West Side. We stood on the sidewalk holding hands beneath a canopy of honey locust and pin oak trees. Their limbs were bare, and their first buds were just beginning to sprout. The fertile smell of spring was in the air. I hoped that these signs presaged a wonderful 1954.

Mohammed looked around and shrugged.

I ushered him to the side to allow a mother pushing a baby carriage to pass. The woman smiled pleasantly at us, and the child waved.

"Nothing out of the ordinary."

"Exactly. And it's absolutely wonderful."

"Tired of Sorayamania, are you?" Mohammed asked, teasing me about all the coverage we'd been getting.

"You know the newspapers, darling. They'll do anything to sell themselves."

"I know that the motto is 'Never let the truth get in the way of telling a good story.' But you truly are the World's Prettiest Queen." Mohammed Reza quoted one of the headlines. "No one is making that up."

"And you truly are one of the great defenders against the onslaught of the dreaded red horde. No communist shall trample us under your watch." I laughed, my mood so light that I didn't even mind seeing members of our security detail trailing fifty feet behind us.

I was used to the media in Tehran, but New York reporters were quite another sort of animal altogether. Yes, we were the Peacock Dynasty, and we were used to strutting and revealing our plumage. But nothing could have prepared us for the onslaught of New York. Yet despite its sometimes overly assertive presence, I was in love with the city. Each time I emerged from a car or a building, a surge of energy coursed through me. The incessant sound of traffic and car horns, the throngs of pedestrians, even the wind surprising me as I went around the corner thrilled me.

We'd just managed to evade a reporter who'd trailed us from our hotel to Fifty-Sixth and Madison Avenue. There, Mohammed was fitted for two dozen suits, thirty pairs of pajamas, and several brocade vests. We'd joked that we were sure his shopping spree would crop up in the next day's news. The same had been true of the three weeks we'd spent earlier in the States. We'd been greeted by an enormous crowd at Idlewild Airport on our arrival, and were motorcaded over the Triboro Bridge and the East River Drive to Gracie Mansion. There the outgoing and incoming mayors competed for our attention. Robert Wagner Jr. was more than taken with me. His gruff charm lacked the refinement I was used to, but I imagined America as a place where the influence of cowboys and gangsters still held sway. He did nothing to dissuade me of that idea. According to all reports, in Washington DC, we solidified our reputation as a very modern pair. I was surprised that the writers found it remarkable that we loved to dance and seemed to revel in one another's company. Our love of American nightclub life seemed to exude from our pores. Who wouldn't be enamored of the US, especially in that postwar time when the country was on the rise?

Everyone seemed to be drinking giddily, and it made me recall what I'd read about the Roaring Twenties.

The accounts of our activities included the fact that the assistant secretary of state became another of my admirers. In my mind, he was just one of many who waited in line to whirl me across the dance floor at the Shoreham Hotel. The next morning, President Eisenhower and his wife Mamie greeted us on the White House lawn, their Weimaraner Heidi prancing around us. Given Eisenhower's military experience, I expected him to conduct himself with straitlaced military bearing and seriousness, but I found him very down-to-earth and humble.

While Washington was the seat of power, it didn't hold my interest. I suppose that Hollywood was the land of artifice, but I found DC to be even more of a land of make-believe. People wore their insincerity like cologne—some subtly, but most too powerfully. A senator's wife, clearly "in her cups," as the Brits like to say, approached me. Steadying herself by grasping my arm, she said in a whiskey-tinged voice, "I've admired you from afar forever. What you're doing in Israel gives hope to all your people. Shalom. Isn't that how you say it?"

Her husband, a fat man with a strange accent, led her away.

It was necessary to be on my best behavior in the nation's capital, but I was eager to let my hair down. I was still very young, and the novelty of wearing ball gowns and tightly coiffed hair piled high on my head like a dunce cap had worn off. I imagined myself more as Audrey Hepburn in *Roman Holiday*, the young princess who escapes her guardians and sets out on adventures. Unlike her character, I already had a husband, but I wanted to capture the young actress's style and flair.

Fortunately, there was Los Angeles to offset the stuffiness and frequently too-formal and fake Washington, DC (which in my mind stood for Dull City). At one point, Mohammed was swept up by my enthusiasm, and we snuck off to the Mocambo Club. There we danced until well after midnight, not even sitting out the challenging, "Shake, Rattle, and Roll." I can only imagine what the society pages in Washington would have made of our surprising (inappropriate is what they would have meant) appearance there. Los Angeles embraced us with great warmth, and I felt the same way. It was good to see Mohammed Reza enjoying himself. I attributed this to his being not just away from his duties, but also from his family's critical eyes.

As much as I'd enjoyed our evenings out among the "regular" people, I will never forget dancing with my teenage crush, Humphrey Bogart. I'm sure that Mohammed would say the same about leading Greer Garson around the floor. This was not our only brush with Hollywood royalty—a group that seemed far more taken with themselves than we were. Skiing in Sun Valley with Gary Cooper and his wife was an absolute delight. I loved the woman's nickname—Rocky—and still felt the bittersweet sting of Hollywood's draw tugging at me. Being a real-life queen was one thing, but being able to play one on screen and then a nun, a femme fatale, and later on a housewife, still held an allure. I wasn't willing to trade my life for that other imagined one, but I would at least have listened to an offer or two.

I'm an old woman now, and it might be said that I over-romanticize those times. So be it. In my mind, those scenes still play in oversized Cinemascope and perhaps too-bright and gaudy Technicolor. That's how memories of our best moments should be. Seeing those stars on a human scale rather than on-screen didn't diminish them. Those people only enlarged the scale of my life, and made me feel more special than some thought I deserved to be. I didn't pay attention to my critics either then nor do I now. And if Mohammed was feeling a freedom and control outside the sphere of influence of Tehran and his family, then so did I.

I was aware that much attention was being paid to me, my clothes, and my appearance—not that that had anything to do with my decision to dye my hair a rusty red that delighted my husband and had tongues and pens wagging in the gossip columns.

One night in Palm Beach, I met the beautiful Jacqueline Kennedy at a gathering. The Kennedys were beyond charming—the very picture of elegance. I loved her light and trilling voice as much as her look. It was the voice of a woman who knew how to make herself heard, but didn't always insist upon it. I was equally impressed with her husband, a senator who limped around the room using a cane as a result of a recent back surgery. He managed to be cordial, although he was clearly in pain. The shah was much taken by him, commenting, "He seems to embody what I most like about this country: vitality, youthfulness, and optimism."

Although I agreed with his opinion of America and its people, I dreaded returning to New York. I guess that in some way, I was content to remain in denial. If the news from the doctors was not going to be to my liking, then I did not want to hear it.

"I know that tomorrow isn't a day that you're eager to face," he added.

"Can't we just enjoy the day? I'd love to take a stroll through Central Park. We can save this talk for later, can't we?"

"Soraya, you knew from the beginning this wasn't simply a holiday." Mohammed sighed deeply.

I clung to him, burying my face in the softness of his cashmere blazer. "Like every little girl, I dreamed of what my life might be like. I never could have imagined that things would be this wonderful. I just don't want it to end."

"I agree, my darling. Our time away has been a gift we've given each other."

"I wish we could stay here together, just us."

"You know that's not possible."

I was happy that my little ploy had worked, and that Mohammed had dropped the subject.

I didn't need any reminders of what was to come the next day. It had been on my mind for weeks.

As we strolled through the park's entrance, Mohammed broke the silence. "I'm certain that the results will be nothing but good news. You'll see."

"I realize that, but knowing it doesn't offer me much comfort." Apparently my ploy had only worked temporarily.

"You agreed that this was the right thing to do."

"I still believe that, but 'right' doesn't make it any easier. It may mean the worst is in store."

Mohammed didn't respond. We stood at the park's inner drive, watching as cars sped past. When the light changed, we walked again.

"Suppose I see the doctors and they do help us hasten the pregnancy. What then? Will the child really be my son? Will we be responsible for raising him, or will he be in the hands of your mother and sisters?" I pointed to a couple and their toddler playing in the grass off the Sheep Meadow. "Can we enjoy simple pleasures like that with our child?"

I didn't want to voice these concerns, but Mohammed's insistence on pressing the issue of the fertility specialists, spoiling for me what had been a wonderful day, had me in a sour mood.

"Soraya, when you married me, you knew I was king."

"Yes, just as I knew that there was a planet called Mercury. Without having experienced either, how could I have known?"

"Regardless. You knew that there would be benefits and drawbacks. As there would be in any marriage. However, I know that having a child will be nothing but beneficial, both politically and personally."

"I'm merely talking about the reality we will both face. I want our child to be ours, not the property of the monarchy. I want to be the child's mother and make the decisions that a mother has the right to make. I don't want the constant meddling ..."

Mohammed scowled at me. "I've been more than understanding. Especially since we've been restored to full authority, and I've granted you anything you've wanted. There are limitations on my generosity."

"You are most kind and generous. I love you for that, but this ..."

"Your father is happily entrenched in Berlin as the ambassador."

"He too appreciates your kindness."

"My son—if we have a boy—will be my heir. Attendant with that fact are certain realities that you may find painful. The child will be a joy to us and to both our families. He will also be a signal to our people that we mean to remain in Tehran and in power."

I looked around. Mohammed had spoken so forcefully that I worried about who might have overheard us. Perhaps more than anything, I worried about the security men. If we showed signs of discord, then who knew who they might tell about it?

"Being here has opened my eyes to a more free way of living, without so many traditions of the past," I whispered.

Mohammed threw his head back in frustration and moaned. "Your enchantment with 'normal' life is just a delusion. Don't be naïve. We won't have this." He gestured toward the carousel we'd stopped in front of. "Wanting that is just not realistic. All the energy you expend hoping to change things would be better spent elsewhere."

"Such as?" I asked, waiting to hear him play the same tired notes.

"Producing the heir that we both want and need."

"But if this is something we're in together, then why are you leaving for Washington?"

"Fortunately, your dancing partner in the Department of State has agreed to meet with me. We're making inroads. Perhaps there may be some aid packages coming our way. We're still in the talking stages. There's much that remains to do."

"It's just that I've so enjoyed being together." I didn't like how I was sounding and feared that Mohammed might interpret my remarks as weakness. In fact, that was exactly what I was being—weak and immature.

"As have I. But don't worry; you won't be alone. Forough will accompany you tomorrow, and Ardeshir will be with me. Once you're done at the hospital, you'll be back in Washington in no time."

The following morning, I shifted uncomfortably, trying to adjust my gown. The paper cover of the examination table clung to my leg.

A swift knock on the door preceded Dr. Stevenson's entrance. A stout little man with a shock of thick hair that rose from his head like a sleeping cap added a comical touch to his overly serious demeanor. His back to me, he snapped on a pair of gloves. Without a word of greeting or explanation, he asked me to raise my legs into the stirrups. I stiffened as the cold metal made contact with my warm flesh. I hugged myself and stared at the ceiling, counting to take my mind off what I was experiencing. After two hundred and eighty, I watched as the doctor's head rose from the hammock of my stretched gown.

"I'll see you in my office in a few minutes after you've dressed."

I scanned his face looking for some clue; anything to let me know if the news was good or bad. The only indication I had was the man furiously scratching notes on his clipboard.

An hour later, I sat in Riverside Park. Forough Zafar sat beside me on the bench, her hands in her lap, head down.

"I really don't know what to say, Your Highness." Forough's voice was nearly drowned out by the sound of a nearby siren. "Are you going to have the surgery?"

"I am inclined not to. Maybe another doctor will find that my fallopian tubes aren't blocked. I'm terrified of something happening to me if I go under the knife."

I looked away from the statue and through the trees to a glint of river and the New Jersey shoreline. I retied the scarf that held my hair in a silken embrace.

Forough started to speak, but then stopped.

I laughed to myself. "Forough." I patted my confessor's hand. "I don't need you to say anything. Listening is enough."

My voice was thin and reedy, and the older woman leaned in to hear me. I cleared my throat and coughed. Forough offered me a handkerchief, and I wiped my mouth. The purse's clasp snapped in the silence. A dead leaf skittered across the sidewalk and then lifted into the air. I watched as it drifted in the breeze, feeling like my dreams were being ferried away with it.

Chapter
TWENTY

A week later, I lay staring at the ceiling of an examination room in London's St. Bartholomew's Hospital, trying not to think about the new set of hands that were probing me. The X-rays had been taken, the blood drawn, and now I felt like a specimen under a microscope, less a person than a condition. I tried to keep my breathing steady, but I felt my heart rapidly percolating.

I shut my eyes and thought of the doughy man with the roseate cheeks and the raspy voice I'd heard so many times on newsreels and the radio. I'd been reading Churchill's memoir and had dozens of questions that I'd hoped to ask him over dinner the previous night. However, the prime minister had peppered my husband with questions about the current political climate in Tehran and the fallout of the Mosaddegh incident. At one point, he raised his glass, which was emptied and filled with alarming regularity, and said to my husband, "Here's to you and to our ongoing struggle against anarchy all around the world. Long may you reign."

Although I had wanted to press him with questions, I knew better. Mohammed Reza had warned me that the UK's allowing nationalization of our oil industry had ruffled more than a few feathers in London and elsewhere. The Brits were particularly angry, and we needed to work carefully to end the rancorous exchanges that had followed. We had been on a mission to restore the West's confidence in us and reinforce the idea that our monarchy could rule wisely.

Churchill leaned into me, his jowly cheeks prominent. I said, "You once referred to Iran as 'the bridge to victory.' I'm hopeful that you will look on us as kindly again."

His face twisted into a mask of puzzlement and then sagged. He shrugged exaggeratedly and then, his eyes twinkling, said, "Your Majesty, I honestly cannot remember making that remark."

I felt my breath catch in my throat.

"However, insofar as those words made a significant impression upon a woman of your sophistication and beauty, I shall indeed take the credit."

I knew that a man of his accomplishments was generally immune to flattery, but I was pleased to see how he had responded. I cast a glance at Mohammed Reza, who was also smiling.

A moment later, I felt the prime minister's hand on mine, and then his mouth pressed close to my ear. "Please disregard anything that woman"—he surreptitiously raised his pinkie finger from his glass to indicate Queen Elizabeth—"may have to say on any subject. She rules but does not govern, and I fear she does not do either very well."

My companion smiled like a schoolboy pleased with a put-down of a teacher whose back was turned to the class.

I didn't quite agree with Churchill. To be honest, I somewhat envied the Queen of England's role—all of the pomp and few of the circumstances.

"I'll see you in my office in a few minutes," the doctor said, startling me out of my reverie. He smiled kindly and then whispered to his nurse. As I dressed behind a folding screen, I looked out the window at the Henry VIII gate. I was aware of the irony of my having passed beneath it in order to get onto the hospital's grounds, since it was named after the king who wreaked havoc on his wives in order to produce an heir.

I'd eagerly agreed to a second examination, this time with specialists in London, hoping that the previous diagnosis and recommended course of treatment was wrong. I still hadn't shared the New York results with my husband. I hoped I could end the charade by telling him at least one version of the truth, instead of evading it entirely.

When I left the doctor's office, devoid of all hope for that resolution, I was glad that Forough was there waiting. With one look, I conveyed the news that the original diagnosis had been confirmed. I was glad that Forough had enough sense to reveal nothing until we were back at the Athenaeum Hotel.

I lay on the bed propped up by pillows. Forough sat in a chair by my bedside, massaging my hands.

"They said that stress contributes, did they not?"

"Yes." I pulled my hands away and rubbed my temples. My head throbbed and my stomach gnawed at me.

"That means that there's still a possibility without ..."

"Of course. There are always possibilities. I just don't know what to say to Mohammed."

"What you've just told me will do: that the stress of the last few years, and in particular these last few months with all this traveling, isn't conducive ..."

I waved my hands to stop her. The sound of the others entering the suite ended the conversation. Mohammed entered the room, and Forough slinked past him and out the door.

"What news, my darling?" He sat beside me and perfunctorily brushed his lips against my cheeks. I caught the smell of cigar smoke and spirits. My stomach churned as I struggled with what to say to him.

"Nothing new. As before, I was told that patience was needed."
When I saw the shah frowning and shaking his head, I changed tactics, "The doctor did say that my past medical history, what our lives have been like, and what we're doing now could all contribute. Too much stress and commotion, I suppose."

"In other words, they know nothing." Mohammed nearly spat the words.

"It's an inexact science."

Mohammed turned on me. "Why must you correct me? All I know is that we haven't gotten the results we wanted."

"I'm saying that if we took some other precautions—that's not the word for it exactly. If we were more relaxed, slowed our pace a bit, my body would be more receptive. That's all. It's like anything else …"

"How can you say that?" Mohammed was nearly shouting his disbelief. "You know what is at stake. There is nothing at all like this."

I began counting, not wanting to say anything in anger.

Feeling as if I'd composed myself, I continued. "Of course, knowing that the fate of your reign and the Pahlavi dynasty is contingent on my getting pregnant contributes to the pressure."

Mohammed collapsed into a chair and kicked his feet onto an ottoman. "Pressure to do the most natural thing in the world."

"Mohammed, you …"

I stopped when I saw Forough shouldering her way into the room with a tray of tea. "Forgive the interruption."

I saw through Forough's transparent attempt to call a time-out. We remained quiet while she poured. I looked at her quizzically, wondering if there was something else she was up to. A moment later my question was answered.

"I think that what the queen is trying to say is that she needs rest. Traveling from hotel to hotel, the flying, all the meetings." The words rushed out of her like the tea from the pot.

"How dare you?" The shah stood, and for a moment I feared that he would strike my lady-in-waiting. I sat wide-eyed while Forough stood calmly regarding the ruler of her country.

"Get out of here immediately. I don't need your meddling."

I sensed that Forough had more that she wanted to say, but her training took hold. "As you wish, Your Majesty."

Forough had put on her bravest face, although she knew well that no one talked over the shah. She exited the room, defeated but unbowed.

Moments later, Mohammed stormed out, slamming the door behind him.

Later that night, he had calmed enough that I felt it safe to try again to explain to him what the doctors had in truth said.

"What is so stressful about your life? You travel in a private aircraft, are ferried about, stay in the best hotels." He sipped his drink and continued. "Your life is far from difficult."

I pointed at his glass. "They say that even alcohol can have an effect. The body is a delicate instrument, easily knocked off balance."

I immediately regretted my choice of words.

"And of course you needn't tell me that you are more delicate than most."

His allusion to my battle with what everyone believed was food poisoning made me even more sure that I had to avoid surgery.

"I just wish you'd consider allowing me to travel back home for a bit," I said.

"And this is how you propose to produce a child—through air mail delivery?"

Sarcasm is the last resort of the frustrated and the foolish. My husband may not have been the latter, but he certainly was the former. His responses were reaffirming my decision to not disclose the full truth.

Two days later, Mohammed and I were in the Hotel Königshof in

Munich. Another city, another argument. I was almost grateful that this time the subject was different.

"What were you thinking?" His voice rose in pitch and volume.

"They asked me the questions. I thought it appropriate to answer."

The shah tossed the newspaper at my feet. "And you felt compelled to speak about the role of women in Iranian society? Do you have any idea what this might mean to my supporters back home?"

"How could I forget my place? After all, I'm not even allowed to decide who's fit to be my aide." I was nearly beyond caring that my words would incite him. There's a little bit of arsonist in all Persian women, I believe. Stoking the fire of my husband's anger aroused a combination of fear and pleasure in me.

"Don't speak of that woman again."

"Forough was a valued member of my court, and you dismissed her without so much as a word to me."

I thought of the tearful farewell I shared with the woman who had become as close to me as my own mother. After what she did for me, taking on Mohammed in the hopes of advancing my cause, I only loved her all the more. She was like a soldier who had thrown herself in front of a bullet to protect me.

The shah knew how much I depended on Forough. "You have your own mother and mine. You don't need another person filling your head with silly notions. I'll not tolerate anyone interfering with business of the state."

I wasn't certain if he was referring to Forough, or to my recent interview. It didn't matter. I saw the circumstances as one and the same.

"And I don't like anyone interfering with my rights as a woman to employ who I like—or to say what I feel."

"So that gives you the right to undermine my authority, speak for us as the rulers of this country, and to antagonize those with whom

I've tried to cultivate a good relationship?" Mohammed's expression was a contorted mask of barely suppressed rage.

"I spoke my mind. I said nothing that I haven't stated to you before and which you seemed to support. If we are going to be perceived by the West as anything but backwards anti-moderns, then …"

"Enough! I know how you work. You're on your own footing here, admired and adored because of your ancestry, and you take the opportunity to outshine me. You knew full well that I don't speak German, and your eloquence would be all the greater."

I shook my head sadly. "If that's what you think, then I can never be anything but guilty. I was trying to help our cause; to let people know that we're not, despite what they seem to think, completely barbarous."

My none-too-veiled reference to the shah's father hit its mark. He skulked off, Ernest Perron in his wake. There would be no attempt to make an heir that night, or the next, I thought. I couldn't believe that Mohammed was jealous of me and the attention I was getting in Germany.

"Get away from me," I said to the woman my husband had installed in Forough's place. I thought of the previous lady-in-waiting that had been forced upon me, and considered this new woman to also be a spy.

I had come to confide my deepest thoughts with Forough, sharing with her the frustrations I felt about my life with Mohammed Reza. Our final conversation served that very purpose.

"I don't know how any of this is going to turn out. I've worn myself into a frazzle trying to please him. Worse, I've come to doubt who I am. Am I a piece of state property? Is that why I feel like I'm a stranger in my own marriage? Yet at other times, I know he loves me dearly."

Forough laughed ruefully. "You could fix all of this if you'd do the one thing he wants. Produce a son, and your worries will be over."

"Right," I said, joining in her sarcasm. "That's what unconditional love is all about, isn't it?"

The truth was, I did believe in unconditional love. I wanted children, but that wasn't a condition of my love for Mohammed. I didn't want that to be a condition of his love for me. I understood well the political realities of the dynasty. Now through his maneuvering, he'd rid himself of Mosaddegh as prime minister and restored himself to full authority over the country. We were a true monarchy, and even before the queen mother so forcibly reminded us of the need to have a clear line of succession, I knew that to be true. While I was making an effort to tell Mohammed the truth about my medical results, he was shattering my pride. The fact that he felt the need to remind me of the privileged life I led and to accuse me of being ungrateful infuriated me beyond words. I was starting to doubt whether I really knew this man whom I worshiped and loved. I knew what he meant to me and knew that in an instant I would without hesitation sacrifice my life for him. Would he have done that for me? Or did both our lives revolve completely around what was in his best interests? I tried to rid myself of those thoughts and of questioning his character. Instead, I tried to focus on how to best deal with my fertility issues.

The flight to Tehran at the conclusion of our journey brought us into conflict again. Instead of the drone of the plane's engines lulling me to sleep, they made me restless. I craned my neck and saw that a single light was on in the cabin. My husband sat bathed in a spot of light. I squinted and made out the title of the book he was reading: Churchill's *The Dawn of Liberation*.

I slid into the seat across the aisle from him. He placed the book in his lap. Beside him, a lump of blankets stirred. I decided to ignore Ernest Perron's presence.

"You're not asleep."

I shook my head slowly. "I have too much on my mind."

"As do I. Even Churchill can't put me to sleep." He tapped the book and smiled. Since London, few moments of pleasantness had passed between us. I was glad for this little bit of humor.

"Very boring, then?"

"Quite the contrary. He offers a blueprint that I'd like to follow." He rubbed his face, yawned and stretched. I looked around the darkened cabin. Ardeshir was awake as well. I smiled at him, and he nodded sleepily.

"We've done well, Soraya. Maybe even better than I'd hoped in normalizing relationships with the West. Moscow is its own challenge, but I'm thinking beyond this summer to the fall."

"Always the chess master."

Mohammed laughed. "Indeed. While we're pieces marching afield, we still have to be very much concerned with those closer to home. The Iraqis, most certainly. Perhaps the Saudis.

"Depending upon when you become pregnant, we'll adjust the schedule. From what I understand, the stress of travel may not be good for you then."

I folded my hands in my lap and looked down at them. I straightened my wedding ring. "That's true." Typical of him, Mohammed had taken part of what I'd said and twisted it to reflect his own version of reality.

"I've been thinking about King Faisal. He could be a very valuable ally." Just as quickly as Mohammed had dropped in a reference to my situation, he immediately returned to affairs of state.

"I agree." I struggled to keep my tone neutral. When Mohammed was like this, he was insensible to anything but himself and his rule.

"That is why I'm thinking of having my daughter accompany us when we visit him."

I immediately felt anxious for the young woman who was his child by Queen Fawzieh, and who had been living abroad since their divorce.

I thought of a dozen responses and questions but hesitated. I was used to Mohammed being preoccupied with matters of politics and policy, but none of that prepared me for what I sensed was coming next.

The shah filled the void. "It's time to consider her marriage. A strategic move would not be the worst of things."

I saw Ardeshir turn in his seat. I knew that the shah couldn't see his young aide, but I watched him intently.

"Has she mentioned a desire to be married? Does she have any interest in Faisal?"

"What my daughter wants and what's good for us are not of a piece. What I'm suggesting makes sense logically. A union between our two families will help provide some stability in the region. Much-needed stability, I might add."

Ardeshir sat up in his chair, his face stricken. I was too involved in my own thoughts to consider Mohammed's thoughts fully, but clearly Ardeshir was not in favor of this plan.

"Logic? Stability? You make it sound as if all you care about is strategy, and not your daughter's interests. She's not a product to be exported, a trade agreement to be hammered out. She's your child."

I had the sense that we shouldn't have been in an aircraft. We should have been bouncing along a rutted road outside our medieval castle.

"And what if she could be happy and provide us with other benefits, as well? There's no harm," Mohammed said dismissively, obviously eager for the conversation to be over.

Realizing this was how my husband thought of his own marriage to me, I struggled to put into words what I was feeling. "Princess Shahnaz and I are not close since I'm not her mother. However, I have to speak up. Shouldn't she be allowed to marry someone she loves? Shouldn't she be allowed to marry someone who loves her? Why can't this be about an affair of the heart, and not of the state?"

The shah stared at me. I was unaware that my voice had risen considerably, but given his angry expression, I knew that I'd erred. Struggling to make him understand, I turned to Ardeshir. "What do you think? Princess Shahnaz and King Faisal? Would such a match be wise? Especially given that she is only fifteen?"

Ardeshir stood in line of sight of the shah. "I always considered King Faisal to be ..."

Ardeshir's resolve wilted and collapsed in face of the shah's harsh glare. He shut his eyes for a moment and stifled a wince. What came out of his mouth were the words of the man the shah had appointed to the position of chamberlain. "Iran and Iraq have many interests in common. Perhaps it is best if their interests were more aligned. The type of marriage being suggested might prove rewarding for all parties." Clearly flustered, Ardeshir wiped his hands on his thighs. His actions were those of a man sorely conflicted about being forced to speak words he didn't truly believe.

"That's correct, Ardeshir. I see that you understand my rationale better than my wife does." Mohammed's self-satisfied expression made me cringe.

Ardeshir spoke again, his voice hesitant. "I know that the princess is a great beauty. If things did not work out as planned, many other suitors, perhaps some more to her liking, would be easily found."

The shah had already turned to his book again. I watched Ardeshir fumbling nervously with papers he'd rolled into a tight scroll. I couldn't contain the smile that crept across my face as his difficult position became clear. The man had his own interest in Princess Shahnaz—a fact I couldn't resist filing away.

"I trust your trip went well."

I squinted in the harsh light of a hallway in Ekhtesasi. The queen mother stood with her arms folded in front of her as she rocked on her heels.

"Would you like to come in?" I was barely awake.

"I won't be but a moment." Unfolding her arms, she produced two small pills.

When I didn't offer up my palm immediately, the old woman wrapped the pills in her fist and shook it, saying, "Take these with your next meal. Unless there's been some development I haven't been told about?"

"No developments. What are they?"

"Red clover and shatavari. They should aid in fertility. There's an old tradition linking them with it."

I held out my hand and watched the pills tumble into it.

"I'm glad you're back for a bit. Now you can turn your attention to what matters most. I don't want to see you wasting any time. That will only add to the rumors currently spreading."

"How do you know about such things—these herbs, I mean?"

The queen mother met my eyes with the full force of her malice. "I know that they are of far more use to you than a barren bride is to my son. That is all you need to know."

Without saying another word, she stalked off. I locked the door. Staring at the pills in my hand, I walked into the bathroom and, hesitating briefly, dropped them into the toilet. I was more certain than ever that this was not the first time that a Pahlavi had tried to poison me. I would do the best I could to make sure that this was the last. How sad my life had become: Everything was in question, everyone a potential suspect.

Chapter
TWENTY-ONE

*T*ell a lie, or tell yourself something often enough, and it becomes true. For two years, following examinations in Russia, Sweden, and France, I'd told Mohammed Reza that the doctors could find nothing wrong with me and that there was nothing they could do beyond tell us to be patient. I'd said this so many times that I believed that lie to be the truth. I'd told myself so many times that if I risked undergoing the procedure, I would end up dead at the hands of certain conniving Pahlavis, who could easily pay off a doctor to botch the surgery.

Each time I thought of lying in a surgical suite, staring up into the lights, I could feel my own heart stopping. For months I was plagued by a horrible dream. I woke up breathless and in tears, my heart racing and my pores oozing sweat. Instead of dreaming about a surgery gone wrong, I'd dreamed of nothing. Just a complete and utter blackness, impenetrable to light, sound, and sensation.

I dreamed of death.

Perhaps it was my heritage, but I'd always believed in signs and portents. I had vivid recollections of Bibi Maryam muttering a quick prayer under her breath whenever someone complimented me as a child. Although my mother forbade me from doing so, my grandmother instructed me to scratch my chin whenever I was praised. I can still see and smell the smoke of burning *esfand* wafting off the iron plate of Bibi Maryam's stove when we returned from the market. She'd burn the seeds to ward off the evil that came from someone commenting favorably on my appearance or behavior.

Along with that came my fear of those with the *cheshmeh shoor*, literally the "salty eye" or "evil eye." Even with my western education and my adoption of all things modern, there were some parts of my Persian upbringing I couldn't escape. Ernest Perron was one person who I considered to be *ghadameh shour* and a possessor of the evil eye. He was so frequently present when bad things happened that I couldn't escape those thoughts.

I can admit that superstition played a part in my decision not to undergo surgery. I believed that no good could come of it, and that people in my husband's circle would take the opportunity to do me harm. While Mohammed had not told me of these threats directly, in Germany he'd commented that he sensed that I was out for myself, hoping to raise my own profile at the expense of his and the throne's. I'd heard rumors that many at court shared that view, particularly his mother and his sisters. Keeping in mind that Ashraf had poisoned me to try to keep Mohammed from marrying me, what would they do now if given half a chance?

I also knew that paranoia is contagious. Mohammed suffered from it, which was understandable given his tenuous position. Seeing how he sent Forough away, and how he had appointed my father to an ambassadorship that removed my parents from Iran left me feeling that I was being plotted against. I was alone and defenseless.

The other way to build up one's defense against paranoia is to build a fortress of facts. When we returned from our overseas journey, I had plenty of time to assess things. I'd seen how Mohammed's advisors worked. They had encouraged him to cast aside Ardeshir's father, the man who played a key role in winning back his throne, and remove him from the prime minister role once he was no longer needed. The shah was well aware of the general's popularity with the people, and feared that he might lose his position of power and influence to him. Ardeshir and Forough had warned me about the rumors that my Bakhtiari heritage, once a prize, had become a liability. Most damning of all, the queen mother told me that I was useless unless I produced an heir.

In the end, I decided this: I wasn't being paranoid; I was being realistic.

My return to Tehran plunged me once again into darkness. Mohammed Reza seldom visited our bedroom, and conversations between us were infrequent and strained. It was as if beneath the thin veneer of our words ran a deep streak called "succession." Without allies and with nothing to do but ponder the succession issue, I finally came upon a solution.

Mohammad had abandoned the idea of his daughter marrying strategically, and Ardeshir and Shahnaz were to be married that October. One evening in late September of 1957, as their wedding date to Ardeshir Zahedi approached, the pressure to produce an heir before she did increased. I asked for and received permission to visit the shah during the day. However, when I arrived at his office, I was displeased to find Ernest Perron with him. I eyed the man suspiciously and then asked, "Can we please speak alone, Mohammed?"

The shah looked up from a sheaf of papers he was flipping through. "Anything you have to say can be stated in front of Ernest. I trust him implicitly. You know that." A smile of self-satisfaction slithered across the man's face.

Knowing that my time was limited, I plunged right in. "You keep telling me that the very future of the dynasty is at stake if I don't get pregnant and produce a male child. Why can we not make it so that if something were to happen to you, I would become the ruler?"

Without looking up, the shah replied, "You know very well that a woman can never rule Iran. It's out of the question."

"If the law states that a woman is prohibited, then why not change the law? If you want to appear to be a strong leader, why not make a bold move that insures your line will continue?"

Mohammed Reza set the papers down. His gaze landed on Perron, who nodded slightly. The shah smiled briefly at me. "Let me see what can be done. I also want you to know that all this will be resolved. It's all very complicated, and will take some time."

Although no more words were exchanged, it was very clear to me that my audience with my husband was over. As I walked out of the room, I caught Perron smiling at me. When I met his eyes, my husband's aide raised his eyebrows quizzically. Unable to bear it any longer, I sauntered out of the room.

As I walked down the hallway, I knew why Mohammed Reza had so readily agreed to my proposal. He'd already dismissed the notion as unviable and was merely placating me. I should have known it would be more complicated than that.

There was no escaping the issue of succession outside the palace walls as well. Although I had long suspected that someone was censoring my incoming mail, a deluge of cards and letters had been coming in with suggestions to aid conception: potions, incantations, positions, times of day. Some were ludicrous, others embarrassing, and still others made me wonder if I should agree to the surgery.

The counteroffer that Mohammed Reza presented to me as the solution arrived not long after my proposal to him. I'd heard whispers of it for a good while, and had worked very hard to ignore them.

Under only the direst of circumstances might I have considered what Mohammed Reza had to offer. What infuriated me nearly as much as what he presented, was how he chose to handle the situation.

As soon as I'd heard the woman's voice, I recoiled. Her tone was a mixture of unctuous insincerity and barely disguised triumph. I sensed that she had something to say that I didn't want to hear, but needed to.

"I'm quite busy." I knew that I should speak with her, and likely would. But still, making matters difficult for her had become almost a reflex.

"I would prefer to speak with you in person, but if you are so busy, I can do this now and be done with it."

"If time is of the essence, then tell me now." I moved from my desk to one of the chairs opposite.

"Time has been of the essence for the past seven years." Ashraf stopped herself and then sighed heavily. "But that's of little consequence."

"Then please get to what is consequential." I was irritated by this intrusion, and fearful of what the message might be.

"My brother has given considerable thought to your failure to produce an heir. Surely you realize that without a known successor to the throne, his position is weakened. You know what the people are demanding."

I wondered if Ashraf was speaking my husband's words or her own. I let her continue uninterrupted.

"He still loves you, and wishes that you continue to be his wife in spite of your shortcomings in this crucial area. One remedy is for him to take another wife who will bear him a son."

I suppose that I should have been shocked and appalled, but I'd been expecting this. I knew that my husband's father had taken more than one wife—perhaps not for this specific reason, but the law allowed a man to have multiple marriage "partners." I hated the practice in theory. Now that it was suggested as a way to solve our own problem, I loathed it even more. I saw no way that I could share my husband with another woman. I couldn't accept the notion that I was to be branded as barren. I wasn't going to be party to a practice that reduced women to being little more than brood mares, a practice that in the eyes of many of our new allies seemed antiquated at best and primitive at worst.

After a few moments, Ashraf asked for my response.

I refused to honor her request and returned the phone to its cradle.

I sat for a few moments, trying to hold myself together and urging myself to think logically. How did this new information fit into my plan of not having the surgery and keeping that decision from Mohammed Reza? I also wondered if maybe I was being unreasonable, refusing to accept the most logical choices presented to me.

A series of ifs cascaded through my mind: If I didn't want to have the surgery. If Mohammed Reza didn't want to wait any longer for me to bear a child. If I wanted to remain married to a man I truly loved. If the country's political stability was threatened.

Wasn't what he was suggesting the most logical answer? But to my mind, logic had little to do with it.

If I was refusing to solve the problem either through surgery or by this latest means, then why? Was I rebelling on behalf of all women? Was I testing the shah, seeing how far I could push him before he abandoned me? Was I thinking that if I so longed for unconditional love, and if he could pass this test, then maybe he truly did love me?

For years, I had wondered if perhaps that was what was preventing me from conceiving. It wasn't the excess of mucus, the clogged and nearly impassable fallopian tubes the doctors went on and on about.

In the end, my refusal to respond to Ashraf was all the answer I gave to my husband. I can see now that some might question, not so much my choice, but my refusal to confront him. I have no good answer for that. I was hurt. I felt guilty about my deception. I wanted and needed to believe that he would express his faith in me, in our future, in our love. He had chosen his own emissary to deliver his offer. I allowed my silence to serve as a statement. If I did not respond, it was because the question had not been put to me.

Mohammed Reza gave no indication of his displeasure with my silence and thereby saying no to his proposition. We'd grown so cold toward one another by that point, I imagine that he thought of it as nothing personal. He was merely making a business offer, and I'd declined. He had other plans to back up any that might fail. That didn't prevent him from sending Ardeshir Zahedi to speak to me about the possibility. Ardeshir didn't say that he was speaking on behalf of the shah, but I suspected as much. He addressed his concerns in the costume of a man about to be married himself to a member of the royal family. After speaking briefly about his own circumstances, he then began to address my situation.

Yet, even as I fretted over my own future and that of my good friend Ardeshir, I knew that I wouldn't change the essential part of myself that believed that love is for life, and that it can and should endure all complications. Perhaps I was clinging to some fairy tale notion of idealized love. Maybe I couldn't accept the political realities of a monarchy.

But one thing I knew for sure: I couldn't accept the idea of multiple partners in a marriage.

As a result of all this, I was profoundly wounded. That made me vulnerable and irrational and more likely to lash out before thinking. I knew I had to keep my wits about me, but it was difficult to do so. I was reminded of when I was a little girl and one of my teeth came loose. How the pain troubled me and how resistant my tongue was to obeying the command to stop poking and probing. How deliciously pleasurable was the self-inflicted pain.

One evening in February of 1958, I stood with the shah in a garden at Golestan Palace. The blue-green waters of a reflecting pool captured the arched windows in its stillness. The distant sounds of the streets of

Tehran carried over the walls, and the trees stood frozen at attention, as anticipatory and mute as Mohammed and I were. Under any other circumstances, it would have been quite beautiful. Instead, an air of foreboding made it difficult for me to breathe.

I followed my husband's gaze to the Marble Throne Veranda. Many years before, his father had the audacity of certain rulers to coronate himself by placing the crown on his head with his own two hands, much like Napoleon had once done. What arrogance that must have taken! Yet, in that moment I understood the impulse: the drive to take command of one's own fate, to seize control in defiance of all reason.

"Perhaps it is best if I leave Tehran for a while. Once the Majils have the constitutional issues worked out, I can return."

My words came in a single tentative breath. I could imagine them taking substance in front of me, hard glittering objects like diamonds, their facets reflecting the light of the just-risen moon. In a moment, those diamonds were reduced to dust.

"I think that is wise."

Instead of moving to comfort me, the shah turned his back on me and walked a few steps away, his hands clasped behind his back as if he was the prisoner.

He had said the last thing I wanted to hear. I'd been hoping for something as simple as my husband saying, "No. Stay." That had proven to be too much to expect. The wind picked up, and the image in the reflecting pool shattered. I drew my sweater more tightly around myself.

Alone in the gathering darkness, I was unwilling or unable to stay still long enough for the first star to appear. My head bowed, I walked into the house, hoping to hear footfalls behind me. However, nothing but the hollow ringing of my own steps reached my ears.

In my haste, I had pushed against Mohammed Reza, and he had

pushed back rather than gather me in his arms. I took some comfort in knowing that I'd made the suggestion, the choice, to leave. When you feel as if you are losing everything, even such a small victory eases some of the pain. To be honest, I wasn't feeling much of anything those days. I was hollowed out, a reed through which the wind blew, sounding little more than a faint anthem to my stubborn pride.

The truth of it was that as much as I was fearful for my own life, as much as I contemplated the idea that a kind of curse had been placed on me, Mohammed Reza and I were engaged in a test of each other's pride and will. That was just the latest battle that we'd waged on and off for years.

He wanted to be the leader of the nation, the singular figure who led his people into modernity and prosperity. I wanted to be his partner in that, to have my input recognized and valued, if not by the people generally, then certainly by him and those in his inner circle. He wanted a wife who was dutiful and willing to sacrifice her needs and desires for his. I wanted a husband who was willing, if to not break, then at least to bend traditional views of women. He wanted me to swallow my pride and agree to his taking another wife. I wanted him to swallow his pride and accept me as I was, childless or not.

As the saying goes, pride goes before a fall. I had just started my descent, and in some ways the sensation of losing this test of wills freed me. I felt a kind of release that comes with relinquishing control.

I had packed just a few things and made certain my goodbyes came across as farewells lacquered with a coating of a defiant "I will be back." My pride wouldn't allow me to let on that I knew in my heart of hearts that I would never see Tehran again as its queen. It took just one more nudge from the universe to let me know that was to be the case.

The morning after I had suggested that I leave, I received an envelope, slid beneath my door. When I looked to see who had delivered it,

I found the hallway empty. I didn't recognize the handwriting, which had only my name in a tight, thin, masculine scrawl on it.

Inside I found a letter from the hospital in New York, addressed to me, inquiring about my decision regarding my infertility surgery. In the margin, in the shah's neat script were penned the words, "You betrayed me?" The letter was dated May 7, 1956, months after my initial visit and now nearly two years later.

At first I was livid, crumpling the letter into a ball and tossing it aside. I tore around the room looking for other things to throw, but each item I picked up seemed to say to me that the accusation was true. I had betrayed my husband's faith in me. I had lied to him, and no matter how good the reason for doing so, I understood his anger. What I found unacceptable was that he didn't even have the strength to confront me personally. Not about the taking of a second wife, and not about his discovery of my deception.

The letter had been sent to him in mid-June, weeks before our final confrontation that resulted in me suggesting I leave. He had known for that long and hadn't said a thing to me. Instead, he shut me out and let others plant seeds in his mind about next steps. It was his pride that didn't allow him to accept the fact that I was human, prone to error and misjudgment, frightened and frustrated.

If he'd chosen to berate me, at least that would have been a sign that he cared. This simple declarative sentence telling me that I betrayed him barely fed the hunger I felt. He may as well have said, "You have brown hair," or "You are part German."

Both of those were traits I possessed, but they weren't essentially who I was.

As I stood in my bedroom, leaning against the door, I sank to the ground. Pounding my thighs with my fists in frustration and anger, I thought: Was this what he thought of me? Was this the conclusion that he came to after all these years? That I was a betrayer, a traitor, someone who committed an act of treason against my king and my people?

Why couldn't he respond as a man would, and not as a head of state? I wanted some kind of trial, a chance to defend myself. Instead, I was summarily convicted. There was no trial, no dramatic moments, just a letter slipped under a door.

It didn't even matter to me who had delivered the message. I imagined that this was one of Ernest Perron's machinations, a way to rub salt in the wound. Whether it was another example of Mohammed's weakness or pride didn't matter. He wouldn't stand up to whatever pressures he was under to be rid of me.

I ask you: Who was the betrayer, and who was the betrayed?

On hands and knees, blinded by my tears, my heart a painful jagged stone piercing my chest, I crawled to the phone and began dialing Ardeshir at his hotel in Switzerland. Realizing that the line was not secure, I hung up before the connection was made. I knew that I couldn't speak openly to my mother or father. I believed that the sooner I left, the better. I wondered briefly what schemes the shah's people had already set in motion, in whose hands my fate resided. Now that I'd started this, what would they do to arrest it or to aid it?

Although I had hoped better of myself, I hated thinking that all the various courtiers and other hangers-on would feel victorious when they learned of my absence. Still, I thought, going away would be good for me. I could use it to forge a plan, a way to ensure that although I was gone, I would not be forgotten. I still held out hope that the simple strategy of trusting in my love for the shah would help me win.

As the plane banked after its takeoff from Mehrabad, I got a good look at the city laid out below me. I remembered again when I was a little girl, and I'd imagine that the small blue plane flying over Isfahan was the shah's. I wondered if there was another little girl now, playing in one of the parks or squares, shielding her eyes from the sun's glare, admiring the empress as she flew overhead. I wished in that moment that I had the power to intervene in that imagined girl's dreams, to let her know that like Icarus, there was a danger in flying too close to the sun. That coming so close to one's dreams could result in the warmth of a winter's sun changing to a burning flame that consumed all it came in contact with.

Chapter
TWENTY-TWO

As the days passed, in spite of my dire circumstances, I still clung to hope. I chided myself for my self-pity, realizing that I wasn't a former royal quite yet. And what of the question mark that the shah had added to the end of his damning notation on the letter? I'd assumed that the comment had been directed at me, but what if he was simply querying his own sense of things? Maybe he was puzzling out what to make of this information about the possibility of surgery aiding my fertility? Had I been too hasty in assuming that he had passed judgment upon me? Might he have been accusing the person who gave him the letter of betrayal?

And exactly who was it that slipped the letter beneath my door? Shams and Ashraf could have had easy access to the shah's office. That oily devil Ernest Perron was my initial suspect. *From fairy tale to detective novel*, I thought ruefully. So typical of the palace intrigues. At least there was some consistency in their approach. The shah's office issued a press release announcing that the queen had gone to St. Moritz on holiday. I played along for a while. That was a nice gesture, letting everyone believe that I was performing perfect stem christie turns down the slopes, when in reality it felt as if I was tumbling downhill in an avalanche. The truth was, I was trying to maintain my balance, maintaining some semblance of control.

After that, I joined my family in Cologne. This was a good idea in some regards, although February's darkness and cold could put a damper on anyone's spirits.

I spent the first few days hiding out in my parents' home. I remembered a bit of old personal magic: If you want to make the phone ring, place yourself far from it. I poured myself a glass of cognac and curled up in the sitting room with a cigarette.

This power over telecommunications, at least, had not abandoned me. As I ran to the front hallway to pick up the receiver, I already knew who it was, as if he had his own special ring. For that reason, I did not say hello but at first only listened. My heart pounding and beads of sweat gathering on the back of my neck, the sound of his voice soothed my anxiety. Answering his greeting, observing basic Persian social pleasantries, I asked after his health and family. Everyone was fine.

"Have you reconsidered my proposal?"

I didn't comment on his unfortunate word choice. Mohammed Reza was determined to take on a second wife.

"You know that I have. And you also know that I have rejected it." If Mohammed was going to use a businesslike tone, then so was I. The unreality of discussing our future life together like a salesperson and a prospective client saddened me. Fortunately, I could keep those emotions from coloring my tone.

"Well, then …" Mohammed Reza's voice registered some surprise and perhaps a bit of disappointment.

"And how does that make you feel?" I asked, hoping that choosing the direct route would allow us both to arrive at a destination—one that he wasn't eager to get to.

"I need to take what you've said into consideration. It's really quite—complicated."

I wanted to scream at him, to let him know that actually, no, things were quite simple. Did he love me enough to deal with the consequences of my choice not to have surgery? Did he care enough about our future together to simply be patient?

I was a haltered horse, a thoroughbred made to run, but was being held back by some other essential part of my nature, something inexplicable to me then.

"Has a decision been reached?" I chose my words carefully. I couldn't ask him if he had decided whether or not (as our predecessors stated it) to put away his wife. I knew that the issue was too bound up with his mother's wishes, with Shams and Ashraf, and no doubt with Ernest Perron.

"Not yet. I will inform you next week."

I was on the verge of asking another question, when I heard the click.

How stubborn is our hope and our hearts! The process repeated itself each day for a week. Every time the phone rang, I expected Mohammed to say that he had reconsidered, that he'd come around to my way of thinking. I even had the audacity to hope that he would say that he loved me. I have no doubt that he wished that my response would be different as well. But we were distant planets, spinning in our own separate orbits.

Then the calls ended.

When hope leaves, illness rushes in to fill the void. I spent the next few days in bed.

My mother's tapping at the door, her inquiries, and her urgings went unanswered. One night, I woke from a bad dream shivering. Knocking over a lamp to reach the phone, I fumbled with the dial, in my frenzy getting the number wrong again and again. Finally, I made the connection. "Can I speak to my husband?"

A pause on the end of the line, a muffled bit of conversation, then another voice that chilled me.

"His majesty is asleep," Ernest Perron said, and I felt my shivering double in intensity. "Please, I …"

"He has asked not to be disturbed unless it is a matter of national emergency." The man's sibilant *s* festered in my ear. "Is there something I might assist you with?"

Cradling the phone, I felt a wave of nausea overtake me. I leaned over the bed, gagging emptily, the bitter taste of bile rising in my throat. The man hadn't referred to me as Your Highness and made no effort at all to acknowledge my role as empress. I knew what that meant.

As I sank back into the bed, my father simultaneously knocked and entered.

"Soraya, are you all right?"

"Just restless," I said, sitting up. Something—Baba, having seated himself at the foot the bed, but most of all, my present reality—reduced me to little-girlhood.

"I just called him, hoping to hear his voice," I confessed, falling into my father's arms.

"Raya," said Baba firmly, holding my teary face up to look me in the eyes. "Remember, you're an empress. You must be strong. The shah loves you. You must be patient. Stop hiding your face. You have nothing to fear. You will go back to your husband in no time, I trust in that. In the meantime, why don't you go out, be seen in public, put a stop to all the tongues wagging about trouble at court?" He kissed the top of my head and left.

I sat awake for a while, thinking over his advice.

The late February chill wisped around the towering spires of the Cologne Cathedral. I joined the thousands of sightseers who had come that day to gawk at this Gothic immensity, recently restored to prewar glory.

Having completed my outdoor sightseeing in record time, I proceeded inside. Behind the high altar, I occupied myself in pacing about the walls of the great reliquary. I appraised the enameled depictions of the flashpoints of sacred history idly, finding little that could take my mind off my own history. I could not help but pause in front of the statue of the three kings.

"Gentlemen," I quietly addressed the bones contained therein, "I gather your journey here was a winding one. Some say you hail originally from Persia. If so, please accept my special greetings. Except that, if so, I don't suppose it's a good sign. Like someone's bidding me: Come on in, climb inside, mix your remains with those of your countrymen."

I screwed up my face at the morbidity of my own wit, and then turned to walk away.

In the touristy semi-hush of the cathedral, I muttered, "Anyway, you were probably from Babylon."

So much for my father's advice.

That night, at least, there were no nightmares and no desperate dialing in the dark, although the urge to do so remained.

The next day, I awoke early, got dressed, and headed downstairs for breakfast. Glenda, the family's long-time housekeeper, started with fright when I walked into the kitchen.

"*Mein Gott!*" She held her hand to her heart and then pressed her doughy face against mine. The scent of cinnamon and allspice had me eager for strudel. I sipped coffee and waited for the fresh-from-the-oven treat, suddenly back in 1939, girlishly kicking my legs in anticipation.

While I waited, my mother joined me.

"You're up and about early." Her tone was level, conferring neither judgment nor hope. "Yes. I thought I might do some shopping today. I hadn't thought things through as I might have." I plucked at the collar of a thin cotton sweater set. "I've been freezing."

"I always admired that lovely fur you got." Eva set down her coffee cup and rested her elbows on the table. "I'm so sorry."

"Mother, there's nothing to be sorry for. You can say it." Eva shook her head in rapid twitches.

"It was a wedding present. From Mohammed Reza." I helped myself to another bite of Glenda's flaky treasure. "Let's not do this, Mother. You were so right to encourage me to go out. I want to shop today and not think of anything else."

My mother and I spent a pleasant afternoon strolling the Friesenplatz and Ringe. Our arms laden with packages, we walked to the Weidengasse to meet Bijan at a Turkish restaurant.

Enjoying our anonymity among the various Indian, Italian, Greek, and Iranian émigrés, we both commented on how we felt as if we might have been back in Isfahan.

Standing in the vestibule, we spotted Bijan waving frantically. His blond hair had darkened slightly, and I noticed that his face was fuller, his eyes now pillowed on burgeoning cheeks.

"So good to see you, sister." Bijan folded me in his arms. "You're smoking again?" He contorted his face into a semi-serious snarl. "And I can see by your face that you're trying to quit."

After receiving our menus, Bijan rubbed his hands together. "So tell me, have there been any other envoys for you to dismiss?"

"As you know, I saw Amir Jang." I struck a match and paused.

"I know. I can't imagine what it was like having to square off against the patriarch of the entire clan," Bijan chuckled. "I'm sure he didn't take kindly to your rejection of the proposal."

Again with that word! I crossed my legs and leaned back in my chair. "He was fine."

Bijan snorted. "Fine? The man was likely apoplectic. They do love the idea of keeping you around and adding another. The old ways!"

"Bijan, please," Eva interrupted. "Show some respect."

"Don't tell me they've convinced you that taking another wife is a fair solution?"

"Of course not. But just because we disagree doesn't mean we can't be civil."

Bijan feigned throwing his menu over his shoulder. "Well spoken, Mother. For a moment, I thought Papa the diplomat had possessed you."

Eva eyed her youngest child. "We all have Soraya's best interests at heart. Remaining the empress is of great importance, but I've never advocated for the solution they're offering. I'm merely suggesting that we not do anything rash and burn any bridges."

During the exchange, I recalled how Amir Jang, ever the politician, had calmly accepted my response. He did suggest that I reconsider. I wondered if he wanted to reach across the table and throttle me, berate me for not having the good sense as he saw it, for all sides to win the day. Or perhaps he was glad to be rid of the Bakhtiari brat and was trying to suppress his joy. If Mohammed himself had come to plead his case, I might have reconsidered.

"And General Yazdanpanah and his wife, and Dr. Ayadi? What of them?" Bijan asked.

"I've chosen not to see them." I lifted my chin to expel a plume of smoke, as if indicating how easy it had been to dismiss those people. "I know what they have to say, and I don't want to hear it." In truth, it wasn't that easy to refuse to see Dr. Ayadi, a man whose honesty I had always appreciated. "But you did receive them, Mother?"

Eva held up two fingers to indicate the number of visits they'd paid.

"Persistent, aren't they?" Bijan turned his attention back to me. "Wasn't he someone you trusted?"

"Once upon a time, yes, but things have changed. I trust no one now." I stubbed out my cigarette and gave Bijan my best fake smile. "Not even you."

Bijan gasped exaggeratedly, "*Moi?*"

"You. You tell us this place has the best *çiğ köfte* ever, and I haven't seen a single plate of it go by."

Bijan shrugged his shoulders exaggeratedly. "There's no accounting for taste."

My jibe at Bijan had the desired effect. The conversation meandered over a variety of topics, but not the Pahlavis and what the shah might be thinking. There was a grain of truth in my statement that I no longer trusted anyone.

The last time I had spoken to Mohammed, there had been such tenderness in his voice. Once again I told him I would not accept another woman in our marriage. I said that I hoped to return home soon, but he hadn't fully committed to that idea. Even with his reluctance, I got the feeling that for once he was speaking from his heart. Over the years, he'd admitted that I alone possessed the ability to disarm him. In leaving Tehran, I hoped that the simplest thing—his missing my presence in his life—would be enough to settle the issue. I clung to the notion that with all the options available to him, he would surely see the wisdom in remaining with me, the woman he loved.

Later, our Mercedes pulled into the driveway and was suddenly overtaken by a swarm of photographers. Eva got out first to distract the paparazzi and news reporters. They unleashed a barrage of questions: "*Wie lange bleiben Sie in Köln?*" "What's to become of your marriage?" "*Was haben Sie von ihrem Mann gehört?*" "Is it true that you are unable to …?"

They went unanswered. I fled into the house, covering my face. "Were there any calls from the palace?" I asked Glenda optimistically.

"No, no calls for today."

A few minutes later, Eva and Bijan entered the house. Eva's concern was etched in her face.

"Mother, I understand you want to comfort me, but when you look at me with those eyes, it makes me think that on top of my own suffering, I have to look after your feelings as well." My mother cast down her face, her eyes suffused with reserved tenderness.

I pinched the bridge of my nose. "I'm sorry. I don't know what overcame me. I'm feeling okay one minute, and we come home to that," I gestured vaguely toward the door, "and the next minute I'm ready to brutalize someone."

"Why not take it out on Shams or the other one? Any of those bitches and bastards," Bijan said, rising to both his mother's and my defense.

"I don't know why you insist on running down every Pahlavi …" I began, and then abandoned the effort out of exhaustion.

"Because they deserve it. Look what they've done to you." Bijan's earnestness touched me, but I had reached my limit for the day and for the foreseeable future. I skulked out of the room, my brother's plaintive apology trailing behind me.

A moment later, Bijan knocked at my door. "Soraya, please let me in."

I waited for a few moments before unlocking the door.

"I'm sorry," he said.

"Don't say that if you don't even know why you're apologizing."

Bijan stood with his hands on his hips, staring wide-eyed at me. "I may not know exactly what offense I've committed, but I do know that you're not yourself."

"How can I be when I'm surrounded by people who have so little faith in me? Between your hateful words and Mama's constant hovering over me like I'm an invalid, I can't get a moment's rest."

"We're all simply trying to offer you our support in whatever meager ways we can." Bijan's sounding like the offended party only made me feel worse.

"Then tell me that I've nothing to fear; that my husband still loves me, always will, and that everything will be okay."

"Fine. Then as you say. All of that is true." Bijan spoke with an earnestness that touched me.

"Oh, Bijan, you don't understand. I have to believe those things are true. Otherwise my whole life has been for naught." I sank onto the bed, and he joined me there.

"If I'm not with him, then who am I?"

"You're my sister, and I love you very much."

Before I could respond, Mater stood in the doorway. Behind her, Baba stood in the hallway.

My father said, "Soraya, you have a phone call. It's Ardeshir. He'd like to speak with you."

I stiffened as Bijan hugged me again and then left the room.

"I'd like to take the call in here, if you don't mind." My voice sounded strange to me, as if it was being broadcast through a tinny speaker. My mother nodded and smiled grimly. It had been nearly two weeks since I'd heard from my friend in Tehran. All of our previous conversations since my departure had been curt, officious even—almost as though we were the ones struggling with the decision.

From Ardeshir's somber tone, I knew immediately, but I scrambled to mentally assemble a wall to keep the news from penetrating.

"It is always a pleasure to hear from you, Ardeshir." I resorted to casual politeness as a first line of defense.

"And I as well, under most any other circumstances." I was certain that Ardeshir was crying, or at the very least on the verge of tears. "This evening the shah has addressed the Iranian people, announcing your divorce to the nation. I don't know if you have heard yet, but I was asked to inform you."

I fell to my knees, still cradling the phone. A moment later, I dropped the receiver and sat back on my heels. Then, as if some genetic switch had been thrown, I rocked back and forth. My forehead touched both the rough edge of a rug and the cool of the walnut floor.

Then I threw my head back and stared at the ceiling. Anyone seeing me would have thought that I was a Muslim at prayer; I was anything but. The tidal pull of my mourning ultimately dragged me under, and just before I drowned, before the blackness overtook me, I emitted a guttural cry that brought everyone running to my side.

My stuttering sobs shook me, and as I bit the inside of my cheek, the coppery taste of blood filled my mouth. At that moment I realized that our hearts don't break at such moments. The stupid muscle kept pumping away, insensible to my prayer that it cease. I was once again unheard and utterly useless, powerless, and out of control. The strangeness of that freedom so frightened me. I longed for the blackness to overtake me so that I might feel something familiar; anything but the vast emptiness that was my uncertain future.

INTERLUDE

Raya's Version

MAY 2001

Chapter
TWENTY-THREE

I can't say for certain whether telling us the story of her divorce was cathartic for Soraya. The four of us—Soraya and I, Dolores, and Estrela—had gathered as usual after dinner, this time lingering in the dining room. A cold front had blown in, and the air howled, rattling the windows. After we had eaten a wonderful dinner of sepia, Dolores warmed up Soraya's audience with a very different kind of story. She told us about the first time she'd seen cuttlefish in its raw state. Estrela laughed at her mother's recounting of her shock at its bizarre appearance. She whispered to me that in her family, they had a Tio or Uncle Cuttlefish, nicknamed for his bulbous nose and bushy walrus-like moustache. Of course, few dared to call him that in his presence.

The two hoteliers seemed intent on being particularly lively that evening, substituting an overstated joviality for their usual low-key pleasantness. I joined in, all of us aided by several glasses of rioja that flushed my cheeks the color of the wine. It seemed as if we were all laboring to offset the sadness that we knew was coming. And we were fascinated as Soraya spelled out her reasons for not undergoing the surgery that might have saved her marriage.

When Soraya was finished, I could see that she was quite drained.

Estrela got up from the table to bank the fire that had diminished in the hearth. As she poked its embers, she asked Soraya if she regretted her decision.

Soraya answered without hesitation. "No. Even if I had given birth to a future shah, he wouldn't have really been my child. I'm certain that the Pahlavis would have taken him away from me. They would have dictated where he was to be educated and all the rest ..." She paused and covered her face with her hands. She sighed heavily, and the three of us got up from our seats to comfort her. Soraya looked up at me and smiled. "If you'll excuse me."

I assumed that Soraya needed to compose herself. I waited in the dining room with our hosts, and in a few minutes, she rejoined us.

"Betrayed him!" Dolores said to Soraya. "What nonsense. The man knew nothing of betrayal." She proceeded to tell us about "her Vincent," who'd been dragged away by Mussolini's troops in 1942 in the aftermath of the civil war. A neighbor, a man who coveted the hotel and often tried to buy it, had claimed that Vincent was a sympathizer with a faction of the Basques who were anti-Republican. The man made up stories about Vincent being a leader of an underground movement bent on undermining Mussolini's regime.

"The last I saw of him, he was being led away behind a horse, his legs in shackles, his hands behind his back. I was holding Estrela, who was crying loud enough to drown out my shouts. Vincent never turned back." Dolores brought her cross to her lips and kissed it. "This was the final gift he gave me."

Soraya said, "It's exquisite. How you must treasure it."

Estrela added, "I wish I had known him. Maybe then I could have avoided my own heartache."

She'd fallen in love with Roberto, a Basque separatist who fled the Navarre region and hid out in Castejón. "I had no idea he was being sought for a bombing. He came here, we met, and I had no reason to ask any questions about those kinds of things." They married, and two years later, Roberto decided he could no longer hide and turned himself in. "I go sometimes to the prison, but Roberto discourages me from doing so. The night he left was the first I'd heard of who he really was, what he believed in, what he was willing to die for."

When it was my turn to relate my romantic history, I took a deep breath. As I tried to gather my thoughts on how best to tell my story and where to begin, embarrassment washed over me. I had sat, night after night, accompanied by Dolores and Estrela, listening intently to Soraya's triumph and defeat. Surely it was a story worthy of the big screen, fit for Hollywood. I had spent my entire adult life defending Soraya in the face of all who criticized her. I had told people that she was human, that what the shah had done to her was devastating, and why she had every right to have been scarred by it all. I still believed that to be true. But in that moment, as I glanced at the mother and daughter sitting before me, their hands rough and their skins weathered, I wondered if I had in fact anything to complain about. The notion of loss is universal. We all share in common the sense of loss in one form or fashion—some greater than others. The truth was that Soraya and I had battled the wars of life in very different ways, but we still were fortunate with so much at our disposal. In no way did I feel less admiration for the woman I had so looked up to all my life. I just did not know if I, myself, was worthy of sympathy.

Soraya's captivating eyes locked on mine. "Go on, Raya." Dolores and Estrela leaned in closer.

"Nothing. I have nothing to say … other than that the man who shattered my heart is not worthy of my wasting this beautiful evening with you fine women. The past is indeed the past. I do believe, as the Dalai Lama puts it: 'Remember that not getting what you want is sometimes a wonderful stroke of luck.'"

Both Estrela and Delores clapped in agreement. Soraya looked at me from the corner of her eye, her face turned as if she had called my bluff.

I decided to brief them on what had happened with Sergio and me, not wanting to go into any great detail. For the most part, I elaborated on my desire to find Soraya in my state of desperation.

Estrela shifted in her seat and reached for her glass. "Like we say in Spain, for every fall, a rise awaits you."

I reflected that that didn't seem to have been true for Soraya, at least not until this point. "What a group we are," Soraya said.

"Men. Their foolish choices." Dolores snuffed out a candle with her fingertips. Throughout my telling, I'd been stealing glances at Soraya, hoping that somehow my tale of woe had meant something more to her than the ones that Dolores and Estrela had told since she could relate to it more. I don't know how I would have been able to assess that—whether it would have been some look in her eye or something she might have said—but I detected nothing beyond her distant look, the familiar carriage of her head and chest. She seemed like an image emblazoned on a coin, or a woman waiting for a crown.

I also thought that Soraya looked as healthy as at any time I'd known her. I don't know if the old wives' tale about the good that fresh air can do for one is true, but it seemed to be so in Soraya's case. Her skin had a healthier glow than I'd seen it possess. Her eyes were bright and signaled an alertness that she had lacked those first few times we had met in Paris. It was as if being away from everything that was familiar to her had somehow restored her. She wasn't drinking any more or any less than she had, so I didn't know what to attribute this change to, but I was glad for it.

Some people seem to possess the power to draw attention to themselves. For better or worse, that was Soraya. I don't think she did this on purpose. There was something elemental about her, a magnetism that had drawn me to her, as it had the other two women. In a way,

Sorayamania still existed, although it was diminished, reduced on our journey to a small circle. For someone who had been spending the recent years of her life in semi-seclusion, this exposure to new people must have seemed more than enough.

Soraya suggested that we all go to the El Toro Rie, a tavern owned by Luca, a man who lived in town. Lately this had become another part of our nightly routine, so none of us were surprised by her suggestion. I went to my room to freshen up. My mother phoned me, and we had a fifteen-minute conversation, during which she asked again when I would come home and find work. After I hung up, I looked for Soraya, but she was not to be found.

Well after darkness had fallen, I walked from the hotel to El Toro Rie. On the way, I had some time to think about Soraya's non-reaction to my story. Part of me wanted her to rush into my arms and console me. Another hoped that she would offer some insight, some explanation that would enable me to better understand what had happened to me and how I could move forward. I didn't know whether to attribute her lack of a response to indifference, inability, or to her simply believing that I had to find my own way. In the end, I decided it was the latter. Considering all that Soraya had been through, it seemed to me that self-preservation was the concept that most rang true for her.

A small group of men sat at the bar, oblivious to my entry. A bull-fight was on the television, the announcer's rapid and high-pitched account riding a crest above the bar patrons' mumbled commentary. Luca stood with a towel over his shoulder, one hand resting on the beer taps, like the others in rapt attention. I waved my arms. When he saw me, he winked and nodded toward the far corner.

Soraya was seated at a table with her back to me and the rest of the bar's patrons. Her red wool jacket and matching beret were hanging from the back of her chair as if a bull had gored them.

When I took a seat opposite her, Soraya didn't acknowledge my presence at all, except to push a bottle toward me. The label read "Orujo," and I presumed the amber liquid Soraya's glass contained was the same.

Without prompting, Luca brought me an empty glass and one filled with water.

"It reminds me of Tresterschnapps." Soraya's voice was husky, and when I lifted the bottle and felt it nearly empty, I understood why.

I poured myself a finger of the liquid and sipped it. "Grappa. Or brandy? It's not really to my liking."

Soraya shrugged indifferently, "A gift from the men of Castejón de Sos. For the company of our pleasure."

I wasn't certain if Soraya was trying to be funny or ironic, or had simply had too much to drink.

I reached for my glass and sat back in surprise at the astringent scent of vodka. I looked at the second glass in front of Soraya, nearly empty and equally colorless. My heart went out to her. I knew that telling her story to us had been difficult. For that reason, I hadn't pressed her for more beyond what she'd already told me. I'd promised myself that I would be a willing listener, but that my days as her interrogator were over. That she was drinking heavily was evidence of the toll that I had exacted from her.

"You barely touched your dinner. Would you like me to order something for you here?" I didn't like sounding maternal toward Soraya, but in this case it couldn't be helped.

"Do you remember what my Bibi Maryam told me?"

I recalled the story of her grandmother telling her to get back on the horse after she had fallen. Soraya went on: "Well, that's what my father told me the night the shah made his announcement."

Even though I didn't like the taste of the brandy, I took another sip since I didn't have anything else to do. With my mouth otherwise engaged, I couldn't ask any questions.

Soraya looked at me expectantly. I remained silent. "Thank you for proving my point," she said at last and then finished off her vodka. For a moment, her eyes seemed to glaze over, but then their clarity and brilliance returned.

"You know, men are masters of misdirection. They tell you things, but only in the most obtuse of ways. With women," Soraya said, her eyes boring into me, "you know exactly where you stand."

"I think you know where I stand: by your side, aiding you in whatever way I can." Although my words seemed stilted and a bit formal, my sentiment was genuine.

"Raya, this escape with you has so enlightened me. I realize that through my life and extended travel, although I thought I had escaped, in reality I remained a captive of my past, and I held on to every bit of it. Getting to know you and trusting in you so much has allowed me for the first time to unload the burden of my life and reveal it in its entirety, truthfully." Soraya squeezed my hand, and again I was amazed by her grip, how her fingers felt like an eagle's talons. "If only there were more time."

She spoke those last words with an airiness that attempted to leaven them, but they felt even more freighted for the attempt.

"Well, we have the drive back to Paris. Have you given any thought to when you'd like to leave once the part for the car comes?" The last time I'd checked in with Miguel, he'd said it would be here in a matter of days.

Soraya shrugged, "I've no place to be other than where I am."

I felt a bit of a sting at that, and Soraya must have noticed it. "That's not to say that where I am isn't very pleasant. As is the company."

Even in her diminished state, her powers to charm were considerable. While I sat there feeling the warm glow of her compliment, she fished in her purse and produced a cigarette and a lighter. Her hands shook considerably as she tried to get it to spark. I considered doing it for her, as I was long since past the point when I thought her smoking was risky. I wanted her to enjoy what simple pleasures she could, while she still could.

"Does this mean that the car is repaired?" Soraya asked through a cloud of smoke. "Nearly so. Miguel has ordered the part he needs. We can be on the road in a day or so if you'd like."

"I'm in no hurry," Soraya said as Dolores and Estrela entered the tavern and joined us at the table.

As the night wore on and more alcohol was consumed, Soraya became someone I'd never thought I would see. As she told stories of her star-studded past, the years seemed to fall away from her face. I could envision her as the much-sought-after guest with the tragic history. That may be overstating the matter, for Soraya was one of those women who possessed such class that it was only in the passage of time that I came to see her in that light.

She regaled us with stories: of the time when she traded the peacock brooch she received on her wedding for a maid's feather duster; hung out with the hipsters at Frank Sinatra's Palm Springs home, Twin Palms; and endured the less-than-polite advances of an up-and-coming actor she referred to as Johnny Good Lookin'.

I have to admit that I became a bit jealous. For so long, Soraya had been mine exclusively, her stories shared only with me. Still, I was glad that she was enjoying herself and could briefly relive some of those glamorous days. I also realized that I was in the hands of master raconteur, or better yet, an orchestra conductor. Each story was like a movement in a symphony, a slight variation on a theme, each with an emotional color from the full spectrum. Soraya knew what this audience wanted from her. She was the celebrity in their midst, and nothing would do but hijinks and hilarity.

Later, long after the posted closing hour of the tavern had passed and the other two women went back home, her mood changed. To say she became that dreaded maudlin drunk would be to put it too strongly. She did, however, slip off into a kind of public reverie that was at odds with how private and guarded she'd been for so long.

"I've lost everyone I ever loved," she said, staring into her drink. "The shah, and later Franco."

I had been wanting to ask more about her relationship with Italian film director Franco Indovina. I knew that she had become his mistress in the mid-sixties, when she was starting to act in some films. Many directors, including Fellini, had been interested in her at the time, drawn to her undiminished beauty. "You haven't talked about him yet; only the one time you mentioned him before. I know that he was the second love of your life."

Soraya's expression dimmed. "Franco wore his feelings not just on his sleeve, but over his whole body. He was so vocal, so spirited, had such a passion for life. That was what I adored about him. I was in a film he was directing, *Three Faces of a Woman*. He was in a loveless marriage, but since he was Catholic, he was unable to leave his wife. So we began an affair that turned into so much more. I knew he would have married me if he could."

"When Mohammed learned of *Three Faces of a Woman*, he was so upset that he had the Savak buy every copy of the print. He wanted me only for himself; even though years had passed, he was still so covetous. Why else would he allow me to retain any title at all in defiance of common practice?"

Ignoring the repetition, all I could do was shrug my shoulders and wonder for myself what it meant that every portrait of her in an official Iranian office or building was removed. Were the reminders too painful for him and his countrymen? I still had many photographs of Sergio and myself together, and as Soraya went on, I speculated about when I might remove them from my wallet, my walls, and from my memory.

"But then Franco died in a plane crash, in 1972," she continued. "His death was so public. His being just one among the hundred and fifteen always troubled me."

"How do you mean?"

"Well, all of Italy was in mourning. It was one of the worst aviation disasters in the country's history: so many lives, so much played out on a public stage. And there were even accusations that it was a bomb plot. The whole thing was dragged out and used by people to advance their own causes. I paid little attention to any of it. I suppose that's why I went into seclusion for so long afterward. I felt the need to mourn privately, to offset all the other noise. I wanted his death to be mine and mine alone. It was selfish, I know, but that's how love can sometimes be."

"It all must have been awful." While I felt sorry for her, I also took a guilty pleasure in her opening up to me; I felt as if I was gaining some admittance to an exclusive club.

"I remember it like it was yesterday. May in Rome is a gorgeous time of year, but with the elections coming up that next weekend, I barely wanted to leave the house. It's funny the things one recalls, but I was listening to the radio, Frank Sinatra singing 'Someone to Watch Over Me.' I'd just gone into the bathroom to take off my makeup when the song just stopped. An announcer came on with the first report about Flight 112. I remembered Franco's flight number because he'd joked that Alitalia made it easy for those coming from Palermo. 'One plus one is two,' he'd said. 'They don't want to tax the brains of the businessmen any more than necessary.'"

Soraya shut her eyes for a moment. "I was still toweling my face when I heard the news. I sank to the floor and knelt there on the tile. I kept looking up, hoping that I'd find myself someplace else, hoping that this wasn't happening. Then I'd sink back down and pray. I prayed that he'd somehow missed the flight."

"I can only imagine what you were going through. How terrifying it must have all been, not knowing."

"The English have an expression they use to describe how they feel when something painfully bad has happened to them. 'I'm gutted,' they say. And that's how I felt then. I recall imagining that I was like one of those fish in the market. I was emptied but still in pain, dully aware that I should get up and do something, but unable to move." Her lips quivered and her effort to hold back her tears had me on the verge as well. She ran her fingers along her mouth to still the trembling.

"For a long time after, I was angry at myself. I could have gone on the trip with Franco. He asked me to join him, but I was feeling drained. After, I wished that I had been there. I couldn't get out of my mind the idea that they were all sitting there, thinking of their arrangements. Who was greeting them at the airport? Would there be a cab? Would that large man with the oversize bag in the overhead do the right thing and not block the aisle? And then nothing. Did he suffer? Did he know in advance? Was his last thought of me?"

Soraya reached for her water glass and brought it to her mouth, her hands trembling. Eventually she regained her composure. She only rarely made eye contact with me when she spoke of the most emotional matters. The rest of the time, she looked into the near distance, as if in a trance. A few minutes passed without either of us speaking.

"I couldn't stay in Rome, of course. The city remains haunted to this day. There's little I can do about that but stay away."

"You didn't attend the funeral?"

For the first time, I aroused her irritation. "How could I, with his ex-wife and children there? I'd say that there was an equal division between mourners and tongue waggers. That he and I truly loved one another didn't matter in the end. I was wracked with guilt. I believed that everyone thought of me as a *comare*—a woman on the side. From the start, he told me that he would divorce his wife, and eventually he was true to his word and left her. Still, everyone thought they knew all about me and my marriage to the shah and this other man in my life—another public figure. I couldn't stand the thought of that scandal taking away from him and what he meant to me."

"Where did you go?"

"I made my pilgrimage back to Germany, to Munich and my mother." Soraya smiled.

"You and your mother remained very close?"

"Yes. She was a great help to me always, and even more so after Franco …"

Even after more than twenty years, she couldn't bring herself to say the word.

I got up from my seat to comfort her. Taking my hand from her shoulder, she brushed her lips against it. "Thank you for indulging me."

"I feel honored to have been able to hear it. Thank you for sharing it all with me."

It would be harsh of me to say that Soraya wallowed in self-pity when she went off on a tangent about how she felt herself to be cursed. She mentioned the captain of a cruise ship who dined with her and her family one night and was found dead in his quarters the next, the victim of a heart attack. Could I blame her for thinking that she was doomed by ill fortune when Franco, the only other man she admitted to having loved, died in a plane crash? And what of her claim that "they" had killed him? After all, from what I knew of all the palace intrigues and the cutthroat nature of that world and how she was dispatched from it, was it paranoia or perceptiveness that made her utter that claim?

As for her belief that she was cursed with bad luck, she brought up the question of whether it was the antibiotics used to treat her illness before her wedding that made her infertile. To hear her say, "Sometimes the cure is worse than the disease," as she gulped down another swallow of her drink, tested my powers to reserve judgment. It's difficult to say what cures and what ails when one feels nothing but pain.

Finally we walked back to the hotel. I have only a vague alcohol-influenced recollection of how Soraya and I parted that night. When I came downstairs late the next morning, Dolores was seated at the reception desk and Estrela was washing the windows in the dining room. When they saw me, they rushed to my side and escorted me into the kitchen. I noticed that they had admitted another guest into what had become Soraya's and my secret hideaway.

Dolores was on the verge of tears, while Estrela kept wringing her hands in her apron and saying, "*Lo siento. Lo siento.*"

At first I had no idea what she was apologizing for. When they brought me a plate of churros and a bowl of hot chocolate, I knew that something bad had happened. I immediately wondered where my friend was.

"Soraya? Is she all right?"

Dolores nodded vigorously, and Estrela shook her head with equal ardor.

"So ... which is it? What's going on?"

"Señorita, Soraya has left."

"Gone?" I asked.

"Yes. We checked her room this morning because she had asked us to rouse her at nine the other day."

In my hungover state, I was trying to figure out if they meant she had asked them a couple of days prior to this to wake her up this day at nine.

"I didn't get an answer when I knocked this morning. I went in and the room was empty. She'd slept in the bed, but everything of hers was gone." Dolores made a sweeping gesture with her hands, as if she had a broom and had cleared away everything.

"Not so," Estrela said. She held up her index finger and exited the kitchen. A moment later she came back with a book and handed it to me. "She left this for you."

It was Stendahl's *The Charterhouse of Parma*, a book she'd found in a small shop just outside of Lourdes. I quickly flipped through the pages, hoping to find a note, but there was none. My heart was racing; I could feel the alcohol leaching out of me, overpowering the smells of the chocolate and the sweets.

"Maybe she's coming back later? She just packed her things ..." My words trailed off. Even in my confused state, I knew that they sounded absurd. I stared down at the book as the breeze blew the pages, exposing the endpapers. Inside the front cover, Soraya had written, "For R. Love, S."

My knees went unsteady beneath me. I sat on a stool and sipped the chocolate, hoping that its heat would wake me out of my befuddlement.

"I'm sorry." Delores handed me a stack of currency. "She left this to pay the bill for you both. We can't possibly take it. It has been too much a pleasure for us all."

Of all I'd been through, and all that Soraya had said to me in the months I'd known her, that gesture made me cry the most. Somehow Soraya's leaving the money pierced the fog from the night before. I remembered her telling me about how ill-prepared she had been to live in the real world. Several weeks after she'd gotten the call that ended her life at court, she'd wandered down a seaside dock in Bermuda. She'd asked a local fisherman if he could take her out to sea for a ride. Of course, she said in that irony-free tone that I'd come to associate with her, she hadn't brought any money along to pay him. Fortunately, he recognized her and, as she put it, "I was able to overcome my imperial helplessness."

After some minutes, the boat pilot did as requested and shut off the motor. "We sat there a while, bobbing up and down, the only sound the waves lapping at the boat's sides. For a long time, throughout my entire marriage in fact, I'd experienced a kind of solitude. What I was experiencing on that boat was true solitude. I was at sea with that old self, the one in which I was so closely associated with the shah. I knew then that I was going to have to leave that person behind. The question was, Who was the person that was returning to shore?"

I spent a few more minutes with Delores and Estrela. I knew they wanted to know if the two of us had had a falling-out, but they didn't ask. The front desk phone rang, and I hoped that it was Soraya, offering some explanation for her sudden departure. A minute later, Estrela returned.

"That was Anna. She said that her brother Luca's car is gone. She believes that he has taken Soraya to the city to catch a flight."

I felt hurt, and wondered why Soraya felt the need to get away when she'd so clearly stated to me that she had no plans and could have remained in Castejón indefinitely.

Feeling depressed, I went to my favorite room in the hotel. It had yet to be remodeled and still had a very deep porcelain claw-foot bathtub. I sat on its edge while the water thundered into it. I looked up at a series of brass shelves and saw a sheaf of paper on one. Knowing that no one else used the room, I knew that I hadn't set them there.

It was a letter from Soraya. It began:

> My Dearest Raya,
>
> The night when I learned of Mohammed's decision, my father said to me, "Words hurt us. Words heal us. Most often, words simply fail us." Last night when you told us all about your troubles, I was too overcome to speak. I worried that I would say something hurtful, and I would not have been able to forgive myself if I had done so.
>
> I believe in my soul that you deserve better. Not just from Sergio, but from me, and from life. I am so

313

happy that I made your acquaintance, and that the two of us together found this place. Please do not worry that I am gone. Please excuse my not saying a proper goodbye. I hope that this last story that I tell you will take the place of those unfortunate formalities.

I have lost too many people in my life to feel comfortable saying goodbye. I have also arrived at a point when I believe that age excuses much. I know that it doesn't really, but if growing old is to have any advantage at all, and there are few that I can see, then I would at least like to believe that I am owed this indiscretion.

I realize that you came to me hoping for answers and that, of course, I can't provide them for you. No one can. What I can do is tell you one last story. As you read this, please imagine that you and I are together after having spent a warm summer day driving along a tree-lined lane for hours. We are sitting in a café together enjoying a coffee, knowing that each of us has found a life-long friend. We spoke very early on about beginnings and endings. For me, this was when my story truly ended.

Please take care of yourself and think of me as fondly as I think of you.

With love,
S

I eased myself into the water, feeling the tension go out of me. I turned to the pages, and there I began to read the ending that Soraya had chosen for herself.

PART IV

Soraya

Chapter
TWENTY-FOUR

hen I was with Mohammed Reza during those tumultuous times, it was difficult for me to understand fully how we were making history and what effect our actions might have. Throughout the winter of 1978 and early 1979, like everyone, I immersed myself in the news of what was taking place in Iran. It made my head spin; it haunted my dreams. Tens of thousands of striking oil workers, the protestors in the streets facing off against armed troops, the eerie shouting of Allahu Akbar now turned into a revolutionary slogan. The newspapers and television programs filled with conflicting reports from each side; death tolls, demands, and ultimatums.

In February, tears ran down my face for my husband and my country as I watched the images coming from the imperial pavilion at Mehrabad Airport. The shah and his third queen, both grimly officious, shook the hands of a few officers, functionaries, and advisers. What the cameras didn't pick up was a pair of palace guards falling to their knees to kiss the shah's feet as he walked to the plane and a future as uncertain as mine had been. I loved Mohammed Reza more than ever when I heard about how, with tears in his own eyes, he had bent to help those men up. I couldn't help but wonder whether, if I had been there long before the departure, I could have made him see not just the political necessity but the moral obligation to help so many others. Maybe things might have turned out differently.

It is true that we are judged by the company we keep, and Mohammed Reza was a terrible judge of those with whom he allied himself. I'd come to think that the role of an adviser is less to give counsel than to unfailingly praise the wisdom of one's leader. He'd gone from his original vision to the grandiosity of his one-party rule, with absolute control over the newspapers, resulting in a photo and story of him on the front page every day. Perhaps it was something inevitable, and I would have been powerless to prevent it. But I would have liked to have tried. As the old Persian saying states: "The sigh that escaped me when he'd wounded me, came back to capture him in return."

One year after the Peacock Dynasty ended, I was in Marbella, jogging along the water's edge in the early morning glow. Something overtook me, and I broke into a sprint. Like a horse suddenly going from a trot to a gallop beneath you, I was surprised and simply held on. It was as if I'd decided once again to be that gazelle-like girl who was chased but never caught by my little brother Bijan and the other children. Bolting at top speed, I shut my eyes tight. The brilliant Spanish sun was dimmed to bluish orange, the sand beneath my feet transformed into a field of poppies. My feet glided over the red blanket of blossoms. I felt my white cotton dress trailing behind me in the wind. Finally, I saw myself as if from a distance, a shrinking speck of white amid the red folds that draped the hills.

I had forgotten that I could run like that. Isn't speed, like innocence, something we possess only as children? I slowed and then stopped, my breathing surprisingly even. I opened my eyes, and the blue-green horizon, the early morning beach, reappeared. I was alone. But then I was always alone, whether I was spinning in the lace and taffeta swirl of a society gala, or there, dipping my heels in the Mediterranean in the quiet shoreline near my villa. I liked it best then, before the resort vacationers with their umbrellas and radios invaded. It was the same solitude that had enveloped me ever since I'd entered court nearly thirty years before.

I flashed back to those images of my husband leaving Iran. I'd been there, those thirty years before, exiting a plane, leaving behind my girlhood, my concerns about schoolwork and social slights. I wasn't alone back then, and I didn't want to be alone any more.

I turned and sprinted back toward the villa, this time with purpose and clarity. I wanted to see him again. I needed to see him again. I felt sure that seeing my eyes, my first love would find the strength to live.

I found Bijan lounging by the pool. My hurried pace echoed off the tiles. Bijan didn't look up from his magazine.

"I'm going to see him," I said, my voice excited like a young girl's.

"See who?"

"I'm going to Egypt. I know he's about to have surgery, but I need to see him."

"I don't think you should do that. You need to keep moving forward."

"I have to. I'm going to call Ardeshir Zahedi."

As I rushed into the house, his voice called after me. "Okay, but be prepared to be disappointed."

I called the Villa de Rose in Montreaux to try to reach my old confidant. We'd been in touch a few times over the years, and I'd kept track of his progress as he moved from being Mohammed's foreign minister to Ambassador to Britain and then to the US. His Excellency was in Egypt, his housekeeper informed me, but he called daily to check for messages.

"Well," I said to her, my determination growing, "I have an urgent one for him."

Out of long habit, and still believing I had the power to make a telephone ring, I sat myself as far from it as possible. That meant joining Bijan poolside. We played backgammon for hours. I was indifferent to the results and Bijan's constant refrain: "Nice shish kabob." His taunting words for incompetent play had no effect. I lost every game, cared less each time, and wondered more and more why Ardeshir was taking so long to get back to me. He was usually so prompt. Could something have gone wrong with the shah?

Bijan convinced me that the way to take my mind off my waiting was to go out to dinner.

"So early?" The sun was just beginning to set.

"We're not as young as we used to be."

Before I could form a reply to this affront, the phone rang.

My sprint into the house was no less impressive than that morning's run on the beach.

"Your Majesty," Ardeshir said formally, "please pardon the delay. I have been at the king's bedside. How can I be of assistance?"

I asked about the shah's condition and was assured that he was resting comfortably, eager for the surgery to end and the recuperation to begin.

Pleasantries and protocol over, I asked deferentially but firmly, "Ardeshir? Is there any way that I can see him?"

"See him?"

"Yes. See him. Visit him. I'd very much like to see Mohammed Reza."

There was a pause and then a sharp intake of breath. "His Majesty is very weak at present. Allow me to make some inquiries. I will see what can be done."

I'd known Ardeshir long enough to understand that his cool

professionalism and formality masked his own excitement about the possibility. In ways large and small, Ardeshir had indirectly over the years confirmed what I suspected—Mohammed Reza had loved me more than any other woman in his life.

Over the next few weeks, I was in an all-too-familiar situation—waiting for a call from Mohammed Reza. Rather than sit around, I established a routine. A run and a swim in the morning, a light lunch, and then another run and swim in the late afternoon. I was in training. Call it pride, call it a romantic delusion, but I wanted Mohammed Reza to see me looking as fit as a young woman. Although I'd been foolish at times and given away most of the dresses that he had bought for me, I'd kept a few sentimental pieces.

I planned to wear a favorite of his, a dress he'd bought for me in Rome in 1953. It had particular meaning for us both. The shah had splurged on it during our brief exile from Mosaddegh's Iran, a time when Mohammed Reza was plagued by concerns about our finances. I stood in the boutique and saw his reflected gaze admiring me. The flared skirt, the jeweled neckline, the princess seaming (a term that delighted Mohammed to no end) were flattering. The green matched my eyes, he said, and then added, "I simply have to have that dress for you."

For me, the dress meant that we might return to those days after Rome, when Mohammed had made good on his promises to me and I truly felt like I was his partner. That was when I seemed to be most alive, most purposeful, most fulfilled.

Of course, waiting in Marbella, I scanned the newspapers, hoping for some word out of Egypt about the shah's condition. I was truly glad to hear, read, or see nothing. Despite how things had turned out in the past, I eagerly anticipated the call, certain that what I wanted would come to me. After all, wasn't I the little girl who'd told my grandfather I was going to marry a prince? Wasn't I once the girl of sixteen who'd realized that dream?

Inch by inch, pound by pound, I got closer to my goal. In mid-July, I was back in Paris. I'd continued my regimen as best I could. I spoke of my hopes to no one but Bijan. Late one evening, alone in my apartment, I went to the closet and pulled out the dress again. The garment bag fluttered like a ghost as it drifted to the floor. I'd just stepped into the dress when the phone rang. Only half-dressed, I staggered to the phone, the fabric clinging to my hips.

"Soraya." Ardeshir's voice was hoarse. I shut my eyes and sank onto the bed, certain that my request had been denied. "I trust that I'm not calling too late. I really don't know what time it is, to be honest." His weariness clutched at my body, pulling me down.

"It's fine. I am awake at all hours. Please, Ardeshir, go on."

"As of today, your shah of shahs lives no more. He was far too young ..."

Ardeshir could not go on, and I don't believe that I would have been able to hear him anyway. The roar inside my head was so great. I had the feeling that I was falling from a high place, very fast.

"I'm so sorry to tell you this, Soraya." Ardeshir had regained some of his composure. "But I hope you'll find some comfort in these words. He did want to see you. In fact, I'm sure that thinking of you kept him going these last months. He just couldn't bear the thought of you seeing him as he was at the end. He'd grown so gaunt, and you know how proud he was."

I stepped out of my dress and looked at my too-human flesh. "Yes," I said through my tears, "I know." I felt a stab of guilt for having been glad that Mohammed Reza had not been well enough to see me immediately. He'd given me more time to prepare, and then, it seemed, more time for me to feel foolish. I quickly dismissed that last self-assessment. I hadn't been foolish at all. I had loved him.

It was impossible for me to attend the funeral. To do so would have been too scandalous and drawn too much attention. I guess I was glad for that, but how ironic that the only men I'd loved had died before me, and I could not be present at their funerals—that I was never able to gain any closure. Still, I couldn't have imagined what it would have been like to be there, to think of his great spirit, his body, boxed and ready to be entombed. I've read about other cultures and their burial rituals, and find the Western ways too confining. It is as if we want the dead to be put away, contained in some place where they can no longer have any effect on us, deny to them in death the freedom denied to them in life. That's foolish. I would have preferred that Mohammed's body had been borne aloft in an airplane, flown over the mountains where his beloved brother had perished, and been left there in the wilderness.

Shortly after the funeral, Ardeshir visited me in Paris. After we'd cried in one another's arms, he related the words that Mohammed Reza had asked him to give me. I hope you can forgive me, Raya, but I can't share those with you. We lived too public a life, Mohammed and I. We let too many outside influences dictate the course our lives would take. Just know that I found great comfort in them, and yet they also made me restless. They became a voice trailing after me, urging me forward. No matter how far I traveled or how fast I ran, I could not escape them.

Having been cast out of my kingdom of happiness, I've spent my days turning everywhere I go into another outpost of my kingdom of sorrow. Please don't follow me there. Not to that kingdom of sorrow. Not to the place where I will live out my last days. Let me be as I was and as I am, a proud and vain woman, unwilling to let the world see my faults and failures.

PART V

Raya

PARIS, JUNE–NOVEMBER, 2001

Chapter
TWENTY-FIVE

I did as Soraya had requested and didn't immediately return to Paris or try to find her. When Luca returned, all he would say was that he escorted her safely to the airport. Her final words to me, to not join her in her kingdom of sorrow, tore at my heart. The thought of her being alone when she needed others around her saddened me in a way that I could not quite grasp. I didn't want to be sad for her, to take up residence in the place she occupied, but there I was.

Dolores and Estrela had asked me to stay on to help them finish up the renovations and redecorations of the Hotel Plaza. I was sorely tempted by their offer. I knew I needed to get back to Paris, but as long I was there, I would help out.

Finally the car was repaired to Miguel's satisfaction and there was no more reason for me to remain any longer. Dolores and Estrela planned a farewell gathering for me. It was a scaled-down version of the soccer match paella party, with about a hundred people crowded into the parking lot. They gave me a gift, a peacock hairpin much like the brooch that Soraya had told them about. Instead of jewels, of course, it was bits of glass, but still lovely. To much applause, I showed it off to those gathered. Overcome by tears, I embraced Dolores and Estrela in turn, the three of us weeping like schoolgirls.

I almost left behind the Stendahl novel that Soraya had given me. Since I was not familiar with the story, it seemed such an odd token, but I had little time to consider what it meant.

Eric and Marie warmly welcomed me back to Paris. They urged me to stay on, but their greeting was followed by other news: They were going to have a child. In preparation, they had taken on another sous chef and a waiter. With all those changes present and future, I knew I wasn't really needed there any longer, and I was glad of that.

I kept in touch with Eric and Marie (and still do), but I knew that Paris in the summer was not something I could endure. Even during the few days I spent there before packing the car again, I purposely avoided the Jardin de Tuilieries. I didn't have the patience for its riot of blossoms, its fertile promise of things to come. It was going to be all too glorious and beautiful. Everyone and everything around me seemed to be pointing toward a better future, and I was just getting used to the idea that I had a place in it. To battle that bit of unfamiliarity, I decided to return to a place I knew well—Barcelona.

The city was big enough and my determination strong enough to weather any possible encounter with Sergio. I found a small apartment in Urquiaona, near La Sagrada Familia, figuring that hiding in plain sight of one of his main work projects would be best. I had been there for only a few weeks when I encountered him at the newspaper stand close to where I lived. On the cover of *Hola* magazine, there was a picture of him with a young Spaniard who worked as a television hostess on several popular programs. I picked up a copy, planning to read more of the details, but then put it back down. As I walked away, emotionless, I remembered that chapter in my life was already closed. I paused and stared at the grandeur of the church that stood before me. Is life not like the Sagrada Familia?

Alluring, sensual, intoxicating—full of the unexpected, and eternally unfinished.

Despite Soraya's final request, I tried multiple times, both when I was in Paris and after I'd moved back to Barcelona, to get in touch with her. I left messages on her cell phone and the home numbers she'd given me. She never replied. I had no way of knowing whether she'd gotten them, and I experienced those moments of wistful and hopeful doubt that come with unreturned messages.

Since my life had taken this new turn, I decided to pursue my passion, even if it meant starting from the bottom. I began investigating design programs, but the thought of more schooling was daunting. One day, when I was walking past a boutique I admired, I approached a woman who I thought was a sales clerk. I asked her if the designer was local. As it turned out, she was not just local, but she was talking with me. Two weeks later, I began working for Maryola as her personal assistant and as a design apprentice, helping with a ready-to-wear line she was hoping to launch the following fall in New York.

Near the end of June, Maryola asked me to attend a meeting at her house near the shore in Premia del Mar. At the last moment, she had to cancel and told me to take the rest of the day for myself. I packed a bathing suit and towel in my shoulder bag and decided to wait out the late afternoon traffic at a beach in town. The perfectly cloudless day went on uninterrupted. The beach was deserted, the children back in school, the tourists elsewhere. I'd been having trouble sleeping for the past few months, being bothered by recent events, and was exhausted. I soon fell asleep. I don't know how long I lay there, but the sound of my phone ringing startled me awake. My thoughts immediately turned tragic, and I was glad to see that it was from an unknown caller.

A man's voice, one completely unknown to me except for his slight unfamiliar accent, greeted me by name.

"May I speak to Miss Raya?"

"Speaking," I said, briefly taken aback by the man's unique manner of speaking.

"I am Her Majesty Soraya's brother. She has asked that I phone you. She wants to see you."

I wondered if his formal introduction was a product of his Persian upbringing or his German background. His referring to Soraya as "Her Majesty" made me realize that he was still living in the shadow of his sister's once-grand stature.

"My sister is not well. She has asked that I look after some matters on her behalf, and calling you was among her requests. She wishes to see you. Can you pay her a visit? Are you in Paris?"

Whether it was because I was still groggy from having been awakened or because I've never been good at dealing with anger or hurt feelings, I fell back on formalities. "That's very kind of her to extend the invitation."

I'd been trying to sort out my feelings regarding Soraya for weeks since she'd left. Perhaps it was because I was caught off-guard—or more likely because he mentioned her not being well—that made me reply, "I'll be there as soon as I can."

"That's quite kind of you. From what Soraya has told me of you, I expected no less."

"Of course. Of course." My fog was beginning to lift, and I was aware of a sharp pain where I'd been lying with my sunglasses pressed against the bridge of my nose.

"She hadn't wanted to speak to you since your trip was over. She needed some time to sort things out in her mind. I tried to talk to her, to change her mind, but you know Soraya. But now …"

I briefly thought of saying "I do, but I don't know Soraya." Instead, I resorted to asking something innocuous. "Why does she want to see me?"

Bijan hesitated, seeming surprised by the turn our conversation had taken. "That's a question I am not able to answer. All I am doing is following instructions. This is Soraya's way of doing things. Dialing the phone herself may have been too much work for her." As he said the last words, he burst into laughter, like a true little brother mocking his sister.

"That sounds like her. Not wanting there to be any loose ends, making sure that everyone is taken care of." Although I was being playful, I spoke in a serious tone.

"Yes, very much like her because that is who she is." Bijan went silent.

Although our conversation was brief and this was my first contact with him, I could tell that he was troubled. I also sensed that he, too, did not fully know his sister.

"I'm in Barcelona right now, but I will leave as soon as I can. I hope to meet you soon."

"Thank you, Raya. What a lovely name ..."

The line went dead.

I gathered my things and stumbled to the car, overcome—not just by my confusion, but about the moment that marked the passing of a segment in my own life. Having attained my girlhood desire of getting to know Soraya, I experienced the inevitable twin feelings of satisfaction and emptiness. Would it always be that way? I'd thought that things between us had come to a conclusion, as indecisive as it was, and I was going to have to live with it. In some ways that lack of resolution seemed in keeping with so much in my life. I hadn't considered the possibility that Soraya would want to tie things up in a pretty package with a neat bow.

I was so distracted that I wound up in the wrong lane to take me back to Barcelona. I had to turn around several times before making it home. I left a message for Maryola, letting her know that it wouldn't be possible for me to work the next two days due to a family emergency. I didn't like lying to her, but in some ways Soraya did seem like family.

I couldn't get a flight out until late the next day. I spent the in-flight hours reading the book that Soraya had given me, hoping to find some clue that would help me put my feelings about her on a more solid footing. The truth was, for all the time I spent with her, she still eluded me in so many ways. *The Charterhouse of Parma* was a classic potboiler: part romance, part novel of court intrigue and war. The lovers are forced to separate by circumstances beyond their control, although they meet at night in the darkness of a church's confessional.

Two sentences from the book were underlined, and I didn't know if that was Soraya's work or another reader's. The first had to do with a man daring to leave behind signs of his affection for a former lover. The second struck me as more profoundly representative of what Soraya had been trying to demonstrate to me. "The pleasures and the cares of the luckiest ambition, even of limitless power, are nothing next to the intimate happiness that tenderness and love give."

I was grateful that I'd been given a privileged glimpse into a priv-ileged life. Hers was certainly a life of beauty and great sorrow, lived large in the public eye. Yet, for all the time I spent with Soraya, for all she shared with me of the court intrigues, the political maneuverings, the jet-setting, it was the grace notes of her small kindnesses that defined her for me.

As much as I tried to, I could not have prepared myself for what I saw when I visited Soraya at her apartment. I was admitted into the space by a middle-aged woman who ushered me into a back bedroom. Soraya sat in a wingback chair, wearing a pair of linen slacks and a floral print blouse. She sat in profile, looking out the window. Much of the healthy glow from when I'd last seen her was lost. Her skin was so sallow it made her bright red lipstick seem even more garish.

I tried to compose myself, but this woman in front of me was not the same vibrant person I'd last seen in Castejón de Sos. It was almost like visiting the house of your childhood and finding that it had fallen into serious disrepair—shrunken and unwelcoming.

That impression disappeared as soon as Soraya turned to look at me. Her smile worked its magic.

"Madam." The maid who had introduced herself as Genevieve addressed her in a soft voice. "You have a guest."

"Not a guest, but a dear friend." Soraya stood and held out her arms.

I stepped into them, and felt her relief exhaling from her body.

"I wasn't certain you'd come. I'm so glad you have."

Soraya's charms weren't diminished by her not feeling well. I had been hurt by her not returning any of my calls for so long, and I tried to put up a wall between us, but I couldn't. Her honest pleasure at my being there won me over.

After Genevieve brought in her medication and some tea, Soraya asked about what I'd been doing. When I explained, she pushed herself back in her chair and said, "I suppose you've wondered why I left as I did."

"You don't owe me any explanations."

"Owed or not, I'd like to tell you a few things."

"As you wish." I felt like I was being put on the spot.

"I truly didn't know what to expect when we first met and the idea of the trip came up. To be honest, other than our Bakhtiari bloodline, I didn't know that we'd have anything in common, mostly due to our differences in age. When you told me about Sergio, I empathized with you. I saw that we'd both had our share of loss, as many do, even if the circumstances were different."

I wanted to stop her and point out that heartache is heartache and one shouldn't compare, but I let it pass.

Soraya shifted in her chair and scanned the room, clearly not comfortable with what she was about to say. "I told you a bit about my decision to not go through with the operation. That meant I was unlikely to have children."

"I'm not certain I understand. What does this have to do …"

Soraya held up her hand to stop me. "Forgive me. The route is a bit circuitous, but trust that I will get you there." She sipped her tea. "The thing is, I could possibly have had children with Mohammed, if I'd had the operation. I chose not to."

"Why?"

Soraya went on. "Mohammed's family wanted me gone. I was growing out of being a naïve girl and was in the process of becoming an empress. My Bakhtiari roots meant that I had strong support from many people all over the country, but Mohammed's family did not like that. And admittedly, I was not strategic or political in the way I dealt with them. The shah loved me, but he had to maintain power. In order to do that, he needed an heir. I refused to be a puppet in their schemes."

Soraya touched my arm. "I'm sorry I didn't say anything to you after you talked about Sergio. I should have, but I couldn't think of what to say. Meeting you, I came to think of what it might be like to have had a daughter, someone with whom I could share so many things. But my failure to comfort you, advise you, do anything for you at that moment made me realize how ill-suited I am to be a parent."

Soraya returned to her chair.

"How can you say that?" I knelt by her side.

"I am tired of pretending."

I was pleased to hear that Soraya looked upon me as a daughter. I was even more pleased because since I had met her, this was the first time we were having a real, human dialogue: no walls, no pretending, and no alcohol.

"What do you mean, 'pretending?'"

"We all do it all the time. We pretend that we are happy, make ourselves sad to get something we want from someone else. We make a show of wanting to be with someone when the reality is we are all alone all the time."

I took several moments to gather myself. I felt like I was finally hearing the truth of Soraya's experiences and beliefs. I didn't like admitting this to myself, but in many ways, I agreed with her.

"I'm not just talking about my mother missing my father after he was gone or how either Bijan or I will feel when the other is gone. I also mean the feelings I had with Mohammed: those times when I felt so isolated from him, so distant, so wanting the opposite from one another."

I returned to my original seat and tried to reconcile everything she had said with what I'd been feeling since Sergio's betrayal. I realized that despite the shah's love for Soraya, he had also used her as a means to an end. Even a great love could also be a conditional love—and this was true for everyone.

Soraya walked toward her closet, and I heard hangers screeching. A moment later, she pulled out a garment bag and unzipped it.

"You remember me describing this one, don't you?" she asked. "I wore it at a summer gala in Antibes. The lovely American senator and his wife, Jackie, were there. Such a shame to have come to that end."

"So much sadness, yes." I could feel Soraya's darkness overtaking me. "You recall telling me about the death dream?"

"Yes. What of it?"

"Do you still have it?" I hadn't told Soraya, but I was plagued by a similar nightmare from time to time.

"I haven't had it in years. Many years, as a matter of fact."

"Why do you think that is?

"I suppose because I'm no longer afraid of death or of dying. I've seen enough of it. I've been alone enough to find it familiar."

Unable to do anything but surrender to them, I let my tears fall.

"I'm sorry. I didn't want you to come here and be sad."

Soraya sat with her hands pressed between her legs. She shifted so her body angled away from me.

"Would you like something to eat?"

I was grateful that she resorted to the customary motherly wound-dressing.

Later, after we'd dined and talked about our friends in Castejón, Soraya fairly insisted that I spend the night.

"I can have Genevieve show you to the spare bedroom. You'll be quite comfortable."

I don't know why, but I didn't want to be that far away from Soraya. All that talk of isolation and loneliness had me feeling slightly out-of-sorts. I was like a child craving to crawl into bed with her mother as if to ward off the bogeyman.

It took a little convincing for Soraya to agree, but soon Genevieve was retrieving sheets and pillows for me. I said that I wasn't tired yet and would fix my sleeping spot myself, so those items sat stacked on one end of the couch. After Soraya bid me good night, I sat looking through a photo album that was sitting on a coffee table.

I leafed through the catalog of Soraya's life and influences. In a formal portrait, her father Khalil sat in a pose that reminded me of the typical high school yearbook shot, three quarters to the camera, his chin resting on his hand. He appeared to be holding a necktie up to his collar, and for a moment I wondered if that was so. In another, Soraya rode in a goat-drawn cart. At first I thought that it had to be from Iran, but when I turned it over, it was labeled "Soraya, age five, the Berlin Zoo." Her companion in the cart wore a type of sailor suit, a kerchief tied around his neck like a cravat. Soraya was laughing; the hat on her head was tilted away from the camera at a jaunty angle. I smiled when I noticed that she was the one with the reins in her hand.

Genevieve came into the room and asked if I needed anything. I told her that I didn't, and asked where Bijan was.

"Running an errand, he said." Genevieve's skepticism added a discordant note. "He said fifteen minutes. That was two hours ago."

With nothing left to do or say, Genevieve bade me good night. I resumed my perusing for a few minutes, when Soraya came out of her bedroom and joined me.

"I can't sleep. My head is throbbing; soon the pills will take effect, I hope. May I join you?"

"Of course."

Soraya sat next to me and began paging through the album, filling me in on some of the details. As she turned the pages, I noticed that her hands were shaking. I continued talking with her about the pictures as if I hadn't noticed her tremors.

"This one is from St. Moritz. Mohammed and I loved to ski," she said.

"It looks like he's wearing tennis whites—the flannel trousers and the sweater. He must have been freezing." Soraya looked a trifle unhappy, or perhaps just cold, bundled up in a large overcoat.

"He claimed he was impervious." She emitted something between a sigh and a laugh. "I wish I had been. Some nights when he came to bed, his feet were like blocks of ice. I'd nearly hit the ceiling when they touched me."

She seemed to skip over the more formal portraits, the magazine covers, and other published shots that I'd seen before. I still couldn't get over how beautiful she was. She preferred to comment on the more candid and informal photos—of her and the shah astride horses, at a picnic lunch, and my favorite, the two of them in a rowboat, apparently on land, Soraya holding an umbrella. They were both wearing sunglasses and serious expressions.

"I told him I would use the umbrella as a sail. He, of course, insisted on being the captain. I said that we'd already run aground, so how would he navigate us out of that one? We were trying so hard to not laugh."

After a few more, Soraya shut the book. "I spend too much time looking back. It's as if instead of ears, I have rearview mirrors. It's not good for one's neck."

"I think it's fun, but maybe only when it's someone else's past."

Soraya considered that for a moment; then her face brightened. "What did you think of the book? It was beautiful, wasn't it? The lovers were separated, but still they managed to see one another in the dark. Well, not really see, but still, you understand."

I looked at the clock. It was nearly two in the morning. The streets outside were silent.

"The witching hour," I said, not knowing really what I meant, but not wanting to get into a discussion of *The Charterhouse of Parma*. Despite my attempt, Soraya continued, "They were no Romeo and Juliet, mind you. No clashing families and all that."

Just as suddenly, the conversation took another turn. "Oh, I don't want you to forget. I'm giving you the paisley dress as a token of my affection. Don't tell me no; I'll never fit into it again."

She walked back into her bedroom, and I sat there, suddenly feeling very weary after the day's travel. I picked up the photo album again. I heard Soraya rustling around, and then suddenly a heavy thud.

I sat at attention.

"Soraya? Do you need my help? Did something fall?" I couldn't imagine what she might keep in her closet that could make such a racket. When she didn't answer, I called out to her again. When she didn't respond, I felt a charge go through my bladder. Tossing the book on the table, I ran into the bedroom.

Soraya lay face-down on the floor, her eyes open, her mouth agape.

I knelt beside her, trying to find a pulse at her throat. She was lying at such an angle that it was difficult for me to get my fingers where I thought they needed to be. Fighting a rising panic, I managed to turn her over, exposing her neck and wrists. The entire time, I kept muttering to myself, "No. No. No."

My breath came in jagged gasps and my thoughts were a torrent. I wanted to call out to the maid, but I couldn't remember her name. I wanted to call in an emergency, but I couldn't think of anything but 911. What was it for Paris? My thoughts turned to Soraya. How was she dressed? Would she want anyone to see her in those bedclothes? Finally, I managed to quiet my trembling fingers long enough to feel each of her pulse points. Nothing. I began to cry. Great heaving sobs tore at my throat. I managed to calm myself enough to remember Genevieve's name. I shouted it over and over again, then, aware that I might rouse the neighbors, I called out more quietly. After a few moments, she rushed into the room, bleary-eyed and uncomprehending. Suddenly, it was as if I couldn't speak French at all. I mimed making a phone call. Genevieve stood there transfixed for a moment, before she sank onto the bed with her head in her hands. I got up and put the phone in her lap and returned to Soraya.

It was clear to me that she was dead. I had no idea what to do. Stupidly, I took the paisley dress that was lying beside Soraya's body and hung it up. Then, thinking that the police or whoever arrived would think it odd that before leaving I went into my dead friend's closet to retrieve a dress, I set it out in the living room with my things.

I couldn't comprehend what had happened. One moment she was talking to me; the next she was dead. When she had told me that she wasn't afraid of death, I'd wanted to hush her. I was afraid that she was tempting the fates.

For all her talk of loneliness and isolation, I was glad that at least I was there with her. What if I had insisted on leaving? Who would have found her? Would Bijan have been the one? Genevieve? How awful for any of us.

Soraya had seemed so happy looking through those old photographs. I longed for the ability to see her as she was in those pictures and not as she was just then.

Hours later, just as the sun was rising, I was finally able to leave. I'd answered what questions I could from the police. The men were officious and just doing their respective jobs, but each flash of a camera was like a knife in my eyes. This was no crime scene, and I wondered what ghoulish fascination possessed them. One of the detectives, noticing me flinching at the sound of the shutter, said to me, "We must be thorough. She was a person of some importance."

I hated his use of the past tense, knowing that even if she were still alive, he would likely have used it anyway. She was still important to me, however; still someone of value to so many.

At one point, I excused myself and went into the bathroom. A ring of lights around the mirror came on when I flipped the switch. The garish light made me nauseous. I could feel a headache coming on, and the sight of my pale drawn face, my eyes raccoon-like with smeared mascara, lent the whole scene a horror movie aspect. A votive candle sat on the counter along with a pack of matches. I lit the candle and turned off the lights. In the pale and flickering light, I stood at the sink, my arms supporting my weight, elbows painfully locked. I didn't care; I wanted to feel that pain.

I stood there for a long time and then rinsed my face. When I stepped out of the bathroom, I saw a figure sitting on the couch, being attended to by Genevieve and some other woman whom I hadn't seen before. It had to be Bijan. I was angry with him. I wanted to ask him why the hell he couldn't have been there that night. I was upset, not about having been thrust into this position, but because he should have been there. She shouldn't have been there with a relative stranger.

She should have died in the arms of a loved one. But I knew I had to let that anger go, along with so many other things.

I gathered my belongings, folded the garment bag with the paisley dress over my arm, and walked to the door as if I had just picked up my dry cleaning. Soraya's body was still on the gurney, covered with a sheet. I looked around the room and saw a vase filled with carnations. I remembered that they were her favorite, and how my mother knew this and told me that they were such a simple but beautiful flower, not ostentatious or flamboyant. I took one of the stems and walked up to where my beautiful friend lay. I tucked the stem beneath one of the straps that held her in place.

When I exited the building, I felt the sting of a chill rain, just as I had those many months ago when I'd first come to Paris. This time, though, I had to fight my way through a crowd of the curious that had gathered. Their cameras' flashes blinded me, and several times I walked right into someone. I could see their mouths working and forming words, but I could make no sense of what they were saying.

Only later did I recognize the pitiable irony of me pushing through them, alternately saying, "Please leave me alone," and "I am no one. I have nothing to say."

Once through the gauntlet, I was finally able to breathe and to think. I walked only a few meters to a tobacco shop and purchased an umbrella. I didn't want the rain to mingle with my tears; there was sadness enough in them. I'm not certain why, but I joined the crowd standing far behind a police barricade. I waited nearly an hour. The rain had intensified and the wind picked up. I was barely able to keep the umbrella from being turned inside out. The onlookers had dwindled to a few. What could I say of us? That we were loyal? Or desperate?

Surely Soraya deserved better than this. The fanfare that sounded from the ambulance and police cars should have been trumpets; the flashing lights, fireworks. What a poor imitation we were of the throngs that had gathered to greet her on her wedding night. I thought of how some had raced along with the car, thumping their hands against the windows. If I was glad of one thing, it was that no one would disturb her peace and her rest that night or ever again.

Chapter
TWENTY-SIX

*I*n the end, Soraya couldn't get what she desired. Through the Bakhtiari grapevine, my mother had heard that Soraya's funeral wishes were for a small gathering. The American Cathedral in Paris was hardly an intimate setting, and the number of dignitaries and royalty included Ashraf, the shah's sister. In Soraya's telling of her story, I'd always felt that Ashraf was guiltier by association than by actual sinning. However, when I saw her sitting there daubing at her eyes, I couldn't stand the thought of her being there, her weeping more for show than from genuine sadness.

I was numb through most of the service, hearing the priest mumbling platitudes about a better place and God's calling her home. Only when Darya Dadvar began singing "Ave Maria," the initial notes a tremulous and impossibly gorgeous sound that reverberated through the church and my body and spirit, did I begin to cry. I'd never really understood the expression "achingly beautiful" until that moment, and I realized that it applied to Soraya as well.

At the end, when the mourners exited behind a coffin borne aloft by men I didn't know and wasn't certain Soraya did either, I saw Ashraf behind a mourning veil. Something about that felt staged to me. I was tempted to dash out of my pew and throw open my coat to reveal the paisley dress I hoped she'd recognize. It wasn't so much what Soraya had told me about Ashraf and her duplicity, but more what Soraya had said about our being alone in life that troubled me. With the exception of Bijan, who was a wreck throughout the service, Soraya had no family there. How could that be? I knew the logical answer to that question, but still I wondered. A small part of me thought it fortunate that she hadn't had any children so that there were none there to feel so great a loss.

Although I had assured myself that my meeting Soraya and hearing her tell her story had served its purpose, after returning from Castejón, I felt lost and empty once again. I resigned from my new post in Barcelona and decided to pay a tribute to my friend. I wanted to carry her with me to that place she had dreamt of returning to.

Days later, I landed in Tehran, still firmly in Soraya's grasp. In many ways, she had eluded me even though through good fortune I'd managed to find her and gotten to know her. I sensed that somehow the place where we'd both been born and lived much of our early lives might have something more to teach me.

So much had changed in my absence of over twenty years. Still, as I wandered through the stalls of the Grand Bazaar, heard the merchants hawking their wares, and felt the jostling of the thousands of buyers, I marveled at how much had remained the same. There were still the fine carpets, enticing perfumes, gorgeous jewelry, and enough spices to flavor my life for eternity.

One thing remained that I wanted and needed, one thing I would never be able to buy, even with all the riches in the world. I could never purchase the answer to the mysteries of the human heart. In the end, we all suffer from loss, but why we must pay for it so unequally can never be known.

When I was a child, my parents had told me that the heart knows what it wants. I had believed them then, but like so many things we don't question when we're young, I had to find out for myself. I needed to search the narrow and crowded alleyways alone and unguided until my heart told me that it was satisfied.

I realized that through knowing Soraya I had gained a sense of myself. The betrayal that I had endured would not cripple me. I wouldn't let it. Instead, it would make me stronger.

In the end, it was of little consequence whether Soraya or I had been betrayed. What mattered was whether we remained true to ourselves. In the language of the stories that give shape to our earliest dreams and desires, I was left to wonder whether we all seek refuge in castles in the air, or if the earthly palaces are just as ephemeral, just as elusive.